Justin Myers is a writer from Shipley, Yorkshire, who now lives in London. After years working in journalism, he began his popular blog *The Guyliner* in 2010. Justin spent five years writing dating and relationship advice for *Gay Times*, before joining British *GQ* as a weekly columnist in 2016. His work has appeared in a number of publications including the *Guardian*, *The i*, *Sunday Times Style*, and the *Irish Times*. His debut novel, *The Last Romeo*, was published in 2018.

Follow Justin online at:
@theguyliner
www.theguyliner.com

Also by Justin Myers

The Last Romeo

The Magnificent Sons

JUSTIN MYERS

PIATKUS

PIATKUS

First published in Great Britain in 2020 by Piatkus
This paperback published in 2021 by Piatkus

1 3 5 7 9 10 8 6 4 2

Epigraph on p.ix from @IanMcKellen, 4:40p.m., 27 January 2018

A CIP catalogue record for this book
is available from the British Library.

ISBN 978-0-349-41695-3

Typeset in Perpetua by M Rules
Printed and bound in Great Britain by Clays Ltd, Elcograf S.p A.

Papers used by Piatkus are from well-managed forests
and other responsible sources.

Piatkus
An imprint of
Little, Brown Book Group
Carmelite House
50 Victoria Embankment
London EC4Y 0DZ

An Hachette UK Company
www.hachette.co.uk

www.littlebrown.co.uk

For dearest Nichola,
and Neil, Luke, Zach, and Claire.
Sunday Club for ever.

The Magnificent Sons

'Life at last begins to make sense,
when you are open and honest.'

—Sir Ian McKellen

prologue.

The hallway smelled like food; last night's dinner, maybe, with a little of this morning's breakfast thrown in. Gravy and fry-ups. Jake followed Evan down the hall into a cramped, untidy breakfast room, with a small kitchen off the back. There was washing-up piled on the side, and half-filled mugs of tea left on a rickety-looking table in the middle of the room, salt and pepper, ketchup, a creased newspaper. Jake imagined his mum's face if she could've seen it; she'd never left the house with a cup unwashed in the sink, let alone out on the table for all to see.

'This way,' Evan said softly, even though he'd said nobody would be in. 'Do you know how to skin up?'

Through another door and they were in the lounge. The TV was old, Jake noticed – older than Granddad's. It was wide enough at the top to accommodate a small lamp and some loose change. The room smelled of cigarettes.

'We *can* smoke in here,' Evan whispered, reading Jake's mind.

'Cool.' Jake tried not to stare. Evan riffled in the drawer of a huge sideboard that dominated one wall. There were birthday cards on the shelves. *Happy 18th Birthday*, some said; others had crude jokes on them. He remembered Evan's 18th, three months earlier, though he hadn't been invited to the party. There was a strict rule in Jake's house – birthday cards came down within a week. Bad luck or something.

Evan handed him a box. 'Here, it's all in there. I'll put some tunes on.'

Jake, of course, did *not* know how to roll a joint. He trembled as he sat on the sofa and opened the box. He'd seen people do this. On TV. On the school bus sometimes. He licked a cigarette paper and joined it to another. He felt very grown up. Almost a 'geezer', like his dad. 'You keep this, uh, *gear* down here?' he asked in amazement. 'Where anyone could find it?'

Evan looked up from the pile of records he was sorting through and laughed. 'You only find something if you look for it. Nobody ever does.'

Jake was messing up the joint. He scattered tobacco like he was garnishing a pizza and hoped for the best. 'Won't the smell . . . ?'

'Oh, it's fine. Nobody will know.' Jake saw Evan select a record. 'Yes.'

'Vinyl,' said Jake, as nonchalantly as possible. 'Retro.'

Evan laughed. 'My brother broke the CD player and I can't afford an iPod. Not retro, just . . . y'know. All there is. My dad's old-school.'

Jake had seen Evan's dad. Always smoking. He was American, had longish hair. He'd nod at Jake sometimes. Knew his dad, probably. *Everyone* knew Jake's dad.

Jake couldn't believe he was here. Too many coincidences had brought him to that room, the box, and the joint he was making a mess of. He'd never been sent to the supervision room before, but forgetting his homework for the third time in a row had been the final straw for his French teacher.

'You're not taking French A level seriously,' she'd hissed, after hauling him out into the corridor.

'I am, miss,' he'd protested, before killing off another distant relative as an excuse. But Madame Jones had a good memory, and thus he was banished to supervision – basically, the holding pen for pupils not naughty enough for detention – along with two girls caught fighting in the toilets, Darren Loughton, who *lived* in supervision, and Evan Kolowski.

Evan had joined Jake's school late in Year 10. They'd never spoken much. He knew Evan was brought up in the States but his parents had suddenly come 'home'. After they'd been liberated from supervision, they'd chatted on the bus and Evan had invited Jake back to his for a smoke. Jake had been gobsmacked. Though the novelty of an American in the class had long worn off, Evan still maintained a loyal fan base. He was tall, handsome. Girls loved him, because he had 'good chat', and many of the boys had a begrudging respect for him – probably because he was good at basketball – although there were the predictable racist comments from some of the white boys whose dads had bulldog tattoos, permanent angry sunburn and spent all day in the Red Lantern. One jibe too many that day had pushed him over the edge and its culprit had accidentally fallen on to the end of Evan's fist. Naturally, Evan had been the only one to get punished, and had found himself in supervision.

They smoked Jake's badly constructed joint without comment before Evan got up to change the record.

'*This* one! "Second Hand News" is an amazing fucking song,' he whooped.

Jake chuckled at the way he'd pronounced 'news'. Nooooz. 'Who's it by?' he asked as sharp, angry guitar strumming started up.

Evan stared back in mock horror. 'Fleetwood *Mac*. My dad loves them.'

Jake couldn't hide his surprise. 'Are *you* into this?'

Evan frowned. 'What, you think cuz I'm American and have a black mom that I'm *exclusively* into hip-hop?' he drawled. 'Niiice stereotyping, bud.'

'No! I . . . oh God, no, sorry.'

Evan grinned. 'I'm fucking with you, Jake. My mom is from Croydon – she's into Janet Jackson and Madonna. But she likes Snoop too, okay? This is *not* a test.' He began to dance.

Jake watched him gyrate, pointing to the sky in time with the beat and giving serious rock-star face throughout the chorus. He was mouthing the words kind of suggestively, Jake thought, as he gazed on in wonder.

'Come on, Jakey, get up!' But Jake stayed where he was, mesmerised, confused by the strange heat that was slowly working its way to every part of his body.

Evan was a good dancer, clicking his fingers and winking as his body twisted. As the song crashed to its finale, Evan slid to the ground and crawled over to Jake, shaking his head wildly. Jake heard the crackle and low rumble of the vinyl under the stylus. The next track, 'Dreams', started up. By the end of it, when the crackling returned, they were kissing.

twelve years later.

one.

Jake wasn't sure he was ready for this horror show, not today, or indeed ever. Hanging out with his family was torture enough at the best of times, but when his baby brother was the focus of the attention – not that this was unusual – his family's 'quirks' went into overdrive. Jake stared out of the train window for the first sign he was near enough to Balham to stand up, and pictured what lay ahead. Trick's birthdays were always ostentatious and, as this was his seventeenth, his mother had taken to labelling it 'the last birthday where he's still my baby'. Her middle name was Marie, but it should've been Drama. No doubt she'd already be on the rosé, teetering on a stepladder hanging up bunting, wearing one of her knitwear 'creations' that could be seen from space, laughing like a drain at one of Dad's terrible jokes, before sneaking off for a cigarette on the back terrace even though she was supposed to have given up in 2013. 'Mum, we all *know*!' was a common cry from his siblings. Dad would be operating in one of two settings: default, full-on geezer mode, handing out tins of beer and rubbing his hands together in anticipation; or holed up in his sports lounge, glued to the planet-sized TV, not listening to anyone. His sister Margo would be partly made-up – she always seemed to be halfway through applying mascara – and chasing Buddy, her six-year-old, round the kitchen with a forkful of unidentifiable food. He imagined himself at the roulette wheel and placed his bets.

Jake messaged Amelia to see if she'd got the cake. He knew she'd text back that of course she fucking had and why was he asking stupid questions, but he wanted to show he appreciated it. Her offer to help came, Jake guessed, from adoring Trick and his (irritating) idiosyncrasies, but also trying to curry favour with his mum, who Amelia was convinced didn't like her. Still. After, what? Three years now? Maybe more. He had spent so long pretending anniversaries weren't important – most of his friends did, too; making it up to their girlfriends seemed part of the courting ritual – that it became a self-fulfilling prophecy.

'She always peers at me like I'm a waxwork and she can't work out who I'm meant to be,' complained Amelia. 'I don't know why.' Jake knew she'd already be there, in the middle of all the chaos, and he felt sorry he'd left her at the mercy of the D'Arcys. Usually she would be fine left with Trick – God knows what they talked about – but Jake knew he'd be upstairs waiting to make his entrance. Just like every year.

Though he referred to his parents' Balham house as 'home', it never felt right coming out of his mouth. Jake had spent more time living away from it than being there; he preferred to think of Walworth, a couple of miles up the road, as his real home, before they moved, when he was fourteen and Dad made what they still referred to in hushed tones as 'the money' building ugly slivers in Dubai, and 'phase two' of their existence as a family began. Jake remembered leaving the comforting courtyards and alleyways of the estate; it had coincided with Trick uttering a full sentence for the first time and being treated like he'd just discovered uranium.

Jake opened the back door to find the dog, Joanie, sitting staring resentfully at the closed kitchen door; she refused to wag her tail even for him. He mussed the fur on the dog's head and strode into the kitchen to find the usual chaos.

He clocked Amelia in one corner trying to slide a far too gooey gateau on to an ugly serving plate while his mother climbed down from the stepladder. The second her feet touched the floor, one of the strings of bunting fell down. He had won that bet.

Margo was decanting crisps from gigantic catering-size packets into melamine bowls. She winked at Jake.

'Trick will go mad when he sees these carbs.'

'Margs, will you give Buddy something to eat?' called Mum. 'He can't wait for everyone else. You don't want him eating junk.'

Margo snorted. 'Yes, *Gran*. If you've got a couple of arms free, you can always do it, Jake.'

Jake scooped up his nephew, tweaked his nose and popped a crisp into his mouth. 'Hello, mate. Want a sandwich?'

Buddy absentmindedly scratched his eye. Tired already. He made a face as he swallowed. 'Chicken crisps are made from hen's eyes. My friend Cassius said. His mum eats vegans.'

'*Is* vegan, Bud.' Margo brushed crumbs off her hands and eyeballed Jake. 'She is *not* vegan. I saw her in Five Guys last week. There was bacon hanging out the sides of her burger.'

Jake buttered bread for Buddy's sandwich. 'How many are coming?' If he knew Trick, a cast of thousands would be in attendance.

'It's very complicated. Use this.' Margo plonked some ham down in front of him. 'The understanding is, close family and *select* friends first. There's a . . . presentation.'

Not a huge surprise. Trick's sixteenth birthday had featured a dance recital and a reading from *The Hunger Games*. 'Can't *wait*. Then what?'

Amelia appeared, licking icing off her finger, and kissed Jake hello. 'Then the rest of the wild teenagers arrive for the night-time festivities, whereupon we hop it. Although I'd rather stay! There's vodka jelly.' Jake's mum and dad had planned a strategic trip to the West End to get out of the way. 'I said you'd be okay to pop in on the teenage dreams later, though, so we need to stay local. Go to one of the pubs on the high street, yeah?'

Jake couldn't believe Trick and his friends were to be left with the run of the house, to have a birthday party. And *vodka*? This wouldn't have happened when he was seventeen – mind you, he'd had barely enough friends at that age to fill the downstairs loo, never mind the whole house.

Mum chewed a biro as she watched everyone set the table, making a mental note to move everything round when left by herself. 'He was strict about the guest list for this part. *Super* close only.'

That's why Mum's best friend Reenie – who had lived in the flat next door in Walworth and popped round most days under the guise of doing some cleaning – was coming, and also Jake's university friend Hannah, who had spent many holidays, and a few months after graduation, camping out in the family's guest room. She seemed to get on with everyone better than Jake did, if he was honest; he'd never quite got over it. She and her boyfriend Dean weren't here yet, though, and he was half-glad – he knew Amelia couldn't understand the concept of Hannah, and Jake having a female friend that he'd never slept with. Also missing at this key stage were his dad and the birthday boy himself, who, as predicted, was stewing upstairs plotting his dramatic descent with his closest acolytes.

Jake signalled to Amelia that he was going to find his dad, and padded through to the front lounge, where Pat, his father, was watching a sport Jake didn't recognise. Shinty? Hoverboarding? His dad would watch anything as long as it involved a vague rulebook and two teams of men pulverising one another.

'Hello, my son!' His eyes stayed on the TV.

'Any idea what's going on tonight, Dad?'

'Naaaaaaaw. Trick's usual theatrics. Bit of acting, maybe. Last year's will be hard to beat.'

Despite sharing two halves of the same name – Trick was named Patrick after his father in a rare moment of sentimentality by Mum, and nicknamed Trick ever since to avoid confusion – to a casual observer the two had nothing in common, but Jake knew his dad had a kind of protective, proud respect for Trick. They were certainly more alike than Jake and his dad. They were loud. If you'd arranged to meet the D'Arcys in a busy pub, you could always find them. Their squawking was a homing device, a booming GPRS. Jake had seen people move tables to get away from his parents' ruination of the chorus of 'Angels' after a few drinks. Jake, however, never raised his voice in their company. He'd never understood why they were so keen to be heard when they didn't have anything interesting to say. His parents found Jake's perceived shyness extremely amusing. 'The quietest are the worst,' was their go-to phrase, accompanied by a friendly poke in the shoulder, before returning to their ear-splitting cackling. In these situations, as a teenager, Jake would pray for a knock at the door by a distressed, yet very serene family, who wanted to talk about a 'mix-up at the hospital'.

Suddenly, from the floor above, doors slammed and there was raucous laughter and choreographed clomping down the stairs.

Pat lifted his eyes from the screen and winked at his firstborn.

'Showtime, kid.'

Trick was tamely dressed for a change: svelte and sleek in a black roll-neck, tucked into black trousers, boasting a flat stomach you could iron on. His shiny dark hair fell in a heavy fringe across eyes thick with guyliner, his lips glimmering with a sparkly frosting and waist adorned with a belt buckle, upon it the phrase 'BITCH PLEASE' in a speech bubble. He was surrounded by two or three friends Jake didn't recognise at first – Jake's contact with them had been restricted to the odd family Sunday lunch, where Trick and his votaries would breeze in, look up from their phones only to roll their eyes in formation before disappearing upstairs – until he spotted Kia. There was a time Kia was the gobby brat from down the road who got into all sorts of trouble with his brother and was, outwardly at least, known to be a boy, with a slightly different name. Now Kia was Kia and a woman, and while Margo said there were mutterings in the local mini-mart and Kia spent a few nights in the D'Arcys' guest room while family stuff had been ironed out, it seemed like everything might be settling down.

Kia stepped forward. 'Okay, guys, fam, once everyone's here we'll move to the sports lounge for tonight's . . . uh,

Trick's *show.*' Trick beamed. Being talked about like he wasn't there was one of his major kinks.

'Marvellous, isn't it?' said Margo, as Trick and his posse posed for photos and complimented one another on their fashion choices like they hadn't all seen each other getting ready upstairs for the last three hours. 'How they've found each other?'

Jake knew that wasn't how it worked. If you were an outsider at school, you didn't 'find each other'; you were thrown together, rejection by the masses being your unifier. He remembered trying to keep his head down and making careful modifications to his personality so any clique he was trying to claw his way into would tolerate him. It hadn't been easy, and success rates had varied, but the alternative was sitting in the lunch room with the crew who got nosebleeds and set fire to stuff, or the ones whose dietary requirements were always to hand on a dog-eared piece of paper and who couldn't go out in direct sunlight. Being on vague nodding terms with someone cooler was much better than being pals with someone you didn't like. If his best friends Charlie and Adyan hadn't started chatting to him in the local park one summer he didn't know what he'd have done – and thankfully, as they went to different schools, there was no pecking order to navigate. They treated him like one of them, albeit more bookish and much fonder of cycling than the wanking competitions they favoured.

Margo continued. 'So different from when we were at school. It wasn't even that long ago.'

'Different?'

Margo gazed into the distance as if remembering. 'Yeah. Can you imagine lads going round full of make-up and nail varnish, or trans kids? They'd have been eaten alive. *You* wouldn't have been able to get away with it. It's so great they can express themselves.'

'I expressed myself with my sneakers, Margs, not a face full of make-up.'

Right on cue Trick and Kia screamed in unison at their phones. 'Okay, well, if Hot Will isn't coming we only have Hannah to wait for. I'll message her.'

Jake turned to Margo. 'The reason they can "express themselves", as you put it, is they go to a private school. They *pay* to be weird. I bet down at the local comp it's business as usual and this generation's version of Colin Barden will be having his inhaler chucked up on the roof.'

'Oh my God, poor Colin. He was *so* unpopular. Hang on . . . are you saying rich people are more tolerant?' Margo scoffed. 'I thought bullying was part of a private school's syllabus!'

Jake watched Trick and Kia do a series of ballet moves. Not more interpretative dance, *please*. 'No, but money talks. If the little preciouses want to walk the corridors dressed like Elsa from *Frozen*, they do.'

Margo shook her head. 'There's a change happening, even in local comps. I can feel it.'

Jake rammed the last of his crisps in his mouth. 'Well, you'll find out soon enough when you're teaching the local dropouts how to hula-hoop.'

'There's much more to training to be a PE teacher than hula-hooping, thank you. I have to teach Humanities as well. Anyway . . . ' She surmised her brother was slipping into one of his infamous sulks. 'I better go find Buddy before the main event; he loves a spectacle.'

Hannah barrelled through the door with three helium balloons – one with a 1 on, one with a 7, and another with 18, but '−1' scrawled underneath in Sharpie. 'Don't panic, D'Arcys! Princess Party is here!' She kissed Jake on the cheek. 'Hi, fave. How are you? Why the serious face?'

'I've been doing my "I can cope with this" grin for an hour-plus. Where've you been?'

'Tube was hotter than Satan's ass-crack – oh, hi, Mrs D – so I got off for a breather. At the pub.' She beamed widely. 'But I'm here now.'

'No Dean?'

'Circuit training. We've lost him to sweat and spandex. Oh, hiiiiii, Tricky baby; happy birthday!' Hannah enveloped Trick in a bear hug and pretended to slobber kisses all over his face. Jake didn't get this dynamic at *all*. 'I was *screaming* at your latest vid. From Sunday? With the Coke float?'

Trick absorbed the adoration like a king. 'Wait till you see tonight's.'

Apart from being an annoyingly conscientious A-level student, Trick's side hustle was making videos, broadcasting to the nation – well, his subscribers – and he was, by all accounts, quite good at it. Jake had watched a couple out of loyalty when Trick had first started his channel, but had found them superficial and aimless. Jake's favourite YouTubers were fitness gurus who did kettlebell swings using a half-packed trolley case or instruction videos on how to fasten a necktie to look like a Danish pastry. Droning on to the camera about last night's TV, celebrity romances and concealer did not appeal. But, as lacking as it was in plot, Trick's followers were genuinely interested in his story.

Kia tapped a fork on her plastic tumbler – presumably to get a bit of hush but it sounded like she was drumming on it like a toddler – and the lights dimmed. On the screen appeared a huge picture of Trick at the age of, Jake guessed, seven. Jake had to admit his brother had been cute: jet-black hair and shining blue eyes; not cherubic and pudgy like other children, but sleek and angular. He was destined to be a beauty; it had helped him get away with murder for years.

Jake looked round as everyone faced front, rapt. Amelia huddled in next to him. Jake breathed in her scent and felt mildly placated. But *still*. How much longer? He never understood this family trait of hanging on Trick's every word. Jake and Margo got on well for siblings three years apart, but she and Trick were closer. Maybe it was because he had left home long ago and they hadn't, but when he heard people talk about 'the D'Arcys' he thought of the other four, not picturing himself among them at all. And the nickname thing had always bugged him. At school, the coolest people had alter egos. As ridiculous as they were, nicknames were labels of belonging; tribal. It was the same at home. Margo was really Megan, but renamed as a toddler, after a character in an old sitcom who she looked like when she sulked. Trick's name was instant cool, Dad was Pat, of course, and Mum was Vee – short for Genevieve, which she'd thought too posh to use every day, but kept the name for her hair salon. Jake, however, was just Jake. No cutesy nickname, no extra moniker, nothing. Not even Jacob, which would've given him somewhere to go, just Jake. If you don't feel part of the pack, even the smallest thing feels like a barrier to entry.

Finally, a video started up, its title flashing up in humongous purple letters:

PATRICK STARCHASER D'ARCY: A LIFE

Jake poked Margo, who was in front of him. 'Starchaser? Where the hell is *that* from?'

'He's always wanted a middle name. We workshopped worse ones, believe me. I quite like it.'

Old home footage now, along with photo collages, YouTube snippets, highlights of birthdays past. The camera loved Trick and he was only too happy to bask in its admiration. Once it was over, Trick stood on a footstool to address his crowd. Photos still flashed behind him, the silence punctuated by the tap of Kia's talons on the laptop as she clicked 'Next'. It was like being at a funeral – the corpse being humility.

Trick surveyed the room with a nervy yet imperious grin.

'It means so much to have you here, special people, who I love. I feel lucky to be celebrated and honoured in this way, year in, year out.'

Day in, day out was more accurate. Eva Peron on the balcony of the Casa Rosada had nothing on this. Jake sighed heavily; Amelia nudged him.

'I'm proud of who I am. To be open. I *never* hide. But over time, I've had big chats with myself about who I am and what I want.' He tugged at his sleeve and wobbled slightly on the stool. 'I've been one hundred per cent supported all my life by my besties and my family. My squad helped me see I needed to make this happen. This is officially my last birthday as a child.'

Jake heard a strangled cry from somewhere in the room. Mother was off already.

'And now, the next part of my journey. The big news, what I'm about to say, may not be a shock, because you know me better than anyone, but today I can say, officially, that I . . . Trick D'Arcy, me, *I* . . . am . . . a gay man.'

The applause was deafening, like a game show audience told there were the keys to a Ferrari under one of their seats. Joanie barked wildly from the porch. Hannah let off party poppers and Dad shouted about 'cracking open the bubbly'. Tears were streaming down Amelia's face. Jake stood still, trying to process. What the hell? Who *cared*? Surely this was a given? Trick had dressed like an explosion in a glitter factory and called Hollywood actors 'gorgey' for years! Like he'd said, no shock. But this was how Trick rolled: a gold star for breathing in and out. Jake felt like he was watching this happen through a debilitating head cold, as everyone lined up to congratulate Trick.

Amelia glared at him in search of a reaction, so Jake forced out 'Brilliant' and took his place in the line-up. Margo squeezed Trick tight before kissing him on the forehead. 'Well done, bro. Can't wait for us to go out on the pull together . . . I'm *joking*! You couldn't handle me.'

Jake held out his hand for Trick to shake. Trick grinned and took it, while Jake lightly slapped his brother on the back. Time to stay something brotherly, familiar. 'God bless you, you little attention-seeker. Obviously we all knew,' Jake found himself saying. 'Shoulda filmed this one! Imagine the clicks! Perfect marketing campaign for you!'

Jake gave a hearty, fraudulent laugh, but Trick's smile evaporated, eyes deadened and he dropped Jake's hand from his grip immediately. He turned away and hugged Reenie, who was next in line. Jake stood mute for a few seconds before backing away. Oops.

'Do you really have to go and check on them?' complained Hannah as Jake finished his pint.

'I promised. Well, *Amelia* did. Mum and Dad won't be back until after midnight.' Jake looked at his watch. 'It's been three hours and they were lining up shots of raspberry liqueur on Mum's hostess trolley when we left. At *six*.'

'I thought Margo was chaperoning! I haven't seen you two for ages.' She nodded at Amelia.

Jake realised neither woman particularly wanted to be left alone together. He pushed his glass away. 'I don't want to leave her by herself.' He absolutely did; the thought of looking into Trick's eyes again didn't appeal. 'I'll be straight back.'

Jake chuckled as he stood at the gate. A few teenagers, dressed like sentient laundry baskets, were smoking at the side of the house, some managing to multi-task and urinate at the same time. The *state* of them.

Trick saw Jake making his way down the hallway, and sighed so wearily Jake heard it over the din of the music.

'What are *you* doing here?'

'*Mum* said, remember? Can you ask your friends to stop piddling up the side of the house like it's the toilets at Glastonbury?'

'Piddling. *Cute.* When have *you* been to Glastonbury? Watching Kasabian on the telly doesn't count, you know.' Trick whirled round and melted into the throng.

Almost every room was full of gangly adolescents – actually, all consenting adults now, Jake supposed – pogoing to songs almost as old as they were, screaming, 'This is sick!' The lounge was in darkness save for the lights of a few mobile phones strobing off the walls. In the kitchen, Kia was pouring vodka into egg cups for a line of giggling girls who all looked young enough to be at nursery. The vodka was expensive; the binge-drinking clearly endorsed by parents glad to be rid of their precocious teens. This was another world. Watching from the doorway was a young man, kind of familiar, tapping a cigarette against its packet, eyes pinhole-small in the kitchen's bright light. Even over the music, Jake could hear somebody puking violently in the downstairs loo.

The teenager noticed Jake and nodded. 'Trick's dad, right?'

Fucking hell, the little shit; he'd said that on purpose, surely? Jake blanched and shook his head, laughing. '*Brother*.'

'Yeah, I know. Just messing. Jake, right?' The young man nodded down at his cigarette. 'Wanna go in the garden and chill?'

Jake hesitated a second too long, and the guy looked startled. 'Oh, not like *that*,' he spluttered. 'Like, a smoke?'

They sat facing one another on patio chairs. His mum must've had one of her attacks of design inspiration when setting up the party; there were candles at strategic points on the decking. The effect was very DIY makeover show.

They shook hands. 'I'm Hot Will.'

He held out a cigarette as Jake stifled a laugh, before taking it – even though he hadn't smoked since he was nineteen. 'I've heard of you. I thought "Hot Will" was something *other* people called you.'

Hot Will smiled. 'Yeah, at first. Turned into, like, a whole *thing*. It's my name now.'

'Why do they call you that?'

Hot Will's mouth fell open. 'Why d'ya think? There were two boys called Will in Year Nine. *I'm* the hot one.'

Jake imagined the street value of this boy's self-belief. 'And what about the other one? Was he stuck with "Ugly Will"?'

Hot Will looked offended that anyone could think him so cruel. 'Of course not!' he exclaimed. 'He was . . . "*Other* Will".'

Jake pulled on the cigarette, trying not to show it was burning his throat. He remembered seeing Hot Will lurking over the years now, one of the hunched, sportswear-clad acolytes who shuffled into rooms, grabbed snacks and exited without a word. They'd all grown up, Kia, Trick and now this one – shapeshifting before Jake's eyes while he remained resolutely, pathetically the same. The younger man had a swagger and a confidence that would've been totally alien to Jake at that age. Only bullies and beauties – usually a killer combination of the two – had it, and Jake had been neither. He suddenly felt unusual . . . what was it? Then he realised: envy. He was jealous of a teenager who smoked like Justin Bieber doing a Robert De Niro impression.

'You having a good time?' Hot Will said now, scratching his stubble. 'What would you usually do on a Saturday night?'

Jake laughed, again, dangerously nearing his quota for the year. 'I can't think of anywhere I'd rather be than babysitting a load of projectile-vomiting hormones in skinny jeans.'

'*I* don't need babysitting. And I would *never* wear skinny jeans.' Silence fell. Hot Will, however, was unfazed and stared off into the distance.

'You *with* someone?'

'Tonight?'

Hot Will crushed his cigarette into the ground – Mum would go nuts when she saw that – and lit another with youthful nonchalance. 'Any time. Generally. *Whenever*.'

'Oh. Yeah. Yes.'

Hot Will looked him up and down, considered him. A pause. What did that look mean? 'Girlfriend?'

Jake's teeth began to chatter, though it wasn't cold. 'Amelia. Yes. Together, uh, three years, I think. Four, maybe.' Why did he keep pretending he couldn't remember?

Hot Will gave a low whistle. 'I'm single.' He had the sadness of a world-weary bachelor in his forties. 'For now.'

'Best way.' Jake stubbed out his cigarette on the bottom of his shoe. Who on Earth was he trying to be? 'So, tell me, *Hot Will*, if there were two Jakes in my class at school, which one would I have been?'

'Which one?'

Jake looked him straight in the eye. 'Yeah. Hot one, or the "other" one?'

Hot Will smiled, then leaned forward to speak. 'I'd need to see the second Jake before making that call.'

'Ha! *Ouch*.'

One set of patio doors slid open; Trick's head appeared, his expression unreadable, but the irritation in his voice unmistakable.

'Hot Will, come do the playlist. Jordan's tunes are *killing* the energy. Come *on*.'

Hot Will stood, took a cigarette out of his packet and placed it in front of Jake. Trick, his head still jutting through the doors like a mouse peering out of its hole, sighed and hissed, 'Seriously', before disappearing.

'See ya, Will,' said Jake, tipping his head to him.

The younger man gave a small salute. '*Hot* Will, remember. Bye . . . ' A discernible pause. '*Hot* Jake, definitely.' He quickly receded into the darkness. Jake lit the cigarette on a candle, at last doing all the coughing he'd held in for Hot Will's benefit. He felt very light-headed, like he'd just shared a lift with a celebrity.

Margo stuck her head out of the back door. 'Honestly, Jake, where've you been? I've got five teenagers in floods of tears and I can't work out why because they're speaking in tongues.' Then: 'Hang on . . . are you *smoking*?'

Jake collapsed on the sofa, listening to Amelia brush her teeth in the bathroom – she was meeting friends for brunch nearby in the morning, so it made sense for her to stay over. He scrolled through Instagram, too tipsy to focus. Margo texted: she'd managed to dispatch the last drunk, puking teenager to their parents. An Instagram post from his brother flashed up, a series of photos posing with his friends, Mum, a spooked-looking Dad peering into the screen and not the lens, his sister, Hannah, Joanie the dog. Everyone. *Nearly* everyone. Underneath:

> Thank u so so so much to every1 supporting me thru my journey. I ❤ all you guys so much >>> mama // poppa // margs // buddy boy // kiki // hot will 🔥 // winston // suze // franky // tobes // ella // jas // angel // hannaaaah // dean // shellie // ameeeelia // dom // kyle // loulou // jord // molly // auntie reeree // jp // my baby joaneeeee // u r all da bessssssst xoxoxox 😍 😘 🕶

Jake read and reread the list, scanning the photos again. Hang on. Dean wasn't even there; why did he get a mention? Was 'joaneeeee' the dog?! There was only one person missing. Him.

So Trick was out of the closet and Jake was in the cold. The omission stung more than it should've. Why had he said what he'd said? Trick was theatrical, effeminate, emotional. Rolling his eyes was his cardio. Nobody with one-liners so sharp could ever be straight. So why did Jake's words hurt him so much? He remembered Trick's face. That day with Evan came back to him, the moments right after, when Jake had come home and stared into the mirror, trying to work out whether anyone would be able to see the change in him. Both he and Evan had looked dead ahead when passing one another in a corridor. Jake had told himself he'd got it out of his system, and assumed Evan had done the same; there had been no more days in supervision, no schleps back to Evan's house for a repeat performance, no further contact at all unless absolutely necessary. But the feeling, the urge . . . Well, despite Jake's protests to himself, they had never left his system, really – if anything they were more intense. And never more so than tonight. Just like the spring when Mum's long-dormant narcissi made an unexpected return to the back garden, a light had gone back on. He knew why Trick was mad. Nobody liked being told who they were.

Jake flicked to Facebook, quickly finding Evan's profile. It was on lockdown so he couldn't see much but a grainy thumbnail photo of a group of people. Begrudging reconnections with hordes of people he'd barely even spoken to at university had taught him that a friend request and a perfunctory message – it would be 'good to catch up' – were as much effort as anyone expected. Jake flopped back on the sofa and drifted into sleep, dreaming about Trick's terrifying slideshow, but instead of pictures of his brother, it was a continuous roll of photographs of Jake, looking guiltier and stupider in each successive one.

two.

Scrolling through pictures tagged with #trickdarcy17, Trick was thrilled. The party had been a success! The two girls throwing up in bin bags right at the end were an extra treat – plenty of social media blackmail potential. Typical for the buzz to die as soon as Jake turned up, though. How did he *do* that? Enter a room and immediately suck the joy from it? Always refusing to join in, and just *be*. Talking to Jake for any length of time was like listening to someone read the back of a cereal packet out loud.

Kia was convinced it was 'eldest child complex'. 'My brother was the same: thought being born first meant you should worship them.'

'He *is* worshipped! Mum sulks for days if he doesn't phone.'

Kia laughed. 'He's mad because you're the fabulous one and he's a . . . what does he do?'

Trick didn't know for sure; it was a family tradition to be dismissive of Jake's job. Dad's building firm, Mum's hairdressing, Margo's teaching vocation – all proper trades you could explain – and obviously Trick was going be an actor and presenter, as well as a content creator. You know, an *interesting* job; stuff you could talk about at parties.

'He's in communications, or something, for . . . uh . . . a big washing powder company that kills wildlife.' No *glamour* to him at all. There was a certain irony about Jake working in communications when during most family gatherings he was, at best, monosyllabic or, more usually, a weapons-grade buzzkill, but Trick hadn't joined the dots sufficiently to make that joke out loud yet.

Kia stroked Trick's leg. 'You okay, babe? We gonna talk about what he said?'

Trick smoothed back his hair. 'He tried to steal my scene.'

Kia said nothing but gave the slightest of nods – her therapist did that and it always made her spill her guts.

'I mean, you *know* how important this is to me. I can't believe he thinks I did it for publicity! Like I need *that*.'

Trick knew he was gay before he even knew what being gay actually was. He always felt different from the children in nursery. They were all so loud, and rambunctious, but there was no grace in what they did, no *flair*. It was so terribly dull. Trick didn't want to run around the playground shouting, holding a truck, or screaming while chasing boys who wanted anyone but *you* to catch them – he wanted to perform, to be seen.

'Patrick has . . . a wonderful flamboyant energy,' was his first teacher's view on parents' evening, while Trick waited outside the classroom practising his catwalk strut, three copies of the children's illustrated encyclopaedia balanced on his head. Trick always knew there had to be more – than what, he didn't know, but he did know whatever was waiting out there for him would *never* be enough. Feeling he was outgrowing his storyline, his enthusiasm dipped toward the end of primary school, so in a panic that the one child who actually seemed to enjoy being there was flagging, his teachers put him in another class, where he met Kia and Hot Will – then just plain old William, but not for long – and realised amazing, theatrical people *did* exist. People just like him who understood that the world was a stage, a performance, and you had to give 110 per cent, even when the spotlight was otherwise engaged.

And then, as puberty took up residence – and after a succession of wet dreams about the guy who sat next to him in double science kissing Hot Will with tongues – Trick finally put a label on it. Gay, but not *just* for the sex. Gay for everything: life, music, fashion, friends. Gay Plus, he liked to call it. Platinum card-holding rejecters of heterosexuality and its dull trappings, like corduroy or leaving the house with no eyeliner on. Jake, in other words.

The prospect of Trick's coming-out had been mulled over for a while – after intense discussions with Hot Will and Kia, he had delayed it a year.

"Live with it a bit, baby boy; it's still new,' Hot Will said as Trick's sixteenth birthday approached – he'd come out himself a few months earlier, to what masqueraded as rapturous congratulations from his parents, but Trick knew different. The ease and charm that made Hot Will so attractive must've been a fluke, because his parents had zero personality, save for their fondness for liquid ecstasy at the tail-end of the nineties and being able to name any techno song from the same period within three seconds of the intro.

Hot Will's parents were irritating former hellraisers who moaned the younger generation didn't do enough drugs and had no rebellious spirit. Time, bitterness and successive Conservative governments had turned them into dinosaurs, even though they were way younger than Trick's own parents.

Hot Will's dad – the apple rolled a marathon's length away from the tree in the hotness stakes – once said he'd watched one of Trick's videos.

'You see, young Patrick, you *overthink* things. You don't just let yourselves chillax. Embrace serendipity, freedom.'

Chillax. Yuk. Easy for him to say with his job as CEO of his own father's company, where he seemed to spend only two days a week. Their moneyed liberalism fooled Hot Will's parents into thinking that flinging an allowance and a frozen king prawn makhani at their teenage son at regular intervals was teaching him how to be a free spirit, and not just feeding their own inherent self-centredness. When Hot Will finally told his parents he was gay, they immediately gave him money for therapy sessions.

'Get all the support you need,' they said, without a trace of irony. Hot Will had donated the money to the content collective; they spent it on lighting. No wonder Hot Will never wanted to be at home.

Burned by his friend's experience, Trick decided coming out at sixteen would be a cliché, anyway. Coming out at seventeen, however, was more grown up, made more sense, like there was something to aim for – or some*one* to aim for.

'You should've seen Jake last night,' squealed Trick. 'Sitting out back with Hot Will *smoking*. So lame. Why can't he be more like *us?*'

Jake never even tried. The Christmas before, Trick had worn his customised Christmas jumper, adorned with body parts of Barbie and Ken dolls acting like baubles on a huge glittery Christmas tree. Yes, he'd been boiling hot in it, but as he always told his followers: 'We must suffer for art.' Trick knew his sartorial expression annoyed Jake, dazzling as ever in his pristine uniform of Oxford shirt and chinos in the perfect shade of migraine. Trick and Kia had taken to calling Jake 'Clean Shirt' behind his back, and Trick had watched in delight as Jake spilled gravy down his front, face wrinkling in displeasure. As he was mopping it up with Mum's second-best napkins, Jake asked Trick about his 'unusual' wardrobe.

'You making a *statement* or something? Just wondered. No offence.'

God, he was so tiresome; his entire conversational repertoire the kind of questions you'd ask one another at a speed-dating night. No offence, indeed – like Jake could ever be controversial enough to offend anyone. Trick had looked round the room. Mum, in her spangly party sweater – so bright that if she stood in the garden, planes would mistake her for Heathrow – Dad's garish Christmas sweater vest, and Margo, upright and uncomfortable in a sleek cocktail gown, even though she wouldn't be leaving the house.

'It's how we roll. You should try making a statement sometime.' Other than a bank statement, Trick had laughed to himself.

Jake had smiled thinly and said one of his dreary conversation destroyers, like 'fair enough', or 'have it your way' – all potential for debate successfully vaccinated against. He had no *bite*. Given how much he sulked in their company, you'd think Jake would be glad to be nothing like them.

Luckily, since meeting Amelia, Jake's visits were rarer, and if he did darken their door, Trick would arrange to be elsewhere or upstairs filming. Watching everyone fawn over him like he was just back from a war – 'A war on style,' he had quipped at Kia one night – was painful. Mum and Dad seemed extra edgy when Jake was around: Mum did this fake giggle after literally everything Jake said and looked at him like he was a big pie she couldn't wait to eat. A personality only a mother could love, he guessed. Dad, too, was a traitor, all bear hugs and clinking beer cans. Lads lads lads. *Pathetic*. All that effort and creeping round, just to make sure he was comfortable, and for no result: Jake would just stand there, limply, like he'd rather be anywhere else – back in his boring, minimalist open prison of a flat, watching documentaries and bookmarking articles about climate change on his iPad. The atmosphere lightened the second the door closed behind him; Trick wished they could get the locks changed.

Kia hunched over the laptop and took a deep breath. 'Oooooh. Your stats are through the roof, babe. I'm so proud.'

Kia and Hot Will were Trick's unofficial partners in his ongoing venture, the eventual goal kind of vague but with a view to world domination or being a billionaire, whichever came first. Hot Will had a flair for shooting and editing and Kia was excellent at picking themes, spotting trends and keeping on top of admin, and they shared the spoils when they came in. It was all down to Trick in front of the camera, though; he was the draw and they all knew it. Despite appearances with close friends or sassing his family, Trick saw himself as quiet – or so he had once claimed to Kia, who had sat with her mouth open in awe for a full five minutes at the *audacity* – but once that ring light was on, and Hot Will did his 'rolling' action, Trick was a superstar. It didn't matter what kind of cynical bullshit Jake came out with, Trick knew who he was now and nothing could change that. Yet. A glitch. A feeling he couldn't shake. A thousand mattresses but still the pea prodded into his back.

When Hot Will finally woke up, Trick breezily asked what he'd said to Jake in the garden. Hot Will had no juice for him.

'We talked about his girlfriend, mainly.'

Trick loved Amelia and couldn't understand why someone as funny and pretty as her was interested in Jake. 'What about her?'

'Oh, you know, stuff. I think he's okay, actually. He looks a bit like Ryan Gosling.'

Trick was aghast. 'You'd have to hit me with a cricket bat a few times before he'd look like Ryan Gosling to me.'

'Hmm.' Hot Will's head was elsewhere, but sensing a chill, he jolted back into the now. 'Anyway, baby boy, let me see the comments on the new vid.'

Hot Will pulled Trick in close as they crowded round the screen. Trick took a deep breath to get as much of Hot Will's scent as possible while they were touching. But in among the deodorant and his sharp fragrance was the inevitable smell of cigarettes, which instantly transported Trick back to his brother's face illuminated by the tiny candles, not pinched and awkward as usual, but relaxed, cheerful. As if reliving it, his eyes tracked to Hot Will's face across from Jake, similarly illuminated but, in there somewhere, something brighter and smouldering. His eyes, Trick remembered now as they broke apart, gleamed with expectation. Flirtatious? Nah, surely not. But Hot Will never looked at *him* like that. Another reason coming out was important: Hot Will was out, proud, with an incredible knack of getting attention, for which there would be a lot of competition. The best way to put yourself in contention was to show you were ready for the next level, whatever that was. Trick feared he would get left behind.

'You ever noticed,' said Trick, giving Hot Will a friendly tap on the shoulder, 'how close together Jake's eyes are? And small? Like two raisins on a dinner plate. Aren't they?' But Hot Will wasn't listening.

three.

To Jake's disappointment, Charlie, Adyan and Dean confirmed what he already knew: he'd handled Trick's coming-out badly.

Adyan tutted as he sat down next to Charlie, the beers on the table wobbling in recognition. 'When my cousin came out we had to act surprised. He thought he'd done such a brilliant job hiding it. He had pictures of Princess Diana on his wall! He wasn't even born when she died.'

Dean ambled over to the table. 'Watch the casual homophobia, boys. Hannah said it was sweet.'

Jake shivered in recollection. 'It was like the *Oscars*. I kept expecting someone to get in my face with a microphone and ask me, "Who are you wearing?"'

'What did your mum and dad say?'

'Usual. Pulitzer Prize for Trick, as per, and a "don't be grumpy" for me. I'm *not* grumpy.' Jake's friends stifled a laugh. '*What*?'

Charlie licked beer foam off his top lip. 'Er . . . well.'

Adyan grimaced. 'Yeah, we definitely *don't* call you Arsey D'Arcy.'

Dean nudged him. 'It's a good thing, what we like about you. Thoughtful, aren't you? Brooding, like . . . uh.'

Charlie coughed. 'Like Mr Darcy off that film! A serious, responsible kind of dude. Remember that movie? Maybe I watched it at school?'

Jake rolled his eyes. Thousands of pounds Charlie's education must've cost. Not for the first time, Jake knew he'd made the right decision staying at the local comp, as draining as it had been. '*Pride and Prejudice*. It's a *book*. Jesus.'

Adyan pointed. 'There you go! Arsey D'Arcy! *Yes*, mate.'

Charlie quickly rearranged his face into a serious expression. 'That brings me nicely to something else. I have serious, *responsible* "man business" to discuss.'

The wedding. Again. It was over a year until Charlie married Holly, but they'd talked about nothing else for centuries. It was thanks to Charlie and Holly that he'd met Amelia, as she'd been at university with Holly – but, honestly, Jake felt he'd lived every moment of his pals' relationship: courtship, proposal, engagement party, buying a flat together.

'Stag.'

The others cheered. 'Yes!' bellowed Dean. 'Where?'

Charlie suddenly looked nervous. 'Depends who arranges it.' He laid a hand on Jake's shoulder. What was this? Jake looked slowly from his friend's hand to his face. An inexplicable rush of emotion brought a lump to his throat. Charlie's eyes looked glassy. 'Mate,' he croaked, 'be my best man. Yeah?'

Nobody ever asked Jake to do things like this. He wasn't sure why. Maybe he always looked too busy, sounded too *arsey*? Maybe he wasn't best man material. Worst man, he felt sometimes. Not man enough?

'Well?'

Jake tried not to get excited. He did his usual thought process: counter the joy, keep it real, this could all be taken away from you any second. His mind was flooded with images of herding thirty drunk stags round a market town – seven different pubs, all called The Grapes. Football chat. The word 'tits' reverberated around his head.

'Are you sure?'

Charlie's arm crept along Jake's shoulder, pulling him in tighter. 'You're the man for the job. Organised. Dependable. The only one I trust not to tie me naked to Tower Bridge.'

Adyan and Dean tapped their glasses on the table, chanting in unison. 'Jake. Jake. Jake.'

Jake looked back at Charlie, desperate to tell him what it meant to be given a chance, to be part of it, recognised as a man who *could*, and would. But it wouldn't do to say it out loud. Too soppy. He filed away his euphoria under 'to enjoy later, alone', and slowly raised his glass in fake resignation to his fate. 'Okay, okay.' He turned back to Charlie. 'It would be an honour, I suppose.'

Charlie beamed. 'Excellent, get the next round in, my dude.'

*

'You'll be brilliant,' Amelia said over dinner the next day. 'Holly hasn't picked her bridesmaids yet.'

She could feel the warmth of Jake's excitement as he squeezed her hand like he was consoling a dying relative. 'Don't worry. I'm sure she'll pick you.'

Jake's serious face almost made Amelia laugh out loud, but she held it in check. Why did men assume that all women wanted to do was dress like Disney princesses and cry hot, fragranced tears at the sight of their besties scrapping over a bouquet? So *basic*. She almost didn't *want* to be asked. Once you'd done it a few times, being a bridesmaid was terminally boring. Amelia spent most of her twenties standing about in dresses that were either too sheer or too unwieldy, being prodded and posed by irritable wedding photographers. She'd suffered lukewarm champagne, cold and chewy wedding breakfasts, and interminable speeches, *dying* to slouch but instead remaining a poised, perfect vision of beauty, her hair coiled atop her head or straightened into submission and tickling her back. Pre-wedding Prosecco, girlie hen-night cocktails – she was *done*. She wanted to dance herself sweaty and drink beer, drifting in and out of the marquee whenever she wanted, not standing to attention all day and night, batting away well-meaning aunties who kept telling her, 'You next!' Did she even *want* to be next? Her friends were coupling up fast; only two minutes ago they were lounging in shared flats, listening to dubstep, and flicking cigarettes into makeshift ashtrays made from old house bricks. Everyone had gone respectable. Her workmates were the same. She was only thirty, though; surely there was time for that later? Not that Jake seemed in any hurry; their relationship trajectory made the concept of limbo look rigorously scheduled.

Amelia jumped at the insistent hum of a message alert. Holly. Of course. Asking that fucking question. Amelia took three goes at typing 'delighted' sincerely before hitting send.

*

Jake was googling 'sophisticated elite cultured stag nights Europe' when his manager Lisa came bowling out of a meeting room looking flustered. As Mannheim-Turner-Zoring's newest director, she was still getting a rough time from her fellow company A-listers.

'They all call me darlin', even the other women, the wankers,' she moaned as she dumped handouts on Jake's desk. 'Latest on the Telveril product recall. Please make it sound as non-lethal and life-threatening as possible. Thanks, babe.'

Jake had worked for MTZ since leaving university, trying a few disciplines before finding his 'calling' in corporate comms. Any scandal, or bad press, he could take the sting out of the tail, and thanks to his serious, confident demeanour – what his family called the 'sulk' – he'd worked his way up.

'Anyone actually died?'

Lisa bowed in mock prayer. 'As of yet, no. Draft the press release and update the website before someone actually *does* throw a seven. Then, me, you and Harry can go over the strategy.'

Ah, Harry. One of his longest relationships that wasn't Amelia or his old pals. They'd started on the graduate scheme together, gone off on secondments, but always ended up back in the same team. They'd hit it off straightaway. Harry was basic – he still used teenage antiperspirant and sometimes had tomato ketchup sandwiches for lunch – but he was funny, handsome and super-smart. They started in sales, which they both hated. They'd meet at the weekend for a couple of 'jars', as Harry called them, to watch football, and Jake would pretend to be interested even though he'd point-blank refuse to watch it with his own father or best mates. They went to comedy gigs together, too, and when on conferences or business trips abroad, they'd always hang out. MTZ notoriously didn't care about graduates who weren't tough enough to survive: they had to be available at a moment's notice, and share hotel rooms. One time, visiting the Madrid office, they'd picked up two women in the hotel bar and taken them back to their room, kissing and fooling around – Jake in the bathroom while Harry bagged the bedroom. Jake's date had eventually got bored and gone back to her room once it was clear no condoms meant no sex, so Jake had stayed in the bathroom, sitting on the loo wrapped in a duvet, falling asleep to the sound of Harry thrusting and grunting as the bed – and his date – squeaked in recognition of the (considerable, energetic) effort.

One trip, the summer before he met Amelia, they'd tried and failed to impress the locals in Cologne, so had gone back to the room secreting currywurst in their jackets, cracking open bottles of lager and flicking through the hotel's entertainment offering.

'I can't believe there's no porn.' Harry had belched loudly and scratched his groin. Jake's eyes had darted back and forth a couple of times – his fight-or-flight reaction. Harry had suddenly had a revelation, and grabbed his laptop from his suitcase. 'As MTZ says: "Let's innovate".'

He'd found an adult website and flicked through the options like he was ordering a takeaway. 'Mum and daughter. Hmmm. Mum and son?! Wow. Priests and nuns. Okay. Errrr. Threesomes! Whaddaya reckon?'

What was this? An elaborate ruse? Was a hidden cameraman about to burst out of the wardrobe? Jake had waited; nothing happened. Harry had selected a video, two disengaged women and a skinny guy rolling around on a bed in a hotel room only slightly dingier than their own.

Jake's eyes had bored into the screen. The man had a woman's name tattooed on his wrist; Jake wondered how 'Araminta' would feel about her name being so prominent in the inevitable money shot.

Jake had noticed Harry's breathing quicken, get deeper.

Was he? No way. Did he dare look? What was he supposed to do? Laugh? Say 'phwoar' and rub himself too? Whatever he did, Jake had been absolutely sure that he shouldn't look at Harry. Too gay. Jake had risked a peek. Harry had taken off his boxers – Jake was now shaking like a bookcase in an earthquake – and was staring intently at the screen. Holy shit. What next? Harry's head had suddenly jerked up and he'd given Jake a drunken, lopsided grin. Somehow he looked more beautiful doing it. Jake had felt trapped. He hadn't wanted this moment to end, but had feared spooking Harry and causing irreparable damage between them. He'd wrestled briefly with his instincts before deciding, uncharacteristically, 'fuck it'.

Soon, Jake's pyjama bottoms were on the floor and he'd pretended to look at the screen too, but his eyes had kept flashing to Harry's face – forehead slicked with sweat, tongue between teeth in bitter concentration – before lowering them to his groin where the action was. Amazing how quickly reality could become unrecognisable. Jake had felt weird being silent, so every few seconds, he'd let out a fake moan. The effect had been like the very last of the air being coughed out of a deflating balloon, but it had worked a charm on Harry who, as they'd both reddened and picked up the pace, had once more looked right at Jake. This time they hadn't looked away, just right into each other's eyes, until it was done.

The next morning, when Jake had woken, Harry was already packed and downstairs at breakfast. At the conference, Harry had flirted with Melissa Gardner from accounts, and Jake had later seen the two of them kissing sloppily in a lift after the evening drinks. Harry hadn't come back to their room that night. Jake had been surprised by his feelings; he had expected shame, maybe, but it hadn't come until way later. The days, weeks and months passed, and, while Harry was still friendly, the invitations to drinks and comedy clubs ceased. Once they'd completed the graduate scheme, they were deemed worthy of a room each on any business trips. Harry began dating Melissa. Eventually Jake stopped thinking about it daily – although, if pressed, he could give a very detailed description of Harry's penis; it was burned into his retinas. Since Trick had come out to rapturous acceptance, though, it was back on his mind; the cost of experiencing these thoughts and feelings alone was trying to find some kind of meaning in them. Trick had said he knew who he was, and was proud of it, and from where Jake had been standing, it had been gimmicky, yes, but obviously liberating. So now, every time Harry brushed past his chair, or sent him an email, or shook his hand at the end of another successful project, instead of it being nothing, it was 'something', like he was back in that hotel room in Cologne. But without the grunts and shrieks of really bad porn ringing off the walls. Small mercies.

Jake's romantic history had never been straightforward; his first kiss was Rosie Flint at the school disco, aged thirteen.

'We're the only ones not getting off,' she'd said by way of chat-up line, so he'd obliged. After, she had said it was 'Okay actually' and left him with his thoughts and, as it turned out, his first ever cold sore.

Most of the girls weren't romantically interested in Jake. While other boys in his year shot up and broadened, Jake stayed weedy and childlike. His mum had always told him it was wrong to stare at girls or 'lech at them like they're pieces of meat', and she often clobbered creeps on public transport, screaming, 'Pervert!', so he tried not to leer, but he did enjoy looking. Their hair, the softness of their faces, the curves of their body, the way the waist went in. Their confidence was self-affirming and joyous, rather than the boys' brash entitlement and masculinity, which felt much more exclusionary. He could talk to girls more easily, and even lightly flirt, but as the hormones kicked in, their attentions turned to the boys becoming men before their eyes, and, to his surprise, so did Jake's. Quite a revelation.

He loved their arms. Still did. Strong, svelte, meaty, wiry, whatever. From shoulder to fingertips, he was an avid fan. He'd watch boys from across the room, eyes trained on their throats as they spoke, both enjoying and fearing the carefree way they'd scratch themselves, sitting with thighs wide on the science-lab stools. Jake was self-conscious of openly mimicking them, but he gave it his best shot. The girls wanted them, and Jake desperately wanted to be wanted. He stood sometimes in the garage at home, lifting his father's dumbbells trying to get those arms that he and the girls loved so much. Pat overestimated his own strength, however, and liked weights to be a challenge, so Jake struggled to manage more than four bicep curls before collapsing to the ground. Being strong was his dad's thing, anyway; Jake was annoyed at himself for thinking he could ever be like him.

Gradually, Jake realised he didn't just want to be *like* the boys. There was something else. He began fantasising about them, but in a totally different way than girls. When imagining sex with women, he pictured himself a romantic hero or master of seduction, that perfect boyfriend asked in for coffee at the end of a date. Even though he didn't like coffee.

With boys, though, it was more . . . primal, almost, with occasional forays into science fiction. He dreamed of stopping time in the changing room before PE lessons and getting closer to Lloyd, Todd or that French guy who turned up in Year 10. Hervé. Fucking *hell*, Hervé. Typically French, Jake thought at the time – a five o'clock shadow by morning break and a manly, musky smell, with a cosmopolitan strut. In Jake's tacky dream sequences, once time was frozen, he'd tiptoe over to his classmates, rendered as statues – 3D printed now, he supposed – to be near them, to feel their heat. The perversion of it embarrassed him, however, so in real life he never dared more than a glance while they got changed.

Once, he'd lingered too long on Hervé's awful cartoon boxers and Hervé had crudely called over: 'You wanna suck my balls, huh, Jake?' It had killed the attraction stone-dead, and the fantasy. Schoolboys never forgot, and it was mentioned at every PE lesson for months – Jake had kept his eyes trained on the wall. Who needed their scrawny legs and weedy chests, anyway?

He'd never told anyone about this attraction, dismissing it as hormones working themselves out – wise beyond his years or, as his mum used to say through a cloud of blue smoke, 'old head on young shoulders'. He'd assumed it would pass when he met the right girl. He still wanted women; if anything, after the incident with Hervé, his lust for women increased. He never panicked about his urges, was more bemused by them. He would lie in bed thinking, Am I actually a poof, then? – adopting the vernacular of the back of the school bus, which helped to keep the idea totally ridiculous. There were gay guys at school, sure, but if they saw something in Jake they never commented on it – they were usually grateful he wasn't calling them names or mimicking their voices like other boys. But Jake had made a conscious decision to distance himself, for reasons he couldn't quite understand. It was a risk, he supposed; yes, they were targeted by the bullies, but popular kids more or less left them alone because they couldn't relate. They were dismissed as weirdos and avoided. It was 'crossing the floor' that attracted attention. Andrew Forker – one-time bookish nerd who wrote poetry for a series of frizzy-haired girlfriends – and his sudden penchant for chunkier shoes, the distinct whiff of ladies' perfume and a smear of badly applied eyeliner attracted attention. Hockey-team Matt having long chats on the bus home with Millie the lesbian caused quite a stir and led to months of speculation about his sexuality – it turned out they were both learning guitar with the same teacher. At primary school, his main tormentor, George Weston, had been open about his distaste for Jake, picking him last for games or punching him whenever he got too close, and Jake had worried this cloud of fists, fury and darkness would follow him. Thankfully, in the last term before moving up to high school, George had clubbed the wrong child over the head with his skateboard – the son of the local police station's desk sergeant – and his educational journey had taken a sharp left turn. At secondary school, then, it had been more about keeping quiet, head down, editing himself to be as inoffensive or unremarkable as possible. Controversy, or attention, could change you for ever. And, overall, aside from the odd blip, like staring at Hervé, Jake assumed he'd been successful. The gay kids at school seemed indifferent to him – he never made their 'top 20 buff guys' lists online, which the girls used as their bible when flirting with boys at school friends' birthday parties – which led him to think his attraction to men couldn't stay around for ever, that it wasn't real. If he stayed focused and acted like everyone wanted him to act, he reasoned, everything would sort itself out. But the confusing dreams and fantasies returned; the soft tongue of Edie from 11C would morph into the forceful kiss of Hervé, and vice versa, and he would sit bolt upright on waking, hands instinctively going first to his mouth, then the embarrassing bump in his pyjamas, as if he was trying to hold in the secret. He realised what he thought an aberration was the norm – at least *part* of the norm – and that the rest of the word wouldn't understand.

four.

They were having a Saturday morning out together in a bakery, munching through a basket of breads, croissants and jams. As Jake watched Amelia butter her walnut loaf, his gaze tracked to the table behind where a blond, moneyed family were working their way through the messiest things on the menu.

Sitting slightly apart from them, but definitely one of them, as his hair was like snow, was a cool little boy, around seven, playing with several dolls and wearing a pair of shades that Trick would no doubt have called *fab-drag-ulous*: bright pink, with shooting stars round the lenses.

His favourite was an *immaculately* groomed doll he referred to as Caress, as he fed her a muffin. Jake filtered out the clacking of crockery and dreary middle-class small talk – 'I wanna be kitchening in the basement and laying the synthetic lawn by September' – to hear the boy's chirpy narration. He was so bright and cute, but was obviously hard work – he was in the middle of demanding a decaf latte for his doll. The rest of the family treated this like standard behaviour. The little boy looked into a compact as his smaller sister watched, rapt.

'Can I try on your glasses, Hector?'

The boy sighed dramatically and handed over his prized shades, mechanically turning the compact round to her as she clumsily put the glasses on with her precious, chubby fingers.

'I like them,' she warbled.

The compact swung back to face its owner. 'I don't *think* so, Maisie,' he deadpanned, whipping the shades off her head. 'Not very *you*.'

Jake stifled a laugh. What a legend.

Amelia looked up from her phone. 'What's funny?'

'Oh, nothing. That little guy at the table behind.'

Amelia turned to look, knocking her coffee cup over in the process. The clatter of porcelain on wood and the ensuing commotion startled the boy, who looked up and caught Jake staring. The boy slowly put his doll to one side, took off his glasses, and reached into his satchel – baby blue with unicorns on – to pull out a crayon and pad. He drew with exaggerated concentration, occasionally peeking to see whether Jake was still watching. Jake was jolted back to those moments at school when he worried about being found out, if the editing failed and you showed yourself to be someone else all along.

'I was partial to playing with a doll in my time,' Jake said finally.

'Were you? That's quite cool.'

'Well, they weren't mine. Reenie's daughter had hundreds. She let me play with them round at hers.' Jake thought back to Gina's legion of flaxen-haired, orange-skinned dolls, painted with bemused smiles, and remembered one afternoon, when his dad had come to collect him, Reenie and Gina at the door, Gina holding out one of her C-list dolls to him.

'Borrow her if you like.'

Did he really remember his heart quickening? He definitely recalled his little hand hesitating. Then, his dad's throaty chuckle, and a refusal on his behalf.

'Ah, more than enough toys at home – we'll never fit this little lady in there. We'll bring some of Jake's over next time, eh?'

That first flush of confusion burned as his dad had scooped him up in his arms, Jake staring over his shoulder as Reenie and Gina waved, getting smaller until the doll was just a dot.

Now, Jake cleared his throat, and thanked the waiter for mopping up the spilled coffee, before glancing up to see Amelia smiling, looking at him anew. He didn't often share secrets.

'What kind of dolls did you play with? Crying baby or pneumatic knockers Barbie?'

'Barbie. Maybe it was the hooters that appealed.' He laughed awkwardly, aware of sounding ridiculous.

Amelia wrinkled her nose. '*Hooters*! Yuk. You don't seem like the kind of boy to play with dolls.'

He smiled. 'Maybe I was just anxious to get my hands on a naked woman.' Amelia winced. Why was he like this? 'Anyway . . . I grew out of it.'

'Well, not entirely. You've always been keen to get your hands on *my* . . . uh . . . hooters.' Amelia chuckled. 'Sometimes I wish I could go back to playing with my dolls all day – they used to have amazing sexy dates with my brother's Action Man. And of course all Freddie was interested in was brushing my dolls' hair. All the signs were there.' Jake bristled at the mention of Amelia's gay brother, but she didn't notice. 'Wouldn't *you* like to do that? Go back to when things were simpler? To Gina's dolls, or your Lego, or whatever?'

Jake smiled. 'Absolutely. Well, the Lego, for sure.' But nothing had been simpler then. At all.

*

Amelia hated not being able to work things out. She was a problem solver. As a teenager, she'd routinely ruin boyfriends' lives by completing unfathomable video games without breaking a sweat and was a dream when working out complicated logistics – probably why she'd been called on to organise so many sodding hen nights. But Jake continued to be a puzzle, even after all these years. At first, she'd found it intriguing. Men were usually all over her, splashing the cash – which she actually found suffocating and demeaning – but when she'd first met Jake, at yet another wedding of two people far too young to be plighting their troth to anything more serious than a Netflix account, she'd felt drawn to him. He was wry and charming, no hint of sleaze; everything he'd said was carefully considered, with grace and purpose. He was funny, but didn't laugh at his own jokes; instead, his eyes had glinted and looked off into middle distance to let the punchline land. His description of the bride's bouquet looking like it had been picked out of the blades of a threshing machine had her screaming – it had been a very unfortunate attempt to use wildflowers and different grasses – and as he'd pulled apart the menu, table settings and bizarre token system for paying for drinks with acidic precision, she'd wanted him to be her best friend for ever. He'd been attentive, too, flagging down canapés or signalling to barmen for another bottle – once he'd checked she'd wanted to share one. He'd asked before pouring her wine; most men would have sloshed it in, trying to get her drunk. When he'd poured it was deliberate, careful, the same amount for each of them. She'd known she wasn't dealing with the usual predator here; this was the kind of man she'd read about in dog-eared copies of *Tatler* in the dentist's, or heard her aunties mourn after another encounter with millennial rudeness in the Co-Op. This was a gentleman. Her neck had flushed in realisation. She had smiled warmly as she'd signalled, yes, she did want a top-up. He'd looked into her eyes as he poured – grateful, maybe, to be finally recognised for who he was. She couldn't tell whether he fancied her and it had infuriated and delighted her. When, at the end of the evening, she had eventually grabbed that tie – expensive, she'd noted, but understated – pulling it, and Jake, toward her, it had felt like the sweetest of victories. He still excited her now, in a way, and she'd feel a strange surge of affection for him whenever she spotted him getting a bit out of his depth – he wasn't great in large groups of strangers and seemed to have a personality transplant whenever he crossed the threshold of his family home – but lately he'd been prone to drifting off, like he was trying to remember the last item on a shopping list while she was talking to him. It was starting to grate. She didn't see why she was kind of . . . secondary in his thoughts. Why couldn't he just talk to her? Sometimes she missed her last ex before Jake – a fucking biblical liar but at least she'd held his attention. But, no, Jake was different in a good way, the *best* of ways. Still, she wasn't sure how much more of this difference – or *in*difference – she could take without screaming.

Over cans of gin and tonic while wrapping a mountain of Christmas presents, she aired her confusion over Jake to her best friend Rudi. There had been no talk of moving in, not even as a joke. Couples who got together after them were already getting intimate with mortgage brokers. 'I thought I was doing everything right, y'know? Not being *that* girl. I never ask about moving in, even after three years. I don't leave my stuff there. *He* bought me a toothbrush to keep there. I don't even have a drawer, officially, and that's fine.'

Rudi sniffed. 'But . . . '

'But is it gonna *progress*? Who's gonna say it? Do I have to start sneakily leaving my knickers there?'

'You should see how fast lesbians are. Man, we move in together really quick. Some go back for a shag after the second date and never leave.' Rudi guffawed.

'I thought that was a stereotype.'

'Stereotypes are stereotypes for a reason. Sometimes they're true.' Rudi crushed her empty can and broke open another. 'At least he's not full of bullshit or fake promises . . . '

Amelia's previous boyfriends had been flaky, consummate liars. Players. Nice cars, big bouquets, but sacks of shit to go alongside. Jake had a quality to him that those who came before had lacked, an air of seriousness and dependability, but he still made her laugh like nobody else. He'd never led her to believe she'd be moving into his flat, or *any* flat, and when she left stuff behind, he'd say she could keep it there if it was easier. Easier. More convenient. But never because he wanted it there. Or her.

That morning in the bakery was the latest example. Amelia preferred to stay in on the weekends she spent at Jake's, with bacon sandwiches, ketchupy kisses and the prospect of sex – satisfactory and consistent but not earth-shattering, she would confess, if ever asked at gunpoint – but Jake liked to be 'up and out'. He refused to get satellite TV so she'd no choice but to switch loungewear for weekend casuals and follow. He'd been barely listening *again*, and after a – what would you call it? A confession? Anyway, after telling her he'd played with dolls as a kid, he'd gone dewy-eyed and the conversation had dried up. Maybe it was supposed to be a deep moment and she'd missed the memo.

Maybe it was about Christmas – for the first time, they were spending it together, as a couple, at the D'Arcys. Amelia's mum lived in Spain now and was 'having the girls over' from her native Manchester for the big day – a mass of divorcees, fake tan and industrial-size cans of Elnett descending on Marbella – and her brother Freddie would be spending it as he always did, at home in Scotland.

'Being with his family always makes Jake tense,' said Amelia as she took the roll of tape from Rudi and smoothed down the wrapping paper.

Rudi tried to untangle her fingers from the tape. 'Are they horrible? Are you sure you want to spend Christmas with them?'

Amelia thought about those terrifying first ten minutes whenever she crossed the threshold. 'They're a bit much when you first meet them, but quite a tight family unit. I never understood how Jake fit in at all. I mean, he *doesn't*.'

Rudi was losing the battle with the tape, adding a rogue gift bow to her troubles. 'Fuck. Tell me.'

'Y'know, when I first met Jake, I expected his family to be like him, kind of . . . I don't know. I was expecting, if I'm honest, starchy, uptight middle-class bores. I thought Jake didn't like hanging out with them because they were dull. Anything but.'

'They a bunch of circus performers or something?'

'No! They're . . . *vivacious*.' Amelia began to describe Jake's salt-of-the-earth dad, but when it came to his mum, she looked off into the distance, much like Jake had been doing lately. 'I can't quite work her out but she's this kind of gaudy, outgoing . . . I guess I'd call her a *bird*. Y'know?'

'I don't think you can call a woman a bird any more.'

Amelia laughed. 'But she *is*. A proper London bird. And Margo's really loud and funny and the little brother's an absolute gem, a proper star.'

'But Jake's a laugh, ain't he?'

'Yes, at *home*. Dry, witty . . . ' Amelia sighed and smoothed the tape over the flap of wrapping paper, thinking of Jake's gentle barbs and deadpan humour as they curled up on the sofa. 'But not with *them*. Kind of goes into himself. But it's only three nights, from Christmas Eve.' Amelia breathed out deeply and held up the parcel to check it was completely covered, remembering the uncharitable thought she'd had as Jake had grazed his card over the reader in the café that day. He was sweet, and gentle, and proper, but when it came to mind-melting confusion, he was worse than every heart-crushing fuckboy she'd ever met.

*

The MTZ Christmas party was the only thing Jake never had to fight for budget to pay for – no way would the directors miss out on a chance to throw back Pouilly-Fumé, dance the Macarena and give lower-ranked female colleagues a few horror stories to scare their daughters stiff with in years to come. By the time it came around, Jake was sick of the whole concept – Irish-themed this year, at the insistence of the new sales director, who was American and drank a pint of Guinness once, and continually used the word 'craic' in his emails – so he was sitting alone having a breather, studying the dance floor. He watched everyone try Irish dancing – thankfully no broken collarbones like last year's Charleston competition – and saw Lisa lining up bright-green shots. Harry suddenly slumped down next to him into the banquette.

'Having a good time?' Jake bellowed above the music.

Harry's nod was drunken, heavy, emphatic.

'I hate this song,' he slurred.

Jake cocked his ear exaggeratedly to show Harry he was listening. '"Fairytale of New York". It's a classic.'

'It's the "faggot" bit.' Harry grabbed his chest. 'It's not right.'

Jake's stomach rumbled. 'Of its time, I guess. Wouldn't be okay now, but I don't think it matters.'

Harry squinted at Jake, trying to focus. 'C*ourse* it matters. Of its time, *yeah*, but it ain't that time any more. They should bleep it. I reckon if Kirsty were still with us, she'd have rerecorded it by now.'

This felt like another test. Like Cologne. Was Harry about to unfurl a huge banner saying, FOOLED YOU, GAY BOY? Jake shrugged. 'Just a song. A word.'

Harry shook his head so hard his cheeks flapped like a St Bernard. 'You're wrong, Jake. Gay people shouldn't have to hear this shit. It's a word that . . . ' He searched for the right phrase. 'Demeans. Ain't right.'

Jake gulped. He wasn't expecting Harry to be a staunch supporter of gay issues, especially after Cologne. Maybe he was only a ten-drink activist.

Harry reared back. 'Got to be inclusive.' He struggled with the 'inclusive' – more consonants than he was expecting – but got there in the end. 'Isn't everybody? *You* are, right?'

Jake looked back uncertainly. 'I am what?' Was Harry about to say he knew? What *did* he know, anyway? Did Jake have some kind of aura? Maybe Harry would ask if he wanted to tug off to porn again. Jake briefly considered how he'd answer.

Then, Harry lurched forward and gave Jake a tight hug. Jake didn't know where to put his hands, unused to the feel of Harry's toned, hard bulk. To his horror, he realised he was on the verge of an erection. He thought of Joanie the dog dragging her arse along the carpet, Excel spreadsheets, a plate of jellied eels – anything to make it go away, but to no avail. Harry landed a slobbery kiss on Jake's ear. 'Love you, mate. You're a good egg.'

Harry stood up and gave an okay sign, before ambling away and grabbing a shot from Lisa. Jake stayed put until it was safe to get up and leave.

At the next post-workout beers with the guys and Hannah, the song started playing, and an emboldened Jake mentioned his new stance, which, as if by magic, now matched Harry's.

'*What?*' shrieked Charlie. 'It's a *song*. Anyway, it doesn't mean *gay*; it's Irish slang.'

Adyan looked thoughtful. 'Nobody says that word any more, anyway, do they? And the song is, like, thirty years old.'

Hannah laughed bitterly. 'Believe me, that word is still used.'

Jake repeated something he'd read on Twitter after he'd spoken to Harry. 'If you imagine it as the last word a gay person hears before they're kicked in the head, it takes on a new significance, don't you think?'

Charlie laughed. 'Whoa, bit much.'

Adyan joined in. 'You getting woke now, Jake? Shall we start calling you "Wake"?'

Jake's eyes met Hannah's, a charge of electricity between them.

'That you guys don't get it, and never will, is part of the problem.' Hannah's voice was threatening.

'Han, you coming out as lesbian now?' Charlie and Adyan

dissolved into laughter. Dean laid his hand on Hannah's arm and shushed them.

Hannah shook him off. 'You don't have to be *gay* to give a fuck about gay or bisexual people. You and Holly might have a baby, Charl; what if they grow up gay, and someone, some fuck-nut in a pub, calls them a faggot? What about our gay friends, huh?'

Jake stayed schtum; Hannah was best not interrupted when in full flow. Charlie blew out his cheeks. 'What . . . uh, gay friends?? I don't have any, do I?'

Hannah faltered for a second. Jake stared straight ahead. 'Well, there's Trick. Jake's brother is seventeen. Gay. Imagine how he feels hearing it on the radio, straight guys saying it's "just a song".'

'Han, Jake's brother doesn't give a shit what we think. You're being dramatic!'

Hannah bit her lip, hissing, 'How's *this* for dramatic?' before getting up and walking out. Dean shrugged in apology and followed. Jake stayed put, mind whirring.

'Trick aside, who *else* do we know who's gay?' said Charlie.

'Dean, if Hannah's not careful,' laughed Adyan.

On the way home, as Jake knew she would, Hannah texted.

Hannah: You shouldn't let them
talk about your brother that way.
It upsets me.
It should upset **you** too. x

Jake: They weren't talking
about Trick.

Just that stupid song.
And I agreed with you!
Anyway, Trick wouldn't
give a toss. x

Hannah: What do you mean?
How would you know? x

Jake: Well he's fine isn't he?
Seems to be doing OK x

Hannah: Not sure tbh.
Some of his Snapchats . . .
I dunno.
I guess. You should stand
up for him more. x

Jake: Snapchat?
Has he added you on Snapchat?
He hasn't added ME. x

Hannah: I wonder why, said
nobody ever.
I'll see you xmas eve. x

Jake: Seriously though have I
done something wrong? x

Hannah: No just think about
what I said. Don't give into
macho bullshit Jake. It's

always been my favourite thing
about you. x

Jake hated making Hannah cross; they never fell out. Hannah was the first person he met who didn't treat his 'differences' like a disease, but appreciated them. Jake had first laid eyes on her in front of his halls. His parents had just driven away in the van, exhaust fumes spelling 'thank God' as they'd sped back to London. Hannah had been sitting on a wall with seven boxes in front of her, eyes closed against the sun, saying 'fuck' to herself over and over.

'You okay?'

Her eyes had flashed open and she'd quickly scanned him head to toe. 'A'right, pal.' Scottish. 'Are you normal?'

'Too normal, some might say.'

'Would they? Good. You look strong enough to help with my boxes but not so strong I wouldn't be able to beat you up if you tried it on.'

'Good to know.'

Everyone else on their course was terrible: stuck-up trust-fund brats who wore expensive puffa jackets in all weathers or overly confident wide boys with grubby fingers and a roll-up behind each ear. Hannah had come to university for a reinvention: her mother was dead and her father had since committed himself to reaching the bottom of as many bottles as possible, as fast as his liver would allow.

'I'm here to start living, Jake,' she'd said, blowing foam off her cappuccino in the student union, just after their first lecture. 'Being here has to work, because I'm never going back.'

When Jake had told her about his family she'd gazed back in wonder. 'When can I meet them? How soon can I start calling your mum by her first name, do you think? Tell me again about her Sunday roasts.'

Introducing Hannah to the D'Arcys had been a revelation. Charlie and Adyan didn't come round to his house that much – they had bigger bedrooms, more powerful speakers and frequently absent parents – so the family had thrown themselves at Hannah, fascinated by this rare portal into Jake's private life. She'd clicked with everyone at once. Maybe they saw in Hannah the oldest child or sibling that could've been; Jake still thought about that every now and again. Hannah treated Trick like her own baby brother, and would give Margo all her old make-up – two part-time jobs at university meant she always had cash at hand and loved the idea of newness. 'Consumerism is my middle name. Shopping was invented for me. Some people drink or do drugs to bleach out their past; I dive headfirst into the MAC counter,' she would say, often, usually while drunk and/or trying to score MDMA at a party. And yet, despite slotting in with the D'Arcys, she understood Jake completely and was fiercely loyal to him. She was his connection to them, in a way, the missing link. Somehow she untwisted the awkwardness Jake felt among his family, acting like his spokesperson and cheerleader all in one. The tension never evaporated entirely, but when Hannah was around it was cirrus clouds up in the sky and not the usual encroaching damp fog. When Jake got his first salary from his graduate job, rather than head to the pub to celebrate with Harry and the rest of the cheaply attired intake, he'd rented a car and picked Hannah up from the call centre where she'd been temping – her career highs were a long time coming but she got them eventually – and taken her for a weekend in the country. Separate rooms. On the first night at dinner in the hotel, she'd leaned over as they'd clinked glasses and had whispered, with a very serious face, 'Jake, tell me straight. You're not going to propose or anything, are you?'

Jake had laughed. 'You're like my sister. A totally less annoying sister. So . . . no.'

Hannah had begun to cry gently. Had she wanted him to make a move? After all this time? He wasn't wondering long.

She'd dabbed at her face with a napkin. 'Oh, thank God,' she'd said. 'I didn't think so but I had to check. It's just . . . this is the nicest thing anyone's ever done for me and I'm not used to that . . . unless they want something.' She'd smiled brightly and tossed the napkin aside. 'I'm so glad I picked you to carry my boxes.'

'I'll always carry your boxes, Hannah.'

She'd held him to that.

The D'Arcys threw their usual drinks party on Christmas Eve, this time to 'welcome Amelia to the family Christmas experience'. If they expected an engagement announcement, they were out of luck – all Jake and Amelia brought with them were three huge tubs of chocolates grabbed from the supermarket on the way.

Amelia was furious. 'You said you were *handling* it, getting stuff. You could at least look like you've made an effort.'

'They won't notice. Trust me.' He felt bad for making her obvious anxiety worse.

Half the street was in attendance, and while any other family would pour a sherry, clink glasses and shove the neighbours back out into the snow, Jake thought, his mum and dad were really going for it. In the kitchen they made cocktails and burned their hands on trays of M&S party food, all with yellow 'reduced to clear' stickers on the packaging, whooping with laughter every time Pat tried to hit the long note on 'All I Want for Christmas is You'. Amelia's nerves weren't going anywhere.

'Just get drunk. It's what I do. Every year.'

Amelia shook her head. 'What if I overdo it and throw up? *Say* something?'

'When would you get a word in?' Amelia had been a little subdued, but if *he* still found them overbearing, with three decades of experience, he couldn't expect her to dive in.

Jake remembered Hannah's text. 'Let's talk to Trick, he likes you. I'll get a round of drinks sorted for everyone. Let's penetrate the pentagram of teenage cool.'

Trick and his regular cohorts stood exchanging impenetrable slang and showing each other their phone screens, just like at his birthday. Jake noticed Trick stiffen slightly as Hot Will greeted Jake with a very polite 'Merry Christmas, Jake', and shook Amelia's hand. As soon as the pleasantries were over, Trick gathered Hot Will close and they stood staring at the two interlopers, lost for words. Jake actually found it hilarious. Fucking teenagers.

'Drinks? Anyone? I was second-favourite mixologist in the student union bar, you know . . . '

Jake tapped their orders into his phone, each request delivered in stilted discomfort. Leaving Amelia to Trick, he sidestepped a swaying Christie from number 47 and headed to the freezing utility room where drinks, mixers and those cheap, dinky French beer bottles were stacked. Soon he was interrupted by Kia and Hot Will gliding in.

'Hey, Jake.' Hot Will grinned. 'Uh, can we change our minds? That okay?'

The last thing Jake needed was to look more unreasonable

than a teenager so he beamed like a children's entertainer. 'Sure! What you after?'

Kia spoke. 'Do you know how to make a Cham Cham?'

Hot Will laughed.

'Errrr. No, I don't,' said Jake, any vestigial coolness evaporating. 'What is it?'

Hot Will traced his fingers over the bottles. 'It's . . . champagne with an itty bit of Chambord liqueur in the top.'

'Very sophisticated. They sound lethal. No champagne . . . but I can do Prosecco.' Jake laughed. 'A kind of *sham* Cham Cham, if you like!'

Hot Will burst out laughing. 'Love it!'

Jake allowed himself the brief delusion he wasn't being mocked. Kia's glower, however, pricked that particular bubble, and the temperature dropped another degree. 'We'll, uh, help take them through.'

'Thanks.' Jake knew Hannah would expect progress by the time she arrived to drop off presents. 'Um, how's Trick getting on?'

Hot Will and Kia looked at one another. '*Getting* on?' said Kia.

Jake opened the Prosecco, hearing Hot Will murmur 'Smooth' as he eased out the cork with a gentle pop. 'Yeah. Since he . . . uh . . . came out? Just wondering. He doesn't say much.'

Kia watched Jake pour, eyes rocketing skyward momentarily as he sent bubbles cascading over the rim. 'You an ally now, Jake?'

'Ally?'

'Yeah. An LGBTQ ally. A gay ally.'

'What are they?'

Kia's lips twitched. 'Basically a *straight* person,' she paused to run her tongue over her teeth, 'who's, um, interested in helping the LGBTQ cause.'

Jake added in the Chambord. 'What do they have to do?'

'In *my* experience? The bare minimum. Not killing a queer person is usually enough. The bar is looooow.'

Jake handed the pair their flutes. 'Well, I *am*, then. I have never killed a . . . ' He stumbled over the next word. He didn't know you were allowed to say that. 'A *queer* person, and never would.'

'Do you walk the walk, though?' Kia sipped from her glass as Jake remembered Harry's impassioned speech. He sensed a trap. He had no choice but to fall into it.

'Uh, well, Amelia's brother is gay and we went to Pride with him once.' Not *strictly* true: they had stood in a really loud pub and guarded Freddie's bag while he'd twerked with strangers. Jake had found glitter in every crevice for weeks after.

Hot Will patted Jake's arm and smiled. 'It's sweet you're thinking of Trick, mate. He'll be so pleased.'

Would he? Why? Jake couldn't wait for this interrogation to end.

Kia sipped her drink. 'Yeah. *Elated*. Do you watch his videos? Start there,' said Kia as she turned away. 'Or . . . you know . . . ask him yourself.'

Hot Will flashed a winning grin. 'Course he's okay. He's got us. Thanks for these.' He raised his glass to Jake and followed Kia, looking back once more before he disappeared into the kitchen.

Christmas Day with the D'Arcys went okay, amazingly. Trick was either in his room filming or quietly scrolling through his phone in his Tigger onesie. Margo was fine as long as she had a Prosecco cocktail in her hand – 'Kia was telling me about these Cham Chams, they're amazing' – Buddy was on his best behaviour in case Santa was watching for next year, and Mum and Dad were minding their Ps and Qs in front of Amelia. It was unusual to have guests at Christmas – only Buddy's dad had managed to infiltrate for a brief spell in the last couple of decades – and Jake's mum seemed to be struggling between trying to impress Amelia and showing no airs and graces. Any sense of superiority had long pre-dated the move off the estate: she and Reenie spent many an afternoon destroying neighbours for not washing their net curtains regularly, and once they moved into the 'new house', they'd done their best to prove they weren't inferior to anyone else. With gentrification now throttling the street, the pressure was even more intense.

Over dinner, they talked New Year plans.

Trick flicked his phone screen with his one hand and shovelled sprouts with the other. 'House party with Kia and Hot Will.'

'Ooh, lovely,' said Vee. 'We're at Reenie's again. She always gets a prawn ring. I eat it out of politeness.'

Margo guffawed. 'Mum, that year I went to Reenie's, you *inhaled* the prawns. I'm staying in, like every other night, but downing my usual Citalopram with a glass of champagne.'

Dad topped up Amelia's glass. 'You two are in Edinburgh, aren't you? Gorgeous city. Me and Vee went there once on a jolly with . . . who was it, Vee? Jeff and Barb?'

Amelia thanked him. 'Yeah, my brother lives there. He's got an *amaaaazing* flat in the city centre.' Jake saw her rein herself in, to avoid sounding like she was bragging. 'Um. Yeah. It's great. We're going to the street party.'

Vee presented her glass for a top-up. 'He's gay, your brother, isn't he, Amelia?'

'Uh . . . yeah.'

Jake held his breath, awaiting whatever clanger his mother was about to drop.

'You hear that, Trick? You should go with 'em!'

Trick wrinkled his nose. Jake gripped the side of his chair. 'What? Why?'

'He might meet some lovely gay men. What's your brother like, Amelia? Has he got a boyfriend?'

Jake slowly closed his eyes in horror. His mother had a habit of chattily firing out extremely personal questions like she were on the phone to Mr Pepperoni on Tooting Broadway, choosing extra toppings for her Hawaiian.

'Not sure,' said Amelia. 'He's quite secretive about his love life.'

Trick tutted loudly. 'He's *old*, for God's sake, Mum. Even older than Jake. Why would I wanna go up *there* to meet men? I have—' He stopped himself. 'Well, I'm busy here.'

Busy keeping an eye on Hot Will, no doubt, thought Jake, glad to see the heat off him for a change.

'Yes,' sighed Amelia, 'he's thirty-three, so . . . ' She saw a chance to change the subject, find some common ground. Accepting the pudding with a nanoscopic nod, she looked up at Vee and said, 'Did Jake . . . have a doll when he was a child?'

Jake sat up straight. 'What? Why? Uh . . . come on.'

Amelia mouthed a *What?* at Jake, and continued: 'Well, you were saying that time. That little boy in the bakery . . . '

Margo rested her hand on Buddy's to stop him banging his spoon on the table. 'Did he? I don't remember.'

Trick's eyes finally tracked up from his screen. 'Well?'

Vee plonked the final dish of trifle down on the table in front of Jake. 'No, I don't think so. Not of his own, anyway,' she said.

'Nah, no dolls, not Jake. But there was . . . uh, Chrysalis,' chuckled his dad, as he spooned trifle into his gaping gob. 'You remember Chrysalis, don'tcha?'

Vee's chest heaved lightly as she started laughing. 'Chrysalis was the . . . Ooh, I'd forgotten about that.'

Amelia turned to Jake. 'What's Chrysalis?'

Jake leaned back in his chair, desperate for a sinkhole to take him into the Earth's core. 'You don't wanna know.'

Vee threw her head back. 'Oh, you *do*. Every time Grandma D'Arcy came round, she'd let you play with one of her handkerchiefs. She always had two. One up her sleeve and another in her handbag, for . . . well, Jake's face usually. Do you remember, Pat? Bless him, we used to piss ourselves.'

Jake's dad began roaring, like he was about to choke on his trifle. 'What did he used to say when he ran about with it?'

Jake thought of his grandmothers. They'd understood him; he could be himself with them. Pegging out washing at his fearsome Essex granny's, or silently cutting out fabulous women from his Irish nana's old copies of *TV Times*, there was nobody watching or judging. Until his grandfathers came home, of course, and the acting began again. Standing at a series of muddy gravesides, and trying not to cry as he'd forced down a curled-up sandwich at the wake, had removed that layer of protection, however, and soon he was a generation up, and alone.

Jake swallowed hard. This was worse than the time they got out the baby photos– which they'd no doubt do again once they'd downed enough Baileys.

'Yes!' said Mum, clearly on a roll. 'You'd always beg, "Let me do Chrysalis," and she'd give you the hanky. You'd tie it round your hand like this.' She picked up a napkin and grabbed one side of it in her fist. 'And you'd parade up and down, saying, "Look at Chrysalis with her big hair," and you'd talk to her . . . well, to your *hand*. Like it was a person. We wet ourselves, to be honest, but you loved it.'

Jake let himself chuckle. 'Yeah, I was a weird child, I guess . . .'

'Not weird, you pudding, it's what kids do, isn't it?' said Pat, his own laughter subsiding. 'We just had to remind you not to take it – sorry, *her* – out with you. People looked.' He surveyed his son for a while, before blinking out of his reverie. 'Anyway, thank God you sorted all that out. I'm done, Vee; mind if I go through?' He jerked his head to the doorway. His wife shrugged.

Amelia chucked Jake under the chin. 'Aw, that's so sweet.'

Trick laughed, tilting his head to show he was concentrating on his brother – a trick Hot Will taught him. 'I can't believe your hand was into *drag*! Fierce fingers. The grande dame of *digits*!'

'Oh, Chrysalis,' chuckled Vee. 'Yes! Brings it all back!'

Jake said again, plainer this time, desperate for the spotlight to land somewhere else: 'Weird child.'

five.

Freddie's flat was huge, and only ten minutes from Edinburgh city centre. High ceilings, large rooms, period features – it had everything. The only problem? It was cold. The central heating was as effective as basking in the heat generated by a wasp's wings.

Freddie showed Jake and Amelia the room they'd be sleeping in, opening the door with a flourish. 'This is Kim's room; she's away at a cottage somewhere until after Hogmanay. That's what we call New Year up *here*.'

Jake laughed inwardly at the condescension. What a prick Freddie could be when he really wanted – which he did, most of the time. Amelia took in the large windows and wooden floorboards. Bookshelves neat, with contents colour coded and alphabetised. In the centre, a huge wooden sleigh bed. Either Kim or the landlord had money to burn. 'Wow, it's sick.'

Freddie's dark eyes flicked over Jake quickly and then to his sister, who had seemed nervous since they'd arrived. Amelia was usually quick and sharp, but in Freddie's company she was reserved, much like she was among Jake's family. Whether it was hero worship, resentment or overexcitement at being in his company again, Jake couldn't tell, but it was the same every time they were all together, which wasn't often. Save for the trip to Pride, Freddie didn't come to London much and their visits to Amelia's mother seldom coincided with his.

'This would cost a fortune in London.' Jake wasn't massively interested in property chat, but he'd learned from nights out with friends that flats and fertility were hot topics among the over-thirties. And Freddie didn't look like he was hankering after being a daddy.

Freddie tutted and laid a hand on Jake's wrist. 'Jacob,' he drawled, 'let's not talk house prices. Let's get you two nice and wasted the Edinburgh way and see in New Year in style.'

Jake shot him a killer smile. '*Hogmanay*, surely?'

Freddie's eyes flashed, acknowledging the defeat. 'Of course.'

One–nil to me, thought Jake, as Freddie flounced out.

Freddie was horrified that Amelia wanted to go to the huge street party – apparently it was 'too touristy', and instead suggested a house party with his friends. The thought of seeing in 2018 with people who found being around Freddie in any way pleasurable didn't sound appealing to Jake, but, to his relief, Amelia played a very out-of-character petulant-little-sister act and won.

'I reserve the right not to buy a ticket,' Freddie had complained over noodles the night before. 'We'll scuttle into a pub within the perimeter and join the masses later.'

'You need a ticket to stand on the street?'

Freddie had peered at Jake over the dessert menu. 'People come from all over the world for the Edinburgh Hogmanay, treasure. It's a big deal.'

Jake understood why Freddie made Amelia nervous. He was very good-looking – a male Amelia with more chiselled features and a buzz cut – but Jake didn't find him attractive; there was something intimidating that dulled his beauty. When Amelia talked about something she'd done at work, or a cool place in London she'd been, Freddie would talk over or try to one-up her. Yet he was captivating. Amelia couldn't seem to look at her brother directly, instead keeping her eyes on Jake with a fixed smile or gawking at some vague point in the distance. Freddie, however, had no such issues, his head swivelling between them like a talk-show host, eyes devouring them until their words trailed off and he could start talking again. He was tactile and, toward the end of the night after a few rounds, was definitely trying to get Jake onside and . . . could it be considered ganging up if Jake wasn't playing? Whatever it was, it was isolating Amelia, and Jake was glad when they were tucked up in crisp white sheets in Kim's draughty room, window sashes rattling.

'It's so lovely to see him,' Amelia said flatly.

Jake squeezed her hand and felt her gradually give in to sleep, knowing it would be a while before he did.

Jake shook all the hands and tried his best to hear the introductions to Freddie's friends over the pub's boisterous din. Ana, small, blonde, deely boppers on over her woolly hat. Samir, smiley, huge brown eyes, enviable quiff, already tipsy. And Lorcan, bright-blue eyes, jawline like Buzz Lightyear and menacingly tall. Did Freddie not know any ugly people? Amelia was looking at the boys appreciatively; he'd never noticed her ogle anyone before. Had she always done it? He couldn't tell if the men were gay; how *did* you tell these days?

Men were unpredictable – Harry had taught him that. Lorcan wore a rugby shirt, Samir a pinky ring. Amelia's first-night awkwardness around her brother had vanished and she was now poking him in the ribs and threatening to reveal his childhood indiscretions. She'd found safety in numbers.

On the street, they stamped their feet for warmth, dodging unsteady tourists seeing it all from behind their camera phones, and found themselves sharing space with two guys in kilts with a gaggle of girls surrounding them.

'Let's have a look under your skirt, then, Angus!' bellowed one distinctly Yorkshire accent.

'Are you a true Scotsman?' screamed another.

Freddie and Lorcan joined in the chanting.

'How embarrassing,' Jake found himself saying, although he wouldn't have minded a peep under the kilt himself.

Samir stood alongside. 'Ah, don't be fooled. They love it. No man out in a kilt at Hogmanay wants to be left alone.'

Jake laughed. 'Are you telling me they're . . . *asking* for it?'

'Trust me. They'll end up getting off with everyone on Princes Street.' He looked straight at Jake. 'It's the only reason I ever wear one. See?' Freddie, Lorcan, Amelia and Ana were now fully integrated, circling the man and one of the women, who were now locked in a very involved kiss, their tongues like tentacles.

Amelia waved. 'We're playing truth or dare! Come on.'

Memories of lame teenage parties. Jake's life had been too uneventful for any shocking truths, so his stock answer was he'd seen a dead body. This was partially true. When Mrs Rennard from the flats hadn't been seen for a few days, eight-year-old Jake peeped through the letterbox and saw the toe of the slipper of his now former neighbour. Tonight, it would have to be dares. He wandered over with Samir. Lorcan was fulfilling his dare of smoking three cigarettes at once.

'Right!' screamed one of the women to the first guy in a kilt. 'Dare you to kiss one of the girls. And whoever it is cannae say no!'

Jake muttered, 'This is possibly one of the most inappropriate times to have women kissing men against their will, to be honest.'

Samir chuckled beside him. 'Totally.'

Clearly hoping to be picked, the woman who set the dare stepped forward, but the guy motioned to Amelia. She looked horrified.

'Um, I'm not single!'

The woman, reeling from rejection, fixed a narrow eye on her. 'I said kiss you, not *fuck* you. Your man won't mind, he's not here.'

Jake seized a rare opportunity to be gallant. 'I *am* here, actually, and . . . y'know, I think she'd prefer to kiss me at midnight. No offence.'

The man in the kilt sized him up. Jake hoped his breeziness would save him from a smacking. He was twice Jake's size and was standing in the middle of Edinburgh in a kilt – Jake knew without looking that under that kilt lay a huge pair of balls, made of iron. Luckily, for Jake, as big as his testes may have been, his sense of righteousness was larger. 'I'm no kissing a man's girlfriend in front of him. It's no right.'

The woman was not to be placated. 'Forfeit!' she screamed, crunching flat a can of lager and opening another in one swift movement. 'And I get to choose it!' Revenge was writ large upon her face. 'Kiss a man! For fifteen seconds!' The crowd whooped. Out of the corner of his eye, Jake saw Freddie and Lorcan high-five; he really hoped he wouldn't be picked. Putting aside how large and scary the guy's mouth was, what would it mean if he was seen kissing another man? Right there on the street? In those seconds, Jake fully catastrophised the scenario. Maybe the kiss would be, like, enchanted and a huge finger – wearing a fur-cuffed leopard-print glove, perhaps – would descend from the sky to point at Jake and tell everyone he fancied men too? Maybe Jake would be branded with a huge rainbow or unicorn on his chest after they pulled apart? If Jake refused would it look like he was protesting too much? Should he kiss back, and be good at it, or purposefully bad? The man was pretty drunk; there was every chance he'd puke in his throat. Jake remembered his only kiss with a man so far. Evan. His mouth. The faint taste of tobacco and Tizer. He was pulled out of this memory when the guy in the kilt barged past, grabbed Samir and went into a full snog, faces twisting every which way. Jake unconsciously touched his own mouth, in relief, perhaps; he'd been spared. Samir responded enthusiastically, manoeuvring the kilt guy round until Jake could see Samir's face, brown eyes open wide. And looking right at Jake. He had seen enough. 'Need the loo, back in a sec.'

He reached a side street with a row of portable loos, queues snaking in front of each one. Everyone coming out of them, mercifully often, looked like they should be at home in bed or perhaps having their stomach pumped. Jake watched in wonder as a drunk woman asked another woman in a huge fur coat if she could 'piss in your handbag'.

And then: 'Been waiting long?'

Samir.

Jake started to feel light-headed, as if the alcohol he'd been throwing down his neck in defence against the cold was finally hitting its target. They chatted as they waited for the loo, checking their watches for midnight.

'I have a confession,' said Samir.

Jake, with a creeping dread, attempted a carefree laugh but it wouldn't come. 'Okay.'

'The dare, before. That was . . . uh. I asked the lady to say that.'

Jake's lips began to go numb. '*What*? Why?'

'It was a ruse.'

'A *ruse*?'

'Aye. To see how you reacted. To check.'

Jake was frozen to the core yet still managed to blush, heat rising from the pit of his stomach. Anyone touching him now would need immediate treatment for first-degree burns. 'Check what?'

Suddenly a voice behind shouted, 'Get a fuckin' move on, you pair of bufties!'

The loo in front was free so Jake leapt in, peeing shakily thanks to a heady combination of sub-zero temperatures and terror. His mind raced. He wanted to take his time, hide, but that would make him very unpopular with the scores of revellers outside. When he was done, waggling his fingers so the antibacterial foam would dry quicker, he looked around but Samir was nowhere to be seen. Phew. Crisis averted, right? Then, a hand on his shoulder.

Samir's eyes were wide; he looked nervous. 'I want to talk to you.'

'What about?' If Jake played dumb as long as possible maybe they'd abandon whatever this was and go back to everyone. Midnight was close. Samir, however, was closer.

'About you.' Samir's eyes were trained on Jake's. 'You're . . . you're gay, aren't you? Or bi, at least? Maybe? I mean . . . ' He scratched his head. 'I *hope* you are. Are you?'

Jake pulled his mouth in tight. 'No, I'm not.' It wasn't very convincing.

Samir leaned in closer. 'Are you sure? I've got a Spidey-Sense about these things.'

Jake looked around them. It was crowded, loud. He couldn't remember how to get back to their group. He ran his hands over his face, trying to think. He could run, maybe, let whatever this opportunity was drop out of his grasp. But it had been said, it was out there, he'd been *seen*. He didn't even care what gave him away. Finally, he grabbed Samir's sleeve and pulled him down the street. 'Come on then, Peter Parker.'

They didn't speak, took left turns and right; the shouts and screams of the crowds became a faraway drone, happening somewhere else. They came to a dark, narrow street, free of Hogmanay drunks. Jake spotted an even smaller alleyway running off it: a fire exit, with steel bars hemming in the staircase. They scooted down it wordlessly. It began to drizzle. There was one streetlight, glowing bright orange. Jake knew this would be momentous, even if they just stood here looking at one another and nothing more.

Samir cleared his throat. 'I want to kiss you. But not if you don't want to.'

Jake's head was a supernova of confusion, curiosity and fear. He looked away and deep into the damp cobbles beneath him and thought of Amelia, back on Princes Street, waiting for *him*. He couldn't do this. He'd never cheated on her, hardly even looked at another woman. Or man. Mostly. Well, there was that guy in the gym but, honestly, he did nothing but strut around the locker room with his tackle flapping about. And this *would* be cheating, wouldn't it? But he could stop it right now; he and Samir could walk back to the group with dignity intact, and he could snuggle into Amelia and feel her faux-fur hood against his chin and smell her perfume and all would be as it should. So what if Samir thought he was gay or bi? Jake hadn't *confirmed* it. But he'd dragged him here. Every second they spent together made the situation more irreversible, risky. But what good was caution now? Flapping penis man aside, he always looked away in the changing rooms, lowered his voice an octave, never hugged his mates when celebrating winning a point at squash; he always did everything 'right', kept it in check. Endless editing. Just once, he wanted to let go. In his head, he apologised to Amelia, made a promise that, after tonight, it would be all about her, he'd never do it again. He just . . . needed to see, feel it, to know whether Evan was a fluke. He would make it up to her, anything she wanted. Anything.

Jake put his hand round Samir's waist and drew him nearer. It felt odd. Firmer. Broader. No crook between hip and waist, much squarer. The fire escape pressed into his back, the damp chill of metal finding its way through his layers until his skin started to numb. Jake found himself surprised by Samir's scent. Musky, spicy, not the florals or freshness of Amelia. The stubble against his own felt alien for a few seconds, before it began to feel perfect, and soon Jake was responding to the forcefulness of Samir's mouth like he'd always kissed that way. Somewhere, on another planet, a crowd started to count down from ten. Everything melted away.

When they broke apart, it was a different year. And Jake felt like the future had got sick of waiting; it had come to hurry him along. It was the most devastating, frightening, exhilarating feeling. That hadn't just been a countdown to another year; it was a warning, telling him that he was running out of time.

'Where have you been?' called Amelia as Jake trotted back as nonchalantly as possible. 'Have you seen Samir? Freddie wants to go home; we're going to watch Ana and Lorcan do the New Year dook in the morning.'

Jake was worried his quivering voice would give him away, so he kissed her on the cheek and grabbed her hand and squeezed it. 'Huge queue for the loos,' he finally managed to croak. 'I went to find another and got lost. Samir was somewhere queuing too. I lost him. Can't believe I missed the chimes. What's a "New Year dook"?'

'It's the *bells.*' Freddie tied his scarf tight round his neck. 'A dook is when a load of fannies with nothing better to do go and jump in the Forth, by the bridge. It's tragic but there are bacon sandwiches. Where did you say Samir was?'

'I, uh, I dunno.'

Freddie's eyes narrowed the tiniest amount. He wasn't stupid. Maybe he could tell. He *was* gay, after all. Did Jake's face give it away? Was Samir's kiss smeared on his face, like paint that only shows up under UV light? He put his hands to his mouth. Freddie's phone beeped.

'That's Sammy boy. Couldn't find us so he's headed to the flat. Silly sausage.' Eyes up to Jake, then back to his phone. 'I'll tell him to open the champers. Let's give 2018 the kick up the arse it needs.'

Jake looked back and saw truth-or-dare girl smooching with one of the kilt guys – did they even *have* names? – and when she spotted him, she pointed at him with gun fingers and winked.

'Hope you got your snog, you gorgeous boy, ye,' she squealed, before giving into kilt boy's kisses once more.

Amelia linked arms with him. 'What did she say?'

'Dunno,' sighed Jake, pulling Amelia into him tighter as they walked behind Freddie. 'I don't really understand the accent, to be honest.' But he turned back and blew her a kiss, feeling like a hero and a traitor all in one.

Jake woke up and looked at the clock. 04:44. Spooky. He'd drunk one glass of champagne in shaky silence earlier, as Freddie's friends trooped in and out of the bathroom, each one coming out even more boring than when they went in, before he and Amelia feigned tiredness and went to bed. There was no noise from the rest of the flat, so he assumed the revelry was over. He reached for the glass of water by his bed to find it empty, so tiptoed through to the kitchen, shivering under his gossamer-thin T-shirt. He was surprised to find Samir rolling a cigarette by the light of the hob. He looked up and smiled.

'Hey.'

Jake gulped. 'Hey.'

Samir was high. 'I won't tell anyone, y'know. It's none of my business.'

Jake stood awkwardly for a moment. 'Okay.'

Samir squinted as he fiddled with the roach. Jake could now see it was a joint in his hand. 'But I must say . . . it was a good New Year's kiss. Hot. *You* are hot.'

Again: 'Okay, er, thank you.' God, he sounded pathetic, like he'd been sent to the shop for his mum and told he could keep the change. 'You are, uh, hot too.' The compliment did not feel natural in his mouth. He ran the tap and filled his glass. Samir stood and came close to him. Jake shivered.

Samir put his mouth to Jake's ear. 'Come to the bathroom. Let's have a quick toke.'

'Can't we just smoke it here?'

Samir chuckled at this wide-eyed innocence. 'No.'

As Samir closed the door behind him, Jake reached for the light cord, but Samir stopped him. 'The fan . . . ' he whispered. 'Makes a right fucking racket.'

'Are you going to light it, then?' History repeating itself, he realised, a joint shared with a boy who wanted to kiss him, and *did*.

He could feel Samir grinning through the dark. 'In a minute. After.'

Jake felt Samir's hands on his face. They kissed again. The stubble still felt strange; the scrape of it against Jake's own was arousing, in a way. Samir first cupped Jake's face in his hands, before running them down Jake's torso as they kissed, making an appreciative noise as he reached Jake's belly. The hands continued to move down. Jake placed his hand under Samir's chin, leaned back and closed his eyes against the dark, while his head filled with brilliant light.

After, Samir flicked ash down the loo as Jake panted into his hands, waiting for his breathing to even out and be quiet again. He wiped sweat from his brow. Samir slipped his boxers back on – the ping of the elastic against his skin a deafening echo off the bathroom walls – and put his finger to Jake's mouth. 'I'll go first. You wait here.'

'Go? Where are you sleeping?'

'With Freddie, of course.'

Jake breathed out as quietly as he could, heart still racing. 'What? Are you . . . ?'

'Hush, little Englishman.' Jake detected a snigger and it unnerved him. 'Well . . . maybe not so little. Don't worry.' He licked his fingers while looking Jake straight in the eye, before quietly unbolting the door, opening it a crack, and slipping out. Jake stood looking at himself in the mirror for a bit, tracking his fingers across the small crease in his forehead, while the wind whipped outside. He brushed his teeth. After what felt like a decent amount of time, he pulled open the door and looked up, immediately springing back. Freddie.

'You all right, Jake?'

Jake didn't know what to say. He began to stutter his reply.

Freddie's eyes tracked Jake's body – he realised he'd forgotten to put his T-shirt back on – and rested on his face. 'You'll catch your death. Get some sleep. We're up in a couple of hours.' He rubbed his stomach. 'I think the champagne didn't agree with me,' he said icily. 'Gonna try and chuck some of it up. Go on, chop-chop! Nap-nap time.'

Jake wrapped his arms round himself against the cold and made his way back to the bedroom, the bed, Amelia, and how everything had been twenty-four hours earlier. Same, but different.

On the train back to London, Amelia was relaxed and happy as she sipped her tea, exclaiming joyously at the food on offer in the at-seat service deal, cheerfully scrolling through her phone and reading out tweets and snippets of news, and marvelling that her brother had found someone so nice.

'Most of his exes are nasty bitches or cheaters. Samir is so different.'

Sadly not, Jake thought. 'Yeah, lovely guy.'

Jake's mind returned to their encounter, imagining he

could feel Samir on him. To see Amelia so settled, blissfully unaware her midnight kiss had gone to another, and that while she slept off her cheap Hogmanay fizz, in the next room, in the dark, he was getting his rocks off with her brother's boyfriend. The guilt felt like hands round his throat, and his heart began to beat faster – in dread, this time, not excitement – and suddenly it felt like if he didn't do or say anything else, he would confess all and forever taint what he could see was already a happy memory for her. He fixed his eyes on his laptop screen in tense concentration, looking through the words, links, pictures, everything. As he'd kissed Samir – actually, his official account of the matter in his own head was that he'd *let* Samir kiss him – he'd promised he would make it up to Amelia. Time to make good on that.

'Have you been to Paris?'

He knew the answer: a succession of exes had spirited Amelia away on romantic breaks in the French capital, but Jake had never attempted to match their extravagant wooing. He cringed in recognition of his romantic neglect.

Amelia looked up, curious. He carried on: 'Eurostar are doing a deal. Half-price, and discounts on hotels.' A deal, wow. *Why* had he said that? He really wasn't a natural when it came to retaining a romantic mystique. 'Do you want to go? Would it be too cheesy?' But she was beaming back at him, spinach in her teeth from her toasted ham hock and cheddar flatbread. Jake motioned at his own teeth in warning and she ran her tongue over hers to dislodge it. 'It's near Valentine's. Can you handle it?'

'God, yes! I've always wanted to go again.' The 'again' stung and she saw it, quickly rectifying. 'With *you*, I mean! Have you been?'

He had. Twice. First a school trip toward the end of A levels. Second time was business. With Harry. It had been fairly unremarkable, zero mutual masturbation.

Amelia suddenly looked unsure. 'Paris is *freezing* in winter.'

Jake winked. 'Everywhere is freezing in winter, but only Paris is as beautiful as Paris. Come *ooooooon*. We'll sink all our savings into scarves, hats and cardigans. Snow boots! I'm booking it. Now. We never do *anything* like this.' What he meant, of course, was that *he* never did anything like this, for her.

'Can you afford it?' Amelia ventured, but Jake wasn't to be dissuaded; he could see the Arc de Triomphe reflected in her eyes. He tapped in his details with glee.

'Can't afford not to. Bargain! Done!' Jake clapped his hands together and smiled in victory. 'We travel on the seventh – a whole week before the dreaded Valentine's mob so we should be fine. Excited?'

'Yes!' Amelia smiled back. It was good to see her happy. 'I am. It's gonna be great.'

On a roll, Jake messaged his brother. Did he understand him more now? Buzzing from the temporary absolution, and feeling invincible, the adrenaline surged as he pressed 'Send'.

Jake: Happy New Year bro.
Hope you had fun
and got a midnight kiss. x

Did he call him 'bro'? Was this something he'd ever done? What *did* they call each other? What would Trick say if he knew what Jake had done on New Year's Eve? Would he be happy? Would it bring them closer together? Was it appropriate to suggest Trick had been kissing someone too? Did he want to think of Trick sucking face with some long-limbed streak of misery in a boozy house party? Not particularly.

An hour later came the reply.

Trick: HNY 🖤

Brief. Sarcastic? No kiss, but a heart emoji. Not personalised. Did this mean . . . anything? Jake sank down in his chair, irritated at the dismissal of this olive branch – were they even at war? The little shit.

He opened Facebook for yet another deathless scroll through the New Year engagements, pregnancy announcements and basic house parties. One notification.

Evan Kolowski has accepted your friend request

six.

It was freezing. *Fucking* freezing. Jake even wore a woolly hat, which Amelia claimed was cute but Jake thought made him look like a serial killer, or a farmhand taking a cigarette break from lambing on the North York Moors. It was their last day in Paris, and the pair of them had spent the first part of their break sizing up possible things to do on either the hen or the stag night.

'I think the girls are gonna insist on a beach, though,' said Amelia as they staggered up Montmartre. 'Won't the boys rather do Ibiza?'

Jake cringed at the idea of beered-up lads running amok in huge clubs of banging techno. 'Well, it will still be hot in Paris in September; Charlie goes bright pink after an hour on the sunlounger, plus he's terrible at handling his booze. I could plan a full programme here. That way, if I keep him busy, he won't get drunk and break his leg. They're all private school, aren't they? Cultured. No? What do you think?'

Amelia seemed to read his anxiety so changed the subject. 'Okay, well, now we've got that nailed, what shall we do today? I was thinking maybe the Eiffel Tower?'

Jake fancied queuing in the freezing cold about as much as

he fancied a razor-blade enema; he'd had a day in the hotel spa in mind, or propping up the bar in an old-school drinking den.

'I read in the guidebook the best way to see Paris is by going up the Tour Montparnasse.'

'Why?'

'Well, if you go up the Eiffel Tower, there's one very important thing missing – the actual tower. You can't see it.'

Amelia scrunched up her face. 'Yeah, and when I get back and Troy and Becky at work ask if I went up the Eiffel Tower, I get the unique opportunity to say, "No, I went up the Tour Mombanass – or *whatever* – instead." I wanna go up the Eiffel Tower. Christ. Put two scarves on. Man up!'

Man up? His scarf was gunmetal; how much more manly could he be? Okay, so his woolly hat had a pom-pom on it, but at least it was black. He gave it one last shot. 'Cruise on the Seine? On one of the *bateaux mouches*? Pompidou Centre?'

Amelia removed her coat from the wardrobe hanger with calm exactness. 'Jake. We've *never* been to Paris together before. Ever. We've been here three days. Literally the first things anyone wants to do in Paris is eat a croissant, smoke a packet of Gauloises and go up the Eiffel Tower. I've been carb-free since New Year; I don't smoke, uh, often; so all I've got is the tower. We're going up it.'

The queue was small, thanks, perhaps, to the icy winds and lacerating sleet. Jake hugged his coat closer to him.

'It's beautiful, isn't it?' cooed Amelia, as Jake looked up at the tower and felt immediately nauseated.

'It looks like it's moving. Is it . . . swaying in the wind?'

Amelia rearranged his scarves. 'Of course it isn't. *Is* it?'

There was a look in her eye Jake couldn't decipher. Not the

standard mischief, excitement or calculation, but nervousness, impatience.

'I'll get this,' she said, when they finally got to the front to buy the tickets. Again, unprecedented. Amelia liked to go halves usually.

'Soooooo, there are, like, three lifts we have to get.'

'*Three*? How long is this gonna take?'

Amelia pressed on with a light cough. 'One to the top of the, uh, legs. Then another up the . . . um . . . next bit, and then the last one right up the middle to the very top! Exciting!'

Jake put his head back and looked straight up the tower, then to the left and watched the first lift precariously making its way, kind of diagonally, up the leg. He wasn't usually afraid of heights – he'd done the London Eye three times without so much as a wobble – so where was this dread coming from? What was wrong with him?

Jake looked down as the ground got further away, then up again at the expanse of metal above. He suddenly felt small, insignificant, a speck of gravy on the silk tie of the universe. Then it dawned on him. The nervousness, the *insistence* they come to the tower. Amelia was expecting him to *propose*, wasn't she? That's why she'd really wanted to come up here on the last day. It made sense. That's what couples did: came to Paris, drank champagne, argued a bit, had sex with the curtains open and then . . . got engaged up the Eiffel Tower. Why else would he have suggested coming to Paris the week before Valentine's? What was she supposed to think? Jake's throat contracted and he felt a pain in his arm. His heart started to beat faster. This was why, this was why. She was waiting for him to ask. She was tired of pretending not to be bothered; rolling her eyes at her friends' sappy engagements was all for show. So far he'd avoided the moving-in chat, been too non-committal, but he now realised she wasn't 'cool with it' at all – she wanted to be like Holly, and Sheena, and Eva, and Sophy, and Mel. She wanted to get married. To him. Husband and wife. Mr and Mrs . . . Black spots danced before his eyes as he imagined it. Mr *and Mrs* D'Arcy. And he had to ask her *now.* Shit.

The lift was slowing. Jake's eyes were sore from the effort of staring at nothing. So what should he do? He didn't even have a ring. He never wore them, thought they were either too 'girly' or intimidating – thank you, not only toxic masculinity but also his dad's mate Scouse Elvis who wore gold sovereigns on every finger – but as little as he knew about women, he knew they expected a ring. Maybe she'd get lost in the moment and not care. And right there, Jake was certain he *was* going to ask, and, in the absence of any reason why not, Amelia would say yes, and then they'd get married and agree to love and honour – did you obey, he couldn't remember – and pretend they were okay, that it was perfect, that he'd never thought about anything or anyone else, this was it, for ever. So why, for the first time, despite everything, did it feel like being with one another was the very worst thing for both of them? Did Amelia feel this too, right now, like he did? He loved her, he knew; he fancied her. She made him laugh and feel proud; opening the door to see her face filled his heart with joy. But he'd done what he'd done and felt the way he'd felt that night in Edinburgh. If he proposed, that would be the end of . . . of what, exactly? What was he losing if he married Amelia? Could he do this? But. But . . . *something*. The thing. There would always be the thing. Evan, twelve years ago.

Harry, five years ago. Samir, just weeks ago. The thing, the men. The truth. Would she ever understand? And not only that. If he married her, stayed with her for ever, there could never be another *anyone*, let alone a man. A door would slam tightly shut, but he'd barely peeked beyond. And why the hell was this lift taking so fucking long? He went through it in his head. Amelia, will you . . . ? He imagined lowering himself to the ground, hand outstretched, knee bent, arctic February wind whipping down the back of his jeans, watching Amelia's face. She would feign confusion at first, probably, that's how it went, then break into a smile as she said what anyone would say when proposed to atop the legs of the Eiffel Tower, whether they wanted to or not. Yes, Jake! Yes!

He couldn't breathe now. They stepped out of the lift, other passengers impatiently thrusting by because Jake was walking so slowly. Amelia was beaming, excited, pulling at his sleeve and saying she wanted to try out the glass floor. In dreams, when stuck in a difficult situation, Jake would throw himself to the ground to wake himself up. As Amelia walked ahead, Jake wondered whether he should try his waking-up technique, before realising he wouldn't have to pretend at all – it was actually happening. He tumbled to the ground, the floor coming up to meet him faster than he'd expected, the urge to resist and break his fall strong, but not strong enough; he was numb. He gasped as his hands slammed down against the floor, and was vaguely aware of a crowd gathering as he hyperventilated and stared down at the dots far below. People. Normal people who didn't think like him or feel like him and would never let themselves get in this situation. Was he flying? Was he *dead*? No, he realised, his face was pressed against the glass floor. Soon Amelia was at his side, face contorted with worry, helping him to his feet. As she shooed away the gathering crowd, Jake got his breath back.

'Heights. Floor. I want to go down. Please.'

He expected resistance but Amelia nodded and took his arm.

Once back on terra firma, Amelia stroked his face and said, 'Haven't you been to the top of the CN Tower?'

'What?'

'Seattle? With work? I saw a photo.'

'That was inside.'

Amelia allowed herself a derisive sigh. '*Yes*, but you were clamped to the window like a stick insect, laughing your face off.'

'It's different here. Windy. I can feel the air.'

Amelia let go of his arm. 'I thought you were dying.'

'It's a heights thing, I swear. I'll go for a walk. Calm down.'

Amelia looked back up at the Eiffel Tower and shivered against the blasting wind. She turned to Jake. 'Okay.' A sigh. 'Where shall we go?'

'By myself, I mean. Just for a bit. Why don't you . . . go shopping? I can . . . get a surprise for you. Make it up to you.' This again. The whole trip was supposed to be consolatory – when would it end?

Amelia looked through him, her expression a cocktail of sympathy, suspicion and worry. Misery, even. He'd ruined her day; he felt terrible, but not terrible enough to stay with her, as he should have. She read it in his face, didn't ask him to change his mind. She nodded slowly, put her shoulders back, turned and walked away. He called after her to text if she got lost, but she didn't look back, instead wrapping her scarf round her even tighter, as if to shut him out of her thoughts.

Jake made for the river and walked along the Seine, feeling

sorry for himself, even though he only had himself to blame. He was cheered to see a British couple having a humdinger of a row as he waited to cross the road on one of the bridges.

'I told you . . . I didn't bring the iPad on purpose,' said the man, whose face told Jake this argument happened a lot. 'We are *not* sitting in a hotel room watching Netflix on the romantic trip of a lifetime.' As soon as the light went green, the woman stalked off in fury as her weary lover trotted behind.

Light snow began as Jake looked for recognisable landmarks, seeing Notre Dame and the Île de la Cité loom into view. As he crossed the river and edged his way through the tourists, the overthinking kicked in. What would happen now? Would he have to go back to Amelia and tell her why he couldn't marry her? And what was that reason? Was he actually gay? No, because he was attracted to women; that feeling hadn't gone anywhere. Did he like danger? Was he just a sexual opportunist? Did this mean he was *dirty*? Would she understand? Did it matter if she didn't? He wanted to give her what she wanted but, as he walked and walked, he had considerable trouble working out exactly what that was. According to his watch he'd been wandering for two, bone-chilling hours. He nipped into a department store to use the loo – all the way on the top floor and with the hugest graffito of male genitalia he'd ever seen etched on the inside of the cubicle door – and realised he was hungry. There was a Starbucks and patisserie in the department store but it felt too sterile to brood in dramatically, and he needed to do plenty of that. If you couldn't sit looking haunted about your future in Paris, where could you? This needed alcohol.

He came upon a bar with unfamiliar pop music piping out of the speakers, and the smell of fries, waffles and crêpes, maybe. The sole barman was pouring beers with glacial nonchalance. Jake waited. He usually got embarrassed and furious in queues; he forever picked the line moving at a snail's pace. Even worse was standing at the front of a queue – or being the *entire* queue – and getting ignored. Amelia often complained at Jake turning on his heels and wheeling out of somewhere because he wasn't served quickly enough. 'You are such a *diva*! How do you get anything done?'

It wasn't impatience, though, just the painful reality of being low on someone's priorities; the unadulterated melodrama of this thought made Jake chuckle, and the barman, now offloading the beers from a grubby tray into the eager hands of a group of loud guys in fake-fur jackets, noticed him, finally. 'You want something?' he drawled, in a French accent. Obviously. Because, well, *Paris*.

His name, as revealed after the second beer, was Corentin, which Jake had to get him to spell, and he was 'really an illustrator', originally from Quimper – again, Jake asked him to spell it out so he could understand – but had lived in Paris since he was a student. He was attractive; Jake soon began to feel that good old sensation, the 'central heating coming on' clank and groan of his hormones starting to race and he realised, quickly, that he was flirting with Corentin and, more excitingly, Corentin was flirting back. Spinning round on his stool after a fourth beer, Jake noticed he'd wandered into a gay bar – same-sex couples at every table and a pair of drag queens in one corner, squabbling over sequins. So he bought another drink, and another, and then Corentin got a round in, and then another, and their faces kept getting closer and their conversations more hushed, and Jake felt like he was waiting to be given the gentlest of shoves over a cliff into . . . whatever he was getting himself into. They laughed about exchanging numbers so they could be intercontinental WhatsApp buddies, and then actually did, and the heat was rising so much Jake's skin was sizzling. This could have gone anywhere or nowhere but it was going *somewhere* and Jake was terrified and intoxicated – in every sense – and it was only when Corentin made a joke about Jake's dimples, or '*fossettes*' as he called them once they'd googled to clarify, that Jake remembered where he was, who he was, and who was waiting for him back at the hotel.

A jolt. Someone walking over his grave, or someone else waiting for him in Paris, alone. It had been hours, and Amelia hadn't texted. 'I have to go.'

Corentin shrugged and smiled – he'd clearly done this before – and as Jake scampered away, he called out, 'Come again in Paris. I will steal for you more beer.'

It was cold, and he was drunk, but his mind had never been so razor sharp. His sense of direction kicked in and he power-marched back to the hotel without looking at his phone once. He knew what he had to do. He knew what he was going to say. Time to make the leap.

Jake gingerly opened the hotel room door. Amelia was sitting up in bed, looking worn out, a novel open on the duvet beside her, a large glass of red in her hand and a couple of shopping bags on the floor. She didn't ask where he'd been. He kissed her on the forehead and she responded by squeezing his wrist gently as he leaned over.

'Feeling better?'

Jake nodded. 'Yes. Much, thank you. I'm so sorry. What did you do?'

Amelia flicked her wine glass. It pinged sharply. 'I went shopping. Got really drunk on *excellent* vino. Sat on the wrong Metro all the way to La Défense. Froze my fucking tits off. Read my book. Finished it. Started my emergency book.' She lifted the novel and tossed it across the room. 'It's *shit*. What about you?'

Jake swallowed. His throat felt claggy. All that talking. All that beer. All that Corentin. 'I've been thinking,' he started. 'I need to—' He stopped as Amelia sat up straight in the bed. 'I have to tell you . . . ask you. No, I mean.' He was drunk. This wouldn't come out right. Amelia looked terrified. He didn't want to be a bad guy. This wasn't the right place, but where would *ever* be the right place?

Amelia took a glug of wine, the red staining her lips; a drop falling down her chin. 'Go on.'

'I think . . . ' Jake breathed deeply. 'I think you and me . . . ' The room started to spin. He remembered Corentin's smile, the clinking of glasses, the feeling. *Fossettes*. But also fear. Change. Openness. The end of everything. 'I think we should move in together. Come live with me!'

seven.

Amelia hissed as her trolley wobbled off into a shelf of steel colanders. 'Oh my God, why is this thing so unwieldy?'

Rudi laughed and waved her hand round the store with a flourish, like a spokesmodel at a car show. 'This shop is *supposed* to be the most hellish experience on Earth; if a couple can withstand this place, they'll never divorce. Is that why you brought me and not Jake?'

Amelia pulled a face. 'Shut up. No! I don't want him worrying that I'm infiltrating his personal space with loads of crap.'

Rudi surveyed the trolley, filled with placemats, cushions, throws, lamps and a house plant. 'What you gonna do? Bring in one thing at a time over a period of weeks, under cover of darkness?'

'Have I gone too far?' Amelia had heard of girlfriends who moved in and demanded a total refurb; the pressure to remain sexy and aloof and not appear a joyless nag was heavy.

Rudi noticed and changed tack. 'No, hon, but you've nothing to prove. You don't have to go full domestic goddess.'

But she did, thought Amelia; she had to make this work. It had to be the right decision. That night in Paris, after Amelia had said yes and Jake had fallen asleep, she'd played out in her head all possible scenarios that could come from moving in with Jake, and she hadn't been sure happy outcomes were the majority. She'd set aside her own nagging doubts, his strange behaviour, and the fact he'd seemed to have asked her out of obligation – who believed in happily ever after, anyway? They worked reasonably well together *now*, and that was all that mattered; she'd approached it with optimism. Once back from Paris, they'd discussed ground rules. Amelia's requests were simple. No nagging about her untidiness; they must employ a cleaner. In return, she'd asked only that he do his own laundry. 'I'm sorry,' she'd barked over the noise of the Tassimo machine, 'I know the mystique can't last for ever, but I'm not ready to sort through your undergarments.'

Jake's solitary demand was that under no circumstances would they ever buy any cushions, pottery or screen-prints featuring the words 'Live! Laugh! Love!' – or any similar adjectives.

Rudi filled the silence. 'This means a lot to you.'

'It does. Now Mum isn't around any more, and Freddie hardly ever comes down, I feel – oh, this is stupid – like I . . . need to belong.'

'It isn't stupid. You *do* belong. Everybody loves you.'

But Amelia wasn't looking for the standard reassuring clichés; she could usually rely on Rudi to cut through the bullshit. 'It's all very well loving me on a night out, or dying of a hangover, or on holiday, but who loves me when I'm eating a bowl of cornflakes or switching off wildlife documentaries because they freak me out? The boring bits.'

'You're never boring.'

'I *am*!' A few people looked up from inspecting bath mats and turned to the source of the exclamation. 'And that's cool. I wanna be boring. I need someone to be there through it, though.'

'And is Jake the right someone?'

'What a question!' Amelia stared at Rudi aghast. 'Come on, I'm done. Hot dog time.'

'You promised me meatballs!'

'Okay, okay.' Amelia, relieved, considered the subject changed.

The first row came four days in. Of course, it was family-related; Amelia should've known. Margo 'dropped round' to see how they were getting on – by Amelia's reckoning she'd come a full hour out of her way – but Jake was out. Over a bottle of beer, Margo asked Amelia to start pumping Jake for ideas for his thirtieth birthday.

'I think he said he was away on business on the actual day. And it's *months* away!'

'Look,' said Margo wearily, 'years of watching Jake's disappointed face on Christmas morning and successive birthdays have taught me it takes planning to meet Mr D'Arcy's satisfaction.'

'Hmmm, but he doesn't like attention, not *that* kind.' Amelia recalled Jake tensing up at least twenty times during that Christmas dinner.

Margo whooped with laughter. 'I love this thing he does where he pretends he can't *stand* attention. Who does he think's impressed? He's a *D'Arcy*! It's what we do!'

Amelia decided silence was the best response to this line.

Margo gathered her handbag. 'Anyway, better be off. Well done for surviving so far. He hates having his personal space invaded – never shared as a kid.'

Jake came in from work in a good mood, crowing about

a successful presentation, so Amelia relayed what Margo had said, thinking he'd laugh it off. Wrong! She saw his face changing: seconds ago, light and relaxed; now, a pressure cooker about to go off.

'What we *do*?' he bellowed. 'It's what *they* do, not me. Showboating at Christmas, singing too loudly at the panto, high-fives for *nothing* like they're in *High School Musical*.'

Amelia was not here to be shouted at so tried to interrupt, but Jake was in full flow.

'You know, sometimes, I'd sit in my bedroom and wonder if I was an alien. I liked reading, being on my phone, not *attention*. They never *got* me.'

Amelia wasn't prepared for this weird confessional-cum-toddler tantrum. 'It's your family and they want to do something nice for you. Thirty is a big one. And you know what they're like.'

'Yeah, I do know. Their parties always end up the same way: everyone drunk and screeching, wading through nostalgia. Someone filming it on their phone for posterity. I can't relate. I'm sick of grinning and bearing it. *Them*.'

For years Amelia had slept beside Jake and never knew the grudges ran this deep. Untangling this would be like tackling that mysterious carrier bag marked 'CABLES, LEADS, WIRES' that she'd found under her bed when moving. She wondered why he'd been so willing to share now. What had changed? Maybe turning thirty was freaking him out; she'd seen it happen a lot to friends.

Jake ploughed on. 'It's a code I can't break, and when I try to get away from it, I'm a spoilsport or too "serious".'

'Jake . . . '

'Or it's all down to my "famous sulks" – I *know* they say

that, by the way.' Amelia blushed as if caught betraying a confidence. Jake looked away. 'They love to diagnose me, but they don't know me at all.' He looked like he was about to say something else but thought better of it. 'I'm not sulking. I'm just not "up" twenty-four/seven.'

Christ, that tortured brow and petted lip. Was this her chief role now they lived together? Jake's unpaid analyst? It seemed there was a lot to unpack; Amelia believed in travelling very light.

She put her arm round him. 'You have *me* now. You can tell me anything.' She hoped he wouldn't hold her to that. 'Is it . . . are you not ready to share your space yet?' She felt Jake stiffen. Fuck.

'Oh, the *sharing* thing. Did that come up?' He didn't hate sharing at all, he said – this was a myth. But as the eldest, his family was obsessed with taking things from him to show him *how* to share. Jake sighed as he explained that as soon as little Margo opened her mouth and pointed in his direction, whatever was in his hand was snatched from it and put into hers in the name of 'sharing'. She never shared back.

Amelia thought there was something faintly ridiculous about resenting your siblings as you headed for your thirties, before she remembered Freddie's superpower of making her feel feeble and stupid with only a few choice sentences. But did Freddie make her this angry? Not once he was out of her eyeline. She lay her head on Jake's back and they stayed like that for a while. Until: 'I think that was our first row.'

Jake turned to her, his face heavy with remorse and a trace of panic. 'It wasn't.' He kissed her hand. 'Whatever happens, I'm never angry at you. Ever.'

*

'Jake, my boy!' Charlie bellowed across the pub.

Jake acknowledged the table of unfamiliar faces, searching for Adyan and Dean among them. He'd run his plans for the stag weekend by Amelia the night before.

'It's a good mix of culture and lads-lads-lads *hell.*' Amelia prodded at Jake's mood board – yes, a mood board, he was a professional – with her nail. 'You can't get more classy-trashy than the Moulin Rouge. I'm surprised you went for Paris in the end, after what happened when we were there.'

Jake thought of that glass floor in the Eiffel Tower and shuddered, before pulling himself together. 'But Charlie will like it, yeah? Loves a gallery and wanging on about wine. I thought the cocktail-making class would appeal to his inner hedonist. Good to do it a bit differently. Like a stag weekend, but *luxe.* Nobody coming back with chlamydia or a criminal record.'

Amelia helped him pack all his plans into the portfolio case. 'They'll love it!'

They did *not* love it. It didn't start well: at introductions, the private school boys were so nasal or throaty, Jake couldn't quite decipher the names; it was a long honking wail of vowels. He definitely caught a Miles and a Hugo, but beyond that, he was presenting his perfect stag weekend to strangers. He was up to Saturday evening, where they would eat a gourmet tasting menu at a beautiful restaurant cut into the rock face round the corner from the Sacré-Cœur, before heading down to the Moulin Rouge, when Miles – or Hugo or Godfrey or Ezekiel or whatever – raised his hand and bade him stop.

'Need me to go over something again?' said Jake brightly, in full organiser mode, like he was at work. He felt less nervous when hiding behind a persona. Force of habit.

Miles swigged his beer. 'No, I don't. I just . . . I'm a bit confused, Jack.'

Charlie nudged him. 'Jake.'

Jake swallowed hard. 'Confused?'

'Yeah, becaaaaause, I was under the impression that we boys – ' he swept his arm round the table like a conductor ' – were going on a *stag* weekend, not a girlie chick-lit spa day.'

Jake began to stammer a response but Miles wasn't waiting. 'This is Charlie's last weekend of freedom. He wants – *we* want – booze, girls, tits, *drugs*. No?'

Charlie stared back at Jake, face flecked with guilt. 'Well, Holly did say this is the last weekend before the wedding I'll be allowed to do MDMA.'

'*Allowed*?' Jake felt self-conscious standing, so slowly sank to his seat. 'But whenever we've talked about Europe we said we'd do the culture, the Louvre, Musée d'Orsay, the lot.'

'Yeah, mate, but, like, with the ladies. Couples. Not a dudes' weekend.'

Jake stared back at his best friend. 'Dudes? Are we *dudes*? Have we *ever* been dudes? I've never seen you on a surfboard.'

Miles butted in again. 'Tits, Jake. Will there *be* any?'

Jake sighed. 'There's the Moulin Rouge.'

Miles snorted. 'That's just trussed-up burlesque for tourists. They won't touch your cock. I want proper breasticles all up in my face. Full-on shirt potatoes as far as the eye can see. Nipples.'

Jake wondered if he had enough budget left to pay for Miles to make a one-way trip to the Bastille. 'You can get a lap dance *anywhere*.'

'No, I *can't*. My Jessa wouldn't stand for it, but abroad, it's a stag, it's okay. It's a free pass, *expected*.'

'Charlie?' Jake reddened in defeat as his friend nodded. 'But . . . I've booked the travel.'

Charlie smiled awkwardly. 'I appreciate it, truly. We can still do Paris, just maybe cut back the cultural stuff, eh? Have a big night out? I still fancy the riverboat, though.'

'Yes, chap! Boozy cruising.' Miles finished his beer. 'And don't forget the . . . '

Jake smiled as wide as he could to show he wasn't a spoil-sport. 'The naked breasts. Fine. I won't.' He looked round the table, everyone's features becoming more porcine by the second. 'You guys are right; I don't know what I was thinking. Let's have a massive blowout. Leave it with me! We're gonna really . . . ' He searched for the words to get them on side. 'We're gonna 'ave it! *Have* it!' He grinned so hard as the group of stags roared in appreciation that his cheeks ached all the way home. Dudes. He had lost out to the *dudes*.

'You're early!' trilled Amelia, flicking through the channels on the TV. 'We really need to get cable installed; channel-hopping through anything less than five thousand stations is really unsatisfying. How did it go?' Jake must've looked even angrier than he felt; Amelia recoiled slightly as she looked up at him. 'All good?'

Jake took a deep breath, worried he might shout in frustration. He counted to five. 'Yep, went down well,' he lied. 'Just a few suggestions to take into consideration. It's gonna be a blast.'

eight.

Things went well at home those first few weeks. Jake checked the hard drive on his computer for shirtless pics of Usher and Jamie Dornan, and shoved his copy of *A Little Life* to the back of the bookshelf. Not hiding or lying – merely not revealing, that's how he saw it. It felt good to make Amelia happy; he knew he could be a drain on people at times, rather than a booster shot. When Charlie was full of apologies after the stags' mutiny, Jake brushed it off. It wasn't about him, it was for Charlie, he told himself; no point playing up to his grumpy reputation. Embracing this new positivity, and feeling more stable and secure than he had for a while, he decided to address what he'd been putting off for months: replying to Evan's message. It wasn't like him to leave somebody on 'read' – he was prone to writing 'sorry for the delay in replying' if he took longer than twenty minutes to get back to someone at work – but it was difficult to know what to say to Evan after all these years. It was a relief, then, when Evan suggested cutting to the chase and meeting up for a beer. Like men did.

The name of the bar Evan suggested was unfamiliar, but Jake recognised the place straightaway, realising the message

Evan was sending by asking him to meet there. It all came flooding back. Summer 2012, before he met Amelia. Hannah had asked if he was free after work to go for a drink.

'I'm in Victoria today; can you be bothered schlepping over? Nice change?'

They had walked arm in arm to a shabby-looking bar with blacked-out windows.

Jake had gawped at the front door, with peeling paint and rusted handles. 'Are you serious? Why?'

'Everywhere else is Olympics tourism bollocks. I doubt this place will be.'

'That's because it's a shithole.'

Hannah had guffawed. 'Where's your sense of adventure? Come on, fave, let's rough it.'

They'd been halfway through their pints and Hannah's story of her latest, unfathomable work vendetta when Jake had taken a proper look at their surroundings.

'Han . . . I think this is a *gay* bar.'

'Noooooo.' She hadn't looked up from her drink.

'It *is*.' Jake had picked up a leaflet at the bar. 'There's a Steps tribute band playing next week . . . '

'I loved Steps.' She'd begun to hum one of their songs, 'One for Sorrow'. Jake had been surprised he recognised it.

'And . . . ' Jake had nodded at the bar staff, who were disinterestedly shining glasses or picking at their goosebumps in T-shirts half a size too tight. 'They all look like Freddie Mercury.'

'So did my granddad. What's your point?'

Jake had put down his drink and held Hannah's gaze. 'Han, look, why are we at a gay bar?'

Hannah had shrugged. 'I thought it might be *fun*.'

'Lots of places are fun. Why here?'

'Maybe I'm turning lesbian.'

Jake had peered around the place. 'There are *zero* women in here.'

Jake had caught the eye of a man across the bar who'd smiled at him slowly. If Jake kept staring, he'd probably wink or lick his lips or something. Or worse. Jake had realised he was getting way ahead of himself; the man could very easily be smiling at a childhood memory. 'God, though, it's a bit *much*.'

Hannah had looked downcast. 'I thought you might like it. A laugh.'

'Like it?! Why would I . . . ? Let's come and gawk at the gay people isn't very you.' He'd been careful not to sound angry or defensive; that would be an admission of guilt. An admission? Guilt? Why was the language around this kind of stuff always so criminal, anyway? He'd tried to defuse the situation. 'I mean, what are you trying to say, Han? You're not trading me in for a gay best friend, are you? Because I'm not turning, not even for you. I'm not gay, sorry.'

Hannah's mouth had tightened. 'No, of course. I *know* that. But . . . ' She'd picked up her drink and swilled the beer round the glass. 'I wouldn't care if you were. I just want you to know.'

Jake had kept his eyes on his drink, like it was the most fascinating thing in the world and not a very flat lager. He'd been silent for a few seconds. His chest had filled with what felt like molten lava and he'd felt breathless and light-headed. He'd seemed to be having an out-of-body experience; he'd known he should say something else but was too busy wondering what had given him away. At university he'd had a fling with a girl called Jessica – Hannah had delighted in christening her 'Basica' because of her daddy-bought designer handbags – and it had gone well until she'd jolted him out of his security.

'I'm so glad you're the kind of guy who's in touch with their feminine side,' she'd warbled, pausing to clink her plastic beaker of the second-cheapest wine from the supermarket with his. 'It's comforting. You're one of the good ones.'

Great, Jake had thought, a good guy – didn't they always finish last? He'd wanted to go back to what Jessica had said again and again, ask her what she'd meant about his feminine side, but he'd been afraid to in case it had looked like he was bothered, or worse, she would explain exactly how she'd arrived at that conclusion, and ruin the illusion he'd been carefully cultivating for years. Sometime he felt the mark of his afternoon with Evan was still on him, like Evan's hand-prints were burned on his bare chest, tongue luminous from his kisses – an indelible stain that everyone else but Jake could see. And here it was again, he'd thought.

'I know you wouldn't mind if I was gay, you'd love it – finally someone to drag to that Kylie night you're always on about in Dalston. I'm afraid I can't help you there. I'm not gay.'

Hannah had smiled sweetly. 'Not even for Kylie? What about Steps?'

The chill had thawed.

'Not even. Let's go.'

As they'd walked toward the safe blandness of the chain pub down the road, Hannah had squeezed his arm tighter than she ever had before, and in the fuzzy summer heat, her eyes had looked wet. Hay fever, she'd said.

Inside, the bar hadn't changed much; the only difference in nearly six years was the posters on the wall – old magazine shots of Debbie Harry, Pete Burns, Madonna and a wide variety of other music icons – were more curled up at the edges. It was fairly empty: an older couple sat at one table in deep conversation, a group of men – mid-forties, he guessed – flicked through magazines at another, and a couple of lone guys leaned at two taller tables scrolling through their phones. One was young and looked like Zac Efron put through a boil wash. The other was not, and did not. Jake nipped to the loo before returning to the bar, ordering a gin and tonic from the barman – not the same one, but certainly from the same bored, detached gene pool – and saw Zac Efron had been replaced by someone he recognised. Evan.

Evan looked more or less the same. Still those browny-grey eyes, hair longer than it had been at school, when he'd worn it shorn to his head. His fingernails, Jake saw as he got closer, were painted a dark green. Jake recoiled for the briefest of seconds – the same reaction he had to seeing two men kissing on TV, or someone saying 'anal sex' within earshot – but pulled it back before Evan noticed, he hoped. The American accent had all but gone, but his relaxed smile was still there. They greeted each other awkwardly – Jake had held out his hand but Evan went for a hug. They started with the basics.

Evan worked for a hotel company, travelled a lot, met his husband – Nuno – on Tinder, and had been married two years. Their first dance was to 'Can't Take My Eyes Off You'. 'Lauryn Hill version,' said Evan with slight embarrassment. 'Nuno wanted "Love is a Losing Game". You know, Amy Winehouse? I don't think he even listened to the lyrics. It was either Lauryn or a dance routine to "Proud Mary", but I put my foot down.'

Jake imagined them in matching tracksuits strolling down Colombia Road – they loved to spend their weekends with friends in east London, because of course they fucking did – and picking out flowers for their no doubt tastefully decorated apartment.

Jake took special notice of Evan's actions, how he carried himself. At school he had been quite subdued, low-key. Enigmatic, maybe. Now, he was more exaggerated; he touched Jake's knee, and sent his eyes rolling to his forehead at certain points during the conversation, the kind of behaviour Jake had repressed or rebuffed over the years. He'd seen it in chat-show hosts and gay characters on TV and, for a while until 2013, in his barber, the best haircut he'd ever had in London – he hated himself for cringing at the time, but had done it anyway, because this was expected, from both sides. At least Evan was being himself, letting down his guard, showing who he was with no shame. As the conversation got more personal, the tension gradually drained from Jake's body until he was almost slumped in the perilously high stool, like a set of bagpipes thrown to one side.

As he told Evan about Amelia, Jake noticed him looking into the distance as if staring at the chemtrails of what Jake had just said. 'Can I just say?' He didn't wait for a reply. 'I'm . . . a bit surprised.'

'Surprised? At what?'

'That you ended up with a woman. Is that wrong of me to say?'

Jake's eye began to twitch. Evan shrugged. 'It felt – what happened between us – a bit more than an experiment. Even if we did both pretend we didn't exist after.'

'I'm sorry about . . . that.' *That*, as if it had been nothing, a small misdemeanour like taking ages to reply to a text, and not aggressive avoidance of one another. It had hurt at the time.

Evan's eyes glimmered for a moment. 'Yeah. Same, I guess.'

He guessed. Nice. He carried on. 'I assumed you'd be . . . gay now. I know that's presumptuous of me; it was just a kiss. I don't think I've got, like, gay superpowers or anything.'

Jake laughed politely, keeping his hands flat on the table so Evan wouldn't see them shaking. What could he say? That blanking Evan in the corridors had been devastating? Was that even true? Or should he say it was fine and all worth it in the end because in the early hours of New Year's Day, he'd finally got a sequel in a draughty bathroom?

'We treated each other badly.'

Evan tilted his head. 'Yeah. I should've known better. We could have helped each other out. Bloody awkward teenagers. Why didn't you say something?'

'Why didn't you?'

'I had my own shit to deal with.'

Jake remembered the hassle Evan used to get at school. Evan dismissed his attempts at empathy.

'Oh, not *that*. I'm used to that racist shit. White boys never disappoint. Except you. I made my peace with it because as long as they were concentrating on my skin, they weren't calling me a queer. Like they did to you – behind your back, usually. Did you know?' Jake had guessed as much. 'So . . . yeah, I distanced myself from it, from you. Like you did from me. Survival.'

'I'm s—'

'Nah, Jake, don't. I was mad at you, yeah. We wasted a lot of time. I thought I might have answered a few questions for you. But, y'know, you're straight, so congrats on that! The world belongs to you!'

Evan drummed his fingers on the table. He'd waited a long time for this audience. It hadn't quite been the reunion Jake had expected, but he realised he'd needed it.

'I'm not straight.'

Evan did an exaggerated double-take like Scooby Doo. 'So . . . explain? Is dear Amelia just a great big beard?'

Jake's heart pounded. He felt very disloyal to Amelia for letting someone say that about her. She was also very proud of the fact that she had never needed to wax her chin, unlike every other woman in her family.

Evan was still talking. 'Does she know? Has she, uh, swallowed the keys for you?'

'Huh?'

'The keys to your closet. Helping to keep you in? Locking your secret away?'

'No, it's not like that. She doesn't know. I . . . get a feeling. It's different from women. I like women, and feel . . . uh . . . aroused by them. I like sex with them. All that. It feels . . . ' Jake had not been ready for this speech. He tried to get back on track. 'Sometimes all I think about is women, but some days . . . I only dream of men. Well, a man. And that's when I get myself into trouble.'

'What kind of trouble?'

Evan's eyes widened as Jake told him about Edinburgh – 'This is proper soap opera shit, are you kidding me?' – and soon Jake felt a rush of guilt for Evan and his own stupid, awkward seventeen-year-old self, and remembered the sting of Harry's rejection and his subsequent confusion after their moment in the hotel room. Samir's closed face all New Year's Day.

Evan chuckled. 'I wish you didn't look so worried or sound so embarrassed. Why haven't you told your friends? So you like both? So what?'

Jake shrugged. 'It's nobody else's business!'

Evan shook his head. 'It is. You can't be yourself. You're snogging your brother-in-law up against a fire escape while your girlfriend is a few feet away.'

'It was the brother-in-law's boyfriend. And he's not really my brother-in-law.'

Evan laughed. 'Details. Okay. But what gives, then?'

Jake stared down into his drink. He wasn't good at explaining himself. 'I know this sounds weird, but it'll be the most interesting thing about me and the effort of telling everyone . . . '

Evan slurped his cocktail. The lights dimmed to signify the evening had officially begun and the drinks were now 50 per cent more expensive. 'You know, my husband believes labels don't matter and we can all be who we wanna be, but I'm not so sure.'

'What do you mean?'

Evan leaned forward, his breath minty from his mojitos. 'Don't get me wrong, labels can be destructive and restrictive, but they also help you define yourself.'

Jake laughed. 'You sound like a wellness blogger on Instagram.'

'Fuck off, Jake. This is bona fide good advice from someone who has *done* this. If you have any chance of living the life you *claim* you want, putting a name on it is the best thing you can do. Do you feel relieved telling me you're bi?'

Jake thought the moment called for an awkward silence, but a techno song he remembered from his teens was doing its best to escape the speakers and jackhammer away any deeper meaning. 'Yes, I do. But . . . I can't be with Amelia any more, can I? Not if I want to . . . '

'Explore? Nope, probably not. Unless she is cool with it. I

say this as someone who's been not a *million* miles away from your situation, don't leave it too long and fuck your*self* up over this. Do it before anyone gets hurt. People aren't *collateral* on your journey to self-discovery, y'know.'

'She's just moved in. She bought cushions.'

'And I'm sure they're gorgeous.'

'I'm going to say something for the first time.' It was incredible how comforting it was to be able to talk to a near-stranger, with no investment in your present.

'I'm all ears.'

Jake cleared his throat. 'Things between me and Amelia. We're not right. I want something else. And she deserves . . . someone else.'

Evan picked mint from between his teeth. 'Well, the sooner you do it, the longer you have to recover – make things right.'

This time they hugged properly, and it wasn't awkward; it felt like home. Evan helped Jake into his cab. 'Thank you for this,' slurred Jake.

'*This*? Funny word for an emotional, confessional reunion, during which you changed sexuality about six times!' Evan winked and closed the door, leaning down to muss Jake's hair through the open window. 'Couldn't resist a chance to take another look at my first crush.' He laughed. 'Now I'll go home and tell my husband all about it. I'll probably say you're a bit uglier.'

'I'd love to meet him.'

Evan's smile was thin, cautious. He'd built a decent life for himself after years of wondering if he ever would. Messed-up school pals he'd swapped saliva with were not part of his long-game, but he did know how Jake was feeling. 'Sure. Sort out your shit and keep me posted. You have my number now. Call me any time. And, remember, tread careful, D'Arcy. Life is long.'

Jake noticed lights still on in the flat as he said goodbye to the cab driver with fake cheer. Amelia was propped up in bed, on her iPad. There was one last unpacked box next to the bed. She saw Jake glance at it.

'Tackling it tomorrow! Promise. Then it's done. It's the last odds-and-ends I scrambled for before I left. Corkscrews and Christmas cracker presents, I bet. Or more bloody cables!'

Jake nodded. Amelia turned back to her screen. He used the moment to take her in, his eyes sweeping across the bedroom. Her perfumes and creams and clothes all in place, like they'd always been there, no trace of what was before. This was forever now. Flashbacks to Paris. What he did say; what he *should've* said. Evan's words rang in his ears like a dream sequence in a terrible soap opera.

'I'll make us a drink.'

He went to the kitchen and made hot chocolate from the machine, heating milk in the microwave to top it up, just the way she liked it. As the machine gurgled, he looked out into the lounge. Bookshelves now groaned with Amelia's books, her scatter cushions – thankfully free of slogans – smothered the sofa. On the worktop, a form for cable TV installation, as she'd threatened, and on the fridge, unfamiliar notes stuck to the door – with magnets she must've brought with her; he didn't have any – in her neat, delicate handwriting. Making herself at home, as was her right. Eventually, he supposed, they'd need to sell this place. Too small for a . . . for a family. He wondered when the conversation would come, how soon before friends enquired whether they'd be getting married.

At Holly and Charlie's wedding, probably. He pictured them chanting 'You next!' like something out of a horror movie, faces zombified from tiredness and the free bar, the word 'commitment' daubed across their chests in party glitter.

He kicked off his shoes and checked his reflection in the door of the microwave to see how rough he looked. Not great. But there was no right or wrong way to look when you were about to break somebody's heart, which he now knew with absolute certainty he was about to do. It had come together right there: the sight of her cosy and contented in the bed, her things around her, ready to devote a lifetime to him and their relationship. He couldn't waste any more of her time. This – she – was not what he wanted.

He allowed himself to whisper, 'Shit', before looking at his watch one more time – 23:48 – and picking up the two mugs, clenching his teeth as the heat from one scorched his thumb, to make his way to the bedroom. By midnight, nothing would ever be the same again.

nine.

'Men? You're *into* them? Is that what you said?'

This was, as it turned out, the hardest thing Jake had ever had to say. It was different from blurting it out to his former school friend; Amelia had skin in the game. So maybe it hadn't been a great idea to casually drop it in the middle of a conversation about how the coffee machine might need descaling – 'I can taste *fragments* in this hot chocolate' was the last thing Amelia had said before Jake had made his revelation. 'Into men', like you'd advertise the fact you'd discovered a new cocktail or tell someone your favourite breed of dog.

'Yeah. *Yes*. Men.'

'*And* women too? Also? Additionally?'

'Yeah.'

'At the same time?'

This was going almost comically slowly. Jake thought how best to make the pennies drop, but he was drying up fast. 'No, not like that.' He was very aware of how quickly he was talking, trying to get it all out before he changed his mind.

'So . . . you're *bi*sexual? You like both? Any?'

Eureka. Almost. 'Both, yes. Not sure about "any". Either?'

Revealing your true sexuality to your girlfriend, it seemed, was like reading out a list of substitutions made in your online groceries order.

'But not just . . . whenever? You don't fancy everyone, at all times?' Amelia was out of bed now, wrapping her dressing gown around her.

'Is there . . . ?' She breathed deeply, steeling herself to ask a difficult question. 'Is there a reason you're telling me this now? Today?' Her face was frozen, awaiting orders on how to react.

'I had to tell you because . . . I've wanted to say it for a long time. Only today did I realise how long. You *know*? Maybe you don't. I don't expect you to . . . absorb it straightaway. I don't think I have.' Babbling, babbling, babbling. At breakneck speed.

Amelia looked down into her mug of hot chocolate. 'Well,' she said finally, 'thank you for telling me. I'm glad you felt you could.'

Jake wasn't sure he'd heard right; he was waiting for the storm. It seemed seasons came and went, ice caps thawed and refroze, while he waited for her to start shouting and screaming. But nothing. Shouldn't she be angry? Sad? Instead, she sat regarding him for a while, before looking down into her cup again and not liking what she found there.

'I need a glass of wine.' She walked over to pat his shoulder, before moving to the bedroom door.

He followed her, tiptoeing like a child up past bedtime, as she padded through to the kitchen, switching on the light and sighing as she opened the fridge. What was she thinking? Was her mind as busy as his right now? What should he do?

Jake coughed to break the silence. 'You're . . . not *upset*?'

Amelia turned to him, brow furrowed. 'No. Unless . . . are you seeing another man? Another *woman*, even?' He told her he wasn't and, incredibly, she just shrugged. Was this how it ended? With a shrug? Grateful as he was for this very grown-up and serene break-up at the breakfast bar, Jake had expected more fireworks. This was more of a dull thud than a big bang.

'Did you expect me to rip your head off? Go into a *frenzy*?'

Jake took the glass of wine Amelia offered him. 'It changes everything.'

Amelia sat opposite and stroked the stem of her wine glass absentmindedly, before moving the cable TV forms aside so she could reach for Jake's hand. Her hands were warm; he realised he was trembling. Amelia's eyes were kind, willing him to speak. But he couldn't.

'It changes nothing, Jake. It's part of you. I don't want us to have secrets. This is what being together is all about. *Living* together. Knowing one another inside out.'

But of course this was her reaction; she was a good person. The best. How could he not have guessed that instead of seeing his sexuality as the end of everything, she would be encouraging and thoughtful? He really didn't know her at all if he'd thought she'd go crazy. He couldn't hear her now; he was desperately trying to work out how to unpick this to a point where she understood. He should've done the relationship part first, shouldn't he? This was like that time he didn't read all the questions before starting that test in sixth form and it turned out the last question was 'Ignore all questions except the first'. Ideally, he'd have explained his feelings in an email and gone round the world for a year, but Amelia was sitting here now, waiting. It was time.

'Part of it, too . . . ' Jake felt like a used car salesman trying to palm off an old banger on to a trusting customer. 'Part of it is getting to know myself.'

'Okay. When did you first know? What were your earliest experiences? Is this about playing with dolls again? Or the thing your mum mentioned. With the hand. Christabel.'

Jake sighed. 'Chrysalis.' What was going on? She was acting like his best gal pal, not his imminently former girlfriend.

And then: 'I think I knew there was something . . .'

Jake gasped more theatrically then he'd usually allow himself in public. 'You did?'

'Well, yeah. Freddie used to say . . . ' Jake's eyes bulged at the mention of him. 'Well, he would make comments.' Jake held his breath. 'But I assumed that was just Freddie being Freddie; he's always enjoyed making me squirm.' Jake was surprised to hear her admit that; he'd always assumed she was oblivious. It made his heart ache for her even more. She carried on. 'You had a *quality* my exes didn't. Sensitive and . . . uh, nice.' Her eyes flicked over him. 'Your . . . uh . . . *fashion* sense threw me a bit, though.'

'That has nothing to do with . . . Anyway, we're getting off track. Please. Can I explain? Just a moment.' To her credit, Amelia did not interrupt with words, but her face spoke volumes. 'This has been inside me a long time. I've hidden it away, sometimes not wanting it to be true, because if it's not true, it's easier. I think there's . . . something not right about you and me at the moment, too, and whether that's made me face up to . . . what I want now or not, I don't know, but I *think* I need to explore this, see if it makes me happier. Feel whole. Does that make sense?'

It would have sounded authentic in a mindfulness seminar, but in the fuzzy gloom of the hob's overhead light, teetering on kitchen stools, it sounded exactly like it was: just words. 'I'll always love you,' said Jake, meaning it, 'but this is what I have to do.'

Amelia slowly withdrew her hand from across the table and moved the half-completed forms back to where they had been, as if pulling up a drawbridge. She didn't say anything for a long time, and drained her wine glass.

'Why didn't you tell me earlier? How far would you have let it go?'

The crack in her voice made his eyes sting. 'I couldn't. I didn't know until today that I couldn't keep it in.'

'You asked me to move in. Did you mean it?'

Jake thought of Evan describing her as a 'beard'; he remembered his panic in Paris, the fight-or-flight feeling, Amelia's face drawn and wary in the light of the hotel room. He felt fraudulent, but owed her a lie. 'Yes, I think so.'

'I . . . I don't want this to sound . . . the way it is going to sound, but . . . ' Her voice was detached, ghostly. 'Are you using being bi as an *excuse* to get rid of me?'

'What?'

Her voice was gravelly from the strain of staying up late. 'If you wanted to go off and "explore" you could just *dump* me. Blame some, oh, I don't know, fear of commitment or whatever men say when they wanna shag someone else.'

'I . . . ' Now probably wasn't the time to interrupt that, no, he wasn't huge on commitment either. 'No, of course I'm not. It's not an excuse. I'm . . . telling you at the same time. It's a . . . like, a coincidence?' Pathetic.

'Why're you telling me you're bi?'

Jake refilled the wine glasses. 'You're my best friend. I had to tell you.'

'*Hannah* is your best friend.' Amelia grabbed her glass and took a huge slug like it was a tequila slammer. 'But, like . . . if you're bi, then *fine*. We can still be together, can't we? Bi equals both. It means you like girls too. *I* am a girl. We're already in a relationship. Why break up?'

Jake struggled to argue with this logic.

'Allow me to answer for you. You want to eat *all* the steaks before you go vegan, don't you? And me, well, I'm in the way, like that box that . . . ' she breathed out slowly ' . . . that I will now never unpack.'

'Amelia . . . ' Jake gulped.

'If you don't wanna be with me, just *say* it. And if you're bi, *cool*. But don't pretend the reason we're over is *because* you're bi. You wanna go and sleep with other people. *Including* men. Right?'

Amelia seemed less and less familiar to him, her speech more detached, already turning into the stranger she would, he guessed, eventually become. She sounded logical, but hurt, talking to him like she was reading out data. They both looked knackered and ugly; two gargoyles grimacing into middle distance. Jake wanted to reach out to her and comfort her as he would any other time, with any other catastrophe.

Jake trailed after her to the bedroom. 'I never wanted to hurt you.'

She didn't acknowledge him, and began putting underwear into an overnight bag.

'Not wanting to hurt you meant I never mentioned . . . it . . . sooner, and now it's hurting you even *more*. I'm sorry. I shouldn't have let it get this far.'

Amelia stopped packing and stared sadly into the dead air before her. 'I thought I did everything right. Never demanded, never nagged. Waited around like a . . . oh, I dunno. Never even left a pair of socks here in case you did what men *usually* do and panic I was trying to get you down the aisle.'

'I know.'

'Never complained, never took the lead, but didn't act like a doormat either. I've pushed my own doubts and worries to one side because I . . . thought this was where I belonged.' Amelia looked around the room. 'Four fucking years. Christ. I'm drained. You are the loveliest, nicest, weirdest guy I've ever met and this has been much harder work than it's looked. You were hiding behind me all this time. And I let it happen. Maybe I was doing the same, clinging on to air. And now . . .' She sat on the bed, deflated. 'I've nowhere to go.'

Jake sat beside her, expecting her to move away. Instead, she stared into space. He said her name a few times.

'I'm so tired,' she said. 'And drunk now. I didn't have dinner, I was busy unpacking. Unpacking! God. This is so sad. I want to be angry, but I'm too sad. I feel sick. I don't understand anything. Why did you have to do this now? Tonight? I was just about to go to sleep. I can't speak about this, to you, any more.'

Jake felt his head collapsing in on itself. To watch her try to figure out what was going on felt cruel. He had to get away, let her be, before she started to hate him. 'Will you be okay? If you . . . Why don't you . . . stay here?'

'Here? What do you mean will I be okay? Where are you going? Are you . . . walking out? Now?'

'Stay here until you're sorted. I don't mind. I'll go to Mum and Dad's.'

Amelia's eyes were huge and round like she'd heard all the world's nastiest secrets. 'Do they know?'

'No, not yet.'

'Everyone will know. They will blame me for this. Like a glittery, socially conscious Typhoid Mary.'

'Course they won't. It's all me. I'll . . . get some things together.'

She looked at her phone. 'It's one in the morning. My life was so different an hour ago. I wish I'd turned the light out earlier.' Amelia turned back to Jake. 'You can't go at this time, knocking them up out of bed like a copper.'

'I've got a key.'

'You *can't*. It's weird.' She was suddenly practical. 'Are you sure I can stay? I don't know what else to do.'

'I'm sure. Just text me when . . . '

'When I'm gone.' Amelia nodded. It was sinking in, slowly. 'That's nice of you. But confusing. You *are* nice, I'd forgotten. That's what I always liked. Nicer than the others. But now . . . not. I have . . . a question. Does Hannah know? *Did* she know? Before me?'

Jake made a mental note of the people he must now tell. Hannah knew, didn't she? The gay bar. Hints over the years.

Amelia's eyes narrowed. 'Ever wondered why me and her never "gelled"?'

Jake said he assumed Amelia didn't believe men and women could be platonic friends without an ulterior motive – she had no male pals aside from a couple of gay guys at her office.

'Oh *no*,' said Amelia, suddenly animated, daring herself to laugh. 'She said, years ago, she was so glad you'd met someone and were happy. I was pleased she liked me; I saw how much she meant to you.'

Jake nodded, waiting for the punchline. Hannah's frankness was unmatched.

'How sweet and grossly sexist of you to think Hannah and I would consider scrapping over you, by the way.' Amelia leaned back against the headboard. 'No, but then another time after that – at some shitty Christmas drinks or something – she got really drunk, as *usual*, and ambled over to say she was thrilled you "sorted yourself out". I'll *never* forget. She looked at me, winked and said, "I always thought he was gay, you know. I've been trying to get him to come out for years," and walked away.'

Jake's blood ran cold; they'd known all along and never said a word.

'So you see,' murmured Amelia, exhausted, eyes beginning to close, 'I knew too, in a way. Always did. How annoying for that *cow* to be proved right after all.'

ten.

Jake's hangover was already kicking in, eyes puffy, and stomach acidic and angry, when he let himself in the back door of his parents' house at 3 a.m. He was planning to steal up to bed, but was surprised to find Kia sitting at the kitchen table in her pyjamas, fingernails clacking on her phone screen, a mug of something hot by her side and an ashtray with two butts in it.

She was just as startled to see him. 'You scared the fuck out of me.'

'You're supposed to smoke outside now, I think.'

Kia's eyes dropped in guilt. 'I know. I didn't wanna wake the dog. Sorry. I was gonna spray air-freshener.'

Jake felt bad his first words to her had been a telling-off. Someone sitting alone, in the kitchen of a house they didn't live in, probably wasn't having a very good night.

'Doesn't matter. I won't tell. I'm gonna make a drink. Want one?' He stared at his parents' bewildering coffee machine. Kia spotted his difficulty and got up to help.

'We film on a Friday,' she said, 'so I usually stay over. What about you?' She pressed the correct sequence of buttons on the machine with a flourish. 'You lost?' Jake felt in the spotlight as Kia studied him for a few seconds. 'This is a very personal question, but have you been crying?'

He had, all the way there. Silently at first, so the soothing tones of the taxi driver's radio masked the sobs. By the time the car was zooming over Battersea Bridge, however, with the lights around him feeling so hopeful and cheering, tears had streamed down his face, shoulders heaving with the effort, like his dad when he got drunk at Christmas and listened to the Darlene Love version of 'Winter Wonderland'.

Kia reached into her pyjama pocket and fished out a small tube. 'Eye rescue gel. We get this stuff free. This one's brilliant. By the morning, you'll be stanning it like it's Ariana Grande. Oh, sorry . . . ' Kia began to speak really slowly as if reading out the *Radio Times* to an elderly relative. '"Stanning" means you'll really like it.'

'I know. I once sat in on a teenage focus group for antibacterial facewash.' He thanked her as he took the tube. 'And, yes, I've been crying. It's a long story.'

Kia tapped her talons on the wooden surface. 'Try me,' she said, lighting another cigarette and blasting a quick burst of Febreze with every drag.

'Okay.' Jake took a deep breath. 'I'm bi. Bi*sexual*, I mean.'

'Yeah, I'm aware of the, uh, terminology.' Kia waited a beat or two. 'How many times you said that out loud?'

Jake sighed. 'Until today, never.'

'Clear delivery.' Kia reviewed it as if leaving a comment under a YouTube video. 'Emotional, but you held it together.'

'Eternally the filmmaker.' Jake chuckled. 'What do you think?'

'What do I *think*?' Kia looked skyward and tapped the eye

gel tube against her chin. 'I think, Okay uh, nice one. That's it. What's it gotta do with me, y'know?'

Jake was disappointed. 'Did you . . . suspect?'

Kia shrugged. 'Never thought about it. You're not a puzzle I ever fancied solving, y'know? Other shit to do. No offence.'

Jake laughed at her brutal honesty.

'Yeah. I mean, look . . . ' Kia leaned in. 'You're, uh, older, white, cisgender . . . '

'What's that?'

Kia ran her tongue over her teeth in mild exasperation. 'Google it. You're gonna *need* to know that. Anyway, yeah, you got a job, money, a family who loves you. You'll be sweet. I'm not saying it isn't hard or nothing, but in the great big queer hierarchy, you're, like, six vitamin shots ahead.'

Jake considered this. 'You are very wise about all this. You and Trick always sound like you shoulda been on *Dawson's Creek*.'

'What's that?'

'Google it.'

Kia had done 'all this' at least twice, she said. First, aged twelve and living as a boy, announcing to her parents what she guessed they already knew: she had always felt different. Not wanting to rock the boat, she tested the water by saying she might be gay, and they made their peace with it. And then, at sixteen, things came to a head and she realised, 'I had to vocalise what I'd always known – I'm a woman. That's the big one. You have no idea. Like telling people you're from another planet or vote Tory.'

Jake felt a brief flash of gratitude that his own life was comparatively simple.

'You do stay here a lot, though,' he said. Kia's face slipped.

'That's not a dig, but is that why? Are they not cool with it, your mum and dad?'

It had taken time, and her sister had helped, although her brother . . . not so much. As long as she stayed out of trouble, her mum and dad were fine, getting there. As for school, Kia laughed bitterly as she explained why she'd left to go to college.

'My mates were amazing but the governors got into a right fucking froth so . . . yeah college. Fuck negativity, you know? But yeah, I *am* here a lot.' The thunderclouds in her eyes began to disperse. 'Your family and me don't have baggage, do we? I don't belong to them so . . . they don't worry about me as hard. Trick has been there for me since day dot. I'm staying here for, uh, a few days, actually; my auntie's visiting.'

'I thought your mum and dad were okay with your . . . with *this*?'

Kia's eyes narrowed at the 'this' but she carried on. 'Oh, I *did.* You don't think it ends here, do you? That you jump out of the closet with, like, a big parade and unicorns and then you're done explaining? My auntie doesn't know yet. So, instead of risking a scene, I came here, out of the way. She'll be gone soon.'

'That's awful. You should be proud of who you are, not hiding it.'

Jake saw Kia sneer slightly at his second-rate mantra. 'It's a reality, Jake. I'm not *hiding*; I'm showing compassion. I don't wanna stress my mum and dad out. It's an act of love, not shame. I still get to be me. Just not there, not this week. Compromise, yeah?'

'Why did you . . . ? Your name. I was wondering . . . ' Jake felt it might be okay to ask this question; there was *something* between them. But he couldn't quite manage it.

'I'm cool with questions if it's genuine curiosity, and not piss-taking,' mused Kia. 'I chose it because it sounds the same as my old one. The spelling, the *spirit*, are totally different, but nasty people . . . they wanna have power over you, because they're scared of you. Maybe *you'll* find this out. I ain't giving these wankers the chance to deadname me . . . ' Kia saw Jake's puzzled face. 'Deadname. Ah, jeez, google it. But yeah, I've taken that power away. They can shout "Keir the Queer" all they want but when it hits me it's "Kia" and a bit of queer never hurt anyone.'

Jake nodded solemnly. 'Am I going to spend the rest of my life doing exactly this, just like you have, probably for the millionth time?'

'Yep.' Kia stretched and yawned. 'You better go to bed. You need energy. You'll be fighting your first fires in the morning.'

On seeing him at the kitchen table, Jake's mum squinted uncertainly. 'Long time since I've come down of a morning and seen you sulking at my breakfast table. What's up?'

Jake rubbed his eyes, sore with four hours' sleep. 'Where's Dad?'

'It's his weekly wet shave, so making a mockery of the bathroom sink, I imagine.' Was something wrong? Something with Amelia? Why hadn't he said he was coming? He always forgot how many questions his mum asked, not waiting for answers. Poirot had nothing on her when she wanted the gory details.

'She's fine, but . . . We've split up.'

'No!'

Was the disappointment in his mum's voice genuine? 'Yes. Go get Dad. *Please*. It won't take long.' No way did he want to do this twice.

He heard the distant quizzical murmuring of his dad as he was disturbed in his bathroom and the heavy footsteps from upstairs while he went to put on a shirt. This was the last point he could change his mind. If he kept quiet now, he could tell Mum and Dad that he and Amelia had rowed, then go home and smooth it over with her. He could roll it back, he was sure; say it was a blip, a wobble, or try to convince Amelia she *was* enough, that this was a phase – sounded believable, right? – maybe even *propose*. She wanted to marry him, no? Was that vain of him to assume? He didn't know. But once he told his parents, it would be real – immovable and irreversible. They wouldn't gloss over it, or forget, or put it down to being out of sorts – they were like elephants. They held grudges against the dead, still remembered the exact location of Reenie's bruises from falling down the steps at the Red Lantern when they were all sixteen. They remembered stuff like it was a sport. So he had to decide now, should he set this in stone or wash it away with the tide? He agonised over this for a few moments – externally all was calm save for an expression reminiscent of a toddler struggling in silence with constipation – his adrenaline rocketing and plummeting every second. And when the words came out, he felt every other option crumbling away, disappearing into 'never was', leaving him only with now, a one-way street, and the baffled faces of his parents, shaving foam drifting from his father's face on to the immaculate tiles, his mother's mouth agape, as if dragging on the phantom cigarette. No going back.

*

Trick rubbed sleep from his eyes and stared up at the ceiling, before looking over to his sofa bed, where Hot Will and Kia snored in perfect unison. Last night's video shoot was boring, but he had to show willing, Kia said, because doing them would eventually pay for the serious things he wanted to say.

Hot Will's favourite thing to shout while filming was, 'Say it with your body, not just your voice. Talk to me with your cock.' Grating and arousing at the same time.

Kia was swaddled in the duvet so Hot Will's leg was hanging out the side. Trick's gaze panned along it, landing at the sports sock on his foot, dangling off and grubby at the sole. Beautiful bastard, thought Trick. He sat up when he heard his mum and dad talking excitedly. They did that in times of extreme happiness – new series of *Strictly Come Dancing* starting, the Grand National, three matches or more on a scratchcard – or great stress and confusion, when the wrong person won *Great British Bake Off* or Dad's favourite sausages were discontinued. It was rare; they were so annoyingly laidback about everything, and impossible to provoke. Every time Trick tried to confront them about something, they'd refuse to engage, telling him whatever it was didn't matter. On hearing about negative or bitchy comments under his videos, their sage advice was always 'ignore them'. It was maddening.

The day he'd realised much of the money that bought their house was made in Dubai, he'd tried to lecture them on LGBTQ rights and they'd been rightly concerned but had shrugged, 'It's a long time ago now, sweetheart.'

Then he heard Margo troop down the stairs and say, 'Hey, what are you doing here?', and what sounded like *Jake* responding. What could've brought him here so early on a Saturday? Death. It had to be. But whose? He did a mental count of black items of clothing in his collection, before recounting to dismiss anything with a logo or slogan. Trick saw Kia was now awake, catching up on messages. Hot Will still snored alongside – leg retracted, Trick noted, mournfully.

'Wow, you look, like, very anti-gorgeous, babe.'

Kia glared up. 'Up half the night. Shouldn't eat pizza. Gluten, man.'

Trick knew it wasn't gluten keeping Kia awake, but she didn't enjoy getting confessional before midday. 'Jake's here.'

Kia leaned back on the sofa bed and closed her eyes. 'I know. I saw him arrive.'

Trick scuttled over to her and tapped her on the forehead.

'Bitch, open those eyes and spill the tea, otherwise I'll tell you my STI story again.'

Kia opened one eye. 'Oh no, honey, you're gonna wanna see this live. Big bro has something to say. Go see. Trust me.'

Trick pulled on some joggers and the nearest hoodie he could find – Hot Will's, as it turned out, that smell again – and tiptoed downstairs. Religion, maybe? Jake had joined some religious sect. Maybe he'd given away all the money he earned in that boring-ass job to a cult. He was the type; he always had a face like a bad credit score. Trick remembered Kia said Jake was trying to get dirt on him at Christmas or something. Scoping him out for gay conversion therapy, maybe! And now he'd come to take him away. Shit!

Trick did his best Jourdan Dunn slink into the kitchen to find the four of them standing in various spots around the room, like the Kardashians posing for the cover of *Elle*. Dad at the sink, Mum at the back door, Margo peering into the toaster. Jake was standing at the island in the middle, fists clenched, a vein popping on his neck that Trick had never spotted before. It was *very* theatrical. Trick briefly wondered who'd play them in a Hollywood version of whatever drama was going down here. To play Jake? A life-size Lego man, a bowl of bran flakes, or the poo emoji, perhaps. They hadn't seen Trick come in.

'What's going on?'

Margo jumped. 'Uh, Jake and Amelia have broken up.'

Trick felt sadder than he thought he would. But he couldn't miss a beat. 'Well, whatever happened, I am Team Amelia.'

*

Jake had never fantasised about how it would go because he never thought he'd tell them. No rehearsed speeches, no counterfactual 'choose your own adventure' guessing, nothing. He realised in future he'd need a better way of doing it than saying, 'So I also like men'. His dad's face screwed up so hard it was like he was peering into a mushroom cloud to find his reading glasses.

His mother finally reacted: 'But you date *girls*!'

'Sometimes. And now I will "date" *boys*, too. I guess. I haven't really thought that far ahead. I'm just *out* of a relationship, remember.'

Trick's mouth fell open. 'You what?'

His mother leaned over the table. 'Did someone molest you? Has a man interfered with you? At work or something?'

As ever, Jake cursed his mother's obsession with tabloid newspapers and true-crime magazines. '*No*, Mum. Fucking hell.'

Dad, now: 'But what about Amelia?'

Tears sprang to Jake's eyes as he thought of Amelia. Awake, now, surely. 'I'm letting her go.'

His parents exchanged a look. 'Did she dump you?' asked his mum. 'Is this why? Do you think you won't be able to get another girlfriend so you're just . . . doing whatever?'

'No, Mum, not just *whatever*. Think of it, like . . . ' He

looked at Margo for inspiration but his sister was pretending her mug of coffee was the most fascinating thing she'd ever seen. 'Right, imagine it like . . . Mum, you like cappuccino, right? And Dad . . . well, every morning Dad has a latte. And that's all he ever has. But me . . . I . . . ' He looked over again at Margo, whose eyes were bulging in recognition of what a terrible analogy this was. Too late, he'd started now. 'I like either. Equally. More or less. Some days I will have . . . a cappuccino, and other days . . . a latte?'

Silence. Jake looked round the room at them all, eyes landing last on his brother. 'Trick? Anything to . . . say?'

Trick looked like he was being manhandled into Room 101. He looked down at the ground like it was clawing at him, trying to take him to the dark depths beyond, then up again as nonchalantly as possible.

'Uh, I need to get breakfast for Kia and Hot Will. They're upstairs. Mum, can I?'

He busied himself putting blueberry muffins on a tray and boiling the kettle.

'Nothing to say to me, Trick?' Surely, thought Jake, if anyone in the room was going to get it, his brother would. He knew he hadn't been there for him when Trick had come out, but he hoped for a miracle now.

'Uh . . . ' Trick looked anxiously at his parents, praying for rescue. 'Yeah, whatever. It's . . . whatever. Congratulations on your . . . *coffee* choices. Or whatever.' He grunted as he lifted the tray. 'See you later,' he mumbled before creeping out of the room to freedom.

His dad spoke, finally: 'I don't understand it, to be honest. How can you like *both*? Shouldn't you pick one? How long have you got to decide?'

'So,' his mum said cautiously, 'you're not gay, you're . . . '

'Bi. Bisexual.'

Jake's dad scratched his chin. 'I see.' He did not see. 'So . . . what about children and stuff? I kind of imagined you carrying on the D'Arcy lineage, you know.' He gave the shortest of chuckles. 'Heirs and spares and whatchamacallit . . . '

'Well . . . this isn't really . . . I mean, I still could . . . ' These were not the questions he'd expected, but at least nobody had made an anal sex comment. Yet. 'Can't Trick do that?'

Another look between his parents. 'We don't really see Trick as the type.' This had clearly been discussed between them before; Dad hated revealing the contents of the late-night chats he and Vee had over a few cans. 'He was meant to be . . . well, himself and you . . . well, you're the, uh, sensible, uh, firstborn kind of . . . man.'

Despite himself, Jake flushed in irritation. 'Hang on. So Trick gets to fulfil his destiny of . . . just being Trick, and I have to be like some . . . brood mare pumping out future generations of D'Arcy?'

Pat looked at his wife. 'What's a brood mare?' Then back to his son. 'Hardly pumping 'em out. You're nearly thirty. Taking your bloody time.'

Jake huffed, feeling like a teenager again, scowling at them falling over in the pub. They couldn't take *anything* seriously.

Pat looked at his watch. 'So what does this mean, then? You'll take it in turns to . . . be with men and women. Is there a percentage?'

'No.' Jake suddenly felt epically tired.

'It's all a bit . . . weird, isn't it?'

'Pat!'

His dad stood up. 'Well, I don't know. Anyway . . . life goes on! I need to go price a job in Woolwich.'

His mum looked relieved to also have an excuse to hand. 'And I've got a full book at the salon. Danielle's opening up but my first cut and colour is in at eleven.'

Was that it? The big moment nixed by pricing a job in Woolwich and mixing a pot of Titian red? Jake wanted to protest, but he saw his parents were itching for the exit.

'Okay, let's talk later.'

When they were alone, Margo whistled as she sponged yogurt off her dressing gown. 'Oh, wow.'

Jake didn't reply.

'That must've been hard. All of it. Keeping it bottled up. I know you've struggled with your, uh, sexuality. It must've been killing you.'

Jake was too tired for a withering look. 'My sexuality must've been killing me? As in, hit me baby one more time?'

'It was *loneliness* killing Britney, dickhead.' Margo put her hands to her head and made a noise like an explosion. 'I know I'm saying this wrong, and you're annoyed. But to finally be coming to terms with who you are is . . . great.'

'Great?' She was trying, he knew that, but siblings were there to be pushed back against. 'What do you mean, *finally*?' he said, drawing circles on the table with his finger. He felt like he'd been sitting there for days. 'I've been handling it. I came to terms with who I was long ago.'

To his surprise, Margo laughed. Quite loudly. Her eyes started to stream. 'Jake. *Jaaaaake*. Oh stop. If that's what "coming to terms with" looks like, I'd hate to see you battling your demons. I've watched you *not* handle this for as long as I can remember.'

Jake felt winded. No way. No fucking way. He *had* hidden it, hadn't he? Quite well, he'd always thought. *Coped*. 'Nah. I mean, you *didn't* know. Did you? It wasn't obvious. Was it? Margo! Why are you looking at the ceiling?'

'Well, I'm kind of hoping a beam of light will come and take me away or a frozen block of poo will drop from a 747 and land on my head. Anything to avoid answering this question.'

Jake found himself laughing. 'You knew, then?'

'Brother mine, I've known you all my life.' Margo finally met his gaze. 'All that stomping to your room, never coming out? Excuse the pun.' They both giggled. 'You were either a constant masturbator, a future serial killer, or a secret gay. As it turns out, you're a tetchy bisexual. But I'm still awarding my detective skills a strong nine-point-five out of ten.'

'Hang on, Miss Marple, you knew I was bisexual just because I was moody? That's . . . just me. It isn't a gay thing! That's not angst. Well, not all of it. That's just *me*.'

Margo clasped her hand to her chest in mock affront. 'Oh. Is it? Are you *sure*?'

'Kind of. I can't *do* what you lot do. I don't have the gene, that urge to show the back of my mouth to strangers and laugh like a dishwasher on the blink. I don't have it in me. My idea of a good time isn't talking about your farts for hours on end, or gossiping about people who died fifty years ago.'

Margo threw a tea towel. 'Great Aunt Isobel was a legend! And don't be jealous just because my farts are more tuneful than yours. I'm the middle child, let me have this glory.'

Jake's eyes were wet with mirth. 'But . . . seriously. It's just not who I am. It was – *is* – like being a potato in a box of avocados.'

'Potatoes make chips! You're on to a winner.'

'Yes, I *know.* I wasn't being self-deprecating.' Jake threw the tea towel back.

'Ooh, you shit. Okay, so . . . real talk: why were you pretending to be straight?'

Jake laughed but he resented the implication he'd been dishonest. 'I wasn't *pretending*, Margo. Nobody *asked*. I like women. And men. I desire both. They appeal to me equally.' He stopped to think. That wasn't how it worked. 'Kind of equally. I dunno. I don't get up in a morning and weigh my sexuality on scales. But I want to be clear: I . . . never doubted my attraction to men; I just . . . couldn't find a way to put it out there, make sense in my head.'

'Okay, I . . . take it back.' Margo cocked her head to one side. 'I'm *Team Jake*, for what it's worth. I thought you were unhappy because you were gay but didn't want to be.'

Jake rubbed her arm. 'Margs, did you ever consider that maybe, just maybe, apart from being bisexual, I might just be a totally miserable fucking bastard?'

Suddenly Margo yelped and dramatically slammed her head into her hands.

'What is it?'

'Amelia!' she cried. 'I'm having lunch with her tomorrow. Holly's hen night committee. Bloody sparkling rosé and passive-aggressive comments about my dress. And now . . . you! Gay. Fuck!'

'I'm not gay. I'm bi—'

'Oh, shut *up*! It isn't all about you!'

eleven.

Jake looked round his teenage room, feeling the walls edge closer like an escape room on a teambuilding weekend. The kind where someone called Pete always either won or shouted from outside that you were too slow and ruining his chances of winning. Jake's room had long been converted into a guest bedroom, but it still had a few reminders he used to sleep there. Remnants of stickers on the door handles, a computer desk with his initials carved into it, a rare act of teenage vandalism. The walls were repapered in generic florals, but if he squinted, he could remember the positions of the posters he'd ripped out of *Nuts* and *Zoo* and stuck on his wall. Pneumatic models in second-skin swimwear, draped over rocks, motorbikes or clambering over cars – the flagrant disregard for motoring health and safety was quite distracting, and Jake's taste in real-life women was more understated. He'd fancied bookish girls at school, the ones that sporting heroes and popular kids used to ignore. Nobody, but nobody, he laughed, would ever ignore a blonde lady in a bikini arriving at school lying backwards on a Ferrari. It seemed like the obvious thing to do at the time: deflect any suggestion he wasn't 100 per cent heterosexual by ramping it up, going as mainstream as possible with the public face of his fantasies. His parents wouldn't have understood his attraction to the girls he actually liked – they responded best to in-your-face sex symbols, intent writ large on face and body – so Jake faked it to avoid any questions. His mum pretended she found the posters sexist and disgusting but he knew there was some kind of twisted pride in there somewhere, for both her and his dad – relief, perhaps, that their sullen, distant teenager was a furtive masturbator with a penchant for porn-star pin-ups, just like the other boys.

Books jutted from the shelves, crammed on, well-thumbed and spines mercilessly cracked – pieces of himself everywhere, but no clues to who he would turn out to be. If he opened the left-hand cupboard, he knew what would fall out. A basketball, unbounced. A putting iron, immaculate. All that cycling gear, too. One day, Reenie's brother who was staying with her – just out of prison, Jake now realised – had acquired a boneshaker of a bike and, taking a shine to the monosyllabic teenager whose physical activity ended at brushing his hair from his eyes like Princess Diana, had asked if Jake wanted it. Jake hadn't been sure – he was a nervous car passenger and a risk-averse pedestrian, never crossing unless there was a green man, but to his surprise he'd found cycling was the cheap therapy he hadn't even known he needed, clearing his head of self-doubt, a chance to scream into the wind all the things he would never say to anyone. After a particularly hard day at school, he'd zoom round the park, then up to Camberwell, slaloming round buses and lorries at the green, then down again to the estate. Once they'd moved to Balham – thanks to *the money* – Dad noticed Jake's nascent cycling enthusiasm and seized the opportunity to forge that connection that had still eluded them, despite fourteen years of coexistence. To encourage this mercifully masculine and aspirational hobby, Pat had brought home a shiny new bike and an array of overpriced, ridiculous cycling gear, proper aficionado's stuff: Lycra, racing helmet, special shoes that looked like an instrument of torture, backpack, hi-vis jacket. Everything but a servant to pedal it for him. Jake had hidden his horror; ingratitude was bad manners in the D'Arcy household and a red rag to a bull for Pat, who'd presented the bike to him like a game show host.

'This'll help you go even faster, see; you can zip up to Highgate in an hour if you wanted.' The zeal in his dad's eyes had made Jake feel sick; he only saw it when Pat wanted him to be something he wasn't.

'Thank you, Dad.' Jake had smiled dumbly and wheeled the bike up and down the drive a few times while Pat had watched. Jake had felt powerless to explain it wasn't about speed, or competitiveness. It wasn't even about fun. It just helped him reassemble his thoughts, repairing everything that chipped away at him during the day; everything he didn't understand became clear on the bike, the old chain cranking right on cue every three seconds. If he was cycling, he didn't have to speak, act or self-edit; he could just unconsciously be. He didn't go fast, or on some kind of manly quest; by the time he arrived home, wobbling up the uneven driveway and climbing off – arse sore from the unwieldy seat – he felt cleansed, and refuelled to begin another twenty-four hours of play-acting. But Dad always did this: looked to identify with Jake through the things he enjoyed. Any flicker of interest in an activity was steered toward fanaticism. Once Jake was bored in a pub's bleak family room one Sunday, so he'd given in to Margo's demands and played pool against her – she'd won, and crowed for three days solid – so Dad had suggested buying a table and whacking it in the old lean-to that eventually was lost to high winds. When he took the family's dog for a walk, Dad would recommend better routes, lusher parks, everything but show Jake a more inventive way to pick up the dog's shit. He knew his dad was only looking for ways into his life, but Pat never tried to be on Jake's level, and was instead intent on dragging him unwillingly to his own.

So despite the initial display of enthusiasm, the shiny new bike had gone unridden until Pat had lost his temper one day when Jake was at school, throwing out the boneshaker. Jake had arrived home to find it gone, and while Margo and Trick would've screamed the place down, Jake had made absolutely no comment, and instead rode its replacement begrudgingly, the mental release more important than slicing off his nose to spite his face. But he'd trundled along, never speeding up, defiantly denying the bike the speed it was built for, missing that familiar clank of the chain with every turn of the pedals. And he'd never 'zipped up to Highgate'. The cycling gear, however, had stayed in the cupboard, labels affixed; its gleaming plastic and bone-dry Lycra menacing and permanent – Jake shivered, imagining it on landfill a zillion years from now. He always liked his rebellions quiet and controlled and this was a classic example; he would never wear any of it.

He must've nodded off, for he was dreaming about Amelia handing him the last unpacked box when he was woken by the distant sound of his sister berating her son for missing the toilet when he peed.

'Just sit on it, sweetheart, it's fine.'

'But I'm a boy! I have to stand,' came the insistent reply. Jake had sat down to pee until he was about Buddy's age. Wetting yourself at school was the ultimate shame – even now, twenty-two years later, he remembered that dark patch on Mark Joseph's beige trousers getting bigger and bigger until someone shouted, 'Miss, Mark's got widdle on him.' So Jake always sat to make sure every last drop was out. One day, driving to Southend, the family had stopped by the roadside so Jake and Margo could pee. Seeing his son squat, Pat had bade him stand up.

'No point having a hosepipe and not watering the plants, Jakey, son,' Pat had boomed, hoisting up his son and ruffling his hair, before standing up against a tree and sluicing its trunk with his own wee. Jake had looked on in awe. It was the manliest, most terrifying thing he'd ever seen, but back then disappointing his dad was unthinkable, so he was soon a convert.

That made him think: the boys. His so-called *dudes*. He couldn't put it off; he should slay as many dragons in one day as he could.

He looked at his watch. They'd be at the football. They'd stopped inviting Jake long ago, sick of his whingeing.

'Mate, if you don't like football, we can still hang around together. Just not here. You're killing the mood.'

Charlie's face was round and leering when he opened FaceTime.

'Jaaaaaaaake! Yaaaaaaaay!' Adyan's head bobbed into view. 'What's up? Desperate for the latest score? Nil-fucking-nil; like watching a load of fucking wardrobes run around.'

'Great, well, I can sleep easier. Errrr, look, what you doing tonight? You free?'

Charlie looked serious. 'Getting pissed so I can have a nice day hungover in bed tomorrow while Holly's out clucking with her hens and chucking back the lady petrol.'

Adyan poked his head into view. 'I will *not* be doing that, obviously.'

'Obviously. Shall we meet up? I'm at Mum's . . . we can do Clapham if you like?'

'Yeah! I wanna talk about the stag, actually.'

Jake kept his face neutral. This fucking stag weekend. That he'd ever been thrilled about organising this seemed impossible. 'Oh yeah?'

'Miles was thinking costumes. So we look like a team.'

Fucking *Miles*. Jake could think of a few costumes suitable for him. A great big phallus, perhaps, or David Cameron. '*Costumes*?'

'Yeah. Like, characters from my favourite film or whatever. Or we could all go as Elvis?'

Jake had a gut-churning flash-forward to a crew of nylon-clad Vegas-and-peanut-butter-sandwich era Elvis Presleys – the incredulous, chic, judgemental eyes of Paris all over them. Then he remembered how much he loved Charlie. 'Absolutely, brilliant idea. Miles is a genius.' Jake clenched his teeth at the lie. 'Let me have a think. So, tonight, yeah?'

The fans behind Charlie and Adyan leaned in, faces pink and lips chapped with the cold. 'Can you poofs say goodnight? I'm trying to watch the fucking game.'

Charlie turned round as if about to say something he'd regret, so Jake shouted, 'No worries! See you later, guys,' and rang off before he witnessed a murder.

Adyan's reaction was the most unexpected. 'I sucked a dick once.'

Charlie and Jake gasped. '*What*?'

Adyan shrugged and swigged his lime and soda. 'Yeah. I'm not bisexual like you, though. I wouldn't do it again.'

'Why did you . . . ? When was *this*? How old?' Was Jake's thunder getting stolen here?

'Oh, like, sixteen or seventeen. Boarding school, innit.'

'I thought it was a myth that everyone sucked each other off?'

'Nah. It's real sometimes. Long weekends. Everyone's kind of crazy. It was more a dare. Anyway, *not* sexy. Tasted . . . gamey. Not for me.'

Jake burst out laughing. 'You're a vegetarian. How do you know what game tastes like?'

'Again, *boarding* school. Dietary "requirements" were *not* a thing. Yeah. Once, actually, a housemaster paid me twenty-five pounds to smoke a cigarette while wearing a washing-up glove too.'

'Oh my God, Ad, that's *abuse*.' Charlie and Jake shot each other horrified looks.

'No! It was one of the lads' A-level art pieces. Everyone else refused.' Adyan chuckled. 'But I really needed that twenty-five quid.'

'What for?'

'Stickers, I think. What else? I was seventeen! Practically an adult. It was a business decision.'

Once the fallout from Adyan's confession dissolved, the questions came thick and fast. Did he fancy them? Did he have wet dreams about them? Had he wanked while thinking of them?

'No, no, and no.' This was a lie. He'd had a few confusing moments over Adyan, especially when they were teenagers, on the rare times he was home. Lovely arms. Now, however, that was cancelled out by an extra decade of getting to know him – he took ten minutes to pick a seat in the pub and would say, 'Aaaah' when he finally sat down.

It went on. Had he shagged someone up the arse yet? Or *been* shagged up the arse? Did it hurt? Would he still have sex with women and could he have threesomes with 'both a bloke and a bird'?

'And more importantly,' said Charlie, 'is it right what Adyan says? Do they . . . does *it* taste gamey?'

On the Tube home, Jake's stomach gurgled from lack of food, too much beer, the dread of facing his parents and, of course, knots of guilt about Amelia. What would she be doing now? What would *they* have been up to, on any other Saturday night? He couldn't remember what they'd done last weekend; it was lifetimes ago, a page ripped out of a book he'd never finish.

Jake crept into the house, hoping everyone might be asleep. He would've stayed at Charlie's, but the prospect of Holly's panicked eyes and the inevitable dragging Charlie off to the kitchen for a staccato-whisper showdown while Jake pretended to sleep on the sofa did not appeal. He heard noises from his mum and Margo's favoured lounge. It had posher, updated versions of the furniture that had been in the Walworth flat. Buddy wasn't allowed in there because he liked to draw in Mum's vintage *Vogue*s, and Jake always felt the pair of them couldn't wait to get him out, like it was a women's space and his dreary masculinity was intruding. Trick, who got special dispensation to do whatever he wanted, was always draped over the arm of a chair – he never sat like a normal person – or helping himself to one of Mum's tiny cans of pre-mixed pink gin and tonic from her glass-doored cupboard.

But it wasn't Margo in there with Mum; it was his dad.

They were talking about him, as far as he could tell. And Amelia. Jake lingered by the door, wondering whether to go in. The decision was made for him when the door swung open and Trick, who'd been uncharacteristically silent, saw him. He looked him up and down before calling back into the room. 'Night, babes, oh, and your problematic hero is home . . . Have fun!' He skipped up the stairs three at a time. 'Don't be too loud with your *Real Housewives* face-off . . . we've got guests and you're all embarrassing.'

Jake trudged to the vacant armchair. Blue corduroy, like the one from all his baby photos. He saw it now. Bright-blond hair, wide innocent blue eyes, hand in his mouth at all times. Made a change from his foot, he guessed. Both his parents were open-mouthed, obviously unsure how much he'd heard; he must've missed some A-grade bitching.

The beer in Jake's belly gave him a new confidence. 'You should shut those gobs before someone throws a peanut in them.' They closed in perfect formation. 'Let's do it, then. What do you want to know?' His parents looked at each other. 'Come on! You two haven't stopped talking as long as I've known you; you once sat chatting all the way through a funeral.'

His dad shook his shoulders like a boxer limbering up but said nothing. His mother reached for a can of gin; the hiss upon opening cut through the air. 'All right, then. I've heard people say they're bi . . . er . . . *sexual* when they're actually gay, to make it easier. Are you really gay?'

'How is this *easier*?'

It was clear they wouldn't talk further without provocation. He could've shrugged and slipped off to bed, but nervous energy, Dutch courage and years of doing that same shrug and trip up the stairs to his room kept him where he was. 'Let me ask *you* something, then. A few months ago we trooped into the sports lounge to watch Trick's announcement and you acted like you were front row at a Beyoncé concert. Ever since Trick was tiny he's been . . . like he is, mincing around like the wicked queen in *Snow White*. Trick has been gay-gay-*sodding*-gay since day one and nobody said a word. We knew he was gay before he could talk. Aside from the fact I'm bisexual, what's the difference? Why is it – and I quote you, Dad – "weird"?'

His dad shrugged. 'You were . . . you. Normal, I guess. Did sports day. Had girlfriends. Went down the pub, friends with a cracking bunch of lads. Trick's an individual, like.'

Jake ploughed on. 'Plenty of bi men do those things. And I *hated* sports day. I have *two* close male friends, neither of whom went to my school.' Pat blanched at the 'whom'. 'They're not *that* blokey and I don't go to the football. Tell me again, what was so different about Trick? Why has he always been allowed to be who he wanted, while you tried to make me something else?'

Pat ran his hands through his hair and stood up, looming over his son. 'This isn't about your brother! And when did we do that?'

Jake realised he could, if pushed, immediately locate on file every instance, but they didn't have all day. 'I read, all the time, but you never randomly brought a book home, took me to an exhibition. Footballs, basketballs, mini golf, despite me never showing an interest in sport, yes, any of that. Trying to turn my bike from something I liked doing into something . . . competitive.'

'We bought you everything you wanted. Within reason.'

'Everything I had the courage to ask for. It isn't the same.'

'Things were different when you were little.' Pat stared off into the distance, as if transporting himself back there. 'Sporty lads . . . seemed to get on better. Got left alone. It was hard out there.'

'It still is.'

'But it was harder *then*. We grew up round it. Gay jokes on telly, lads getting beaten up for not fitting in. Back when me and your mum got married, there were adverts about AIDS everywhere. Being gay . . . it looked like a lonely life. Drugs. I dunno. We looked at what was around us.' He sat down again. Vee chewed the inside of her cheek. Pat sighed deeply. 'Remember that geezer lived in the flat above the Snax Box caff, Vee? Got the shit kicked out of him in Vauxhall? We didn't want that for you, Jake.'

'His name was Simon, his nan came in the salon,' said Vee flatly, the memory of it seeming to drain her. 'We used to look out for him, but you'd hear it sometimes, them calling him a pansy, or worse. Then they got him.'

Pat's mouth gaped as he turned from his wife and back to his son. 'I didn't care *what* you did but I didn't want anyone to hurt you. You're sensitive. *Were* sensitive. You weren't like other lads.'

'Neither was Trick. You were ashamed of *me*.'

'No.' His mum's voice rang out sharp and clear. She wound the hem of her pullover – one of her favourites: leopard-skin with gold lamé epaulettes – round her finger. 'I had three miscarriages between your sister and Trick.'

Jake felt a lump in his throat. She'd never told him that before. He had vague memories of Reenie's ashen face as she gave him and Margo Jammie Dodgers round hers – they weren't usually allowed biscuits before a meal – and told them their mum wasn't well but would be back on her feet soon.

Vee went on: 'When that happens, you care less about stuff. You're just glad they're all right. I was older, even if I weren't wiser.'

Pat reached out to rub his wife's arm; she relaxed at his touch. 'Times changed: civil partnerships and whatnot. Your mum's friend Barry had one. We're *not* against gays. Trick was always so confident and sure of himself. We were in a better position then, moved here, could send him to a nice school.'

Jake laughed at the idea that a bit of money had turned his parents into liberals overnight. 'Come on! You can't blame the estate for *everything*. Working-class gay people exist, Dad. You let Trick get on with it because he's loud and showy – like the rest of you.'

'I'm not loud!' Pat shouted, before cringing at his own absurdity.

'You *are*. All the gang together. Trick wanted attention and you gave it to him. I didn't. I just wanted to be left alone and you've never got your heads round that.'

'It's weird, having a kid who ain't nothing like you.' His mum's eyes were pinhole-tiny through tiredness. 'Me and your dad ain't shy, like you *say*, but you were so quiet, reserved, didn't like getting yourself dirty. It was cute in a way. But you were hard to work out. I still don't think we have.'

His dad opened a beer. 'This is a bit deep for this time of night, you know. Can we put some music on?'

'No.'

'Oh.' Pat looked down at his belly, and prodded it. He would no doubt claim he was on a diet in the morning, like he did every time after a big night on the ale. 'Can I be candid,

Jake? I'm a working man. An honest guy. Here's my hand – ' he held out his hand to shake, one of his regular tricks when he was drunk ' – and here's my heart. But . . . from an early age, it was like you thought you were better than . . . well, everyone. We were never sure how to take it, really.'

Jake watched his father sway. 'Dad, first chance you got, you moved us to a six-bedroom house – didn't *you* think you were better than everyone?'

'Yeah, but I've stayed the same. Here's my hand, here's my— No, hang on, I've done that.'

Jake took a deep breath. How was it possible to be this tired and yet feel like he could run ten marathons? 'Can I ask you a question? Why does this bother you? What difference will it make to your life? Why are you so worried?'

Pat waggled a drunken finger. 'That's *three* questions.'

His mum tipped her can of gin right back to get to the dregs. 'If you're a bisexual we'll never know where we are from one minute to the next – will it be a man or a woman you're bringing home?'

Jake found it unlikely he'd bring *anyone* home in the next hundred years. 'Why do you need to know "where you are", as long as I know where *I* am? Think of it as a lovely surprise, or a guessing game. Maybe put out the yellow guest towels – they're gender-neutral.'

'But we won't know what to say. What will we tell friends? That you like . . . just *anyone*?'

Jake stood up. 'Either you'll adapt or you won't. It isn't hard. I'm the same person. Everyone I date will be a good person, I hope. If what your friends think is more important then I don't know what to say. Honestly. Night.' He swept out, proud of his big exit, his parents mouths agape just as they had been when he'd walked in. More agape, even. Agaper. When he got to the third step, however, he turned back.

'Uh, Mum, can I borrow your phone charger again? I forgot mine.' Damn. Big moment ruined. Now he knew how Trick felt.

twelve.

Amelia was ready to go by Sunday afternoon. She'd wanted to go quicker, but there was so much *stuff*. Rudi helped as much as she could, but every time she held up an item – whether a colander, a bread knife, or an Annie Leibovitz retrospective (all Jake's) – Amelia crumpled like an old tissue, leaving the room for five minutes to compose herself.

She packed boxes robotically and waited on hold for men from storage companies to get round to telling her the cost of keeping her stuff for . . . Well, who knew how long? They called her 'darlin' and she could hear their chairs creak while they scratched their arses or rearranged their testicles, quoting exorbitant fees to store the piffling artefacts she'd accumulated in thirty years on the planet. Almost thirty-one, in fact. This wasn't fair. It wasn't right.

Rudi was a patient listener, doing her best to motivate. On the second day, they sat on the lounge floor and leaned against Jake's pathologically tasteful sofas, eating takeaway pizza and aiming to replace their entire blood supply with unidentifiable white wine. Rudi asked if she'd 'known, or suspected'.

Amelia suddenly found the double pepperoni harder to swallow, relaying Hannah's words from years before, and

Freddie's sneer, before venturing her own opinion: 'I assumed he . . . behaved *that* way because he was a gentleman. Hardly ever shouted at me. Never hassled me for sex. I mean, I guess I know why now.'

'That's not a sign he's bi . . . they want sex as much as anyone else. But it might be a sign he was unhappy.' Rudi scrabbled for more dirt, thinking it would be less painful for Amelia if she came up with more minuses. 'He was . . . a bit moody? Right?'

'Not exactly . . . ' pondered Amelia. 'He could be quiet, a sulker, lost in his thoughts – sharp sometimes – but not moody. Apart from at his mum's.'

Amelia regained her composure and loaded almost an entire slice of pizza into her mouth. 'What about you?' she said. 'Didn't your *gaydar* sound?'

Rudi laughed. It was harder to tell with men, she said, everything in her was wired up not to care; signals didn't come through. 'I only looked for superficial things. How he dressed. Things he liked doing. Conversation. How he acted when another gay guy was in the room.'

Amelia noted Rudi *had* indeed been actively looking for signs but stowed that info for the moment. 'He's not *gay*, though. He says he's *bi*. It's not *all* women he's lost interest in. Just this one.' Amelia stood and poured the last of the wine into her glass before opening another bottle in one continuous movement. 'I don't wanna talk about this any more. I need to tape up the chest of drawers, wrap some plates in bubble-wrap, then call the man with the van and get the fuck out.'

Amelia left the room, her heart sinking at the thought of this situation following her around for life, like a disfigurement. Her friends, her family – what would they say at work? Why couldn't he have had some gross affair with a colleague like every other bastard she'd dated? Why must this be so . . . niche? A nice clean break for him, vanishing until she'd erased every trace of herself from his flat. She was tempted to vandalise something, but instead she sat on the bed and looked into her lap until she had the strength to pick up the packing tape and finish what she'd started. What *he'd* started, she thought, as she tugged at the tape dispenser with renewed fury.

Amelia had planned to swerve the lunch with the girls. For a start, Margo would be there and while they got on *generally*, she knew it would be awkward. As it turned out, Rudi discovered Margo wasn't going because Buddy was ill, so after two bottles of plonk she felt empowered enough to endure it. She regretted this wave of bravery as soon as she arrived. Hannah was there, for reasons Amelia couldn't fathom in her drunken fug until she remembered Dean was a good friend of Charlie's, and the sea of concerned looks from Holly and everyone else made her feel like she was drowning. At the doorway, Rudi grabbed Amelia's hand, and they wobbled toward the table with all the enthusiasm of a turkey checking into the abattoir on December 1st. The conversation washed over Amelia's head, and she nodded along to the hen weekend plans – Barcelona, some Airbnb villa she couldn't afford, cocktails at swanky bars and other dreary 'hen do' ephemera – startled awake in time to hear one of the girls say she'd 'found a great gay club to go to on the final night'.

Every single eye at the table slammed in Amelia's direction. Was she to be the group's leading authority on boys who liked boys now? First the brother, now the boyfriend! Magic! They were poised, unsure how to react until they got the nod, as if Amelia were a Roman emperor. Since the arrival of her third large glass of wine, Amelia was feeling very talkative.

'Penny,' she drawled. Was this even Penny? Or someone else? It didn't matter. 'This is a *girls'* blowout, Holly's last weekend of freedom before she saddles herself to Charlie and his habit of wearing *briefs*.' A light chuckle from further down the table. Hannah. 'We don't want a gay club, where the men only fancy our *shoes*.'

'Amen.' Hannah again.

'I've had . . . a *rough* weekend. We wanna go to a club with a load of women and be the sexiest creatures in the entire place. I want the crowd to chant our names – well, the fake names we give them – and wanna either *be* us or shag us.'

'But—'

'No.' Amelia leaned forward and raised a shaky finger to shush the non-believer. 'No. We've earned it. Holly *deserves* it. Whaddya reckon?'

Holly looked down at the table meekly. 'Well, I guess we can go somewhere like that for a *couple* of hours.'

Amelia raised her glass. 'Great, leave that night to me, I'll book the lot and inbox you for cash later.'

Rudi nudged her proudly. 'This could be the making of you, you know. Show 'em how a break-up is done. Maybe you could try a rebound shag?'

Amelia shot a quick dagger at her friend. 'Literally too soon, Rudi.' She took a sip of wine. 'Who with?'

Rudi laughed hoarsely. 'Jamal is single again!'

Another set of daggers. 'Rudi, No.' A *glug* of wine. 'He photographs his *food*.'

As Amelia and Rudi left, Hannah was just behind them. 'Have you phoned a cab?' They nodded. Rudi coughed to break the silence. 'Do you wanna share?' Amelia shot her a pop-eyed Bette Davis stare.

'Um, no, look, Amelia, I just wanna say—'

'*Don't.*'

'No, I must. I think you're a great girl. I hope everything works out for you, and—'

'Okay, thanks.' Amelia's eyes were glazed doughnuts. 'And what?'

'Well – ' Hannah looked like she was trying to pass a kidney stone ' – I've never forgiven myself for what I said . . . back when you first started going out. I was drunk. And . . . a bit worried. You must've felt like shit.'

Amelia lazily licked her lips, her tongue already furry with pre-hangover. 'Well, you were wrong anyway,' she slurred. 'He's not gay. He's *biiiiii*. Ambidextrous. Know what, Hannah? I should've listened in the first place.' The cab drew up and Amelia clambered in, while Rudi patted Hannah on the shoulder and scrabbled in after.

'Let's go home.'

Amelia sighed at full power. 'I don't have one.'

Rudi pulled her in for a hug. 'You do, always will. My spare room is all about Amelia for as long as you need it.'

Amelia smiled and breathed in the light florals of Rudi's cologne, wishing, for what she hoped would be the last time, that it were Jake's familiar, clean, angelic, citrus scent.

'What about Pete Thingy? Rebound-worthy?'

Amelia closed her eyes. '*No*, Rudes. Flat Earther.'

*

Vee stood at the back door, having a crafty cigarette while the house was quiet, and thought about her firstborn. Looking for signs. Jake had kept schtum about romantic liaisons throughout his teenage years and early twenties. Coming back from prom, he'd been red-faced and surly when his dad had asked him if he'd 'clicked'.

'Only his fingers,' had been Margo's retort, already giving Dorothy Parker a run for her money. Vee could see where Trick got his viper's tongue from – Margo was chief babysitter back then.

At university there had been a ray of . . . it felt wrong to call it hope, really, but something, when Hannah came along. She was everything Jake wasn't: boisterous, outgoing, cheeky. Jake seemed to light up around her and they really connected, but the men Hannah favoured were at least a foot taller than Vee's pride and joy. And then, when Jake left home properly, silence. Until Amelia. The first one he'd brought home. Vee was kind of in awe of her, not just because she was very pretty, but because this felt momentous. Obviously Vee thought all her children were works of art, with features that could make a hardened serial killer cry, but Jake wasn't as obviously handsome as the other two. Trick was always going to be something out of the ordinary, with those cheekbones and slight features and his beautiful mouth. She would sometimes stand at the kitchen sink wringing out cloths extra hard at the thought of some awful person coming along and kissing Trick, claiming that arresting mouth for their own. Margo, too, had turned heads. Pat's sisters had all been stunning too, though, and they'd known it. But Jake . . . well, his lack of confidence always seemed to knock him down from a 9 to a 7. His features weren't distinctive enough, really – he looked more like Pat than the others and it was obvious Pat was disappointed they mirrored each other only in looks – absolutely none of his other traits had filtered through. Vee often thought that was for the best. So when Amelia was presented as his new girlfriend, Vee was gobsmacked. It didn't feel quite right somehow, but as their relationship developed, she watched Jake blossom. He finally broadened, his jawline took shape and the faintest hint of lines around his eyes gave him character. He became a man before her eyes, but the changes were skin-deep. He was still painfully quiet and awkward at times. Vee felt Amelia was a sticking plaster, not a cure, and felt sorry for her in a way. She couldn't be herself around Amelia; she wanted to tell her, 'I'm not sure this is right for either of you', and to run away and find the man she deserved. A better man – no, not better, but more *suitable* – than her own son. Amelia made her feel like a traitor.

Just as Vee was stubbing out a Marlboro Red into a teacup with a picture of a kitten on it, Jake appeared, obviously sneaking out. She pretended not to notice the holdall in his hand.

'I didn't realise you were in, thought you were at Reenie's.'

'She cancelled. Slipped disc is playing up. I've been thinking.'

Jake wondered if his mother had been possessed by a very tired demon; she sounded weird. 'What about?'

'About you.' She took her cigarettes out of her handbag and offered Jake one. He thought about it. His mum lit herself one and took a long drag, clearly enjoying eking out the drama. 'I've been thinking about everything you said, last night. I want you to remember something.'

'What?'

His mum tensed up; she was looking for the words. She wasn't good at things like this sober, or without the protection of the back of a salon chair between her and her client. 'I watched you grow into a bump and saw your little knuckles from inside my belly. Me and your Auntie Reenie talked about you all the time, like you were real, way before you were born. Imagined what you were like. You were like a celebrity we were dying to meet. How handsome you'd be, we'd say, how successful. We was right, mostly.' She looked at him again. 'Quiet one. Old head on young shoulders, we used to say.'

'I know, I remember.' Jake felt a rush of affection. He wanted to reach out for her hand. Vee sensed it and gently shook her head; she needed to finish this.

'This is why it's . . . why we're not . . . Well. We had it all planned out for you. But they wasn't our plans to make.' Vee registered her son's awkwardness. 'Never mind, we'll talk later. Go on. Piss off.' She jerked her head toward the garden gate and winked. 'Where are you going, anyway?'

Jake pulled his phone out of his pocket. 'I'm going home, Mum. Amelia messaged. She's gone.'

His mum looked sad, but resilient. 'Maybe you should stay a bit longer, so we can work things out? I'll work on your dad.'

Jake shook his head. 'I need to give you some time. And I've got work.'

It took a good fifteen minutes once the taxi left his mum's house before the lump in Jake's throat finally melted and he could breathe easily again.

*

Trick watched Jake leave from the window while Kia tutted at the PlayStation. 'He going, then?'

'Yeah, back to his lair of heterosexuality so he can go turn all his jeans into denim cut-offs and hang up his rainbow flag,' said Trick without emotion. 'About time.'

'What do you think, then? About his . . . news?' Kia readied herself for the lie – that he didn't care or thought it was ridiculous – but she could see it had floored him. He was ashen, had hardly spoken. Once you got Trick started on something, he was unstoppable, like his own endless DVD commentary, but this? He really hadn't seen it coming, and she *knew* he hated surprises. She had been by Trick's side during his coming-out as much as time and energy had allowed – shoulders used for crying on can get tired and she had her own emotional state to think about – because he'd done the same for her. When sleepless nights became sleepless weeks, and she was in perpetual fear the floor was about to be whipped away from under her, that she'd never be her true self. He'd said, 'I'm with you', and listened, and even though she could happily smack the shit out of him sometimes she'd stand with him for ever, because he knew how much 'the before' hurt her. They were still going through it, really, but the end was in sight; they had to believe that. So now, when he replied, she would accept it as the truth, until he was ready to be honest.

'His news?' Trick laughed. It was his on-camera laugh, his 'the sponsors are watching' giggle. 'It's *fake* news. He's pushing thirty and trying to look interesting.'

He whipped the curtains shut, hard. 'Sad really.'

*

Jake unlocked the door to his flat and breathed in to get the last of Amelia's scent, but the place smelled only of cardboard boxes and disrupted dust. He walked from room to room – it didn't take long – and felt sad and dramatic, like he was in an ABBA video. He opened the fridge, resentful that Amelia hadn't left any milk for a cup of tea, before realising how insensitive that was. He apologised to the air she'd inhabited only a few hours earlier, and reached in his pocket to see if he had change. Locating a couple of pound coins, he pulled out his phone to read her message again, but found one from Hannah instead.

Hannah: Errrrrrrrrr HELLO
FAVE why haven't you phoned
me yet?!?!
I'm so happyyyyyyy.
Call. Me. Now. xxxx

Oh shit, yeah, he'd forgotten to tell Hannah. The milk would have to wait. Like Kia said, you didn't just come out once. He cleared his throat a few times and practised saying 'hello' to make sure his voice was even – forever self-editing – before pressing the call button, and doing it all over again.

'Hey, Han. Hey . . . look . . . ha ha, Jesus. Stop screaming, *please*!'

thirteen.

For years, Hannah had been prepared to swoop on Jake's flat, armed with ice cream, Prosecco and a box of tissues to be that all-important shoulder on which to blub, but by the time the news finally made it to her – via Holly, who'd heard it from Charlie, and not direct from Amelia, which was *very* telling – it seemed Jake was already doing just fine. Holly warned her Jake was not to be disturbed, that he was telling only people close to him, which made Hannah want to crush untold champagne glasses between her fingers. But she resolved to let him be until, after the most desperately awkward hens' lunch featuring an Amelia who could barely stand up by the time she left, Hannah could wait no more.

Hannah had often mused with boyfriends on when Jake would either come out or join a monastery. She had watched his flirting with women at university – resulting in a few one-night stands but little else, other than poor po-faced Basica – and had conceded he couldn't possibly be a card-carrying heterosexual. There was no edge, no drive. Women loved him, all right – Jake was funny, charming, and not bad-looking if you liked that sort of thing – but he never used it to his advantage. Hannah was always assuring her ex, Blair, that there was nothing happening between her and Jake – one of many reasons he ended up with his suitcases in the hall – and decided if Jake was secretly gay, she'd have to do something about it. Their outing to the gay bar had not been the dewy-eyed confessional she'd expected. Instead, she'd clocked genuine fear in Jake's eyes and worried she'd pushed him further back into the closet. Then he'd met Amelia, and stayed with her, and that seemed to be that. Until now.

'I suppose bisexual makes more sense,' Dean had said as they'd sat flicking through the channels looking for something to watch, eager to distract Hannah from barrelling round to Jake's. 'Why do you think he never tried it on with you?'

Hannah wasn't quite sure. He wasn't her type anyway.

'I always knew I was safe with you,' she said to Jake as she parked herself on his sofa and searched his eyes for his true feelings. 'That's why I thought you were gay. You weren't uneasy around me, after something, like other men were.'

Jake laughed. 'How do you know I wasn't?'

'Because you always told me the truth. When we went to that fairy-tale characters' party and I tried on that huge dress to be Beauty from *Beauty and the Beast*, remember?'

'Yellow one?'

'Yeah. What was it you said?'

'I don't remember.' Jake cringed in anticipation. He'd never had much of a filter around Hannah.

'I *do*. You said I looked more like the Beast in a banana costume than Beauty.'

Jake covered his mouth. 'I was just being mean. You actually looked radiant.'

Hannah rolled her eyes. 'Like a *radiator*; yes, I remember you saying that too.' She peered over the top of her glass. 'Are you annoyed I'm not that . . . *surprised*?'

Jake shrank into himself the tiniest amount. 'A little.'

'I don't know why. It's not a contest. I tried to tell you I knew. All those times you'd turn up at mine, drunk, feeling sorry for yourself – I thought you were going to do it then. I was waiting for it. And then there was the bar drama, or *non*-drama, and Amelia. I thought I'd got it wrong! I thought you'd figure it out!'

Jake was transported to the previous summer, to his brother's face as he'd held out his hand to shake – just minutes after Trick had come out to his entire family – and dismissed it as a publicity stunt. This was how it felt for the world to be in on the secret, to have you figured out before you had a chance yourself. That day, he'd made Trick feel like this. It felt cheap. Low.

'I have an idea,' said Hannah. 'And I don't want you to freak out. But I think you need a shag. Like, a man one, and I can help you.'

'A man-shag?

'Yes. Do you know what a hook-up is?'

Jake whooped with laughter. 'Hannah, I have switched a TV on before, you know. Of course I do! So what?'

'So far your contact with men has been secret snogs and weird crotch grinding. You need some normality, and that will come right here, from your mobile phone.'

'And that is normality?' Jake didn't seem keen. 'Aw, don't make me do that. I don't wanna go to some stranger's flat.'

'Can I just say, it's not all about sex; but getting to know other gay people. Meet them at *your* flat!'

'What if they dismember me?'

Hannah held her hand out for Jake's phone. 'You're *not* going to get murdered.'

Hannah's solution? Play flatmate to Jake for one night only. It would be made clear to Jake's date that his flatmate was coming back at a certain time – 'How long do you think it will take you?' Hannah asked. 'Are you likely to want to go for seconds?' – so the window for any maiming or killing would be narrow.

'I'm so glad I can be here for this . . . huge moment,' cooed Hannah as a date was set.

Jake had resigned himself to his fate, his face a weary depiction of someone about to face the firing squad. 'Okay, Hannah, but . . . you know you can't stay and watch, right?'

The scene was set: clean sheets; masculine-scented aroma diffuser on the coffee table, wine. Once again, an hour before, Hannah dismissed Jake's concerns over serial killers or rubber-mask enthusiasts who would truss him up and steal his laptop.

'He's just a lad after a shag, like most of them. You don't have to go the full way; just . . . get your fingers lightly burned so you can learn from the sting.' Before she left, Hannah noticed Jake filling small bowls – his best ones – with something from a large paper bag. 'What are those?'

'Snacks!' Jake held up a bowl of peanuts in one hand, Japanese crackers in the other, like an angler with his catch of the day. 'You know, to show I'm normal!' He threw a peanut in the air and caught it his mouth. Hannah stayed silent. 'That's okay, right?'

While the man – Ryan – was on his way, Jake became mildly frantic, running around the flat rearranging cushions, turning on and then switching off music, fiddling with the lighting until, finally, he flopped on to the sofa, quickly sniffing his armpits. And then he saw it. The photograph on the shelf. July 2016. A festival. Jake smiling broadly, the ghost of facial sunburn to come making its presence felt, and huddled into him, eyes shining – 'make-up free, except for eyeliner, mascara, a bit of lip gloss and, uh, concealer, my *natural* look' – was Amelia. Two years ago. That was nothing. He had underwear older than that – stuff in the fridge too, probably. Now everything was different. What would he have said back then if someone had told him what was going to happen? He got up and turned the photo to face the books behind.

'I'm sorry,' he muttered to the rear of the photo frame. 'I really am.' Then BZZZZZZZZZ, holy shit, there was a man at the door. For *sex*.

Ryan peered round the room with uncertainty. Jake was relieved to see he too looked like the kind of guy who would be wary of being murdered by a stranger.

'So . . . um. What are you into?'

'*Into*?'

Ryan scratched his chest distractedly. 'Yes. What do you want to, uh, do . . . ?'

'Oh!' Jake reddened. He was doing that a lot lately. 'I don't think I want to do *everything*. Not yet. Not with someone I don't know.'

'No, of course.' Ryan's eyes swept the room again. Trying to weigh up where the action was going to happen, perhaps, or maybe looking for valuables. 'I'm not very into kissing.'

'Oh, aren't you?'

'No. Have you ever seen *Pretty Woman*?'

'No.'

Ryan's eyes popped in surprise. 'Oh! It's my favourite film.

Anyway, Vivian, the, uh . . . main character, is not into kissing her . . . uh . . . hook-up because she thinks it's intimate.'

Jake, in a very quick flash of cruelty, began to wonder about Ryan's IQ. 'And you think the same?'

Ryan laughed. 'Oh no! But I saw a bag of peanuts over there and I'm allergic.' Awkward silence. Jake ran his tongue over his teeth. He'd brushed, like, three times in the last hour so he should be clear of peanuts, but he nodded.

'So if you don't want to do everything, what *do* you want to do?'

Jake struggled for the words. He motioned at his crotch and made a halfhearted masturbation motion. Ryan looked back blankly, eyes flicking from crotch to Jake's face like he was at a tennis match. 'Right. Just that, then?'

'Um. Maybe a . . . um . . . '

'Is this your first time?'

'No! I'm just not very good at talking about sex without sounding like an instruction manual.'

Ryan sighed. 'Same. But needs must and it's quicker than semaphore. You want me to suck you off, then, yeah?'

'And . . . vice versa?' Jesus. How much more unsexy could this get? Perhaps his parents were about to walk into the room and take their seats on the sofa to watch the whole thing play out.

'Then lead on . . . '

Despite it all, the sex was . . . good. Yes, definitely, a change from the clandestine bunk-ups he'd had before; well, he was in a bed for a start. He fumbled a little at first, not quite knowing what he was doing. During, he wondered how far to let go. He remembered reading in a magazine years before that making too much noise during sex wasn't manly – sometimes Amelia would prod him during sex to check he was still breathing – but this was such a huge occasion he couldn't help but let out the odd grunt or squeal of delight – the sound reminded him of going round to his parents' house and hearing the distant sound of Buddy sitting in a different room watching *Peppa Pig* videos. Ryan didn't seem put off and certainly didn't hang about. Twenty minutes after stepping through the door, he was pulling his (red, small, branded) underpants over his hips.

'That felt like it might've been your first time.'

Oh God! Oh *God*. Had he actually been terrible at it? He'd worried about how hard or gentle he should be when . . . using his wrists? Had he been overly rough?

Ryan registered Jake's expression. 'No, it was fine. Good even! I could tell you were nervous. You were trembling.'

'Oh, no, sorry. Yes it was. My first proper . . . Well, not quite, but you know. Late starter. Sorry about the trembling.'

Ryan smiled. 'Don't be. The vibrations felt quite nice against my balls.'

Hannah's face was flush with excitement when she returned and saw the rumpled bedclothes. She sniffed, claiming she could smell sex.

'That's not a thing, Han.'

'Well? How was it? What did you actually, er . . . do?'

The tightness in Jake's guts told him they weren't ready to be spilled; he wasn't ready to share. To him, it was enough that he'd done it. He'd never spoken about his sexual exploits with women with the boys, in all the years he'd been with Amelia, and although the experience was hugely different, he saw no reason to switch to a new moral code. Hannah wanted to share this so badly, and he wanted to include her, but he couldn't talk about dick size, technique or who came first – he had, in all the excitement, taken longer than he'd expected, despite Ryan's insistent tugging and writhing – until he'd come to terms with it a little. But he didn't want to dim her enthusiasm.

'What were you expecting me to say?' Jake chuckled. 'That I span round on it at breakneck speed until we both came in an explosion so fierce they're evacuating every street within a five-mile radius?'

Hannah bit her lip, embarrassed. 'Nooooooo, but, well, this is the first time to my knowledge that you've had a proper sexual, uh, encounter with a guy. You know, not a sneaky snog or an anonymous blowie, but a full-on real, uh, thing. And I want it to be perfect. So . . . was it?'

'Hannah, how many men or women do you know who would say their first time was everything they'd ever wanted? I'll get there in my own time.'

'But what was it like?'

'I can't go into the ins and outs with you' – there was a break for adolescent laughter – 'I'm not like that. You understand, don't you? I mean, we'd never talk about sex with women like this, would we? Why is this different?'

'Dicks! We *both* suck them now!'

Once he'd stopped laughing, he laid his hand on Hannah's arm. 'Seriously, though, Han; I've never been one to kiss and tell, whoever it was. I'm still the same person, I'm afraid, I just . . . yeah, what you said. The dick thing.'

Hannah nodded. 'I want us to share everything.'

But as much as he loved her, Jake knew they couldn't share everything. Not this time. He couldn't let Hannah organise his hook-ups and introduce him to the LGBT world she thought she knew; he had to make his own way. He had to make friends with someone with experience, to make him feel less alone. Then he remembered the kiss that started everything, in a way. Evan. *Call me anytime*, he'd said. Time to take Evan up on his offer.

fourteen.

His dad's words that being gay was a 'lonely life' had been ringing in Jake's ears ever since that first night. He resolved to break that curse by talking to as many people as possible. Emboldened by what Evan called Jake's 'cheap white wingman' (wine) or his 'belchy butch buddy' (beer), Jake's customary aloofness was relegated to a mere guest star. Once lubricated, and, not before, he would say hello and chat freely with whoever happened to be in his vicinity – whether they liked it or not. To his surprise, most of them did.

For weeks, he clung to the familiar and would only drink in the bar where he'd first reunited with Evan – scene of his attempted outing by Hannah; so much for finding his own way – but one night Evan warned him he could look at those curling posters and sit on sticky leatherette no longer, a change was coming. They were just leaving when a slightly tipsy Jake went bowling into one of the tall tables at the exit, at which sat a man on a stool, with a bottle of Prosecco in an ice bucket and two glasses, one of which slopped some of its contents on to the table top. He was older, rounder and more world-weary than everyone else in the room. Enter Bertie – brand-new friend number one.

Dismissing the men's apologies, Bertie swigged from what was left in his glass and took the bottle in his hand, hovering over the second glass. 'Make it up to me by having a drink with an old man who's bored out of his tits. We can ask for a third.'

'We were just—'

'Tell me to get fucked if you like' – the F-word made Jake gasp; he looked far too *refined* for swearing – 'but I'm not trying to pick you up. I prefer men with more timber in the hold and less . . . straw on the roof. And, yes, I'm mixing up my analogies there.'

Jake laughed. 'What do you mean?'

'I'm saying I don't like my bananas green. You're safe. Take a seat, gentlemen.'

They sat. Bertie was fifty-one. 'In dog years, I'm dead.' Divorced twice. 'Lady the first time. Very sad, but mercifully brief. She got custody of the Kenwood mixer. No other issue, thank God. Second time? The love of my life. That ring on my finger, however, drained my battery and when he'd powered up, he was off.'

Jake laughed but was aware this was a performance; Bertie's supposed nonchalance came from a place of pain – there was still the tiniest trace of it in his eyes.

Jake felt a connection, and, falteringly at first, explained his own situation. Bertie nodded wisely. 'I could tell you were new.'

Jake suppressed a flutter of irritation – that old thing about being worked out before you were ready; people really loved that take, didn't they? Even so, he couldn't resist asking what gave him away.

Bertie tittered. 'You joined *me*. What's the story, then? Bi-curious?'

Jake's Prosecco started to take effect and his annoyance evaporated. He winked at Bertie. 'More than curious.'

Bertie smiled. 'Bi-*enthusiastic*, then?' He paused. 'I'm sorry. I'm becoming that gay man I scuttled away from in nightclubs as a young beanpole. Nosy, verging on creepy. I'm waiting for my friend Ramón and he's late so I'm in a funny mood. Drink his share of the bubbles then you can tell me all about your *journey*. I love a journey; I'm forever on coach trips.' He filled their glasses.

Evan thanked him, and then Jake gave a quick primer on his experience so far. He had it down to about three minutes now. The one hook-up with Ryan, three nights of vaguely sexy chat on Grindr with a man who couldn't meet up because he had to wait in for a parcel, and some arduous flirting across the bar with a host of potential suitors, but little more.

'I guess I'm a bit shy,' he concluded. 'And new.'

Bertie roared with laughter as he saw Evan roll his eyes. 'Oh, little one, you must watch that air of "clueless newness".' He cast his eyes up and down Jake like he was inspecting a boiler repair. 'Your whole, um, *aesthetic* is quite the catnip. For some, anyway.'

Evan slammed the table. '*This* is what I've been trying to tell him!'

Jake never looked in the mirror and considered himself irresistible; usually he styled his hair using his reflection in the microwave to avoid excessive self-scrutiny. But he liked the sound of this. 'What do you mean? Am I . . . a *bear* or something?'

When Bertie's coughing laughing fit had subsided, he explained. 'Well, petal, a straight-acting guy like you – I hesitate to say "bloke" but you get the idea – new to it all but . . . well, from where I'm perched, fairly controlled and calm . . . it's what lots of men want. You can't "tell" you're gay . . . *sorry*, bi, at all! Catnip to the anti-camp brigade and the bros and the dudes. As depressing as it is, you could go a long way with that act.'

Jake smiled but he felt wrong-footed. 'It's not an act.'

Bertie bowed his head in acknowledgement. 'Oh, I know, sweetheart. I'm just speaking from experience. *Straight* still wins. Camp fairies like me have our place but you'll be the boy the rugby bloke will want his first time with.'

Jake looked at Evan, who was laughing. 'I don't even . . . why rugby blokes?'

'I apologise, Jake; I'm being insensitive. My heart is in the right place, assuming I actually have one.' Bertie chuckled and drained the bottle. 'I know it's different now, with the apps and the equality and the visibility and what have you . . . but, in a way, it's actually the same as it ever was. History repeating. People are like spaghetti. Everyone is straight until they get hot and wet.'

Jake offered to buy Bertie a drink. 'Another time. I have had enough of waiting for Ramón. My cat is calling.' He stood up, brushing imaginary crumbs from his shirt. 'Here's my card. Call any . . . Oh, millennials don't call, do you? Add me on WhatsApp, then.' He nodded towards Evan. 'Lovely to meet you both. If you like theatre, I have a dear friend who can always get me a box somewhere so long as it's

Tuesday.' He patted Evan on the shoulder and looked at Jake. 'As dear Whitney said, teach him well and let him lead the way. I think.'

Jake wondered if he'd dreamed Bertie up but sure enough, within a few days, he and Evan were meeting Bertie for coffee in a theatre bar – 'I can't do coffee shops, darling, allergic to the smell of incinerated panini' – and he was inviting them to a book launch or a 'little pre-drinks before a lovely new play, and then a delightful little after-party when the curtain comes down, all we have to do is skip the play itself'. He was funny, bawdy and avuncular and never seemed to want anything more from them than a laugh in the right place and first refusal of the biscotti that came with their flat whites.

After so many years averting his gaze when confronted by attractive men, it was weird to be allowed – encouraged, almost – to look at them properly. Before, Jake had stolen glances, snatching quick looks at body parts – a flick of the eye to their arms (always first port of call) then face, torso, down to shoes. The fear he would get caught had been in no way exhilarating; overt objectification was only allowed if you were heterosexual, it had seemed, and was very much controlled by men. Now, Jake thought he'd perfected the flirtatious look: stare a second or two longer than acceptable, up and down, then when they caught his eye, a winning smile and lazily blinking like he was coming round from a dream. The effect was . . . not quite right. If anything, he looked like he was staring into a washing machine on the spin cycle and his languorous blinking was more 'someone getting up off the floor after falling from a ladder', as Evan had put it. 'I know you've been locked out of heaven for a long time, but you look like a bulldog pressed up against a butcher's shop window. Please locate some chill.'

If Evan's offer of 'anytime' had been out of politeness, he and his husband Nuno were doing a good job of play-acting. Nuno was a little older and terrifyingly smart and had explained to Jake why he was in a better position than most to be coming out as bisexual. 'Younger guys have got their heads round pansexuality, and the ones who've been around longer won't want a new man on the scene to have a bad time. Well, *most* of them.'

Evan chipped in: 'Maybe try to stop blurting out that you're bisexual within ten seconds of meeting someone, though. Don't spill all your tea in one go.'

In the absence of an instruction manual, Jake assumed asserting his identity was part of the process. 'Should I get it printed on a T-shirt? Make sure everyone gets the memo?' He laughed. 'I didn't realise there were so many *rules*.'

Evan's laugh was long and hollow. 'Ah, mate. *Mate*.'

Evan had to admit, he was quite enjoying showing Jake the ropes – since getting married he and Nuno had solemnly agreed their partying was behind them, although as far as Evan was concerned, it didn't mean cheese and crackers in front of the TV every night. Anyway, this was a *project*, in a way, a kind of absolution for with him and Jake, to wish away the teenage years wasted. Nuno waved them off at the front door. 'Have fun playing Pygmalion this evening; I shall be here, alone, sugar-soaping the skirting boards.'

Jake's experience with gay venues had been minimal – and under very different circumstances. Before contacting Evan, he'd got the Tube into Soho and lurked outside the odd bar but had never plucked up the courage to go inside. Patrons had shoved past and greeted bouncers like old friends, but he'd felt on the outside looking in – same old story. He'd made it inside just once, and stood alone chugging consecutive pints, willing someone to chat to him but also hoping they'd stay away – it was only knowing Evan wasn't far away that had later helped coax Jake out of his shell. After his third drink, he'd left, feeling unsatisfied and lost. Weird, really, because Jake had been to gay clubs before, with Charlie; they were his favourite place to score MDMA. Charlie knew a huge, muscly bloke called Keith, with a shiny bald head and who looked like he'd been a pro-wrestler in a former life – he could always be found in a club called Gunt, a vast hangar underneath some railway arches in south London. Jake would follow, head down, as Charlie's fairly decent pecs and winning posh-boy smile pushed through the teeming crowd, like an apologetic snowplough. Charlie was unfazed by the attention, or more likely oblivious to it, and once his transaction was done – lots of air kissing, hand-dancing and telling Keith he looked 'hench' – they would do a quick tour of the dance floor, where Charlie would shake his hips a couple of times, then beckon Jake to leave. Perhaps someone in the crowd found it arousing, but while he was full of admiration at his friend's nonchalance, Jake's feelings for Charlie had long been fraternal.

'Jake,' Charlie would say, almost every time, 'you need to get less shy about your moves if I'm gonna take you with me again.' But Jake wasn't sure he'd ever find the right tune. At night, he'd dream of being back there, though, in the middle of the dance floor, but Amelia would be with him, dancing up close to him while the crowd watched.

Callum came along just as Jake was still hovering around in that Venn diagram overlap between shyness and exuberance.

It was Jake's third time in a gay club as anything other than a straight man chaperoning a drug deal. The place was a kind of hybrid multi-purpose place that was half-club, half-bar – guys huddled in corners laughing, and through an archway he could see guys, and a few girls, outside, pulling on cigarettes and fanning themselves in the humid night. It was much less intimidating than Jake remembered all the other places being. Whether he felt less intimidated because he'd come out now, he couldn't tell, but it was joyous.

According to Evan it was 'ideal for people just getting their head around things. Everyone is friendly and usually quite fit. A good mix, you know?'

The dance floor moved in unison – he recognised the song but it had been remixed into oblivion – but not everyone looked the same, which had been perfect for Evan.

'I'm sorry if it's a bit far for you, but when I go out, I like to go *east*-east London,' Evan had explained. 'There's piss all out there for me as it is but I can relax more here.' Jake saw the top of a drag queen's wig as its owner bopped, and the arms raised in the air ranged from snooker-ball smooth to comically hirsute. He drank it all in, not quite believing his eyes, like the first time he'd flown to New York and seen Manhattan spring up before him, like distant Lego, and the tiny Statue of Liberty. A fever dream, but real.

They were on their way to the bar when Jake spotted Trick, Kia and Hot Will huddled together. Jake had never stopped to even think where Trick and his crew might go when they flounced out of the house dressed like half-eaten takeaways, but this didn't seem their kind of place. Were they too young to be here or was he too old? Trick wasn't eighteen yet!

'Don't be such a cop!' said Evan, craning his neck to get a

better look after Jake subtly pointed them out. 'He looks a bit like you did at that age, but taller.'

Jake couldn't help but chuckle. 'I must *never* tell him that; it would kill him.'

Jake managed to manhandle Evan to another part of the bar out of the teens' eyeline. Jake tried to catch the eye of one of the hottest barman but was roundly ignored. As he jostled for space, a guy standing beside him gave a piercing snap of his fingers. The barman looked over and, instead of telling the man to fuck off, as Jake would've when working in the student union, he grinned and blew a kiss, saying he'd be there in a minute. Jake felt both impressed and inadequate. He turned to peek at this magician.

The man had a perfectly coiffed pompadour and was dressed entirely in black, save for a couple of glittery pin badges affixed to the breast pocket of his shirt. He was attractive, yes, but Jake didn't get that telltale buzz that signified a man had crush potential. Time to try out his all-new sociable patter. 'I should call you the hunk whisperer.'

The man was blank for a beat before beaming back with a Hollywood-white-teeth smile. 'You saying you're a hunk, hon?'

Owned. Jake reddened.

The man prodded Jake in the ribs with the back of his hand – to check whether any abs were present, Jake later realised – and howled with laughter. 'Sorry, sweets, I was being a bitch. And you *are* a hunk!'

Handshakes. Names.

'Hello, Callum.'

Just then, one of Callum's nearby acolytes – red-faced, perspiring, and too much product in his hair – leaned in and bellowed, 'Don't you mean *MG*?!' Jake saw Callum do a full body-cringe.

'What's MG? Like Oh-em-gee?' Jake wasn't sure he wanted to be friends with someone who talked like a Facebook status from 2012.

Callum's face showed a flicker of . . . something as he nudged his pal out of the way. 'Sorry about him, sniffed the barman's apron for the first time. MG is a private joke that has never been funny.'

Jake pointed at Evan. 'This is my friend. Evan. We're together. Well . . . not *together* together.' Jesus. Why couldn't he stop himself?

Callum grinned again – those icy whites. 'Lovely! Once I've directed the barman at you with my magical powers, grab your drinks and sit with us! We've got an *area*. Should be table service but I might as well wait for male pattern baldness to claim me. What do you say, Ethan?'

'Evan.'

'Exactly. See you in a mo.'

The barman served Jake, and Evan leaned in. 'Are you sure about him?'

Jake shook him off, beaming. 'Remember what Bertie said: I'm catnip! Let's go get some pu— Oh no, hang on, that doesn't work.'

Evan peered over at Callum's area, teeming with immaculately groomed piranhas. 'Are they really the kitty-cats you want to attract? Do you fancy him?'

'Of course not! I don't! Honestly. Just want to get to know people. See what all *this* is about.'

Evan sighed. 'Well, you're certainly gonna get a crash course.'

Callum knew *everybody*. When he wasn't talking to Jake and Evan, he was raising his glass in the vague direction of the dance floor and, Jake was excited to see, received hand waves, kisses blown or even a 'whoop-whoop' in return. He was a stylist – 'People who look like shit beg me to make them look even more like shit, but expensive shit,' he joked – and lived in Elephant and Castle.

He tapped Evan's wedding ring. 'Is that real or do you enjoy breaking strangers' hearts on the Tube?'

'What do you mean?'

Callum gave a long, dramatic sigh. 'Such a downer when you spy a fitty on the train and look down to see a wedding ring – only thing worse would be an electronic tag. I preferred it when only women wore them, keep a bit of mystery going.'

Evan gave an abrupt laugh. 'It's real.'

'If you say so.'

Jake was hitting his stride; he whooped as Callum filled his glass for what must've been the fourth or fifth time. Amelia would've loved this; she was always going on wild nights out with the gay guys from her work, or Rudi and her girlfriends.

'They're just so much . . . no offence,' she had said once, 'but, um, nicer to be around than straight people. What can I say?'

Suddenly Evan said he was tired and heading home. 'Remember Bertie said about that literary salon for queer authors tomorrow? Me and Nuno are going. Fancy it?'

Jake noticed Callum hovering as they spoke, talking to the chatty pal from earlier but, if Jake wasn't mistaken, very much keeping one ear on Jake's conversation.

'Yeah, why not? Hopefully I won't be too hungover.'

'Or lost a few brain cells after talking to this lot,' Evan hissed.

'Meow.'

Evan spoke lower. 'Well . . . what's the one thing they have in common?'

Jake turned to face the group. 'Uh . . . quite a lot of them have blond hair.'

Evan rolled his eyes. 'Yeah, that's nearly it. Keep going.'

Callum popped up and slid an arm round Jake's waist. 'Don't worry, *honey*,' he cooed, in a near-perfect impression of someone who gave two fucks, 'you head off. I'll look after him.'

Evan kissed Jake on both cheeks. 'Goodnight, catnip.'

As he departed Callum turned to Jake and grinned. 'Your friend seems nice. Do you fancy a cheeky line?'

Oh God, really? It had been a while. Jake had had some disastrous nights out with drugs in the past. Despite always being Charlie's accomplice on drug hunts, his own relationship was one best left to distance. He was always *that* friend who ended up curled in a ball puking up, or annoying everyone in the smoking area by repeatedly asking how their night was going. 'We told you, bruv, ten seconds ago. Our night is amazing. *Still*.'

The last time they went *out* out, he spent the entire journey home from Dalston impersonating a satnav and getting right on the cab driver's tits, so Amelia sat him down the next morning and said she wasn't sure drugs agreed with him and maybe they should both consciously uncouple from them.

But Amelia wasn't here, or indeed anywhere. And yet. He was about to politely decline when he happened to look in the mirror behind Callum and saw, amid the crowd, Hot Will dancing on a podium, while his brother and Kia pretended to be paparazzi, laughing hard and squealing. They didn't have a care in the world. No doubts, no 'baggage', as Bertie had called it – no comedowns would hold *them* back. He'd done worse, he'd done more, in much more hostile environments than this. Shitty rock festivals, awful open-mic nights, a crap rave in a shed three miles from Alton Towers and in the rain.

'Okay.'

Callum leaned in, twisting his hand round Jake's midriff again, his mouth coming close to his ear. 'Hold your hand out, baby.' He slipped the pouch into Jake's clammy hand. 'You go first. I trust you.'

Jake licked his lips and laughed. 'Everyone's being so nice. Thank you. I'm a bit new to all this.' Jesus, he sounded like Dorothy from *The Wizard of Oz*; if he was going to keep up being catnip, he was going to have to control his gushing.

'Why wouldn't they be nice?' Callum's forehead attempted to crinkle; Jake could immediately tell expensive chemistry was doing all it could to prevent it. 'Let me guess, you've been told . . . by person or persons unknown or whatever . . . that gay men are evil and spiteful and out to ruin your life and get you hooked on GHB at a chem-sex party.' Callum laughed. 'But that's only partially true. No . . . we need to swell the ranks more than ever. Those Pride floats won't fill themselves.'

Jake coughed. 'Um, well, I'm, I mean, I'm actually bi.'

Callum grimaced before dissolving into laughter. 'Oh no, not bi. Sorry, we can't be pals.' He registered Jake's face. 'I'm joking. Why not call yourself fluid or something? Make it a bit more of a story.'

'Another newbie for your collection, MG?' said Callum's friend, as Jake walked away.

'Don't call me that, Glanville,' snapped Callum, 'or I'll show you what it *really* means.' Once more, as he'd been doing all night, he raised his glass toward the dance floor in celebration.

fifteen.

Trick was hot and bothered. It had been relentlessly scorching for days now, and half the crowd in the bar was a delightful shade of crimson, clad in last year's floral shirts, and the previous season's sunglasses sliding down their sweaty heads. He knew he'd have to decree the place officially *over* sooner or later on behalf of Kia, who felt less safe the more mainstream somewhere became. He wasn't all that interested in being *out* out anyway – he was way happier hanging around dodgy old pubs with his mates, buying drinks from barmaids too tired or anarchic to bother too much how old he was. Night buses home were the stuff of nightmares, but Kia told him he'd have plenty of time to sit at home and talk to his internet friends when he was a pensioner: while they could walk, and dance, and be 'out there', they should take every opportunity. So after sweet-talking one of his parents – sometimes both – into slipping some money into his account, they'd head off, every Saturday – Friday nights reserved for filming and eating pizza until they nearly threw up – and come to nights like this, for no other reason than coming out meant they *could*. That's what it had all been about, after all. The journey. He'd had it all worked out: come out, live his truth, fall in love, take a year off after A levels, go to university, very possibly fall out of love and then in love with someone else, be fabulous, then get an amazing job in TV, film, music or something else creative and live happily ever after. This was *not* how things had panned out so far.

His family was almost *too* cool with his being gay; there'd been a complete lack of resistance. He'd get dressed up to go out and clomp through to the lounge to say goodbye to his parents and get a thumbs-up from his dad – genuine, too, not the sarcastic one he gave to van drivers who cut him up on the Old Kent Road – and enthusiastic cooing from his mum. 'Where did you get it? I love your hair like that!' He knew he was lucky – his mate Dermot was flung out of the house at fifteen, Hot Will barely spoke to his parents except to ask for money, and Kia's story had been a series of long talks, slamming doors and tears to get to where she was. But there was something not quite right, only made worse when Jake came home looking like he'd slept in a hedge and told them he was gay. No, not gay, bi, of *course*. His mum and dad reacted like it was . . . not the worst thing in the world, but up there. A shock.

'Are *you* surprised?' Kia had asked, in the immediate aftermath.

Trick had had to think. Had there been signs? 'Jake is barely on my radar. Pluto is more in my thoughts.' But this wasn't true; he'd thought about it a lot. He would admit this to nobody else, but he was furious Jake had somehow managed to turn his permafrost, miserable demeanour into a personality. A tortured, secret bisexual like out of a book – a really heavy one, that Trick would love, sometimes, to drop right on his brother's head.

Hot Will had given his view. 'He's not miserable at all! A bit serious, maybe. I feel we really *connected* when we shared a smoke at your birthday.' Kia and Trick had looked at one another – Trick found this 'everyone is awesome' side of Hot Will very draining. 'He has good chat.'

Trick had blanched. 'He never *speaks*. Literally sits there like an extra chair. With a broken leg. Talking to him is like an anaesthetic; you black out within ten seconds. You don't even need to count backwards.'

'Nah, he's deep. There's *levels*. You need to get on his.'

Trick had poked out his tongue. 'My lift doesn't go down that far, honey, and I ain't taking the stairs.'

Not only that, he was an idiot for ditching Amelia – why give up such a babe, just in case you *might* sleep with a man one day? Too much information!

One night, Trick popped by his mum's salon to see if she needed a hand closing up.

'Oh, you are a good son,' she cooed as she put the kettle on. But Trick had an ulterior motive. He couldn't talk to her at home; he'd just get shut down by Margo, who used to be on Trick's side but was chanting for Jake these days. Very disappointing. After sipping his weak tea out of politeness, Trick went in.

'Why are you and Dad so *down* on Jake's . . . like, bi thing?'

'What do you mean?'

'Well . . . ' Trick had to be careful here; while his mother would talk about literally anything – he remembered a particular painful evening listening to her explain to Hot Will about her latest urinary tract infection – when Jake was mentioned she got awkward. Jake had skipped Mother's Day – unforgivable, what a selfish prick – and Trick knew he was messaging Mum much less than usual. Despite outward appearances, Trick always suspected the apron strings between Jake and his mother were the strongest and most tightly wound of the three. Firstborn, after all. *Worst*-born. 'I mean, it's had a *negative* rating from you two. You don't seem thrilled. So, like, if not being straight is the biggest disaster in the world for Jake, why wasn't it for me?'

Vee slurped her own tea. 'Well, you've always known your own mind. And you've always been so open and happy.'

Right, well, that was not remotely an answer. 'Yes, *Mother*, I get this. But why is Jake too *good* to be gay? Is that even a thing?! He won't even *say* he's gay.'

'You and Jake are different. We . . . didn't expect it. No parent wants to see their child upset and he seems very angry and upset with us. You took everything in your stride. And I *assure* you, nobody is too good to be gay.'

'Do you reckon he's bi now, gay later?' mused Hot Will one day.

Trick laughed derisively, like a cat coughing up a hairball. 'If he is, I'm not sure how much later he can leave it. He's middle-aged!'

'Harsh,' said Hot Will. 'It must be harder for him. I mean, he's, like, quite old but . . . inexperienced. He'll need to meet someone straight away, probably. I reckon he'd be a good boyfriend, though. For *someone*.'

Trick and Kia screamed in B-major. '*What*?'

'Seriously! He's got money and is, like, cultured. He's kind of masculine, but not too much of a geezer. And . . . oh, I dunno.'

Bile rose to Trick's throat. Was Hot Will *into* Jake? No way. Honestly, sometimes Trick wished life were a photo so he could crop Jake out of it. This was another problem. Hot Will. Coming out on his birthday was supposed to be the beginning of . . . well, Trick wasn't sure what. Something. While there was definitely only sibling vibes between him and Kia, Trick had sensed something else from Hot Will. He was super tactile, and his hello and goodbye hugs gave Trick this feeling of heat rising right up from his toes until it tingled at every point on his body making contact with Hot Will's. Unlike Kia, who replied with twenty skull emojis if you messaged her after 10 p.m., Hot Will never got testy when Trick buzzed him late at night, greeting him with 'Yo my bromo' – a cheesy in-joke they'd invented in Year 9. His confidence made Trick feel safe. At first, Trick wanted to *be* him: any haircut on Hot Will's head would land in a slightly remixed version upon Trick's own a week or two later. Trick would beg his mum and dad for whatever slight variation on Hot Will's clothes and accessories he could lay his hands on. Hot Will was the most down-to-earth rich kid Trick knew. In fact, Trick was almost certain the universal acceptance of his coming-out at school was down to Hot Will. The other boys never had a problem with Trick, anyway; his school persona – attractive, theatrical but sexually non-threatening – had earned him respect and even the most dude-acious bros bumped fists with him in the corridor, using his nickname. Hot Will was the god of them all, of course, because he was good at football – which he claimed to hate and only played because you were guaranteed to see dick at least once a week in the locker room – plus there was a rumour he'd chipped the front tooth of someone who called him 'fag' back in Year 8.

But for whatever reason, beyond congratulatory hugs, telling him how proud he was and offering to buy his drinks all night, contact with Hot Will remained miserably platonic.

Trick wasn't exactly pining for him, and had got his own sexual experiences underway with varying levels of success in the meantime, but the thought of Hot Will belonging to someone else one day, compromising their closeness, pulverised what was left of his broken heart.

'Stop looking so bored.' Kia slumped down in the seat next to Trick and placed a vodka and coke in front of him. 'Drink me and enjoy the show.'

Trick grunted. He could be unpredictable when drunk. Lately their nights had been ending with Trick getting green eye watching a random chat up Hot Will or joining in a stand-up row with some transphobe who decided Kia was taking up the valuable space he had set aside for being a massive wanker.

'Why are we here again, anyway?' Kia asked. 'Everyone is so old.'

Trick stared blankly ahead at the so-called VIP area, another bottle of fizz popping, and his brother in the middle, dazzling with perspiration and joy, in his usual outfit of librarian cosplay. Trick had never felt an outsider in his own world before. This was all supposed to be *his*; why was he so peripheral?

'Because *he's* here.'

Was Callum the one? No. But that didn't make it any easier for Trick. He remembered their first Grindr conversation like it was yesterday. It had begun, as these things tend to do, with at least one lie to sweeten the pill, this time a little white one from Trick to smooth over any age difference concerns. Well, sixteen and nineteen weren't *that* far off – a few seasons of *Game of Thrones* apart.

Callum: Yknow u seem really
grown up and mature. Much
more sane and sorted than
other 19 year olds.

Sane and sorted. This was music to Trick's rose-gold hoops.

Trick: Yeah guys my age are
so boring and obsessed with
themselves. There's more to life
than selfies.

Trick knew this was what people wanted to hear. Everyone thought they were somehow above selfie culture, even though they took upward of 100 selfies a day.

Callum: Look I dont normally do
this but me n my squad are goin
Burger Queen this friday, its
our regular. you should join.
Let's get drunk. its super glam n
you'd fit right in

It was like Beyoncé inviting you to her birthday party. Like playing a scratchcard or doing Halloween fancy-dress, you had to take a chance to snare the prize, so Trick told Hot Will and Kia he was busy – 'Doing what? *We* are your "busy",' had been Kia's shocked take – and went along. Callum surpassed Trick's expectations. He was exciting, popular and, crucially, talked to him like he was an adult. He was as far removed from Trick's own crew as possible; he wasn't still working things out, or talking through 'issues', or going wild like a health nut on cheat day – he was level-headed, sorted and comfortable in his own skin. Trick didn't know he craved stability until it presented itself to him in the sleek, assured form of Callum clicking his fingers at the ridiculous barman who looked like a serrano ham with tattoos. Over that first drink, Callum told him 'men as gorgeous as you won't be lonely long' – it had thrilled Trick to be thought of as a man – and listened to him talk about coming out, his home life and friends with the sympathetic ear of a daytime-television agony aunt, but with tight black shirts instead of mumsy dresses.

On the second night they met, Trick freaked out at a party in a miserable 'luxury' development in Battersea where loads of guys in bad underwear crowded round a breakfast bar watching someone wrap drugs in Rizla paper. Callum took his hand, and whispered in his ear, 'You're different, I like it', before taking him home and relieving him of the last remaining crumb of his virginity with a respectful and methodical recognition that this moment would be remembered for ever. Trick never forgot the feeling of accomplishment as he stared out at London's skyscrapers from the huge windows of Callum's apartment, the residual tingle of Callum's bristles all over him like a heat map, half-listening to Callum pee in the en suite and trying to control his own heartbeat. He'd made it. So soon. *This* was how it was always going to be. Just like Instagram.

Trick never admitted it to Kia or Hot Will, but his dream was to be just like Dimitri and Cunliffe – the Manstronio-McGregors – two incredibly hot American Instagrammers who got married on Dimitri's twenty-third birthday. Well, it was a makeshift wedding, just a ceremony, really; gay marriage wasn't legal in the state where they lived. They had a beautiful beach house and all their friends – impossibly thin, china-veneered and each with clear, anime-hero eyes – gathered to watch them commit. After a short reading by a YouTuber who reimagined Jane Austen novels as Carly Rae Jepsen songs, the happy couple got matching tattoos on their ring fingers, of both their names. Well, obviously, as their fingers were too slender, they had room only for the first few letters, so each had 'DIM CUN' weaving round their smooth, tanned digits. Their dogs, ironically named Carrie and Big after characters in a TV show, were ring-bearers, and SweetMouthPete, a leading gaming blogger, was best man – although nobody talked about him any more because Pete was later caught on camera making racist remarks, while dressed as a hot dog in an incomprehensible sponsorship deal at a fan conference.

Whenever he looked at the DimCun Instagram, Trick imagined himself in the photos with Callum, who had the optimum look for selfies – expertly sculpted abs and a perfect jawline, even better than Hot Will's jawline, actually – and zero blemishes. Even though Kia spent a good half-hour on Trick's face before they went out, when he took a selfie he could see what she called 'slight imperfections, silly' as huge welts on his face.

'I've tried every filter and brightening tool but still I look like a robber's dog,' Trick would moan. 'We need a cement mixer.'

'Calm down; you're beautiful. My make-up needs are waaaaaay bigger than yours.' As much as he loved them, Kia could be very matter-of-fact to the point of buzzkill, and Hot Will was too 'yeah whatever, mate, you look gorge' to talk about this kind of stuff deeply. Trick saw enough Instagram comments to know even total dogs could get the 'you look lovely, hun' reassurance whenever they wanted. Nothing was real.

Wanting round two, Trick had dragged Kia and Hot Will on a 'pub crawl', which, surprise surprise, had ended up in Burger Queen to see if they could find him. The 'door bitch', the delectable yet terrifying Heidi Strange, had recognised him as one of Callum's acolytes and waved them through. What a buzz! When they'd found him, Callum had been as sweet as he'd been before, but said he was in the middle of some friendship dramas and pledged to come grab Trick later. As Trick had been about to leave, Callum had come over, given his number, apologised and said they'd chat soon. Knowing instinctively playing it cool would be his reward, Trick had sat on his hands to prevent himself from texting him. They'd had sex again twice, and both times afterward Callum had brought him a vodka and coke to sip while he called a taxi for him. Trick had been embarrassed giving his postcode, as it was 'only down the road, really' and he could've got the bus, but Callum had shrugged it off. 'Worth it to have you home safe, little one,' he'd whispered. Trick had thought his head would explode with happiness.

Kia had been quick to notice things had escalated. 'You talk about him all the time. If I didn't know any better . . . '

Trick had hugged his knees to him. 'What?'

'Dunno. Are you . . . catching feelings? You're acting like you're in love.'

'Aw, Ki,' Trick had said dreamily. 'I wish you could meet someone too.'

Kia had laughed sharply, like one of Joanie's warning barks when she saw another dog on the TV. 'You're *too* kind.'

*

Was it love? What *was* love? He tried to tackle the subject with his mum. She was always making discreet enquiries about what the 'talent' had been like the night before, along with attempting to matchmake with any vaguely queer guy who walked past the salon, let alone came in.

'Ooh, I had a gorgeous one in today, Trick,' she cooed while making him a quick sandwich. 'Your age, *smashing* hair, nice skinny jeans but fillin' 'em out, if you know what I mean.'

'Mother! I *always* know what you mean, God.'

'I mean his thighs! Lovely bum.' She peered at her son's behind. 'Don't worry, yours will come through one of these days.'

Trick's hands unconsciously went to his own posterior. He was yet to gain any particular shape in any direction, really; Kia once called him a 'sex pencil'.

'Mother, I am *trying* to be serious.'

Vee put on her best listening face. The scrape of the chair as she pulled it back to take a seat opposite him cut into the ominous silence and Trick giggled.

'Okay, shoot.'

Trick tapped the top of the bread. 'Um. Can you be in love at seventeen? Is it too young?' He prepared a couple of acerbic comebacks in case Mum dismissed him, but to his surprise, she breathed deeply, like she'd been dreading this question all her life.

'Too young? No, course not,' she began cautiously.

'Then why do old farts always say young people don't know what love is?'

'Well, um, speaking as an *old fart* . . . as a person gets older and has more experience of love, they look back and reassess the love they felt when they were young, and say it couldn't possibly have been the real thing.'

'But it might have been?'

'Yeah. Maybe. I mean, love feels different every time. So you fall out of love with *that* person and the cycle starts again and you, kind of, *crave* that feeling of a love you once had. You want to believe the love you feel now is the proper one, but only time and distance can tell you that. And by then, well, you're making different mistakes.'

'Mum . . . have you been possessed by a Valentine's card?'

Vee laughed and dabbed at the crumbs on her plate. 'You asked! It's a big joke, really. You want the love to be as intense as it was, and all the while convincing yourself that this is the real thing, this time.'

Trick blinked away whatever was in his eye. 'Mum, that's like poetry. I mean, like the poetry we make up on the fridge door with those magnetic letters but . . . ' Trick didn't think he could eat his sandwich now; his throat was too full. 'You should do videos.'

Vee looked off into the distance. 'Love's like a cold, really. No vaccine. Slightly different every time. But fucks you all the same.'

Callum was always the same whenever they chatted on WhatsApp or saw each other out – peppy, enthusiastic, attentive – but Trick imagined a growing coolness that felt like watching a car, handbrake off, roll backward into a lake. All he could do was let it happen. One night – *the* night, the last night – he saw Glanville, the friend of Callum's he loathed the most, huddled over a phone gleefully showing a dick pic to another of the faceless, identikit cohorts always to be found sunbathing in Callum's halo. Trick had never taken a picture of his penis, so he knew it wasn't *his*, but he felt bad for the poor soul whose trust had been broken.

'That's private,' stammered Trick. 'You can't do that.'

'And *you* can't sit with us, so fuck off. Don't worry, it's not you. It's *big*.' The guys burst out laughing.

Trick stopped in time before stamping his foot. 'Why are you so mean?'

Glanville leaned over and flicked Trick's ear like there was a fly on it. 'Go home, baby Patrick,' he said. 'It's a school night.'

Trick's hands balled up into fists. 'You're like . . . the *Mean Girls*! You're . . . the mean gays!' Being around these men drained him of his acidic superpower; he sounded petulant and ridiculous.

Callum spotted the commotion and came over. Trick noticed he retrieved the phone from Glanville's hand and put it in his own pocket.

'Watch out, Callum; she's angry!' Glanville screeched with laughter. 'She'll be calling *you* a mean gay next. Big MG!'

Trick felt tears come. 'They were looking at a . . . it's . . . *private*. It's wrong.'

Callum smiled at Trick. There was kindness, but finality. 'I'm afraid, well, nothing's private on the internet. When you send pictures of your cock to strangers . . . '

'But . . . ' Trick sounded like a child protesting the injustice of bedtime. 'But whoever he sent it to wasn't a stranger to him . . . '

Callum slid his arm round Trick's waist and turned away from Glanville's leer. 'No, but . . . maybe it's best if *I* am one, where you're concerned, for a while.' His voice was apologetic but firm. 'Go home and get some rest. It's been a long night.'

Now, Trick cringed at the memory, how childish and naive he must've seemed. Hot Will climbed down from the podium and threw his arm round Trick. 'Come on, baby boy.' The pair watched as Jake returned from the bathroom and leaned in to Callum. 'We've seen enough.'

'This isn't how it was supposed to be,' said Trick miserably. 'That's my night out they're having over there.'

Hot Will pinched his cheek and kissed him lightly on the forehead, breaking Trick's heart all over again. 'I know.'

Kia linked arms in between then and they swayed and sang as they plodded towards the bus stop. 'Love you guys. My favourite queens.'

The three friends slept entwined with one another that night, a mass of sportswear, running make-up and tears. Trick needed to believe it wouldn't always be this way. The future depended on it.

sixteen.

How weird to stop for a minute or two and consider 'before', the way things used to be. When he was going out with Amelia, Jake had embraced routine: he went to the gym on the same nights, saw Amelia on the same nights and their weekends would often follow the same pattern: a forty-five-minute debate over first whether and then where to go for brunch, followed by said brunch, wandering about, a drink in a pub, then either a clutch of convenience food to warm up at his or the promise of a takeaway, or, once or twice a month, a night out. Like, *out* out. Looking back, perhaps it was boring, or behaviour you might expect of someone twice his age, but Jake had found it comforting. Growing up in a circus taught him to appreciate the mundane. Now, however, no two nights were the same and, frankly, he was exhausted. No sooner had he got in from work or the gym and eased himself into the tasteful loungewear that Amelia had called his 'porridge look', than there'd be a message from Bertie or Evan or, if the weekend was coming up, Callum. The messages said different things but the tune, to Jake, was always the same. 'Come!' they seemed to be saying. 'Come embrace what you've missed.' He didn't need telling twice.

He felt guilty he'd never done more with Amelia – she'd always said they should chase excitement while they could – but it had taken him this long to realise the only way to appreciate the luxury of comfort and security was to take yourself out of it for a while. So when chances came, he imagined the alternative, which was staring at the cable TV he had forgotten to cancel, and he took them.

To complicate things even further, there was Rana. His boss's assistant. Gorgeous and smart, he had admired her from afar for years, along with everyone else. Jake often winced as he heard other men discuss Rana over their canteen lunches, in their crass, tabloid terms. Nothing like his own intentions, which, Jake told himself, had only ever been wholesome and romantic. The leering that came naturally to them had never quite felt right. Before Amelia came along, he'd wondered whether to ask Rana out, but all he did about it was stand near her at work events, leaving drinks, and sales presentations and wait for a miracle to happen. It never did and, as far as Jake knew, Rana had no interest in him whatsoever. Until that day.

Harry was making his usual performance about leaving the office – for some reason he liked everyone to observe he was shooting off in his gym gear.

'Staying late again, Jake?' he called as he swaggered out the door, a sinewy stress-ball teeming with heterosexuality. Jake noted he only washed his gym shorts after every other session. Sometimes when Jake closed his eyes all he could see were those shorts and the thighs behind them, like sunspots. 'You'll be putting the rest of us to shame.'

'Nothing to go home for,' Jake replied, joking, but sounding more serious than he'd intended. Anyone else would likely have picked up on it and asked if he was okay, but Harry being Harry, who probably wore mirrors on the inside of his sunglasses, shrugged and laughed. 'Tell me about it, bro.' And off he went to spend two hours on a chest that would strain just the right amount against his work shirts. Jake was watching Harry leave – and objectifying him intensely – when it happened.

Jake definitely wasn't imagining it – Rana had winked. He replayed the scene in his head. Rana walked over, smiled, dropped a folder on his desk, said Lisa needed it by . . . when? He couldn't remember now. Shit. Anyway, she said a date at some point in the inconveniently near future and, then . . . she winked, before smiling again. And walking away. Rana had never winked at him before. Did she wink at everyone? She didn't seem the type. She and Jake got on well; as Lisa's assistant she was always batting away requests for meetings and they had their own system between them. He'd go over and ask how packed Lisa's diary was, she would laugh politely at his quips (usually stolen off Twitter) and tell him – every time – that Lisa had left instructions to be disturbed only for chocolate or Jude Law. But winking, that was something else. Had the wink been conspiratorial – like, 'Oh, wow, isn't Lisa an unreasonable dragon for wanting these documents back so soon?' – or was it salacious? His dad winked a lot – usually at his children while Vee was venting at them, or at his wife while he goosed her at the sink, pretending they didn't know the children could see. Jake never winked back. He was thinking about this too much. It couldn't have been attraction, because Rana was way out of his league – hang on, did he have a league now? Who was in it? Had Amelia been in it or was she a fluke? What did you have to do to get into this league? Slip him a phone number? Be very direct and ask him out? Neither of these things had ever happened before. Wink? Maybe. For what must've been the first time in his life, a piece of his dad's wisdom came to him – something he'd overheard him say to one of his workers.

'If you want to know what someone means, ask 'em. Then you'll know what they want. No shame in getting things straight. Make a joke of it if you have to.' At the time, Pat had been talking about a mansard roof, but this felt appropriate. And so, scarcely believing he was about to do this, he picked up the folder, and wandered over to Rana's desk. She waited until he was practically sitting on it before she looked up.

'You got something in your eye?'

Rana put her hand up to her face; a shiny red nail brushed the corner of her brow. 'Have I?'

Jake tilted his head to one side and tried to control his breathing. He remembered how to do this, right? 'Dunno. I was asking *you*.'

'Why?'

Jake cocked his head back in the direction of his desk. 'You winked at me. When you gave me this.' Quick nonchalant waggle of the folder. 'Thought you might need some eye drops; I've got some.' Jake cringed, almost closing his eyes in horror, but just as they narrowed, he realised this – whatever *this* was – was working.

'Oh, no,' said Rana, placing her hands back in front of her – poised, confident, ready. 'I *was* winking. At you. Yes.'

'I should speak to HR about you.'

'I'll make an appointment for you if you like. When are you free?'

Jake swallowed hard. Was this . . . ? Too soon after Amelia? When would be long enough? What was the grieving process? Someone from work, too. Wasn't it tacky? Rana looked back impassively, waiting for his response. If he could see her smile, then he would know, one way or the other. She was beautiful, funny and sharp. Lightning couldn't strike twice, could it? The women he fancied from afar usually stayed just that – far away. Fate brought him Amelia and he'd clung on as long as he could but didn't think he'd harness that power again. Without thinking, he winked with his left eye, trying very hard to make sure the right eye didn't close along with it. 'You tell me.'

She smiled. Slowly, it crept along her face, like a sunrise does before it gets carried away with itself and takes over the whole sky within seconds. The smile hit her eyes and Rana took a little breath and said, 'Wednesday at seven. Let's discuss it further then.'

As Jake walked back to his desk, it took all his strength not to do a fist-pump. Whatever it was, he still had it, and it was exciting to see somebody still wanted it. He would deal with the rest of his feelings later.

Jake, Bertie and Evan were at the opening night of a star-studded play in the West End, with free drinks as far as the eye could see. 'Sometimes knowing everybody is a curse, and I pray for matches and accelerant, and sometimes it means we go to the theatre for free,' trilled Bertie as he grabbed a glass from a passing silver tray.

To his surprise, Bertie was encouraging about Rana. 'Why wouldn't I be? I think it's marvellous. She sounds delightful.'

'But is it too soon? After Amelia?'

'Too soon?' Bertie studied Jake's face. 'There are no rules.'

But Jake couldn't shake the worrying feeling he was about to make a mistake. Did he have to tell Rana he was bi?

Evan put his arm round Jake. 'The trouble is, we don't know the etiquette. We're not bi. It's hard because they don't tend to shout about it.'

The wine was going to Jake's head and it was only the interval. 'Why the hell not?'

'Why do you think?'

Bertie got a faraway look in his eye. 'I had a bisexual friend. Lovely, lovely Ross. He always said to me, "It's all right for you. You look out there and see loads of men just like you; I don't see anyone like me." Sad, really.'

'Well, maybe I could meet him!' Jake became excited. 'I know how he feels.'

'Oh no, he's long gone.'

A tear sprang to Jake's eye. 'Did he die?'

Bertie cackled. 'No! No, he lost the use of one of his arms in a bike crash, went to volunteer in the Balkans, met a lovely woman from Basingstoke and now they're doing the two-point-four toddlers and a Renault Megane somewhere in Gloucestershire.' Bertie noticed Jake swaying. 'Don't get so drunk you forget the ending. This is a serious play, not *Guys and Dolls*, you know.'

Jake looked round the bar, taking in the buzz. 'I know! Sorry! It's just so exciting.'

Evan nudged him. 'Every time we come out, you act like you haven't been to the theatre before!'

He had, of course, but mainly touristy blockbusters or pantomimes.

The bell rang for the second act and Bertie signalled to the barman. 'Don't your family like the theatre? Not even musicals?'

'Yeah, they do but . . . I never really went along. Wasn't my kind of thing.' Jake shivered as he remembered turning his nose up at tickets or invitations to 'make a night of it', and his mum's disappointed face.

'But it is *now*?' Bertie looked suspicious.

'Definitely.'

Evan drained his drink. 'You know if your bisexuality is just a cover to get knockdown royal-circle tickets for the West End, there are easier ways to do it.'

Jake laughed. 'No! I had nobody to go with before.'

'Except your family.'

Jake began to feel a bit stupid. *Why* hadn't he gone? The thought of saying out loud the real reason was terrifying.

'Don't tell me you thought going to the theatre would make you look gay?' At Jake's silence, Bertie stopped trying to grab the barman's attention and turned back to Jake, giving him a long look. 'You have *got* to be joking. This isn't a thing, surely? I'm sorry but being straight sounds absolutely exhausting. Just go to the fucking theatre if you must. Plenty of heterosexuals do! Why do you think *The Mousetrap* has been running so long? Some of those sets must be older than God's dog, not to mention the poor cast.'

The pressure lifted and Jake laughed too loudly; people turned to stare. Bertie's head swivelled like an owl's and they all looked away. He continued: 'I sympathise to a degree . . . but even though I was straight *on paper* I couldn't hide. It was all over my face, and my heart. And you from such a theatrical family! Freedom hiding in plain sight. Silly boy. Anyway, get a glass of water to go back in with. Someone dies in this act. A gay character, of course.'

Jake didn't mention Rana to Callum; he wasn't sure how he'd react. Callum didn't seem to have many female friends, and his circle of pals – which was in a constant state of evolution; Jake had learned not to get too attached – didn't do deep conversation. Callum was always saying, 'I can't be doing with anybody's drama tonight', which Jake was grateful for – some nights he didn't want to answer questions, or think about who and where he was, and getting lost in Callum's social life was just the tonic. Callum's messages would come right on cue, usually on a Saturday, with a précis, a postcode and a promise it would be 'tremendous fun, otherwise I wouldn't disrupt your busy schedule'.

Sometimes Jake thought it was too good to be true, that Callum and his friends were only humouring him, some kind of elaborate scam. Years of invisibility at school had convinced him he was an acquired taste, not a fast friend. Jake always had the lingering memory that he'd broken someone's heart to feel this free, and disappointed his mum and dad for his own selfish gains, so why should someone like Callum do him any favours when there were better looking, more interesting men queueing round the block for his attention? Whatever was in it for Callum, Jake was reaping the benefits. He had finally graduated from sitting and tapping his feet to the music, to standing and shuffling – first infinitesimally, then with actual side-to-side movements – and finally, thanks to Callum's encouragement he was now comfortable enough to defrost the not-too-shabby moves he'd kept on ice for years, and it didn't even matter to him that there were other men on the dance floor much better at it than he was.

'You have to get up for this one,' hissed Callum. 'It's sacrilege otherwise.' Jake let himself be hauled into the centre, as Callum and another guy he would probably never see again whooped round him. It was 'Atomic', by Blondie, one of his mum's favourites. One of *his* favourites, now. He mimed along, raising his hands to the ceiling, delirious not from double vodkas but from the unadulterated joy that came from being allowed to melt into the crowd, yet still feel at the epicentre of it all.

Back at Callum's table, buoyed by the success of his first dance, he asked the question. He was drunk.

'I gotta ask. Why are you so nice to me? Inviting me out? I didn't think it would be easy to make friends . . . well, gay friends.'

Callum shrugged. 'Why wouldn't I? It's hard these days competing with Netflix and Twitter. People ignore the phone, cancel plans.'

Jake tried to sit up straight, but his shoulders collapsed; he looked like an old duvet. 'I don't.'

'No,' said Callum. '*You* never do that. *I* never do that. But people do. So when you meet someone a bit different, and you get on, you keep at it. I didn't know anybody when I got to London and it was hard. I've been there.'

'Yeah, but I'm *from* London. I was born in St Thomas's!'

Callum laughed. 'Oh, you're from *a* London, but not *this* London, not *my* one. So welcome!' He ran his eyes over Jake. 'Why did you think I was being nice to you?'

Jake prodded his own belly through his shirt. A tiny sweat patch was appearing; it was incredibly hot inside and outside – everywhere. 'I thought it might be . . . I dunno.'

Callum clapped his hands in delight. 'Of course! A sex thing! Because all gay men want to shag each other! Yes?'

Jake reddened with embarrassment, but Callum moved closer.

'Let's test your theory, then.' Callum leaned in and kissed Jake. There was tongue. Callum smelled expensive. His fingers were bony as they rested on Jake's chest. And then it was over. Callum leaned back. 'Well?'

Jake looked down at his crotch. 'Yeah, nothing. I don't see you in that way.' He glanced back up to see Glanville watching them from his own seat. Callum's face flickered with irritation for a millisecond. 'Good, there we go. We can get on with being friends, can't we? You're a different kind of friend, that's all.' He held out his glass to be clinked. 'I like changing things up.'

A month's worth of excitement in one weekend usually meant by the time he got to the end of it, Jake was frazzled. He would wake up feeling like he'd lived – even if just a little – and that there were possibilities. What would next week bring? he would wonder, blinking against the searing summer sun while the coffee machine clunked and clicked into life. But there was Sunday to get through first, and what was waiting for him every other Sunday? The one reminder of who he used to be, an attempt at bridge building and keeping his mum happy, back to his old familiar role: Sunday lunch with the rest of the D'Arcys.

*

Margo's teacher training, with just a few weeks left to go, was wearing her out. 'At least once a day someone asks if it's allowed for PE teachers to be fat, or "what's your BMI, miss?"' she complained. 'I forgot what pieces of shit children are. Except my Buddy, of course.'

Hot Will, joining them for lunch that day, gave a sharp intake of breath. 'Eeesh. That is dark.' He turned to Jake, who was barely awake. 'You a bit hungover today, Jake? Out last night?' Jake flinched as a mountain of mashed potato thudded on to his plate, wielded by his mother. 'Who were you with?'

'Er . . . Callum, a friend.' Jake looked up and saw his dad's jaw harden – it was the same every time he made some vaguely gay or bi remark. Jake could hear Vee's lips pursing in expectation. '*Just* a friend, Mum. And, no . . . not a special one.' He looked over at his dad, the tension in his shoulders slowly releasing. He was reminded of all those spring mornings in the park, his dad kicking a football at him while Jake watched it sail over his head, utterly uninterested.

'Can you not *try* to kick it, Jakey?' his dad had always complained, shoulders rigid, but Jake either could not or would not comply. It would've been the easiest thing in the world to kick it back. Sure he'd have made a fool of himself missing the ball or falling on his arse, but all Dad wanted was the effort. But it was no use. Sport was something other people enjoyed, the insiders, who came to it naturally. Footballs were kicked *at* Jake, not *to* him, by boys who knew he wouldn't and couldn't stop them.

Trick had never been forced to endure the kick-abouts; he made it clear early on that his feet were made for high kicks and ruby slippers, not booting a football. And Jake knew Dad appreciated that singlemindedness, Trick's determination, if nothing else. Jake's rejection seemed born of the desire to be awkward, whereas Trick's was self-expression, the assertion that there was no alternative.

Jake remembered Trick dressing up as Kylie Minogue from

the 'Can't Get You out of My Head' video in an old sheet, and Dad's rapturous applause as Trick mimed along, in one of his famous 'back garden shows', while the neighbourhood kids the next day would shove Jake and tell him his little brother was a poof and a princess and that it must run in the family. Kevin Tully, who had a face that looked like a torn-open bag of crisps, its contents spilling out, was the main culprit. His spirit was invoked that Sunday, when Vee said he'd been in the salon.

'I remember him,' said Trick dully. 'He used to call me a gaylord every time he saw me.'

His mum was aghast. 'Did he? Kevin Tully? But he's our Jake's age. How old were you?'

Trick looked straight at Jake. 'It started when I was about . . . three. I used to play with his sister's kid. They lived round the corner. Don't you remember?'

Jake nodded. 'I remember Kevin. He was a Neanderthal.'

Trick held his gaze. 'He did it all the time. Like, years. Even after he had his own kids. Did he say it to you too, Jake? Call you names?' Hot Will leaned forward and put his hand over Trick's. There was a discernible glow to Trick's face; the skin-on-skin contact re-energised him.

Jake looked away, feeling he was intruding on a private moment, and shook his head. 'Not to my face.' But Kevin had said it about Trick, over and over and over. Once, when home from university, Jake had gone into the street to shout Trick in for dinner, and seen him playing with a little girl – Kevin's niece, Jake supposed now – and Kevin looming over them. He hadn't changed much; he still looked like a haggis drawn from memory, with a face you'd never tire of pouring cement on. He was saying something to the children. Trick had been in his customary drag of pink roller-skates and a glittery shawl, his glossy black hair scraped back with an Alice band.

'Come on, Trick,' Jake had shouted in as gruff and low a voice as possible, standing with legs further apart than usual, as if in warrior stance. 'Mum wants you. Dinner time.'

Kevin had leered back, pleased with himself. 'Run along, princess, here's your queen.'

Jake had seen that Trick's eyes were red and raw, and his heart had jolted a little as his baby brother had run toward him, glad of the reprieve. 'Bye, Lucy,' he'd called behind him. 'See you after.'

Jake hadn't said what he'd wanted to say, what he should've said. Years of editing, fading into the background and shying away from scenes were hard to shake off. If he responded, what would happen? Men like Kevin Tully wouldn't have an epiphany; they thrived on their power. The joy his jibe brought him had shown in his car-crash of a face, spiteful features glowing at the memory of it. The most likely outcome was Jake would get punched in the street, and he quite liked his nose the shape it was. So instead, heart racing and bile rising, he'd turned away and started walking before Trick had caught up, holding out his hand behind him for his brother to take. Trick hadn't; instead, he'd trotted behind, before overtaking at the front gate and zooming upstairs to wash his face and reapply his cheek-glitter.

After dinner, as Trick had made to race out the door and back to his friend, Jake had called him back.

'Hey, mate.' *Mate*. Bloody hell. 'You know some people might not understand why a boy wears . . . things like this.'

Trick had stared back blankly, eyes huge, his breathing quick and impatient, the angel wings he was now wearing rising and falling in synchronicity. Jake had carried on. 'Maybe just do that, uh, kind of thing in the house, or in the garden, where you can really enjoy yourself, so mean people can't see.'

Trick had looked down at his own body, his outfit, as if for the first time. His reply had been bright, but sharp. 'I want them to see.'

As he'd watched Trick skip away, back out into the big bad world, Jake had realised he'd asked the impossible – and had been wrong to do so.

Cringing at the recollection of his insensitivity all these years later, Jake wondered how to make it up to his brother. Maybe he wouldn't even remember. 'Mum, next time Kevin comes in the salon,' said Jake, 'shave all his hair off.'

'Yeah!' Trick added flatly. 'And make him eat it.'

That was the longest exchange they'd had in at least a year without an insult. Though the moment had passed in seconds, Jake was already nostalgic for it.

Talk turned to Jake's thirtieth birthday, which was coming up. Vee and Pat had big ideas of going 'somewhere fancy' or having a party, but the thought of being ostentatious and, dare he say it, overtly joyous after the year he'd had didn't sit well. 'I'm away on a business trip with Lisa on the actual day. I don't want any fuss,' he said, but the persisting tinge of wistfulness fuelled by bonding with Trick over Kevin Tully gave him a brainwave. 'What about the carvery we used to go to when we were little?'

'Really? But it's . . . nothing special. Why on Earth do you want to go *there*?' Vee remembered the last time they'd gone, the week before Pat got back from Dubai for good, before they'd moved off the estate. Reenie's Mark had a car for 'some reason' – Vee remembered a court appearance came not too long after this – so they'd piled into it and she'd watched

Margo and Jake demolish the 'all you can eat' salad bar while Trick had screamed in protest in his pushchair. As they'd battled post-food comas, Jake had sat reading, ignoring Margo's pleas to play football in the car park with her.

Jake sighed. 'It seems life was simpler then.' He recalled Amelia mentioning months ago about wanting to play with her dolls again. 'I know things have become kind of . . . ' Vee held her breath in case he was gearing up to talk about things properly, at last. 'Um, complicated. So I thought it would be fun to bring back some good memories, remember how we used to be.'

'What? Back to basics?' Vee laughed. 'Life was only simpler for you because you had no responsibility. But, yeah, might be nice to go somewhere old-school.'

Trick's face creased up like he'd licked the sugary dust from an empty bag of fizzy cola bottles. 'You can't be serious. I'm not *queueing* for meat and coming out smelling like roast potatoes. Mother, this is the *limit*. He's trolling us.' He ran his hands through his hair at the thought. 'How can it "bring back good memories"? I don't remember it at all. And I'm *glad*.'

Vee chuckled. 'Well, let's make some new memories, then.'

Trick made a gagging sound. 'Mother! Making memories is lame. What's the point? Making them for when, for who? Just so you can be chill on your deathbed? Fuck that; I don't wanna make memories, I wanna make *noise*.'

Vee regarded her youngest son coolly. 'Well, you've never wasted an opportunity to make plenty of that.'

Trick took this as his cue to leave, slinking out like a cat who has eaten not only his own dinner but everyone else's too. Hot Will shrugged and followed.

'Forget it, then; maybe he's right.' Jake began to clear the table. 'Silly idea.'

'No, not at all. I'll work on him . . . or we can leave the miserable bugger at home.' Vee got a strange look in her eye. 'You could . . . bring someone. If there is someone?'

Jake readied himself. He didn't want to hide any more. If he let them in, maybe they would show an interest and start getting used to the idea. Margo and Trick were open books as far as he could see, and it didn't do them any harm. D'Arcy confessionals were a staple of the kitchen table. 'Well . . . nobody that I'd bring to my birthday, but . . . I have been on a couple of dates with a girl from work.'

He heard his mum gasp; the contents of the dishwasher jangled in sympathy. Jake looked at his dad, his face a picture of confusion and joy – like his accumulator had just come in.

'Oooh.' Silence. A plane flew over, a child in the garden next door whooped as they splatted on to their backside in their paddling pool. 'So have you dropped the gay thing then, son?' Pat looked devastatingly hopeful. 'Not that we mind. It's . . . it's a hard life. My cousin Kenny, for example. Up in Manchester and off doing God knows what.'

'He's gay? I didn't know.' Jake had met him once, at Margo's communion. 'What do you mean "God knows what"? He's probably just *shopping*, Dad. I haven't dropped anything. I was never gay. Why does this make you so happy?'

His dad did a perfect impression of mock innocence. 'What? What makes me happy?'

'That I'm seeing a woman. I can see it in your face. Relief. What if it were a guy?'

'*Are* you seeing a man too?' His mum closed the dishwasher door and glided into view.

Jake rolled his eyes and saw Margo had her head in her hands. 'Mother, I am bisexual, not polyamorous, or in a permanent state of orgy. I don't have sex with everyone at once. Do you ask Trick questions like this?'

Pat was red in the face, his hands clenched into tight dumplings, knuckles grey. 'Excuse me if I'm happy that . . . there's a new girl on the scene. Even if it is too soon.'

Vee looked back blankly, half-rinsed gravy boat dripping brown sludge on to the linoleum. 'It's nothing to do with Trick.'

Jake stood up. Margo recoiled slightly. 'It is! What if I'd come out first? Would Trick be getting a hard time, or is it because I'm attracted to men *and* women?'

'We're still learning, Jake. The . . . uh . . . "bi" thing – it's a lot to get our heads round,' his dad muttered.

Jake shook his head. 'I can't spend more time waiting for you to catch up.' He patted his sister's shoulder. 'Bye, Margs.' Margo slowly nodded her head.

As he left the kitchen, he turned back. 'Just ask yourselves why Trick's life is one great big gay picnic and mine is inconvenient because you've run out of straight sons and don't have a *spare*.' He didn't wait to see their reactions, but in the hall, he turned to see Trick standing outside his own door. Listening, obviously. They didn't acknowledge one another.

*

As he watched Jake disappear out the door, no doubt off to a bar full of people who looked just like him and hung on everything he said, only one word burned into Trick's mind. Picnic. *Picnic*. Oh, it was a picnic, definitely all right. Uncomfortable, at the mercy of the elements, continually annoyed by insects and surrounded by formerly delicious things now rapidly rotting or incubating harmful bacteria. Trick looked down at his nails and saw the polish was chipped on his middle finger. He raised it anyway, to the space his brother's atoms had occupied a few seconds earlier. 'Picnic?' he finally murmured. 'You absolute *cunt*.'

seventeen.

It was Friday afternoon, when the entire workforce was trying to look busy for the remaining three hours on the clock. Papers were shuffled, emails scrolled through; someone refilled the printer and did a coffee run. Finally, some excitement: a mocked-up storyboard for a new diversity campaign. Jake had been away when it was briefed and was reluctant to interfere in anything Harry was working on in case it threatened his feeble masculinity.

When Harry and Lisa called him over to ask for his thoughts, Jake's heart sank. First of all, he was moments from completing a level on the word game on his phone, and secondly, nobody asking your opinion an hour or two before home time wants anything but a nod of approval, but he had to play along, listening as Lisa and Harry excitedly explained the concept. The plot was gossamer-thin, as these things usually were, but one aspect jarred – a character in the story who'd been making inappropriate remarks about a gay colleague actually turned out to be gay himself. Jake traced along the frame with his fingers, as if touching it would help it make more sense. Jake remembered Evan warning him about this kind of thing, and Trick and Kia talking about 'stealthy homophobia'. Even to his untrained eye – he'd never had to think about this before – this looked like a classic case. It was tone-deaf; he couldn't believe they thought this okay. He looked in amazement at Lisa, an actual company director, and Harry, a self-described LGBTQ ally. Their smiles were fixed; all they wanted was a scrap of positivity and his ordeal would be over. With a pain in his chest, and a building fury he was surprised to be feeling, he managed to choke out the word. 'Cool.'

Back at his desk, his mind fizzed. He should've said something. They'd asked his opinion; he should've given it, told them the truth, what anyone with an ounce of sensitivity would've seen screaming out. He wondered how many times before – from the other side of the fence, as minimal as his journey beyond it had been so far – he had let things like this go, not seen who it could hurt. As Harry and Lisa started to put the boards away with satisfied murmurings, Jake mentally scrolled through recent campaigns, words they'd used. Had he been doing all he could? It was too late to go back in time and tell Kevin Tully to sod off with his tabloid homophobia, but he could seize *this* moment.

Harry and Lisa didn't see him approach. How should he do it? He'd never called this out before. He began with an apology. 'Sorry, guys. I . . . I have to say. I think we need to look at this again.' Explaining, he knew he'd lost Harry straight away.

'No, it's *mocking* homophobia, innit?' he reasoned. 'Like, saying how stupid it is.'

Jake kept his breathing even, resisting the temptation to tell Harry how stupid he sounded. 'No, you *see*, it's suggesting homophobic people are secretly gay, which in *itself* is homophobic.'

'Take it *easy*. Nobody will see it that way at all.'

Jake bit his tongue at the 'take it easy'. He had been calm, reasonable; he could do this, make this case, he knew he could. '*I* see it that way. And I . . . ' The room seemed library-silent. 'I have a stake in this.'

Harry's eyebrows shot up. 'You do?'

'Yes. Recently I . . . ' Jake's heart raced. 'I'm bisexual.'

Lisa was strangely quiet, aside from the air rushing in between her teeth. He turned to her. 'OK . . . well, thank you for telling us. But . . . maybe you're overreacting? The message is more important than the method, right?'

Jake trembled. 'Like a brick through the window is fine as long as it's got a tenner wrapped round it?'

Lisa looked at the board and back to Jake. She was not convinced. 'What do you think, Harry? Any stake in this?'

He looked a tad nervous. Jake saw his eyes pulse. 'I don't think it's that deep, mate.'

Not. That. Deep. Jake bowed his head the tiniest degree. He could be nothing if not gracious in defeat. 'Okay. Well, I just thought I'd mention it.'

Jake went back to his desk and tried to hold in the tears he could feel en route. He hadn't expected to lose, not so quickly. He'd assumed once he told them he was bisexual, they'd see him as some kind of . . . What would he call it? An authority? Whatever, but he was the target of the campaign and the only insider available to give their viewpoint. Yet they'd overruled him all the same. He kicked himself for thinking it would make any difference, and now they *knew*. Shit.

He felt a presence at his elbow. He could see Harry's brilliant white, tight shirt and broad chest reflected in his screen.

'I'm sorry, mate.' He crouched down, his head level with Jake's. 'I heard you and Amelia split up.'

Where had this come from? Did Harry and Rana ever talk?

'Moving in kills the vibe,' Harry continued. 'That's what broke me and Melissa up.'

This was brand-new information to Jake. He was strangely glad to hear it, and for very selfish reasons. He felt excited, and cursed himself for his own predictability, lameness and, astoundingly, yet another tingle of arousal.

'Don't worry, bro.' Harry slapped his back, dragging Jake back into his grim reality. 'It'll be okay. I think you're dead brave for speaking up. I . . . you might have a point. I'll see what I can do about the campaign, yeah?'

Jake nodded, blinking away the one tear that had broken through.

'You go get a seat; I'll head to the bar.'

Rana looked amazing. Men peered over the shoulders of their girlfriends at her as she made her way to an empty table in a corner. The bar area was busy, a leather-fronted semicircle of impatience and persistence, with red-faced men waving debit cards in the hope of being noticed. As Jake waited to be served – he was more patient these days, even though he hated queuing; shame Callum wasn't here to snap his fingers – he looked out at the crowded room. Straight couples, mainly. A few girls' nights out and, in the corner where Rana was sitting, a group of men doubled up in laughter at their own crummy jokes – that explained the empty table. He watched everyone, women nibbling on their boyfriends' ears and men lethargically grabbing their behinds in response, the brashness, the lack of care or self-consciousness, everyone competing to be the loudest and boldest in the room. A man dropped a pint glass and a horde of onlookers cheered like they were at a cup final. This was how it was, wasn't it? How it had always been. But Jake saw it through a different filter now. The atmosphere in the room was as much about the people who *weren't* here. There was a feeling of belonging, a confidence, a sense they knew this was their world. Obviously there was plenty of that in gay clubs, but they too had that thing in common that bound them all. Where did Jake fit in? He was a double agent, an assimilator even – after only a few minutes there, walking back to Rana, drinks in hand, he was conscious of a swagger he'd never noticed before. He had slipped back into autopilot. What was that song the guy in halls with a heavy fringe used to play loud at night, for a whole week after his girlfriend dumped him? Come back to what you know, it said. And he had, so quickly. Back to the world he'd known but never got on with. It felt like a betrayal – to Evan, Bertie and Callum. Amelia, too. How easy it would be to be the old Jake again. Rana was obviously *interested* and he enjoyed being with her. What harm would it do? But it would be repeating the process and he knew right then that eventually, whether it was weeks, months or years, he would be having that conversation again – to a different face, leaving a nasty taste in someone else's mouth. And yet when she said, 'Do you want to come back to mine?', he couldn't say no because, despite his doubts, he really wanted to.

Rana was the only woman Jake had slept with except Amelia in five years. He'd forgotten how good it could be, how exciting. The feeling of a new body, not being able to guess what it would do next. The unpredictability, like that scrape, pressure and sting of putting new shoes on for the first time – the thrill and beauty of the newness outweighing the comfort of the familiar. After, as they lay in silence listening to traffic outside, he marvelled at having sex with a woman again so soon after Amelia. He hadn't expected that. He felt at ease with Rana; he knew what he was doing, didn't have to hide. That's inequality for you, he thought.

He felt what he always felt when attracted to a woman: a lurch in his stomach, a somersault, a rush of affection, an urge to be next to them, make them laugh, charm them. With men, it had been different. He felt a heat, a tingling, a coyness he hoped would radiate and make him the one they wanted to charm.

He remembered an excruciating moment in a bar recently where a guy had asked him what he was drinking.

'Uh, beer?'

The man had scrunched his eyes up and persisted. '*Yes*, but what? As in . . . would you like one?'

'You want to buy me a drink?'

'Yes!' The man had moved closer.

'Why?'

The man had sighed. 'Because I've inherited a million pounds but the only condition is I have to spend it all before midnight. Why do you *think*?'

And then Jake had realised he was being chatted up, properly, made a move on, by a man. It felt different. He'd tried to make his face match his excitement but by then the man had turned his back and was talking to someone else.

He'd heard someone – Glanville, probably – say bisexual people were greedy, but it wasn't that. They knew the best of both worlds, and the worst. If anything, they had a fuller picture of what it was like to be attractive, aroused and alive. Jake couldn't believe he'd wasted so much time living half a life, closing off the east wing, letting his emotions be dormant, with a cloth over them. No more.

He stroked Rana's bare skin and felt her breathing settle into contentment, and he realised the truth: the lurch he felt wasn't strong enough with Rana. It was all there, in the right place, but it was the wrong time. He remembered Amelia's words that night in the kitchen.

'Don't pretend the reason we're over is *because* you're bi. You wanna go and sleep with other people' He'd proven her right, barely explored at all. He just didn't want *her* any more. What a coward he was. Jake moved Rana off him gently, trying not to disturb her, but she sat up quickly, watching him pull on his clothes, getting caught up his trousers in a whirl of frustration. That it was midnight and about 27 degrees didn't help.

Rana finally spoke. 'You going, then? You can stay, y'know.'

'I can't.' He gritted his teeth and tried not to say more in case he made it worse. All he could hear was Amelia, her voice in his head, her face before his eyes.

'Look . . . I know about the bisexual thing, you know. I don't care. You're cool.'

Bloody Lisa. The compliment crushed him even more. 'Thank you. It's not that. Honestly. And it's not you. I just . . . '

Rana struck a match and lit a candle. The smell of fire filled the room. 'Your ex, then? You still love her?'

It was easier to say yes. Rana pulled the covers up round her and looked away. 'It's okay. Me too. With my ex, I mean. I thought you were different, that's all.'

So had he.

'I'm sorry. I . . . hope this won't make things difficult.'

'At work?' Rana's eyes glimmered in the candlelight. 'Don't *worry*. I won't make things difficult for you. I like my job too much.'

Jake felt so shitty and noxious, he had no choice but to tear out of the room without looking back.

*

Kia never wanted to hear the word 'picnic' again. It had acquired a ridiculous quality now, like when you're drunk and say your own name over and over and realise how weird it is that your name is basically a sound – that it may as well be clicks, whistles or gentle purrs. Shame, really, as all Kia wanted to do was head to the supermarket, buy pre-packed sandwiches and cider and sit on the common and enjoy the gorgeous weather, but mentioning picnics to Trick brought it all up again. At first, he was angry, dismissing Jake as clueless, but after a while, he took it to heart. Kia saw his face change as he processed it, questioning himself. For this latest therapy session, they were cross-legged on one of Hot Will's mum's cashmere throws, on the scrubbier part of Tooting Common by the railway. As Hot Will was the only one who was legal – he looked the oldest, anyway – and had what Kia called 'a straight-septable air', he was sent to buy more cider.

'Is it . . . am I?' Kia steeled herself as Trick tried to get the words out. 'Is my life a *picnic*? Am I . . . y'know, privileged?'

The trouble with this question, in Kia's experience, was that people having to ask it undoubtedly were and, also, usually preferred to remain ignorant of that fact. She'd seen many a friend's face crumple – like a child prematurely realising Santa couldn't possibly get into their house through the central heating – when they realised they were drowning in it. So she was kind because, well, otherwise it got awkward and she had no time for that. She faced her friend, taking his hands in hers.

'Your own experience has *not* been a picnic. To me, Jake envies your freedom, how you express. He doesn't have it in him. I bet his underwear needs replacing, too.'

'But am I privileged? Isn't *Jake* the privileged one?'

Kia sighed. Why was everyone such hard work? 'It's not a competition. You're both lucky in your own ways. Privileged, yeah. All it means is less bad things happen to you than to other people, but bad things *do* still happen. So, yeah, be grateful, and try to deal with the problems you do have and . . . '

'And what?'

Kia looked at her friend to take the full force of his expression, which read, as plain as day, 'not getting it'. Would he ever? And how? 'And be nice to people who have more problems than you.' If he could ever work out who that was, of course.

'But what am I gonna do about . . . ?'

'Forget him for now.' Kia squeezed Trick's hand as she saw Hot Will returning. 'It'll be fine.' This wouldn't be solved in a day, and she didn't want to die trying.

*

Airports and hangovers. God, no. Jake's head pounded; he was at that stage of dehydration and tiredness where mild panic starts to set in, and every twinge is immediately triaged by your brain. Heart attack? Indigestion? Yellow fever? No, several hundred bellinis, porn star martinis and, inexplicably, at 2 a.m., that pint of lager that always seems like a good idea but is, in fact, the cheque your body can't cash. Callum kept the drinks flowing, and Jake became sick of saying, 'But I have to go to Brussels for work in the morning.'

'You're only thirty once,' Callum squealed after Jake declined the chance of an after-party.

'I know, but tomorrow I'm gonna feel thirty twice over. Sixty, I mean.'

'Yes,' hissed Callum, his gallop well and truly halted. 'I can add, thanks.' He kissed Jake lightly on the cheek and left him to his taxi, skulking off with Glanville in search of something, or someone, more exciting.

The terminal teemed with a cast of thousands hand-selected to annoy Jake as much as possible. Every baby he looked at screamed in response, pensioners ambled along watching videos out loud on their phones; he was half-expecting a marching band to strike up and parade through the terminal. Jake blinked away sweat and squinted at his cracked phone screen, scrolling through emails to find the booking reference Rana had sent to him.

Here you go, Jake. Safe flight.

No kiss. He punched his reference number into the automatic check-in machine. Then his phone screen went blank. He shook the phone to wake it up but it didn't respond. He must've forgotten to charge it. Perhaps the constant buzz of well-wishers sending him birthday congratulations had forced it into meltdown. The last one he remembered seeing the night before was from Hannah.

Hannah: Jake my fave you keep phoning me from your pocket. hope your/you're/UR having fun and fyi je suis furious you didn't invite me.

Happy birthday for tmrw you
handsome bastard.
When we celebrating? xx

'Why is your phone off?' A voice ahead of him. Shiny black shoes in his eyeline. Not Lisa. Not Lisa at all. A *man*. Jake looked up – a considerable effort as his head felt like it was filled with wet cement – and saw . . . Harry.

'What are *you* doing here?'

Lisa's husband had been in an accident – not serious, but with a broken limb so Lisa was on hand to help her beloved navigate their insanely tall and narrow townhouse with more steps than Bell Rock Lighthouse.

'So the trip's off?'

Harry shook his head and gestured toward a disappointingly shabby cabin-sized suitcase. 'Nah. I'm coming! Boys on tour. It's gonna be magic.'

Since the disagreement – and subsequent détente – over the storyboard, Jake somehow felt his interest in Harry renewed. This was the last distraction he needed, so he tried to suppress this unwelcome reignited sexual desire by picking out things about Harry he *didn't* like. Surprisingly, it wasn't that hard, noticing quirks that either weren't present before or had been obscured by his unrequited lust. He was an elaborate swearer, for one. Nobody was ever a wanker or a dickhead, but a 'cock-womble' or a 'spunk-trombone'. The first three hundred times it was amusing, but as his compounds got more laboured, it became twee and witless. Deeply unsexy. Jake imagined Harry and his turned-up-collar friends knocking back frothy pints of 'beerage' and coming up with new ways of calling a spade anything but. The image turned his stomach, irritation spreading through Jake like a poison. He tried to imagine Harry's peach-perfect butt sagging before his eyes – although it did no such thing, it was a masterpiece in navy polyester – or the adorable dimple in his chin morphing into a crude gash. Jake liked to pretend Harry's eyes were dull, expressionless buttons, not shiny and charming; that any power Harry had over Jake was draining fast. And yet, as they boarded the plane and Harry fucked about with his luggage in the overhead locker three rows in front, then sat in the seat intended for Lisa, Jake felt a tremor reverberate through his body. The familiar dread, excitement and nervousness – and, yes, the *heat* – but with a twist. There was history, a precedent. Their first trip alone since all those years ago in Cologne. Jake's eyes bored into his iPad, the concentration of his stare the only thing keeping the plane in flight, he told himself, but his mind kept replaying Harry's own eyes locking with his, in that room, in Cologne. His breathing clear as a bell in Jake's ears, like they were still there. Luckily, present-day Harry broke this reverie, spilling pineapple juice down his front during the one millisecond of turbulence. 'God, what a fuck-pony I am,' he exclaimed, and Jake's purely fraternal feelings were temporarily restored.

'So!' Harry sighed as the two men flopped into the back of the waiting car after a day of meetings, which ponged of whatever cigarette the driver had just extinguished. 'We hitting the town?'

Jake's hangover was in for the long haul. 'Hmmm, not for me.'

Harry looked disappointed. 'Aw, come on. Night out will do you the world of good. Why are you so hungover anyway?'

Telling Harry it was his birthday sounded ridiculous after not mentioning it all day.

Harry slapped Jake's knee. '*What*? We *have* to celebrate. Look, if you're too fuckeroonied for Brussels, let's go to the hotel to get elegantly slaughtered.'

Drunk. In a hotel. On mainland Europe. With Harry. Uh-oh. Sequels were never as good as the first one, were they?

'I'll expense it! Lisa owes me.'

'I don't know why she made you come; I could've done it on my own. No offence!'

The car swerved into the hotel driveway. Harry looked sheepish. 'My idea. I said it was unfair to send you by yourself. Especially on your birthday.'

So he *had* known. Opting not to ruin the moment, Jake didn't flag it, but it made his heart beat faster. 'Thank you.'

Harry's voice dropped an octave and became more beguiling, harmonising with the hum of the engine, the silence shocking them when it was suddenly switched off. 'We gotta look out for each other, haven't we? Boys on tour.'

The hotel bar's atmosphere made the local mortuary look like Rio de Janeiro at Mardi Gras, the sole bartender resenting their presence as he shook cocktails – well, more lightly rattled.

Harry was unfazed, knocking back drinks like he was in Ibiza. 'I . . . er . . . saw you and Rana getting cosy. I was jealous, tell the truth.'

Jake concentrated so hard on the napkin in front of him he expected it to fly across the room. Fucking hell. What? W . . . wow. *Jealous?* His voice was helium-sharp. 'Were you?'

'Course. Rana's the fittest girl in the office. How was it?'

Jake's lungs deflated. Back to banter. 'A gentleman never tells.' He was glad Rana didn't either. 'Too soon after Amelia.'

'Oh, mate.'

Harry didn't do commiserating; he was a congratulator, a back-slapper. He was always the first to leave meetings that contained bad news.

'Hang on.' Harry went to the bar, returning three minutes later with a bottle of champagne. 'It's your birthday. You're *free*. Let's celebrate.' Back in congratulatory mode so quickly, Jake mused; he probably wore cartoon socks to funerals.

'Harry . . . '

'Told ya. Expensing it. I'll clear it with Lisa.'

Jake believed him; nobody in the office could resist that charm.

'Let's head up to the room, play some music.' Harry jerked his head to the exit. A lock of hair fell over his face with impeccable timing.

Jake's blood suddenly felt volcanic. 'Uh, *whose* room?'

Harry shrugged. 'Any.' Then, registering Jake's expression, broke into a smile half lascivious, half sheepish. 'Um, I'll leave my laptop closed this time.'

A first acknowledgement of what happened in Cologne! This evening was full of wows. Did Harry think about it often? Did it . . . mean anything? The hurricane in Jake's head spiralled. He stood, slowly, and walked to the lift, trying not to strut. He didn't know what would happen next and, for once, he was perfectly fine with that.

Jake had always been suspicious of the term 'one thing led to another'. What did it even mean? Of course one thing would lead to another – it's how time worked, everything had to go somewhere. Harry watched, eyes dark and unreadable – but not hostile – as Jake searched for his socks and tried to understand what had just happened.

'Do you have to go?' drawled Harry, oozing post-champagne and ejaculation confidence.

Jake tried to keep his voice light. 'It'd look a bit weird creeping out of the room in the morning.' No weirder than making his escape at one in the morning, he thought, as he buttoned up his shirt.

At first they had talked about nothing in particular, slating MTZ and their basic hospitality budget – the hotel room was the usual soulless magazine chic of the corporate layover, walls painted one shade brighter than pigswill – before things had taken a deeper turn. Harry was glad to see the back of Melissa, he said, but lonely. Very lonely. The 'very' felt like a threat. Then he gave a strangled cough and said, 'I hope you don't mind me asking . . . '

Here we go, thought Jake.

'You know you're bisexual, yeah? What's it . . . like? Kissing a dude?'

The 'dude' felt unnecessarily masculine for the moment, like Harry was double-daring his mates in the pub. Dudes. Blokes. No matter what Charlie and the other stags said, Jake had never been one, never been *it*. His dad's mates were blokes, their heterosexuality unspoken yet all-encompassing, and their sons – carbon copies who they'd all 'die for', unless the football was on – were *lads*. 'Out with the lads.' Jake was lost in thoughts of denim, T-shirt tans and over-gelled fringes when he realised Harry was waiting for an answer. Maybe if Harry had to repeat it he'd lose his nerve. But he didn't. He said it again.

'Well, it's . . . Why do you want to know?'

Harry leaned closer and suddenly the vestigial pong of his cheap deodorant was the most alluring smell on earth, like his pheromones got the biggest glow-up ever and all turned up at once to show a fuckboy ex what he'd been missing. The champagne coated his tongue, but Jake spoke clearly as he asked again. 'Why?'

Jake felt himself propelled into the future, watching this scene play out over and over. Would this come back to haunt him throughout his life, like teenage photographs, wearing skinny jeans hanging halfway down his arse and a checked cardigan? He'd read novels, seen the coming-of-age movies: would his sexuality forever be a training ground for straight men who had three drinks and 'a couple of questions'. Harry, however, had just the one: 'Is it different?'

This was the dream, wasn't it? The crush finally saying the magic words? He found himself saying, 'Do you want me to tell you – or show you?'

Harry answered with actions, not words.

Harry was an aggressive kisser – it was always the way at first, Jake was learning – and Jake remembered the odd, disconcerting, yet fantastic feeling of Harry over him.

Harry's body did, as far as he could tell, live up to its promise, but at first Jake was afraid to touch it for more than milliseconds at a time, in case any prolonged contact instigated gay panic, or regret, or broke Harry out of the magic spell that made him want to do this. As Harry's kisses got wilder, Jake got braver, and he let his hands rest longer on Harry's arse or cling to his back, and as he felt Harry's firm shoulders press into his own, the impossibility of it made him more excited. White cotton shirts, meeting-room tables, comedy-club banquettes and seatbelts in taxis had kept them respectably apart for years, but, Jake realised now, as Harry's sweat mixed with his, the heat between them had never cooled. Since Cologne, it had felt one-sided, something to make Jake ashamed. Long nights spent awake trying to rationalise what had felt like a hallucination. Once, he'd got up in the middle of the night and looked in his old work diary on his laptop to check he'd been to Cologne at all, running the date over in his mind. What had he worn? What had he eaten? Had he really looked down into Harry's lap and seen what he'd seen that night, or was he home alone, in the UK, wishing it true? Now, he pulled Harry in so tight not even a thread of cotton could get between them, and Harry responded, pushing back until both their chests ached. It had been real, all of it, all along, Jake knew. This was the night they'd been waiting for. Harry clasped his hands round Jake's face and their eyes locked. The deal was done. Fuck, thought Jake, while Harry collapsed on to him; this is what it's supposed to feel like.

They lay next to each other poker-straight. The room's eerie silence interrupted only by the soft rustle of Harry wiping himself dry with the sheet.

'So now I know,' blurted Harry.

'Now we *both* know.'

'It was cool.' A pause. 'I'm not sure . . . ' His words trailed off into the dark.

Jake decided to make it easy for him. 'Not something you'd need to do again, though?'

Harry was silent for a while, then: 'I'm not saying that. But . . . '

Despite the inevitable distancing, Jake felt strangely bound to Harry in that moment. He wanted to protect Harry from the self-loathing that had dogged him for years. 'It's fine.'

The champagne bucket gleamed as a car drove by, its headlights flashing into the room.

'It was . . . uh, nice, though, definitely. Different,' said Harry as Jake finally located that errant sock. 'I'm not gay, you know.'

Christ. 'No, I know, Harry. Neither am I, remember?' He debated whether to go back and kiss him. He really wanted to. His head pulsed as he mulled it over. Go back go back go back. He might kiss you back. But, no, he didn't want to push it. Click.

Nice. Different. Quite the five-star review. Jake smiled all the way down the corridor, feeling musky and tingly, until he reached his own room; here the walls were painted the most depressing shade of panic attack – green with faux-cheery yellow paintwork and borders. He felt woozy. His balls ached, and the end of his dick prickled with nostalgia and disappointment that it was over. That was the trouble with dreams coming true – what did you pray for next?

At breakfast the next morning, Harry arrived second and sat at another table. During the morning's meetings, he was silent, not even trying to pick holes in Jake's proposals like he usually did. It was as though Harry was suddenly scared of him. Jake tried to catch his eye a few times, and when successful Harry would smile back awkwardly. Jake couldn't help but chuckle inwardly at Harry sitting as far away from him as possible in the cab back to the airport. He was tempted to lean over and say, 'Too late to be shy, mate; I've already seen your cum-face', but instead he wound down the window and watched the breeze pummel Harry's hair as he fruitlessly tried to smooth it back into place. The reassigning of power was cute, but Jake couldn't help but feel used. He didn't want to be an experiment or a one-off. In the departure lounge, Harry concentrated on his book – reading a grand total of four pages, Jake saw – and on the plane home he sat on a different row so he could stretch his legs. On landing, Harry slapped him on the back, gave a cheery, 'See you, mate', and jumped into a taxi. On the way home, Jake leaned back in the cab and closed his eyes, the print of Harry's hand still burning his back.

eighteen.

Ramón was Bertie's oldest friend, but he'd never understood why Bertie's weeknights were taken up with escorting younger men to the theatre or propping up bars looking for conversation.

'But, darling, you don't even like younger men. What do you *get* from this? Why do you care what young queers think or do? Leave them to it.'

Bertie always shrugged. 'I don't want to lose touch. I find younger *people* interesting. Not just men.'

Ramón excised a bit of fluff from his otherwise immaculate lapel. 'It's a waste of time. You're out every night with these entitled *millennials*, or whatever. Then they go home to have sex while you're on the last Northern Line home, hoping the cat hasn't crapped in the hallway.'

'The cat always goes in the litter tray. And it's not about sex.' Which it wasn't. Bertie loved his friends, but many of them had disappeared into their own bubble, like they'd wrung out all the outside world had to offer and wanted to exist only in a world of members' bars, expensive holidays and high-carb dinners in vulgar restaurants – their lives ruled by opulence and indigestion. Bertie, however, did the same job he'd always done and still lived in that small flat in Crouch End, and he was happy. They'd all evolved, which was great, but he didn't aspire to be on their level. He wasn't sure it was worth the effort.

'You'll get a reputation as a creepy old man. A funny uncle. There's always an ulterior motive.'

'Not for me.' Bertie smiled, more out of habit. They had this conversation a lot. 'Getting old is an honour. Being around people my own age who don't *realise* that is much more draining than kids who never think twice about it.'

From where Bertie was sitting, perched on his chaise longue while Jake lounged on his sofa, swamped by cushions, Jake's Brussels trip sounded wonderful, and very different from the time Bertie finally managed to unravel the layers of the onion that was *his* straight crush's sexuality. He still remembered the awkward wriggling of that long-lusted-after body all over him, a hairy, jittery xylophone clattering against his ribs. The kisses, fantasised over for what felt like centuries, had been too wet, soft and brief – designed to satisfy a checklist but not arouse. His crush had been too rough, yet hesitant, and Bertie realised he could've been anyone; this was not, as it was for him, a long-awaited meeting of bodies and melding of fantasies. It was functional. The crush wanted to make sense of his urges, and Bertie had been there. Like Jake, he'd gathered his clothes and stolen off into the night – albeit out on to the bustling grime of Hackney Road and not a chocolate-mousse-carpeted hotel corridor in Brussels.

'How do you feel about it now?'

Jake sat his mug down on the coffee table. On a coaster,

too, Bertie noticed; this boy hadn't been dragged up, whatever faults his family had. 'Excited. But confused. Harry is obviously ashamed.'

'How do you know? Has he told you?' So much of early experiences of same-sex shagging was guesswork and cod psychology, full of assumption and embarrassment. 'Is it different from the other time? When you watched the video together?' The video. *Video*. Showing his age, Ramón would say.

'He totally ignored me then. He's not now. Just . . . funny little smiles and he even does gun fingers at me. I think I preferred awkward silence to the forced jollity. I feel a bit . . . used.'

Bertie remained patient and made a mental note to double-check on Google later that 'gun fingers' was not a death threat. 'Has he been mean?'

'No.'

'Okay, well . . . I sense awkwardness. If he's not turned to violence or tried to silence you . . . ' Bertie flinched, recalling the bloody nose his crush had given him once he'd realised what he'd just done ' . . . then maybe he's not sure how to deal with it. How to deal with *you*. What do you want? Another run?'

Jake smiled. 'I wonder sometimes if it was worth it. Not in a . . . depressing way, but . . . it's all very confusing. Did Harry only do this because I said I was bisexual? Would it have happened anyway? Life was simpler when I was with Amelia.'

Bertie drained his cup. 'It most certainly was not. For either of you. Can I speak frankly?' Jake nodded. 'I don't want to say it's all about being young because it *isn't* but sometimes it feels like it *is*. This power you have, the magnetism, it's temporary. A blink. I'm not saying go have lots of sex because it's not just about shagging, but have *some* and have it without regret. Don't take it for granted. Have a think about Harry and what his actions might mean.' He registered Jake's bewildered expression. 'I know. I'm wasting my breath. I wouldn't listen to me either. I didn't. I got this talk from some weary old queen in Soho one night. Sunken cheeks but bright eyes. I ignored it. That's what being young is all about. Ignore the advice, ignore *me*. Make it your own.'

Jake sat back and nodded, like he was taking it all in. Bertie saw relief wash over his face. This was what he liked about Jake, and his other young friends; they made you feel so wise, with your only qualifications being you'd made bigger, stupider mistakes a generation before them, and hadn't learned a thing.

Jake had wondered whether to swerve Trick's eighteenth birthday. Aside from popping in to collect a card and a worried kiss from his mother, Jake's thirtieth passed without remark, the idea of reliving younger days in the carvery forgotten. It was easier, Jake decided, to lie low and let them gather their thoughts, or mourn the son they'd assumed he was going to be, or whatever they were doing. Bertie had insisted he go to Trick's birthday, though.

'Bury the hatchet with your folks, and not in their back.'

The stag weekend approached, too, making Jake even more nervous – at least he knew how his family operated, as painful as it could be. The rampant stags, led by ham-faced Miles, however, were an unknown quantity. Even Bertie admitted it would be tough. 'Death by toxic heterosexuality. But you must go, be there for Charlie. He's your best friend and he needs you.'

'I know.' Jake felt ashamed he was even thinking about

backing out. 'I don't feel I can be myself with that lot. My friends remind me of who I used to be. Ask so many questions.' He couldn't remember the last time he'd seen Hannah, either. 'And . . . when I'm with guys, like you and Evan and . . . my other friends . . . I'm happy. You *get* me.'

Bertie felt winded by the rom-com sentiment but smiled at Jake kindly. 'Look, they might not get who you are *now*, but don't write them off. You need "forever friends", trust me; someone who knew you before, who gets your essence. Now, go, get Trick an amazing present, turn up, and put the badness behind you.'

Bertie was right, plus maybe now Trick was officially a man, they'd understand each other better. Jake laughed at his own delusion – all men were a mystery to him, why should his baby brother be any different? Vee had hired the function room above a restaurant in Elephant and Castle and promised Trick 'all the boring people' would make their exit by 9 p.m. Margo told Jake that Trick was on edge about the party being a flop. His usual nonsense. Trick had never thrown an under-attended party in his life. His gatherings were a hot ticket; every year they became more ostentatious, crammed with internet friends, close associates and, of course, his 'crew'. Jake was fleetingly engulfed by envy as he remembered Trick's birthdays past – picnics in parks that turned into mini Glastonburys, wild barbecues with people clamouring at the gate to get in – anything he wanted, as soon as he asked. Jake, however, asked for nothing, and he got it.

It was burning hot outside – it had rained only once in the last month and London was melting and irritable, so Jake was sweating when he arrived. His mum was relieved to see him, a quick look between his parents established that the last Sunday roast, and Jake's absence since, was not to be mentioned.

'You've come at the right time. The last balloon has just been blown up. Thank God I don't smoke any more; my lungs would be shot.'

Jake let the fib go and hugged them both warily, as you'd embrace someone wearing an explosive vest. The room was already hotting up; with over a hundred teenage bodies in there it would soon be like the last hours of Pompeii.

'I should say hello to Trick.' His parents looked at each other.

'Maybe leave it a while; he doesn't really like being approached until he's had enough time to pretend he hasn't seen you.'

'Of course.' Jake remembered his brother's entitlement could be seen from space, his charitable thoughts evaporating. He kept Bertie's words close.

Once the place started filling up and he'd tired of Margo moaning about her lack of social life – she was literally about to go to Barcelona, for God's sake – Jake made his way over to Trick, who was in the corner with Hot Will, leafing through birthday cards like Ariana Grande would her fan mail. Jake handed over the card and gift, remembering last year's, expertly wrapped by Amelia. His attempt was a little less refined, but he hoped the contents would make up for it.

Trick took the package like it was a landmine. He may have been mad at his brother but he was still brought up to be grateful. 'Thank you.' Jake sensed the effort was killing him.

Hot Will said his hellos – every syllable loaded with intent, as usual – and watched as Trick carefully unwrapped the present, saw the boxes, then looked back up at Jake.

'Seriously, this is great.'

Jake felt ancient as he stuttered his way through the gift's main selling points – some kind of contraption to make any video you took on-the-go broadcast quality that'd taken the woman in the shop a good twenty minutes to explain, and a microphone for voiceovers. 'I hope this is okay. Do you already have those?'

Hot Will surveyed the haul. 'We do, but not ones as good as these, to be honest. What do you say, Trick?'

Trick was blushing as he glanced from Hot Will to Jake. 'Yes. Really sick. Brilliant. Thank you.'

Hot Will laughed. 'Give him a hug, then!'

Approaching each other as you would a hungry guard dog, yet both compelled to do as they were told, the brothers embraced. Jake could see hanging around any longer would cause Trick to combust with embarrassment, so he made his excuses and moved away.

Vee took her son's arm. 'How did it go?'

Jake watched Trick clasp Hot Will's elbow in delight, eyes glowing. 'Success! I think.'

The room reached rainforest humidity by 9 p.m. Jake looked out on to the dance floor and saw Margo pouring a bright orange drink down her neck, egged on by two girls who looked about fourteen.

After another forty-five minutes, he could stand the heat, music and incessant screaming no more, so grabbed a pint – he'd lost count of how many he was on – and went outside. The pavement was packed with more teenagers screeching about slaying, faves, how 'dead' they were and Trick's ranking among the world's greatest sass queens. Jake was about to go back inside and brave the tropics when he saw a metal staircase – a fire escape, he guessed – and climbed it cautiously, every step creaking, as the crowd below carried on acting like he was invisible. At the top, there was a kind of terrace, and a door which, Jake now realised, led back into the party he'd just been so anxious to abscond from. Jake tried to catch his breath, which quickly left him once he saw he was not alone.

Hot Will was standing at the farthest end, taking a long, dramatic pull on a cigarette and looking out at the view – which was no view at all, as it was almost dark, only a few strands of fiery sunset remaining. Streetlights twinkled. Jake saw he was shivering, which seemed odd; it was just as hot outside as it had been indoors. No, not shivering. Trembling. Hot Will had seen him come up.

'Hello.'

Hot Will spun round, feigning surprise. Jake had heard he was going to Manchester to study drama, which was fortunate; his acting needed serious work.

'Hello,' said Hot Will. 'We always end up alone at Trick's birthdays, don't we?'

Jake gave an awkward laugh and looked over his shoulder as if debating whether to leave. 'Yeah.'

'What a year it's been, eh?' Jake grunted in response. 'Can I ask you something?'

'You just did, didn't you?' Jake smiled and winked.

Hot Will laughed politely at the dad-joke. Again. 'Very good. I'll ask anyway. What's your type?'

'My type?'

'Yeah. Since you . . . you know, came to the dark side. Or, like, part of you did, anyway. What's your *thing*? What kinda men are you into?'

Jake's tongue was lead. 'Well, Will . . . sorry, Hot Will, I've never thought about it.' A lie. 'I don't think I have a type.' And another. 'Why ask?'

'I like talking. You'll just go with *anything* then, is it?'

Jake laughed nervously. 'No. I haven't really . . . uh . . . met anyone that I'd call my type.'

'Ah.' The flinty scratch of the lighter being sparked. 'No tunes in your playlist, yet, then?'

Every muscle in Jake's body was clenched. A toffee-hammer could shatter him. Any response would be a trap, like being back in marketing seminars all over again. 'If you like.'

Hot Will placed the unlit cigarette in his hand back in the packet and moved a step toward Jake, who instinctively edged back a little. Where was this going?

Jake took a deep breath. 'This . . . sense of self you have. Some might call it barefaced cheek. Admirable. I'm kind of envious. Why are you up here alone?'

Hot Will's mouth dallied with the idea of smiling. 'Boy trouble.' He moved closer again.

Jake inched back slightly, stomach churning, adrenalin surging and making him feel dizzy. This was unexpected; Jake wasn't sure he wanted to get this deep. He didn't remember ever inhabiting this much space, or being as frank as Hot Will was, until he was well into his twenties, let alone a teenager. As Hot Will's face loomed, he saw another instead: Trick's. His eyes shining at Hot Will's touch, his immediate reaction to – and compliance with – Hot Will's requests. 'Is it something to do with my brother?'

'Fuck, no. Trick's my best friend. My boy. Why would *we* be together?' Hot Will raised a brow. 'Because we're both gay? Do you have sex with *all* your friends now that you're bi?'

He had him there. 'I mean, well, no. But I assumed . . . you're all quite . . . tactile. Don't you ever wonder if something might happen between you?'

Hot Will disregarded the question. 'We're not that different, you and me.' This felt like a line practised often, alone in his room; his voice was shaking now. Jake could see Hot Will had no idea where this was going either.

'We're *very* different. I'm old enough to be your dad.' His voice sounded weird inside his own head.

'Only if you were a very early starter; I'm nineteen in September. No, I mean, you're just out, it's only a year or two for me. Not even. It's a Year Zero thing. We're equals.'

'What's Year Zero?' Jake braced himself for a graphic explanation of some weird sex act Hot Will had seen on Tumblr.

'Got it from some dating blogger. Stages, not ages. Like, we come out at different times in our life, so it's about what stage you're at, not your *age*. See? And you're, like, Year Zero, fresh out the box. I'm not too far ahead. Like, zero-point-five.'

Jake felt sweat trickle down his back. 'I'm thirty.'

'Don't be basic. I'm not into you because you're a *daddy*, or whatever. I'm into you because you're *you*.'

Whoa. What? Did he . . . ? Jake stepped back, suddenly feeling much more sober. 'You're *into* me?'

Hot Will tutted and finally lit that cigarette, before offering Jake one. He took it. 'I'm afraid so.'

A stream of sweat down his back now. How to play this? 'You are *very* confident.'

'Yeah, you said.'

Jake's mind raced. What if it were a young woman Hot Will's age saying these things, up here alone? He'd have run a mile already, wouldn't he? Jake remembered some girls in his year at school had much older boyfriends. Gawky manbabies, their only advantages a driving licence, the need of an electric razor and one-third of some rented dive in Lewisham. This array of losers would line up outside school in their clapped-out motors, leering out of the window at their approaching victims. Jake would watch them drive away, horns blaring and music blasting, and resolved never to be like them. Why was this, now, any different? But flirting with men was new – being flirted at *by* them even newer. Scarier. He didn't know the rules. How did you let someone down gently without it getting ugly? Year Zero? Every *day* was zero, blank page after blank page. Jake realised he was weighing this up for much longer than was appropriate, and that Hot Will was waiting for him to say something. 'You're at school. It would be creepy; you are *eighteen*.'

'Stop firing *numbers* at me, man. I don't *care*. I did my last exam a *month* ago. In a few weeks I'll be at university. Shall we book something in for then?' Hot Will put himself in front of Jake and took his wrist; the noise of the surrounding teens began to fade in and out. Jake could feel Hot Will's pulse pumping alongside his own, both slightly out of time with each other. Distorted echoes. Jake could also sense Hot Will's vulnerability, despite all his swagger. Jake was new to this, yes, and trembling as much as Hot Will, but he knew that no matter how cinematic the moment, this could go no further. Not just for himself, or even Hot Will, whose only scars would be from his own mortification in the morning, but for Trick. It was all Jake could think of at that second: Trick; Trick; Trick. He knew unrequited passion when he saw it, had felt it often enough. And Trick had it, bad.

'Will . . . ' He paused to think; this had to land right. 'We all make mistakes when we're drunk; I don't think this would be a good mistake for either of us. But especially for—'

Suddenly, another voice: 'Hot Will, Trick is doing the presentation now.'

The pair of them whirled round to see Hannah standing in the fire-exit doorway, leaning against the frame with exhaustion, like she'd done a day down the salt mines.

Jake could hear his own breathing: shallow, hesitant. Then Trick appeared behind Hannah at the door.

'Han, what's . . . ? Hot Will? Is that . . . ?'

Hannah sighed deeply, backing into the room and yanking the door towards her. 'It's nobody, babe; I just wanted some air.' Slam.

Hot Will spoke first. 'I'd better . . . '

'Yeah, look, I'm sorry – I'm flattered . . . ' Flattered! So patronising. 'But it wouldn't be right.' Hot Will looked offended. 'No, I mean, I'm sure it would've been lovely.' Lovely! The most daytime TV of compliments; he saw Hot Will's nose wrinkle. 'But you and Trick have issues you need to address and . . . I only have one brother and I don't want to hurt him.'

Hot Will chuckled, his bravado returning. 'Aw, mate, you have no idea.'

Jake stayed put, holding his breath until he heard the jangle and clunk of Hot Will closing the fire exit behind him. He sensed he wasn't alone.

'Your hair's looking . . . higher.' Hannah. 'Is that intentional or does bisexuality make your hair naturally more voluminous? Maybe I should try it.'

Jake turned to his friend. She was glowering; she'd never looked at him like that before.

'In all honesty, fave . . . what are you up to?'

'Nothing! I swear! I've been . . . nervous about coming tonight. I got too drunk. We just got chatting.'

Hannah eyed him with suspicion. 'Look, I know you love your secret trysts, and fire escapes are, like, your kink, but this is too much.'

Jake forgot himself for a second. 'He told me he was *into* me. It was a weird moment. I got a bit lost in it.'

'So I saw.' Hannah's face hardened in impatience. 'Earth calling Jake. Seriously, Jake, there are . . . so many klaxons. Please don't double down on this. Don't make me denounce you in the tabloids.'

Jake had heard enough. 'You're making it sound dirty. You saw three seconds. We just *talked*. I'd never do anything to hurt Trick. I'm gonna get a cab.' He descended the staircase, miserably punching at his phone keypad.

Hannah ran after him. 'Jake! Look, we need to talk . . . '

Jake realised how drunk he was. 'We already have. You're not listening.' He kept walking.

Hannah watched him go, understanding less about her best friend than she ever had.

*

'I think I'd rather you got off with anyone else. My *dad*, even.'

Hot Will rubbed his eyes in the hope it would make everything disappear. It didn't. Trick was sitting bolt upright in bed, guyliner smudged, hair in disarray. A saturated canvas of misery and betrayal.

'Nothing happened. Our lips didn't touch. Your brother is still pure. I thought you didn't care about Jake, anyway.'

Trick's voice was small, closed. A decade of emotion compressed into seven words: 'I don't. But I care about you.'

Not this. Not again. Hot Will sighed and turned to see if Kia was awake yet. She wasn't – unless she was waiting to see how the conversation panned out before delivering her pronouncements. 'You and me are like brothers.'

'*Brothers*?' Trick's eyes flashed. 'We are *not*! I *hate* my brother.'

'No, you don't.' Hot Will got up and sat alongside Trick, nudging him until his friend's head fell on his shoulder. 'I'm not gonna say he's not that bad when you get to know him, cos you know that anyway. But . . . I'm sorry. I was drunk and made a tit of myself. Jake was a gentleman.'

'You know I love you, Hot Will.'

'I love you too, man. We're better than brothers, better than twins, even. We're soulmates. I guess . . . '

Trick's ears pricked up. 'What?'

Time for Hot Will to take it home but also make things clear. 'What me and you have is perfect, it's real. Fuck a friend and fuck it up is what I always say, you know that.'

The heat of Trick's resigned sigh caught Hot Will's neck. 'Yeah.'

'Come on, let's wake Kia, get some bubble tea and grade everyone's looks from last night.'

But Kia, he now saw, already had one eye open. How much had she heard? 'You did *what*, now?'

Oh. *That* much.

nineteen.

Amelia thought she'd seen the last of sad faces, panicked eyes, hushed tones and exaggerated coughing when she walked into a room. Finally, her friends were treating her like a normal person. Now, however, there was a whole new audience to her humiliation: the hens, Holly's clutch of pals who didn't know Amelia but had heard *plenty* about her. Amelia opted to rise above, reclining majestically in the sun, the essence of poise and restraint, while all around her, women who didn't get out much gargled lethal cocktails and talked about men. 'We spend too much time talking about dick,' Amelia said to Holly on the first night as they waited at baggage reclaim.

'*I* don't.' Rudi poked her head between them.

Holly painted on her best 'don't fuck with me' smile. She'd gone full fembot. 'Look, hon, I know, but it's a hen weekend. We talk about our boys, well, except for Rudi, and, you know if you . . . were still . . . ' Amelia almost enjoyed watching Holly tie herself up in knots. 'Um, *with* someone, you would too. Don't stress, babe. We're here for a good time, yeah?'

In other words, don't make a scene, or go on about hating

men, or spoil my romantic idyll. Amelia's smile didn't reach her eyes. 'Sure, Hol. You're right.'

As Holly walked away, Rudi leaned in for a hug. 'And . . . breathe.'

'What do you think it'll take for everyone to stop talking about their fellas?'

Rudi looked thoughtful. 'We should bring in a rule – like the Bechdel test.'

'Yeah, can we go an hour, maybe two, without any of the girls talking about a man?' Amelia toyed with the sunglasses in her hand like a cat batting a dead mouse. 'Know what, Rudes, I think I've failed that test every day of my life.'

Margo and Hannah had been what Amelia's mother would call 'civil' – the kind of conversation you'd have in the queue for a checkout. No mention of Jake. What did they think would happen if his name cropped up? That she'd claw at her empty ring finger, screaming, 'Whyyyyyyyy?'. On the roof terrace of a ridiculously expensive private members' club overlooking the harbour, Amelia now saw Margo and Hannah huddled in a corner, looking appalled by the experience. She quite wanted to go over and hang out. Would it be weird? She was about to get up when Holly sidled over, handing her a drink and some suncream.

'You need to top up, sweets,' she trilled. Holly had an incredible knack of making terms of endearments sound like threats.

Amelia knew Holly had something to say, but rather than coax it out, she sat spraying and rubbing lotion over her arms and legs, adrenaline surging in anticipation. Amelia found something deliciously sadistic about the silence, like waiting for a wasp to settle so you could squish it with an espadrille.

Eventually, however, the awkwardness became stifling, so she cracked.

'Hol, this place is gorgeous. How did you manage it?'

Holly gurned, her 'cocktail number four' face. 'Don't ask. I've made a lot of PR promises I hope my boss doesn't spot.' Holly surveyed the scene. 'I hope everyone behaves. You having fun?'

Amelia lied that she was. Holly smiled back like a saint. 'I was meaning to say. The wedding. I'm so *happy* you're gonna be there.' Her chirpy tone rang the faintest of alarm bells, but Amelia suppressed her irritation.

'You make it sound like I've got a terminal illness. I'm your bridesmaid. Where else would I be?'

'Of course, of course.' Holly made a face like she'd found an anchovy in a cupcake. 'But, well, I was saying to Charlie . . . if you wanted to swerve bridesmaid duty, we'd understand.'

Tempting, but Amelia wanted to make Holly work for this. 'Well, I don't. Choosing that sodding dress robbed me of three Saturdays I'll never get back.'

Holly blanched at this slight against the happiest day of her life. 'You're so funny!' Concerned face. 'But, yeah, with Jake being Charlie's best man, it might be hard for you . . . '

Amelia felt a rush of affection for Holly; she was trying her best, bless her. 'Aw, no, don't worry. I'm a big girl. We're both adults.'

Holly's face thunked from penthouse to basement in three seconds flat. 'No . . . um. Yes. Um. I mean, for Jake. I mean . . . now he's come out, a reminder of his past might be too painful.'

His past? Her, in other words. Amelia felt bilious. 'A *reminder*? Of *what*?'

'Well . . . being straight. Charlie says Jake's found it difficult to adjust. We don't want him feeling excluded.'

Amelia looked into the bottom of her glass, sad it was empty so she couldn't tip its contents over Holly's wilting flower crown. Here she was, at her hen weekend, which had cost a fortune, to be told she should respect her ex-boyfriend's feelings, only months after he'd hopped into a taxi and out of her life, on to his new one without a single word since. She'd put her possessions into storage, moved into Rudi's box room with her smallest suitcase, and schlepped around looking for a house-share – disappointed for her childhood self who'd expected to be a proud home-owner by now. It had been *hard*. She felt jilted, but with no wedding dress to try on when drunk and alone. Soon, she knew, she wouldn't feel Jake's absence at all. She already enjoyed watching what she wanted on TV, and taking her time as she went round the farmers' market, not having to deal with his aversion to long queues or his million over-compensating thank-yous to the hot guy on the olive stall at the market. But she did miss the security and invisibility being in a couple gave you. You didn't stick out, feel like a burden; you just *were*. Now, alone, here, she felt very seen. But avoiding awkward questions was no reason to stay in a crap relationship, which, Amelia had come to realise, hers had been.

She allowed a smile to bleed across her face. 'Hol, I'll do all I can to make Jake feel welcome. There's no hard feelings.' I'm not allowed any, she thought.

Holly looked relieved. 'He's been so *brave*, hasn't he? Charlie's worried they're losing touch. We want Jake to have a brilliant day. It's important to show solidarity.'

Amelia gave herself a surreptitious pinch to make sure this was actually happening.

'Yeah.' It was all she could manage.

Mission accomplished, Holly clinked her glass against Amelia's empty one, the resulting chime hollow and shrill, and slunk off to the other hens. Rudi, observing from across the terrace, narrowed her eyes and blew Amelia a kiss. Amelia returned it, and decided it was time to face the near-miss in-laws.

*

Hannah and Margo looked out from their corner.

'We're the only ones not in heels,' muttered Margo.

'Well, Barcelona is cobbly as fuck so they'll regret that.'

Margo shivered despite the heat. 'I wish we could smoke. Shall we nip downstairs and have one?'

'I don't smoke, Margs.'

Margo guffawed. 'Hannah! We've stood outside parties going twos-up on a fag since I was seventeen. Don't get it twisted. You're a social smoker.'

Hannah was about to protest when she saw Amelia on her way over.

An exchange of 'Hey!'s and other pleasantries, followed by the obligatory appreciation of each other's outfits, topped off by claims that they were 'nothing really, only cheap' and other self-deprecating comments about how the other was better dressed. Once that was over, there was an uneasy hush.

For a second, the devil took Amelia's tongue. 'I'll ask it, shall I?'

Hannah and Margo gaped at each other. 'What?'

'The question. Jake.' She had to break the spell. 'How is he?' The pair looked at each other again and Amelia wondered whether they were worried about betraying secrets; she toyed with turning her back to let them discuss how to proceed. 'It seems strange not to ask. Jake is our common ground. Holly was saying . . . ' Amelia shuddered at the thought. 'She said Charlie doesn't see him much.'

Margo and Hannah exchanged panicked witness-protection glares yet again. It was clear Hannah wasn't seeing much of Jake either. Amelia hated that this made her curious – she didn't want to start giving a fuck about Jake again – but styled it out with a nod and a smile. She considered leaving them to it, but willed herself on. 'Can I say . . . ? Look, this doesn't need to be awkward.'

Hannah opened her mouth to speak but Amelia ploughed on. 'Jake and I broke up, but it was nothing to do with you, with *us*. So instead of pretending we don't know each other, let's have a good time.'

They looked back blankly, like it was a trap. Amelia reckoned she could quite easily toss ice cubes into their slackened jaws.

'I mean . . . everyone over there's talking about boyfriends but they clam up in front of me because they think I'm jealous or . . . I don't know what. I can't be normal around them. Apart from Rudi and, I guess, three drinks ago, Holly, you're the only two I can have a laugh with. So . . . '

Hannah got up and hugged her. 'We're glad you feel that way. Fuck Jake, anyway.'

'Yeah!' screeched Margo. 'He's off doing his own thing now. We hardly see him unless he pops in for a quick argument with Mum and Dad, or Trick.'

Amelia gave a thin smile. That he was fighting back against the family was interesting; he'd always kept it all in. No wonder Margo looked knackered. 'But he's getting on okay? Generally?' Amelia saw Margo interpret this as prying into his love life, which wasn't the intention, but she *was* curious.

'Oh . . . um . . . he's got lots of fabulous new gay friends that he won't let us meet because we're *embarrassing* or whatever – as if – and he was dating a woman from work but it all went south pretty quickly. Typical Jake.'

Amelia felt pressure behind her eyes. What? A *woman*? Already? New gay friends? How? What was 'typical' about this? None of this behaviour sounded like Jake at all. The other two babbled on.

'To be honest, I thought having a gay best friend would be more exciting than this,' laughed Hannah.

Could they hear themselves? And, seriously, who the *hell* was this 'woman from work'?

'I know, right?' laughed Margo. 'I thought dropping out of uni twice, having a baby, dumping my boyfriend and moving back home made *me* the nightmare child, but try having not one gay brother, but two! Love 'em but attention-seeking doesn't even cover it.'

'He's bi,' murmured Amelia, feeling strangely protective, forgetting for a moment how annoyed she was.

'What?'

To hear them dismiss him felt wrong; she fought the urge to defend him. Maybe she'd been successfully gaslighted by Holly after all. She composed herself. 'I'm getting on with my life,' said Amelia. 'I wish Jake nothing but the best.'

The rest of the afternoon, they drank and laughed, and even slipped outside for cigarettes. But on the way back to the apartment, once the Prosecco buzz had faded and her skin itched as it always did when she spent too long outside,

Amelia's anger swelled. Why was the onus on her to compromise, hide her feelings, pretend to be cool and avoid making everyone uncomfortable? Something felt off about this, like her heartbreak meant nothing, because poor Jake was finally *free* and everyone wanted to be his cheerleader. He'd told her he wanted to 'explore', but his explorations didn't seem to have gone much further than the end of the garden – and the *lady* garden at that. Bastard.

Rudi let herself into the room as Amelia was thinking this over. 'This is bullshit!' she exclaimed in frustration.

'What is?' Rudi looked concerned.

'Oh, not you too. Don't tiptoe – come trample over egg shells with me. I don't mind.'

'What? Are you high. Did you . . . ?'

'No, sadly. My sugar rush comes from discovering Jake's been dating a *woman*!'

'Oh.' Rudi sat on the bed next to her. 'Honey, he's bi. He didn't leave you for another man.'

'I thought . . . he wanted to be with *guys*. I didn't realise he was . . . *replacing* me.' Amelia flopped on the bed, head fuzzy with cosmopolitans, holiday heat and nicotine. 'Which one of those bitches took the duty-free gin? Go tell her it's time to play.'

Rudi threw her head back in laughter. '*This* bitch has it. Let's go.'

At the airport, they said their goodbyes, hugging and smooching like parting lovers.

'I'll message you tomorrow,' shouted Hannah as she jumped into her cab. Amelia knew she would do nothing of the sort – or if she did, it would be a one-off – but she felt at peace. She'd turned a corner; they'd stopped seeing her as a victim, or a dangerous toxin.

'I can't believe he's ghosting his mates,' she said as she dropped down next to Rudi on the Tube back into London. 'I feel a bit spiteful. What's it called?'

'Oooh, *schadenfreude*. But taking comfort from their misery rather than, like, loving it. Am I right?' Rudi winked at Amelia.

'Nice to know they're getting a taste of it too.' Amelia reached for her phone. 'Anyway. Whatever.'

Rudi burst into laughter. '*Now* are you ready for your rebound shag?'

'Not this again. Who?'

'Ben Peters? From uni. He's just moved to London.'

'Rudi, you're such a cow. I shagged him once and it was terrible. He made me go on top and as it was going in he said . . . ' Amelia winced at the memory but felt rumblings of laughter within. 'He said . . . "Ruin me". *Ruin* him. Oh God.' Soon the pair of them were shaking with mirth so hard, the couple opposite moved seats.

*

Jake hadn't been around this many heterosexual men since PE lessons at school but, unlike his precious adolescent moments lusting after Hervé, this was an anti-aphrodisiac. Paris was hot, like *way* hot, and of course there was no beach. The stags were huge, overgrown babies – every time one walked into a room, it was like a sudden hurricane and the place would descend into disarray. One night in, and already the apartment was full of socks, empty beer bottles and various electrical gadgets charging – Jake was continually tripping over wires or stubbing his toe on an iPad. One stag even brought a PlayStation. On the first night, Jake organised a meal at a reasonably priced bistro near the Arc de Triomphe. The food was excellent and typically French, but the stags demanded burgers and made yucky faces at the silver salvers of oysters and shrimps, with one even complaining his steak tartare wasn't cooked.

'They have to be putting this on,' Jake whispered to Adyan. 'I've seen farmed salmon more cultured than this.'

'Yeah.' Adyan sighed. 'I think Magaluf might have been a better bet.'

Jake had revised his itinerary to include some of Miles and Charlie's requests, including a strip bar. When the time came, and Jake said he was going to go for a walk instead, the stags gawped back in amazement.

'I thought you said he still liked girls?' said Miles, who, Jake now noticed, had a head shaped like a toaster.

Charlie dug him in the ribs. 'He does. He doesn't wanna go, that's all.'

'I am actually here, you know.' Jake felt he was letting Charlie down. 'I'm not into that kind of thing.'

Miles scoffed. 'Come on, it's a stag. You're single. It's just *boobies*. Still like those, don't you? All for one.'

Jake trooped behind, spying out of the corner of his eye their hasty rearrangement of their ill-fitting underwear in anticipation of their imminent erections. Once there, they behaved like they'd never seen naked women before. Jake had never seen anything like it. A very nice young woman named Patricia in a red wig noticed his shellshock and tapped his hand as she lay his drink down next to him. 'Are you gay? It's okay if you are.'

Jake laughed. It really would've been easier to say yes. 'No . . . it's my first time. I'm not hugely into it, to be honest.'

Patricia winked. 'Me neither. But we pretend, *non*? Wanna dance?'

As the stags whooped his name, Patricia treated him to a very modest lap dance. 'I will keep on the bra, it's cheaper for you.' Jake was relieved to find it mildly erotic, if exploitative, and when it was over, Patricia smiled sweetly and relieved Jake of his euros, thanking him for being a gentleman. 'I think your friends are ready to go,' she said, nodding over at a phalanx of burly bouncers hauling out Miles and Marshall for throwing up into their own laps.

The stags spent the next day sleeping off hangovers while Jake and Adyan shopped and did some sightseeing. Jake couldn't remember exactly where Corentin's bar was but kept hoping he would see it. When they got back, the other stags were voting whether to overrule Jake's meticulously planned clubbing night to go to another pole-dancing place instead. Jake knew staying in Pigalle had been a mistake – too much temptation.

Charlie spoke up. 'If I wanna look at naked women, I can go online or, like, have a shower with my new wife. Let's dance while we can. Jake's gone to a lot of trouble.'

From hours spent reading Paris tourism blogs, Jake had located a cool, compact club – so he could keep control of this herd of idiots – that played good music, was a mix of tourists and locals and, crucially, was near the Eiffel Tower, so the guys could say they'd been to Paris proper. Julius, who was the younger brother of one of Charlie's equally toffee-nosed school friends and had a face like a dropped pie, had moaned for much of the weekend about not seeing the tower. Eventually Jake had snapped, 'Look up from your phone every now and again, or go stand on a hill', to which the stags had all responded with a loud high-pitched, 'Oooooooh'.

Jake had always been told he was quite a good dancer but got embarrassed when his mum or Reenie dragged him up for a carpet-boogie at family get-togethers. He was almost *too* good, and men would eye him with envy, before starting to make fun of him. In the days before *Strictly Come Dancing*, being a good dancer wasn't manly where he came from; it was letting the side down, so Jake had mainly stayed on the sidelines until Callum had managed to coax him out of his shell. Tonight, however, he had reverted to type.

As Jake watched the stags shuffle awkwardly on the light-up dance floor to perhaps rather *too* avant-garde French techno, he was aware of a woman standing next to him.

'Are they yours?' She was English.

Jake turned to her and rolled his eyes with a dramatic flourish. 'The zoo let me have them for the weekend – I return them to their cages, and keepers, tomorrow.'

Her name was Kirsty; she lived in Paris but came from Woking. 'Sleeping, I call it, but I'm not a natural comedian.' She had eyes like Amelia's, Jake noticed, but blonde hair, and was slightly stouter. She was beautiful and, it slowly dawned on Jake, chatting him up. It was different from being chatted up by a man. He felt safe and in control now, even though Kirsty was doing the running. With men, he felt on the back foot; they were more unpredictable, more willing to try any tired line or cliché. Not for the first time, he wondered whether he'd ever made anyone that uncomfortable. He hoped not.

They were on their second round of drinks when Jake

noticed they had an audience. All dance moves exhausted, some stags leaned against pillars, chucking back beers, nodding over and pointing. Some gave encouraging leers, which Kirsty couldn't see, while a couple, Jake saw, were looking . . . what was it? Envious? Disapproving? Hard to tell.

Kirsty talked more about where she lived, what she liked doing, and Jake realised she was going to ask him to come home with her. Or at the very least, kiss him and encourage *him* to ask if he could. Jake felt that familiar tingling, the lurch in the belly. He dismissed thoughts of Amelia, Harry, Rana, Samir; the past fell away. Feeling the guys' eyes burning into him, he leaned in closer.

'Um, look, I'm very annoyed to say, but I'm desperate for the loo. When I get back shall we . . . go somewhere else for a drink? Without my motley menagerie?' He felt smooth, desired, capable – for the first time in quite a while.

Kirsty's eyes flicked to the stags, whose voyeurism was becoming very unsubtle. 'Sounds good.' She leaned in and pecked Jake on the lips.

In the bathroom, grotty and lit by a solitary bulb ten miles up, Jake looked in the cracked mirror, splashed cold water on his wrists – a Bertie trick to cool down quicker, apparently – smoothed down his hair and rolled back his shoulders to make his pecs more prominent, such as they were. Okay, good. He was back.

When he returned, the stags had dispersed – some to separate tables, others back on the dance floor. Where Kirsty had been was an empty space, her half-finished gin and tonic still there, ice unmelted. Jake sat down, confused. Maybe she was in the bathroom.

After a few minutes, Miles strode over. 'Hello, Jakey. You been jilted?' This sounded like a loaded question. Soon Charlie was on his way over too, looking worried. Miles carried on slurring, tongue fat and wet, his halitosis acute. 'Hope I didn't cockblock you there.' God, he was disgusting. A toad swathed in Fred Perry.

Charlie tried to pull Miles away. He was seconds too late. 'It's just,' drawled Miles, his breath lifting the top two layers of Jake's skin, 'I thought she should know she was barking up the wrong tree.'

The truth dawned on Jake. He moved toward Miles until they bumped chests, Charlie trying to get between them. 'You *fucker*. You gross piece of shit. Why would you do that?'

Miles's sneer was priceless, the perfect embodiment of bitter entitlement. 'You're *greedy*. Leave the girls for *us*. No woman wants a gay boy. She needed warning.'

'What the fuck do you know?' Jake hissed.

Miles's expression was utter delight. 'Do the maths, old chap; she didn't stick around, did she?'

Jake lunged at Miles but Charlie pulled him off. The club's security team started barking into their radios. Jake turned to Charlie, shaking him off. 'Did you know about this?'

Charlie looked like he was struggling not to say the wrong thing. He lost the battle. 'Well, you're like half *gay*, so . . . it was a bit misleading of you.'

Every vein in Jake's body surged with fire and fury. He looked round at those red, pinched faces, judging him. 'Fuck you, Charlie. I can't believe you still don't get this.'

'Mate . . . '

'Don't *mate* me. Fuck off. Fuck all of you. Get yourself a new best man.' With a sudden burst of energy, he elbowed his way through the crowded dance floor and outside, gasping in the oppressive summer air.

He was lost. Getting out his phone to navigate, he slowed down to catch his breath, before his battery decided the party was over, and his phone blinked off. Only an over-the-top Harry swearword would do. 'Fucker*ation*.'

He wandered the streets, sobering up rapidly. He felt he'd gone backwards, back to editing himself and trying to be something he wasn't to avoid standing out. This wasn't right. It was a sticky night and couples were out in force, shouting, kissing, arguing and clinging on to one another. He bought cigarettes and sat smoking on the steps of beautiful churches, bought coffee at dilapidated all-night cafés and, as the sun rose, stared into the Seine in the hope its ripples would give him answers. But, no, even in this beautiful dawn light it still looked like sludge – echoing Jake's feelings exactly. All he could think of was being here before with Amelia. He flopped down on to a bench and looked up at the Eiffel Tower. Should he have climbed it and asked Amelia to marry him? Where would he be now? He thought of Harry's kisses on his neck and his urgent, excited whisper of, 'I can't believe I'm doing this.' Rana's disappointed face leered out of the orange sky. No, he decided, feeling reborn under the tower as it twinkled in the sun, I was right not to climb you; I was right to sleep with Harry, and Rana. As awful as this weekend was shaping up to be, he was happy to be the man he was now and not the one he could've been. But he still needed to make it up to Amelia; maybe he always would.

Jake let himself into the apartment to find Charlie sitting alone on the sofa, ashen-faced.

'Oh, mate, thank God.' There were apologies; they felt sincere. 'Holly will kill me if you don't come to the wedding.'

'I'll be there.'

'What happened last night?'

Jake took his shoes off slowly. 'You lot happened. Your *dudes*. The constant jibes. I sat through the lot, things I'd never do – gay, straight or bi – to make you happy, because you're my best friend. So I should be asking: what happened to you to let them treat me like that?'

Charlie went pale. 'I know, I know. I'll have a word. I appreciate everything, I do. I know it's been hard. Miles is a piece of shit.'

'Yes he is. Get better friends. And I'm serious about the best man gig.'

Despite Charlie's protests and reassurances that everything was cool and that Miles would be 'dealt with', Jake knew it was the right decision. He thought about it on the way back to the apartment, he couldn't let his and Amelia's break-up become the main entertainment. If Jake melted into the background, Amelia would have more chance to shine as a bridesmaid. She deserved that. Eventually, Charlie accepted it.

'I really want to understand, you know. All this. *You*.' Catching Jake looking at the luggage by the door, Charlie said the other lads were out on the boat cruise. Jake had forgotten he'd organised it. 'They get a free bottle of wine each so I doubt we'll be seeing them soon.' Charlie nudged his friend. 'Can I ask . . . what's been going on with you? You been avoiding me?'

Jake shrugged. 'I used to hide a part of me away and even though I was out, I still felt I was doing that with you. I was frightened of being rejected, I suppose.'

'Nobody would reject you. Nobody has.'

Jake gave a long, resigned sigh. 'There's more to rejection than being ignored or abused. It's sneaky, done on the down-low; it's not always a shunning. It's not just rejection of the person, but the idea. Being doubted. Saying you're not who you say you are. I can see it on people's faces.'

'Why do you think that would happen? Didn't you feel you could trust us?'

'Ah, Chas. I thought it would happen because it already *has*, loads, while I was growing up – so I fell into line.'

Feeling more at ease with his old friend, Jake opened up about why it had taken him so long to come out.

'I was sure I was different but couldn't tell anyone. I've wasted a lot of time. It was always hanging over me as a teenager; I was waiting for it to go away. All my life I've felt I wasn't like everybody else and . . . people were pretty keen to show me I was right.'

Charlie looked aghast. He wanted names and addresses of everyone who'd been mean. Why hadn't Jake said before?

'What would have you have done, anyway?'

'Kicked their fucking heads in, man. I love you. You're my . . . my *boy*. I swear.' Charlie dabbed at his eyes. 'I wanna kill anyone who hurts you.'

'Well, as much as I don't need rescuing by a straight hero, I appreciate the offer.'

Charlie's voice became strained. 'Honestly, I'd die if anything happened to you.'

Jake's eyes widened. 'Are you sure about that? Actual death? A bit dramatic for you, Chas. You been watching *Top Gun* again?'

Charlie nodded emphatically. 'I'm for real. I was losing it

last night when you went AWOL. Don't shut me out. *Fuck*, mate. When you're angry, tell me. If I need schooling, tell me. I know you've gotta do your thing and I can't always be part of it but me and Holly are there for you, yeah? Ride or fucking die.'

Jake looked at his friend. He was trying. 'Thanks.'

'Are you crying?'

'No.'

'You are. Stop it. I can't cry on my stag. It's illegal. I'll never live it down. Can *we* get some wine now? Proper stuff? Vintage. Plenty of noughts at the end?'

'Yeah.'

'When that lot get back, I'll tell Miles to fuck off again, and then, if you're sure that's what you want, I'll speak to Adyan about the best man substitution.'

'Substitution? You make everything about football.'

Charlie hugged his friend in relief and socked him on the arm. 'Oi! Red card to my favourite bisexual.'

twenty.

One thing Bertie never understood about his younger friends was their approach to punctuality. They assumed the ability to warn you they would be late by text made it okay to turn up late, but for Bertie it was even more rude. Eventually, he saw Jake nudging through the crowded bar, and behind him . . . someone else, small, svelte and immaculately groomed. He looked like a reality TV star.

'Oh, hello! No Evan?'

Jake smiled brightly but Bertie could see he was nervous about this collision of two worlds. 'No, he's helping Nuno with something domesticated, so I asked my friend Callum to step in. Shame to waste the ticket.'

Ah, so this was the famous Callum. Bertie had heard Evan's side of the story – a thumbs-down – and Jake had gushed about him many times. He sounded like hard work, but didn't everybody? Bertie was gracious in welcoming the stranger; this was Jake's night and he didn't want to spoil it. Feeling guilty that Bertie always did the hard labour arranging their theatre nights, Jake had offered to get tickets. He was a novice and paid way over the odds, but he claimed they were decent seats, and the play featured a famous theatre actress singing very loudly about heartbreak, so Bertie's boxes ticked themselves.

There was no time now to do anything but order interval drinks – Bertie gasped when Callum requested a triple vodka and cherry coke – and race to their seats in the scorching auditorium. The seats had not lived up to their promise: if any cast member stood anywhere other than the stage's dead centre, the only thing worth looking at was a flower arrangement.

At the interval, Callum's eyes darted round the bar at the other gay men while Bertie quizzed Jake about Paris. Hearing about Jake gazing wistfully at the Eiffel Tower at sunrise just about sent Bertie over the edge.

'Why would you even ask yourself whether you did the right thing? You have so much to be optimistic about but you do love to torture yourself – stop being such a playwright!'

Jake laughed and clutched his chest. 'I've waited all my life to be dramatic; *please* don't take this from me.'

The conversation turned to Harry, as it often did. Bertie was fascinated by the erotic-novel feel of it all – his life was devoid of titillation for the most part.

'He asked me if I wanted to go for a drink after work.'

'And?'

It had been weird. Jake was both confused and furious with himself that he *did* actually want to go. And yet. He couldn't let bygones be bygones and sip beer like nothing had happened.

He had looked back at Harry coolly. 'Are you sure you want to go for a drink? That all you're after?'

Harry had looked puzzled, anxious. He could only do 'up', of course, not serious. Harry wasn't the kind of man used to difficult questions; the most taxing thing he had to think about was whether to have a latte or an Americano every morning. And that took him long enough; the queue often snaked behind him in resentment. He'd stuttered a bit, so Jake had decided to help him out. He'd glanced about the office to check the floor was empty – the rats had long since deserted the sinking ship.

'I'm just a bit surprised, because not that long ago – oh hang on, on my thirtieth birthday – we had sex, *actual* sex, remember? Since then we've hardly spoken. And now . . . you want to take me out?'

'But . . . '

Jake had felt like he was charged with lightning. He couldn't believe what he was saying but he knew he had to.

'I think we should keep things strictly business, don't you?' It had been almost delicious to see Harry squirm so hard, but for a moment Jake had recognised that anguish on Harry's face. Like there was so much to say but he couldn't get it out.

Disregarding it hurt harder than the feel of Lego underfoot, but Jake had held firm, until, finally, Harry had nodded gently, said, 'Fair enough', grabbed his jacket and strode away, shoulders hunched. At the doorway, he'd turned back. 'I just wanted to let you know, that diversity campaign . . . they're having another look. You were right; we're taking out that part you mentioned.'

Jake had stared after him, watching yet another opportunity walk away from him.

The three-minute bell rang. Bertie finished his drink and saw Jake was awaiting his reaction. 'I applaud your new assertiveness, long overdue. But why did you do that?'

Jake's face fell. 'Well . . . he can't just ignore me for ages then try to sleep with me again.'

Bertie pretended to mull this over like a high court judge. 'Mmmm. And of course that's what he was doing by asking you to the pub, is it?'

Jake blushed. 'Well, why else?'

'Why else indeed? You are, after all, utterly irresistible. Maybe he wanted to talk. But . . . if you didn't want to, you're right to head him off. Of course.' Bertie felt bad as he watched Jake slowly place his glass on the bar; he knew how full of doubt he would be. But perhaps he needed that doubt, to think of someone else beyond himself. Bertie turned to Callum, who'd been mute throughout. 'And what do you think of the Harry situation?'

Callum looked caught in the headlights. 'Well, um, I don't know, really.' None of the usual sass Bertie had heard so much about. Then it dawned on Bertie: Callum didn't know who Harry was; Jake had never confided in him. Bertie felt both honoured and ashamed.

*

'Sorry I couldn't come. How was the play?' Evan laid out the stir-fry in front of Jake with a flourish.

'Oh, fine.' It had not been fine. Callum had been silent at drinks after and even turned down the offer of a nightcap. 'Look, um, I wanted to talk to you, actually. Charlie wants me to bring someone to the wedding.'

Evan suppressed a cackle. 'Just to ramp up the drama? Like the wedding's gonna need it.'

'I asked Bertie but he said he didn't want to be the "spectacle", whatever that means. Something about being too old.'

'That's all he ever says.'

'And I can't take Callum, he's not . . . great around strangers and, well, a bit much.'

Evan knew what *that* meant but he decided to chide Jake about it another day. 'So who are you left with?'

'Ah, well.' Jake tapped his fork against the edge of his plate until Evan's stare bade him stop. 'I wondered if I could borrow *you*? One night only? Would Nuno mind? I'll pay for your hotel, and I'm gonna hire a car and drive down.'

Evan raised his eyebrow. 'Me? Go to a wedding with my first crush who's just decided he likes boys too? Yeah, I'm sure Nuno will be delighted.' Evan burst into hysterics. 'Also . . . you *drive*? So butch!'

The next night at dinner, Evan asked Nuno, who said it was fine. They carried on eating.

Nuno studied Evan across the table. 'I don't make life too boring for you, do I, sweetheart?'

Evan stopped mid-chew – his mouth would've gaped if it hadn't been full of rigatoni. 'What? No! What do you mean?'

'Well – ' Nuno swallowed his food and ran his tongue round his mouth to clear any debris ' – keeping you indoors when you could be out having fun. You don't regret shacking up with me, even though I don't party any more?'

'You don't "keep me in". I go out all the time.'

Nuno looked slightly uncomfortable. 'I know. But you don't mind that I *don't*? It's okay?'

'Yes, of course!'

Nuno breathed slowly. 'Jake is a very good-looking young man.'

'My *love*.' Evan put down his fork and laid his hand on Nuno's. 'He is, if you like that sort of thing. And I *don't* any more. I spend a lot of time with Jake because . . . he's at the beginning of everything, when it's exciting, and confusing, and does your head in. It gives me a buzz, and . . . '

'And?'

'It makes me feel I'm doing something good. Being there for him when nobody was for me; he's got a big hill to climb. Bi guys get it from all angles.' They both paused to let the obvious joke pass. 'You believe me, don't you?'

Nuno smiled. 'I do. Go, then, to this wedding, and make the rest of the guests wish they were Jake, just so they could be with you.'

Evan laughed. 'Oh, *you*.'

Evan: Cinders, you shall go to the ball and Nuno has lent you his Prince.

Jake: Amazing!! How did you manage it?

Evan: Well Nuno knows I'm only attracted to nice people. He knows you wouldn't be my type.

Jake: Charming!

Evan: You certainly aren't. But I'll be your +1 if it means free food and fizz. Separate bedrooms too please!

Jake: Obviously!

*

It was happening more often, Callum noticed, flopping down into his seat on the Tube. The look. *Looks*, plural. Furtive glances telling him he'd been 'seen' by a kindred spirit, whether they knew it or not. He remembered himself at a very young age, feeling something in the air as he clutched his mother's hand on the bus and turning his head to see a man, or another boy, who felt like . . . home. Sometimes it was terrifying if they looked or sounded weird or attracted too much attention. Callum found it ironic that all he'd wanted to do when he was little was fade into the background, not be noticed, and now here he was in his late summer uniform – neon peach shorts cut right up to his clavicle. These encounters always went the same: a boy would sit opposite him on the train, he could be two, twelve or twenty-two – today's was around fourteen, he guessed – and Callum would see something in their eyes that told him his existence had, quite unintentionally, made this boy ask himself a question, one Callum would never answer. It was like flicking a switch and watching power reach their eyes. What was it today? Fascination or terror? Recognition or denial? Would young potential gay men look at him and think, I want to be like him? The young boy let his eyes drop, giving an almost imperceptible shudder and looking away. That result was on the increase too, Callum noticed. It only made him more determined to be the best version of himself.

His phone buzzed. Jake.

Jake: What time did you say you were getting here?

Tonight was a momentous occasion – for the first time Callum would see inside Jake's flat, where he was prone to scurrying off to night after night.

'There's a new club I want to try in north London,' Callum had announced. 'If we do pre-drinks at yours it means we can head straight there and not sober up on the journey.' Callum and Jake did not operate within sobriety; their time together was usually spent in the vicinity of alcohol and clubs, boozing in Callum's flat before barhopping until just before daybreak, whereupon the whole evening would turn into a pumpkin and Jake would be spirited away by himself, turning and waving out the back window like an evacuee. This was how it went sometimes. Everybody assumed coming out meant an instant dive into promiscuity, but Jake's? What was it? Frigidity? Abstinence? Whichever, it was pretty common. All that sexuality at their disposal but no instruction manual, you see.

'Very different kettle of fish from his baby brother, isn't he?' Glanville had said one evening as they'd watched Jake climb into his cab.

Callum hated it when Glanville brought up Trick near Jake, even if he was out of earshot. 'Yes.'

'Is that the attraction? To the V-*Bi*-P? That he's not interested?'

'I've told you before: there is no "attraction" to Jake.' This was more or less true. Callum had wondered if there could be something and, when they had kissed, and Jake had pulled a face like he'd sucked an old bathroom sponge, Callum had been rather offended. *Very* offended. But soon he'd realised they would never work. Jake was too green, too busy working himself out. A slightly different bewilderment than Trick but not a million miles away. 'Jake and I are just friends.'

Glanville had hissed. 'I suppose you did Trick a favour – got the first of *many* heartbreaks out of the way nice and quickly.'

Callum had shivered as he'd remembered Trick's crestfallen look they last time they'd spoken. 'Yes.'

The source of Glanville's hatred for Jake was hard to pin down, but it wasn't unusual of him to reject newcomers. Glanville hated *explaining* himself. 'You pick up so many strays, we'll have to start doing an induction,' he'd said one night as Trick had sat quaking and clueless.

Once, when Callum had made the mistake of wondering why they'd never been invited to Jake's house, Glanville had laughed. 'Oh, silly! It's right in front of your face. What would the neighbours say? He's embarrassed by you, by the gay stuff, wants to keep his hetero options open.'

Was that true? Callum remembered he'd been looking forward to the theatre after Jake's last-minute invitation, a rare foray into Jake's weekday universe, just to be somewhere else, to *do* something else. Something civilised, out of the usual circle. He was tired of gossip; all the one-liners were on their third or fourth circuit. But it was a flop. The play was boring, and Bertie and Jake's conversation was too deep; it was like rejoining your favourite soap after a year away. Callum kind of knew who everyone was but the situations were alien. Why'd he never told him about Harry?

'We only see him after dark, and I don't *think* he's a vampire,' Glanville had said. 'He'll be running back to his straight mates and dating women once his experiment's over.'

'Whatever, Glanville.'

Remembering the exchange now, Callum caught the teenager on the Tube peering at him again with curious fascination. A flash of rage took hold. 'What the fuck are you looking at? Eh?'

*

Jake was nervous as he waited for them to arrive. He wasn't too keen on the idea of the gang screeching too loudly so the neighbours could hear, but Callum had been insistent that Jake host. He'd overheard Glanville and the crew tearing people to shreds for little more than wearing the wrong fragrance – what would they say about his pad? After hours spent rearranging bookshelves, shifting the sofa, and agonising over Spotify playlists to appease them all, he opened the door to find Callum there alone.

'Just you?'

Callum gasped. '*Just*? I am never *just* anything!' He sashayed inside, like a cat pretending it had never even *seen* a litter tray. 'Glanville refuses to cross the river and I'm tired of everyone else, to be honest. I want some grown-up chat. That's okay, isn't it?'

He looked a little lost. Jake wondered if anything was wrong, but Callum never got personal, making it clear he preferred asking questions, not answering them. Jake didn't find him that intimidating any more, really, but there was a sense that prying too hard into Callum's life could prove fatal.

'Of course, I'll get us some drinks.'

Callum sat daintily on the edge of the sofa while Jake poured cocktails.

'What you doing next weekend? Fancy a night to remember?'

There was something called a 'circuit party' happening and Callum had VIP passes.

'You'll love it,' he said, gurning as the alcohol slammed the back of his throat. 'Lots of lovely men in shorts and little else.'

Jake looked down at his midriff and sucked it in. 'Doesn't sound like my sort of thing.'

'Nothing is *ever* your sort of thing. You're being very 80:20.' '80:20' was Callum's way of joking Jake wasn't being gay enough. 'If you're truly bi,' he'd said one night after debuting the phrase for the first time, 'ditch your self-loathing and be more 50:50.'

Jake explained about the wedding; Callum's face folded up in bemusement. He couldn't understand a) *why* he was going to the wedding and b) why he was taking Evan.

'It's like you were immunised against fun at birth. Evan is nice but has a husband. Who's *he* going to pull? That's the whole point of weddings, isn't it?' And then, an idea. '*I* could come! I'm good at parties. I can work a room.'

Couldn't he just. '*You?*' Jake regretted his tone immediately. Amazement, disbelief, like Callum had never even been *considered*, as if it were the most ridiculous suggestion in the world.

Callum registered it all. 'Yes! Why's that so surprising? I can't believe you didn't come to me first!'

Jake took in Callum's zebra-print shirt, open to the navel, his buff and plucked chest exposed. He imagined the wedding. Callum's voice carrying across the reception; the outfit he'd wear; the photobombing; the slating of everybody's clothes. He thought of Amelia watching, thinking, Is this why you broke my heart? And Margo's eyes popping out of her head that he'd brought someone who was . . . well, just like Trick. Jake felt embarrassed and ashamed at feeling like this, but he couldn't take the chance of drawing too much attention to himself. It had to be someone low-key, who wouldn't ruffle feathers or create whispers. Someone . . . dependable. Someone, he now guiltily admitted to himself, less obviously gay. That first night in the bar, Evan had warned him everyone needed someone to look down on when they first came out. 'Just make sure you hide it and get over it fast.' But this time he'd failed.

Callum's face slipped for a second, realising he was being assessed.

'Glanville thinks you're ashamed of me. I hate that bastard being right, but he is, isn't he?'

'No, it's not that . . . not at all.' Jake didn't sound very convincing. 'It's just . . . people have, uh, preconceptions about sexuality and . . . well, I don't want to put you in that position.'

Callum's laugh was derisory. 'Are you taking the piss? What do you know about my "sexuality" or the positions I've been in? You think you're the first dude who's ever said I was too gay for them?'

'I never said that!'

Callum placed his empty glass on the table. No coaster. 'Trouble is, you don't know shit about me, or what it's like to be gay. You're just a tourist, babe. You dip in and out. You haven't put the hours in; you just breeze up in your Ford Focus and go home once you're done. Guys like you are the grey squirrels to our red.'

Jake saw the hurt in Callum's eyes. 'I *don't* do that. I've – uh – thrown myself into it. I'm not a part-timer. I go to stuff with Bertie and Evan. I even went to an LGBTQ book club once.' It sounded better in his head. He slipped to the kitchen to mix even more potent cocktails, relying on alcohol to solve the problem.

'I hope you're nicer to your camp little brother than you are to me.'

Jake looked up with a jolt. 'What do *you* know about my brother?'

'I know everyone, remember.' Callum's face seemed loaded with intent but instead of unleashing whatever it was, he coughed and shook his shoulders as if shivering. Jake realised it could well have been Trick standing there in front of him. What would he say to him if it were? 'I'm sorry if I upset you.'

Callum looked up. 'Not as sorry as I am.'

Shame gripped Jake's chest. He excused himself to go to the bathroom. 'I'm a bad fucking person,' he said out loud, as he washed his hands, before there was a loud rapping at the door. Jake came back into the lounge just as Callum was breezing back in with the fixed grin of a hostage, followed by Jake's father.

Holy shit.

He'd been on a job in Swiss Cottage, he said, and it had overrun so he thought he'd pop in. Pat looked gingerly round Jake's lounge – its stark flatpack minimalism very different from the mishmash of decorating trends, tech and opulence he was used to at home.

'Uh, Dad, this is—'

His dad interrupted him. 'Callum, yes, we met, didn't we, bruv?' Callum beamed at this heterosexual endearment. 'Grandparents from Sligo. Not far from where my mum came from.'

'Jake, you never said your dad was so handsome! You look alike!'

The horrendous ash cloud of this truth hung between them.

Pat broke the silence. 'I came to give you this.' He held out his hand. Jake looked at it like it was a mousetrap. Seeing his son's puzzlement, he explained. 'A few months back, you put me in touch with your landlord about that renovation, remember?' Jake did, vaguely; a lifetime ago. 'Anyway, we got the job and it paid out, so this is for you. Get yourself a drink.'

Jake now saw his father was holding two crisp fifty-pound notes. 'What do you mean?'

Pat looked exasperated. 'You know, you must know, traders, when someone gets us a job, we get you a drink.'

Jake peered at the money again; it seemed radioactive. 'Dad, that's a hundred quid. The only place a drink costs a hundred quid is a six-star hotel in Dubai.'

Callum leaned in. 'Well, we could go to a spendy cocktail bar. A couple of rounds at the Langham!'

Pat thrust his hand forward. 'There you go! Callum's got it! Go to a bleedin' cocktail bar!'

Jake said he wouldn't feel comfortable taking a kickback, that it wasn't right; his father's shoulders slumped before he placed the notes on Jake's coffee table.

'I'm not *bribing* you, Jake. You ain't gonna owe me any favours or wake up with a horse's head in your bed. It's just what we do, what *I* do. How we do business, show gratitude. I thought you knew. It's no big deal.' He looked for the exit. 'Anyway, better be off. Traffic. Your mum. Y'know.' Jake was still staring at the money. 'It's not fake, y'know. Have a few drinks.'

'Okay.'

'It was a *delight* to meet you, Mr Jake's Dad,' cooed Callum, holding out his hand. Laying it on thicker now, Jake saw, as revenge for his judgement earlier.

Pat took Callum's proffered paw, winked and bowed. 'You too, son. Make sure he spends that cash, won'tcha?'

Callum grinned from January to May. 'Like my life depends on it.'

Unable to stay in the same room as this weird pay-off he didn't understand, Jake followed his dad to the door to see him out.

'Your friend seems like a good boy.'

'He's just a friend.'

Pat brushed his son's arm with his hand. 'I know. That's what I said. He's funny.' Jake shrugged.

As Pat bleeped the van door open, he turned back. He looked pained, but he spoke with purpose. 'Y'know, son . . . ' He thought about whether to go on. 'You . . . uh, you haven't really tried to get to know us either. Two-way thing, innit?'

Jake stared back blankly. A reply, an apology, anything – it caught in his throat and refused to budge. His dad hoisted one buttock into the van.

'See you later, son. Don't forget to have that drink.'

Jake stood on the pavement and watched the van go. When he went back inside, Callum was gone.

*

'Okay, so these are what we call *embellishments*,' cooed Trick as he gently pressed the last glittery star sticker on to Buddy's face. 'But if that word is too long for you to say, let's call it *glitz*. Okay?'

His nephew gave a solemn nod before breaking out in a huge smile. Trick had an amazing day planned for Buddy while Margo was at Holly and Charlie's wedding. A fashion show!

Face-painting! Going to the shops in disguise! A cartoon marathon with bottomless popcorn and fizzy drinks! Kia was already there, filling bowls with sugary crap, and Hot Will was on his way. Then, they got to play at being parents for the day. Buddy and Trick had been besties since, when Buddy was about three, he'd given Trick a hug and said, 'I love your face.' Trick would do anything for anyone who told him he was beautiful; he really loved a compliment.

Kia took in Buddy's new look. 'I am *living* for this,' she squealed. 'Now, Trick, you need to get your lashes on so we can review them for the vid later.'

As they negotiated with the lash glue – largely unsuccessfully – they heard the door open downstairs and Jake's voice calling out to Margo. He'd hired a car and was driving them down to Kent for the wedding. Kia and Trick bowled over to the window to get a look at Evan, who was waiting outside by the car, eyes closed against the sun.

'God, he's buff.' Kia was drooling.

'Kia, my mum's already got a window cleaner so can you put your tongue back in your mouth? We need to do the lash-essssss, bish.'

Buddy ran to show his mother his makeover, which, for Trick, was pretty low-key. White T-shirt with a Wonder Woman logo ironed on to the front, bright-blue shorts, glittery face stickers, obviously, and, of course, a dinky neon tiara. A starter kit to fabulousness, really. Trick heard Margo tell Buddy he looked amazing, but Jake's voice sounded abrupt, and Margo could be heard chipping back in defence.

Trick sighed. 'I suppose we'd better go and see what Masc4Masc Mary is bitching about now.'

They descended to find Margo, Buddy and Jake in the hall,

Margo rocking a scarlet dress, and Jake looking, well, nice, Trick supposed. He stood in his corporate uniform of pristine white shirt – he had a woman from Camden come to collect them every Sunday, Trick had heard his mother say – and crisp navy trousers that fitted him perfectly, his shoes as shiny and threatening as ever. His only other concessions to colour were – gasp! – a pink tie and his red, angry face. Pickled beetroot with tempestuous eyebrows.

'What's all this?'

Trick shook his head. 'All what?'

Jake motioned at Buddy. 'This . . . outfit. It's a bit . . . girly.'

Trick patted Buddy on the shoulder. 'Hun, do me a favour and go to my room and go on my phone to get me to the next level on Bunny Quest. You're way better at it than me.' Buddy trooped off up the stairs, happily. Trick turned to Jake. 'It isn't *girly*, Misogyny FM, not that it's a problem if it is; he's a superhero. We're doing a superhero day.'

'Everyone stares when you're out dressed like that, you know. Do you *want* Buddy to get it in the neck at school?'

Trick folded his arms. 'I've been to pick him up from school looking way more drag-u-mazing than this. The kids are cool. They think we're famous. Anyway, Buzz Killington, what do you care?'

Margo searched for a diversion. 'Why *are* you dressed up, anyway?'

'Oh!' exclaimed Trick, glad of an opportunity to sell his concept. 'Well, I'm doing a vid about drag make-up and whether it's easy to put on and do you have to be a drag act or can you just, y'know, borrow the look. I got samples. It looks good, don't it? Except for my shitty lashes, which won't stick.'

Margo took a breath. 'See? Explanation given and accepted.'

Jake wasn't giving up. Didn't she see how *harmful* it was for Buddy? Didn't Trick remember what people used to say to him when he used to go out in a tutu? Had they both forgotten Kevin Tully? And all the others? Trick listened and watched as his brother worked himself up more and more.

'Margs, save your breath. I should've known Jake would be all up in here with some next-level shit, as usual.' He turned to his brother. 'Yeah, Kevin Tully, big *deal*. The only way to stop dicks like Kevin is not to give in. I'm not letting him win. Not like . . . '

Jake's eyes were wide. 'Like I did? That's how you get through it, Trick. You keep your head down, fit in . . . '

'And end up like you!' Trick shouted so loud it made Margo jump. 'I don't wanna be like you. You're *ashamed*. Of me, of yourself, of the whole *bi* thing.' Trick turbo-rolled his eyes for effect. 'I mean, congrats, you're just like every white gay guy in their thirties. You think everyone should be like you? Sit there quiet for *literally* decades and then come out and say, '"Oh, I'm not like everyone else!" Groundbreaking.'

Jake turned away from him. 'Aren't you always moaning to Mum that people call you names when you're out? Don't you wanna blend in?'

'That's different. It's *homophobia*.' Trick stepped forward. 'And it's you who wants to blend in, with . . . ' he waved his hand dismissively over the length of Jake's body ' . . . this insurance salesman drag *you* love so much. You shouldn't wear trousers that tight if you're bow-legged, by the way – you look like a tin opener.'

Margo stifled a giggle.

'You don't know what I've been through. How hard it was for me being undercover.'

'Right, fine,' said Trick. 'It's crappy masculinity and heteronormative bullshit. Free yourself from it! It's not *my* problem, it's everyone else's.'

'Your trouble is you've had it easy. Sometimes I think Mum and Dad created a monster. You wouldn't last two minutes on the estate.'

Trick didn't like arguing – his speciality was a withering one-liner and a sashay away – but right now, he had the energy, and he had the time. Mr Clean-shirt needed telling.

'Why are you so butt-hurt I didn't get the shit kicked out of me on the estate? What do you want me to *do*? Go back in time and tell Dad to lose his money in a poker game?'

'What I'm *saying* is you have no idea what it was like.'

'I know you are! Then why aren't you actually *fucking* glad I didn't have to deal with that? You worried your baby brother is made of stronger stuff?'

Jake shook his head. 'Nobody ever backed me up like they do you. Flattered my ego. It may have been the Trick show for the last eighteen years, but you're in for a nasty shock out in the real world.'

'And won't you be only too pleased to see me get it?' Trick raised his hands to the sky. 'You know the weirdest thing? This oppression is total *bollocks*. Everything came naturally for you, fell into your lap without you even asking, and always will, cos you're *normal* and never rock the boat. But you're still complaining.'

There was a knock at the door, Hot Will's elegant silhouette unmistakable through the frosted glass. Trick glared at his brother, who exhaled in acceptance of his defeat. 'Like I said,' Trick hissed, '*everything* falls into your lap.'

*

Evan smiled at Margo as they got into the car. 'You took your time!'

Margo blew a kiss at Evan and glowered at the back of her brother's head as he started the engine. 'You know something, Jake? Every time I think we've turned a corner, you pull some shit like this. Why can't you cross that threshold without a war?'

Jake didn't answer.

'I'm serious. I think I preferred the twenty years of silence. I kinda miss the Incredible Sulk. Wasn't coming out supposed to make you happy? I wanna support you but you're getting harder and harder to like.' She turned to Evan. 'How do *you* cope with the moods? The irrational anger? One step forward, two steps back?'

Evan looked uncomfortable.

The penny dropped. 'I see,' sighed Margo as she slumped back in her seat. 'Just us, then.'

Jake slowed the car and pulled over. 'Should I go back?' His voice was uneven, face turned toward the window. 'Talk to Trick? I can fix it. I didn't mean what I said.'

Margo looked at her watch. 'No, I'll call him in a bit. He gave you a pretty good going-over. Just tell me . . . when are you gonna start getting over this?'

Jake sighed. 'That's not how it works. I can't . . . just move on, shrug stuff off, forget. Not overnight. It's . . . not linear.' He looked at Evan in search of support.

Evan looked back to Margo. 'He's not wrong. You don't just come out and instantly feel a weight's been lifted. It's up and down. Good days, bad days. Sometimes . . . ' He looked at Jake again. 'Sometimes you hurt people.'

Jake stared back at the window. 'I'm working on it. I

shouldn't have said what I said, I know. Just don't be mad at me, please. Not you. *Please.*' He was trying not to cry. Margo decided not to mention it. The engine started again.

'Fine.' Margo breathed out, reaching into her bag and retrieving a bottle of Prosecco. 'I'm opening this. And, no, I don't have any glasses so I'm afraid I *cannot* share.'

twenty-one.

Amelia had hoped once the hen weekend was over, her involvement in Holly's wedding would be minimal until the big day. Wrong! One of the other bridesmaids – who knew Holly from school and seemed *very* put out not to be chief bouquet carrier – cooked up a host of other events meant to forge unbreakable bonds between them all. Amelia knew these tenuous 'bonds' would vaporise once the last bottle of post-wedding fizz went flat but accepted her fate. In the weeks leading up to the wedding, Amelia's social life was jettisoned in favour of flower-crown making, an execrable life-drawing session featuring a supposed 'hunk' with a Neolithic, dangly scrotum, and a chocolate tasting 'class' – the perfect evening out for a bunch of perma-dieting women five days before a wedding, Amelia thought. And, of course, just like the hen weekend, the deathless dissection of every man they'd ever met. Dads, exes, one-night stands; men who'd forgotten these women existed and had long since married inferior photocopied versions. Usually Rudi shut them down by talking about her girlfriends – instigating the 'time for lesbian deflection', as she liked to call it – but after the third 'bride tribe' get-together, Rudi invented immovable deadlines and bailed.

'I like them, they're really funny,' she said, as Amelia raced out to a butter-churning lesson, 'but we're spending *so* much time together. What the hell are we gonna talk about at the wedding?'

'What else?' hollered Amelia over her shoulder. '*MEN*!'

Amelia felt guilty harbouring unkind thoughts about one of her best friends. When she and Holly had met, pissed in a student bar that served triple vodkas for 65 pence, and shared a Marlboro, they hadn't talked about men at all. They'd talked about telly, art, music, clothes, cool women, and pretended they were both into the same things, like you do when you want someone to like you back. Marriage, men and the rest of that stuff had seemed a million years away, but one by one, the posed, robotic, engagement photos pinged up on Facebook and Instagram, and tasteful wedding invitations thudded on to the mat a year or so later. The race to conform, embrace mediocrity, be like everyone else – she didn't understand it. All her friends seemed happy, the love looked genuine, but Amelia had never felt that way about *anyone*. She realised now she'd always known she would never have that with Jake, as much as they'd cared for one another. Maybe she'd have gone along with it – donned the white dress, made the flower-crown – had Jake not experienced his sexual epiphany. That would have been worse than how this actually turned out, surely? Maybe Jake had done her a favour? She batted away the sentimentality. She was allowed to be angry.

On the morning of the wedding, she let Holly's overbearing friend – Jane or Jen or something; Amelia kept getting her name wrong on purpose to delightful effect – get hot and bothered about nonexistent crises, while she remained an oasis of calm. Holly kept looking over to check Amelia wasn't on the brink of a meltdown because her ex was two floors down. Rather than rip Holly's head off when she asked for the hundredth time if she was okay, Amelia winked and said, 'Yes! I'm so happy for you. It's going to be a beautiful day.'

She first caught sight of Jake from the bedroom window; he was standing out on the lawn in front of the hotel with Charlie, Adyan, Dean, and a taller, cuter guy she didn't recognise. He'd brought a date, then. What a cheek. Holly said he might, because Charlie didn't 'want him to feel alone'. Amelia couldn't decide whether this was a wise move or a *dick* move. Nobody seemed worried about *her* being alone.

Holly joined her at the window. 'Are you okay?' One hundred and one.

Amelia turned to look at her friend, whose face was a mask of fear, excitement and 'please don't ruin my day for me'.

'It's going to be a beautiful day,' she said, squeezing her friend's arm through the lace and, for once, meaning it.

*

Evan was the perfect plus one. Polite to the aunties, ate everything on his plate and kept Margo's glass filled. Jake wasn't enjoying himself that much. He was still smarting from the showdown with Trick. He'd said some terrible things; had he even meant them? Did it really matter what anyone wore? Why wasn't he happier Trick had the confidence that had eluded him? And he'd been right, in a way, hadn't he, about things falling into his lap – Evan was back in his life, Bertie was the sympathetic uncle he'd never had, and, until their bust-up, Callum ensured he never spent the weekends staring at the walls. But what hurt the most was that Trick was right that keeping quiet and hiding himself hadn't done him much good. He felt guilty he'd never been the big brother Trick had needed to squash Kevin Tully. Trick always looked after himself, he thought, but had he always been okay, or just pretending? If Jake used keeping a low profile to cope, maybe Trick's theatrics were his coping mechanism. Trick made him feel inferior, he realised, because he knew he couldn't rely on Jake to crack a few skulls. He should've turned back when he had the chance. An apology never sounded as sincere when it came after a sunrise. He couldn't do anything about that now, but he *could* do one thing he should've done a while ago – talk to Amelia. He'd thought of nothing else since he saw her walk down the aisle, radiant, eyes fixed front, he knew, to avoid catching his. The bad blood between them hurt him more now he knew she was sitting just a few tables away.

Jake looked out at the ornate banqueting room, one wall made of windows looking out on to a terrace and immaculate lawn, with beautiful views of . . . well, wherever it was. His eye then found Amelia, talking to another bridesmaid at the doorway. He nudged Evan. 'Does this remind you of your wedding?'

'Not exactly. It was a bit . . . less. And not quite so many pumpkins.' Holly insisted the theme of the wedding was autumn, and most certainly *not* Halloween, the concept seeming even more ridiculous given it was an unseasonable twenty-five degrees outside. 'I can't imagine how much this must've *cost*.'

'Holly and Charlie have lived off microwave rice since last October.' Jake craned to get a better view of the room. 'Every time I try to catch Amelia's eye she looks the other way. Do you think she's doing it intentionally?''

Evan breathed deeply. 'Wouldn't *you*? Maybe you're best leaving her alone.'

Jake watched Amelia again, still deep in conversation, recognising the signs she was getting irritated. She straightened her spine and started nodding slowly. Her expression was patient but he knew there was a roiling sea beneath. Still able to read her so easily, he felt a strange pang. Grief? Regret? It didn't have a label, but it packed a punch. He tapped his breast pocket and looked down at the small square of colour tucked inside. Charlie had handed it to Jake that morning, out on the lawn.

'We're all wearing one.'

Jake had peered at the pink, blue and purple scrap of fabric. 'Mmmm, it's nice. It even goes with my tie!'

Charlie had looked on the verge of choking up. Was he drunk already? 'It's the bisexual flag,' he'd said unevenly. 'We're wearing it for you. Because I love you and I want you to know.'

Jake had laughed and replied, 'You silly old sod,' but when they'd hugged, he'd felt invincible.

As everyone waited for pudding – he and Evan were seated as far away from Amelia as it was possible to be without being in France – Jake saw her disappear into a small ante-room off the main hall. Now was his chance.

'Don't be long,' hissed Evan. 'I have limited middle-class chit-chat. Heterosexuality is very ageing. Everyone here looks about fifty or like a buy-to-let landlord.'

Margo tapped Evan's hand. 'Refill, babes. Let him go ruin another day for Amelia if he wants. We can *dance*. I've requested "Heart of Glass".'

Jake mouthed 'sorry' at Evan, took a deep breath and

sprang across to the door. He plunged the handle down – bursting in seeming a better idea than creeping in with his tail between his legs. Piles of sparkling, pastel-coloured packages were stacked precariously to the ceiling on a pathetically small table, with just as many again under it and spilling across the floor, giant confetti made of consumerism and last-minute purchases. Amelia was on all fours trying to read the tag on one of the gifts. She didn't look up.

'Your Auntie Karen says she's left the price on whatever she's got you so wants me to take it off. Pointless. Like you can't just google it or go straight to Argos to find out anyway.'

Jake coughed. Amelia hurriedly stood and brushed imaginary dust off her knees before letting her dress fall back over them. She didn't say anything.

'I wanted to talk,' said Jake. 'We're gonna be here all night. I don't want an atmosphere.' You'd need a Samurai sword to slice through the current atmosphere, but Jake ploughed on. 'I know you must be upset and that's why you've been ignoring me and I totally get it.'

Amelia stood calmly, waiting for him to finish. 'Upset?' Her voice was eerily monotone, ethereal almost. 'I've *not* been ignoring you. I've been busy. There's more to being a bridesmaid than standing about, you know.' The hint of a smile at her lips. 'But how *brilliantly* vain to think it was for your benefit. Upset? I haven't been given the *chance*. No crying or sulking. No hysterics, no whispering about you, nothing.'

'Uh.' Jake wished he were in a toy machine at the arcade, that a giant claw could come and lift him out to freedom. This was a mistake.

'You enjoying yourself?' Amelia got back on her knees and again riffled through the pile of gifts. 'Everyone greeting you like you're Kate Middleton visiting a community centre. Nobody's done that to me, you notice? It's like I'm contagious.'

'Everyone has been kind. I was nervous.'

'Were *you*?' Amelia's look was pure fire. 'Did they say you could back out if you wanted, or "pop in just for a bit"?'

'No.'

'Oh, just *me*, then.' Amelia's held aloft the present she'd been searching for and peaking into the seams of the wrapping. 'A knife block. That'll be a fucker to re-wrap.' She remembered where she was.

'And you brought a date! How *lovely*. You'll notice my arm has only the world's smallest satin handbag on it.'

Jake explained Evan was just a friend, but Amelia shrugged. 'They said I didn't *have* to be a bridesmaid, in case I needed to *duck out* because I got too upset.' Amelia sat up, her dress up round her knees again. 'What good *friends,* thinking only of me and not just worried my jilted face would ruin their wedding photos.'

She stood again. 'You know, if you'd left me for another woman nobody out there would be shaking your hand and congratulating you for getting rid. You'd be an outcast, the villain. Where you *belong*, some might say. But we have to accept it – well, *I* do – because it's about being *yourself*. You're walking away from a burning building, on your journey, but I'm still trapped inside it.'

Jake's cheeks reddened. 'I didn't know they asked you to back out. I'm sorry. But you know we weren't right together. I should've handled it better. I guess, once I'd made up my mind, I couldn't let anything stand in my way.'

'Tell me this.' Amelia began to restack the presents. 'Why

do you get to stand in *my* way? Why can't I be angry like any fucking normal person would be after they get dumped? I can't get *closure*, not because I miss you or still want you – cos I don't – but because I can't rage against what you did without looking like a selfish bitch.'

'You're not selfish.' Jake looked down at his feet. 'I don't want you to think this has been a breeze for me either. I felt – still feel – guilty about how much pain I caused you.'

Amelia's eyes met his briefly.

'And many a time,' Jake continued, 'I've had to dash off to the loos at work for a bit of a cry.'

Amelia's lip curled in derision. 'Why do people *do* that? *Tell* you they've been crying after the fact? It's just showing off for people who want to look deep. It's bollocks. You cried. So *what*? I cried too. Should we have cried into buckets or measuring jugs and compared them? A prize going to the biggest pool of tears? Honestly, Jake.'

Jake laughed awkwardly. 'Okay, you have a point. I just wanted you to know that I have been thinking about you. It wasn't like I expected. Harder. I still don't know where I fit in.'

She turned her back on him. 'Determined not to let me have my rage, aren't you?'

'Have it! Go wild!'

Amelia laughed so hard she almost spat. 'Oh, but I *can't*. That's not how it *works*!'

Jake was running out of ideas on how to defuse this bomb. 'You're determined to make me work for this, aren't you?'

'Oh *yes*. Of course! Do you know something?' She turned to face him again now. 'Do you know how much *effort* being neutral and calm takes, when everyone is watching you?

Trying not to show too much emotion, because the first time you do, a man thinks you're unhinged, or a bunny boiler, or highly strung, out to wreck his life because you don't just sit there and *take* everything. And then, of course, if you don't show spirit, or aren't *vivacious* enough, you're a cold, miserable bitch. Frigid, unfeeling. So you keep that balance, and for nearly four years I tried to do that – trying to be *ideal* and uncomplicated and desirable like a fucking Zen master. All for nothing.'

'I'm sorry. So sorry.'

Amelia nodded. 'Good to hear. I refuse to blend into the background, Jake. I know you never wanted that but . . . you should be standing up for me. Not a fucking word from you all these months.'

Jake opened up his mouth to speak but Amelia's eyes flashed to say she wasn't done.

'*Nothing* before the wedding to say, "Hope you're okay that I'm gonna be there too" or whatever. You never checked in. You. Dumped. *Me*. I shouldn't have any work to do here. You just expected to *glide* in, that everything would be fine. And now you come and follow me into some little room I can't escape from, while I am *busy*, and interrupt me for a heart-to-heart. You're out of order.'

'You're right. And I should've messaged you. I . . . didn't have the words.' Jake swallowed hard. 'But . . . I don't regret coming out. Only that it hurt you.'

Amelia sighed in resignation. 'I don't *want* you to regret it. You shouldn't. Of course not. But I don't think it's fair that I'm somehow the villain. I didn't do anything wrong. You were living . . . a lie, and I was your cover.'

'It wasn't a lie. I did love you and care for you . . . I still do, actually. How can I make it up to you? How can I give you what you need?'

'Basically everyone out there thinks I'm a nasty old witch who drove you away and I'm now some fucking damaged Miss Havisham who will never get over you. I don't want revenge, or a favour. I want us to be adults, to be honest.'

Amelia tossed the present back into the pile. There was a faint, but definite tinkle of glass shattering. 'We're going to talk to everyone; once these vultures see we're "together", they'll be crowding round us.'

'What do you want me to say?'

'*We* will say the truth. That we loved each other but not for ever, and that I didn't stop you coming out, and I'm allowed to be pissed off even though . . . I kind of don't have the energy any more, because we're gonna be friends.'

Jake felt tears sting his eyes. Tears of happiness, strangely. 'Is that the truth? Are we gonna stay friends?'

Amelia's eyes looked moist too. 'This is not forgiveness. Or a clean slate.' Jake nodded. 'But since we've got through this . . . let's see.'

*

Margo returned from the bar with two shots of vodka. Over the last couple of hours, she and Evan had covered almost every inch of one another's backstory – Margo was in Evan's sister's class at school and vaguely remembered him from back then.

Evan looked at the shots. 'Is this a good idea?'

Margo banged her fists on the table. 'Tomorrow I'll go home and be Mummy again. It's an excellent idea.' She looked over at Jake, who was still talking to Amelia. 'What's the deal with you two? What does your husband think about you being here?'

'We're just friends. It's been nice catching up, nicer than I imagined. I'm glad he finally came out.'

Margo made the vodka disappear. 'You knew back then, did you?' She clocked Evan's expression. 'Oh . . . I see. *Intimately*. He's a dark horse.'

'Nah. He's not. He's just a little bit complicated. He'll be fine.'

'Hmmm. Glad *he* will be.' Margo counted down from three and they slugged the shots. 'I called Trick to check on Buddy.'

Evan became transfixed by the undulating hips of one of the groomsmen. 'How's he doing?'

Margo huffed. 'Buddy? Fine. Trick? Not so much. In fact, Hot Will answered because Trick was still crying too hard.'

'Shit.'

'Shit is right.' Margo stared over at her brother again. 'I'm not sure how much more of this any of us can take.'

*

'Have we done everybody?' Jake flopped on to a chair.

'I suppose we could, easily, between us,' Amelia deadpanned. Her eyes scanned the room. 'Everyone who matters, I think. After today I'll never see any of them ever again. Maybe I'll catch the bouquet to really piss on Holly's chips.'

Jake hated that their friends had acted this way. 'I know they've handled this badly, and if it makes you feel better, Charlie has had his moments, but they were stuck in the middle. Don't walk out of their life in anger. They're good people, y'know.' He was telling the truth. Charlie really had tried; he should've trusted them more when he first came out instead of hiding his other friends away.

Amelia looked wistful. 'It's not just that. I wanna change everything in my life I'm not *feeling*. It starts with being fake at weddings I don't care about, in dresses I don't like.' She looked down at her 'autumnal' frock. 'Whatever this colour is, it does *not* suit me. I'm done with this ride. I want something new.' She looked over at Evan, who was chatting to Hannah. 'Now, go get drunk with the boys for a bit. Your date – who is hot, by the way – looks bored to death and I hear you and Hannah have some talking to do. I need to tweet.'

'I've missed not hearing from you. I was trying to wave at you in the church, didn't you see?' Hannah offered him the cigarette she was smoking, but he refused. 'Ah yes, you only smoke on fire escapes with teenagers.'

Jake laughed. 'God, don't. Nothing happened. I'm sorry I was angry at you. I just . . . hate being misunderstood. It's happening a lot.'

Hannah tried her best not to look too hurt. 'I always thought I'd be part of it, could help you through it. Where've you been, fave?'

Jake kissed her hand. It smelled of her perfume, nicotine and the chewing gum she rubbed between her fingers so Dean wouldn't know she'd smoked. 'I . . . didn't mean to shut you out. To be honest, I needed to get far away from my old life.'

'Am I being an interfering witch?'

'No! I just needed to find my own way.' Jake groaned. 'I know, I sound like I should be wearing yoga pants and essential oils. And you are a very *good* witch.'

Hannah hugged him. 'I am. Love you, fave.'

'Same.'

Enlivened by his ceasefires, and thanks to a drinking competition with Margo, Jake was in a shambolic state by the end of the night. Amelia watched him pogoing to the Spice Girls – the deejay was in his fifties and refusing song requests. 'I'm a people pleaser but I'm not Spotify.' Jake's date had disappeared into the dancing masses and Amelia couldn't see Hannah either. The lingering spousal sense of duty kicked in; she decided it was time to put Jake to bed. His drunken, mooncalf smile as she approached made her stomach flutter.

'Come on,' she bellowed, like a matron dispensing a suppository, 'let's go.'

They limped along, two steps back for every one they advanced, as Jake dished out the usual drunk's plaudits. How beautiful she looked, how wonderful she was, how amazing it was they were friends. That he loved her. She wasn't drunk enough to reciprocate, and this speedy return to overfamiliarity irked her. Here he was, lubricated by booze and emotionally liberated, wearing his heart on his sleeve now she'd assuaged his guilt. She fought the urge to drop him to the ground, reminding herself it was healthier to move on. He was silent, suddenly, as they reached his room. He was waiting for her to say something.

'And I love you too, of course,' she said stiffly, despite it being the truth, in a way.

Jake started to cry, snotty, racking sobs. His eyes streamed, and he burbled apologies, followed by ridiculous sentimental statements. 'Maybe we *can* be together. We had something good, didn't we?'

Oh, for God's sake. One afternoon and a free bar really was all it took, is that what he thought? 'Jake . . . you don't mean that. We talked about this. You're drunk and confused. Clinging to familiarity. Please . . . stop.'

Amelia coaxed Jake into the room and heaved him on to the

bed, removing his shoes but leaving him fully clothed. Once his sniffles subsided, his eyes closed almost immediately.

Amelia slipped back to the main part of the hotel just in time to see Holly blundering out, gasping for air.

'Babe,' she whimpered, 'help me.' She leaned forward and vomited twenty per cent of her drinks' budget into a pumpkin. Amelia got Holly to her feet, rearranged her fallen strands of hair and handed her some chewing gum, and knew Jake had been right about one thing: whatever her friends had done, she was stuck with them for ever.

'I love you, y'know.' Holly nestled against Amelia's shoulder. Two declarations of love in the space of ten minutes; her cup truly did runneth over. 'Have you had a good time?'

'I love you too.' Amelia glanced up at the sky. 'It's been a beautiful day.'

twenty-two.

Nobody said much in the car on the way home. Evan ducked out at Morden, ostensibly to get the Tube to meet friends but more likely to escape the oppressive atmosphere of a double D'Arcy hangover.

Jake pulled up outside his mum and dad's house and sat with the engine running. Margo didn't budge.

'You not coming in?'

'No. I've got to take the car back. Hire place shuts at twelve.'

Margo had a very withering sigh and she let the back of his neck have it now, as she opened her car door and struggled out with her bag and suit carrier, the red wine stains on her dress peeking through the undone zip, like they were judging her.

She stood on the pavement. Jake opened his window. She didn't lean down.

'You could make things up with Trick. Now. Sooner the better. He was very upset yesterday.'

'I know. I have to get the car back.'

'I wish you would try to understand each other better.' The sigh again. 'You're brothers. You can't go on like this for ever. *We* can't.'

Jake couldn't face looking in the rear-view mirror until he'd turned the corner and knew for sure he wouldn't be able to see her.

Showering for the second time that day in an effort to feel better, Jake dressed and flopped down on to his sofa. The full day ahead of him. He messaged Bertie. No answer. He thought about messaging Callum, but decided against it. He had homework to do. He reached for his laptop.

The first video he selected, totally at random, Trick happily chatted away about this 'amazing' – he said that a lot, along with 'sick' – influencers' event he'd been to, reeling off a roll-call of names that Jake supposed would be recognisable to anyone from Trick's generation, but to him sounded like ingredients on the side of a can of energy drink. On and on it went: Trick, devouring the camera, supposedly touching the hearts and minds of his adoring millions. In another one, Trick mentioned a book he'd been reading, about the Stonewall riots. He actually seemed quite . . . intelligent. Jake knew his brother went around talking like autocorrect come to life, but he'd assumed he was blagging it. Yet here he was speaking with great authority – or so it appeared to Jake, who had to stop to google every couple of minutes – about this huge part of LGBTQ history. Jake opened a beer and sat back to watch more. Things took a darker turn occasionally, with Jake seeing Trick's first tear as he recounted what sounded like the date from hell – a romantic stroll in the park, only for the guy to go home with a guy who they bumped into out walking his dog – and there was a eulogy to an ended relationship that teemed with childish, fruitless optimism, which made Jake's stomach groan in sympathy. He didn't know if he could watch another; even though they were public, they felt like an intrusion. But, as he opened another beer, he clicked one more time.

The video began with Trick brightly saying hello to his fans, thanking them for watching, asking them how they were. Jake found himself mouthing, 'I'm fine.' Trick spoke about his week and where he'd been, and Jake was expecting him to pick up some lip balm or one of those huge pool inflatables shaped like a flamingo and say how much he loved it, but suddenly Trick went quiet and looked into the distance – a direct view, Jake knew, of his *Doctor Who* figurines, and stationery he never used. 'You know what?' Trick said finally, peering straight into the lens, his eyes appearing old, tired and out of place with his baby-soft skin and angular jaw. 'This *hasn't* been a great week. I could sit here and say it's been epic but . . . I never lie to you guys. You know that.'

Jake moved closer to the screen.

'I don't have any regrets about coming out. I just didn't expect it to be this hard. I don't know how to deal with boys, really. Nobody talks about loneliness or feeling insecure or self-consciousness. Even when I'm out, and everyone is having fun and dancing, I'm, like, why does this feel so closed off to me? Is everyone else okay or are they pretending?'

It was strange and uncomfortable to hear Trick admit this. He was usually a dazzling, loud presence – jockeying for, and getting, the attention in a family where competition was tough. To hear him say he felt an outsider in a world that seemed, to Jake, custom-made for Trick, hit hard. By the time Trick's tears finally came slipping silently down his velvety cheek, Jake's were not far behind. He paused the video.

'Fucking hell,' he said out loud. 'Being a teenager is worse than I remember.' He hit play again.

Trick's voice cracked now, like a radio not quite tuned to the right station. He didn't take his eyes off the camera.

'You need someone to go through this with you. You need acceptance. I know we say it doesn't matter what people think, but it matters what *some* people think. The ones you need to tell you it's gonna be okay, or that it might *not* be okay. The truth. To fight for you. Make you feel . . . uh, not special because that sounds *extra* and, like, miss me with your comments calling me a snowflake, we all need someone who "gets" us. Someone who understands it's not a . . . a picnic. Not at all.'

Jake held his breath. Fuck. That *burned*. Any hope that this was a dismissal of Hot Will or another teenage crush disappeared.

'What really hurts is when you have someone in your life who *should* get you, and is there for others but, like, not for me. Even though they're blood. I always thought outsiders stuck together but . . . I forgot we love to turn on each other. That's the thing. Sorry to get deep, and I swear I'm gonna be okay, but you can't make someone love you, so I'm gonna stop trying. Right now.'

The video ended with Trick saying he was going to do his best to see the positives and start again. He looked straight into the lens for a moment; Jake felt he was in the room. Then Trick gave his regular salute and the screen went dark.

Jake let the tears stream down his face unhindered for a minute or two, then went to the fridge for another beer. Empty. He didn't want to be here any more. He wanted to be there, back before he'd known himself. He dried his eyes, reached for a jacket, and headed for the Tube station.

He found himself back in Elephant and Castle. Home. Nearly. Jake glanced towards Callum's ugly glass slab of an apartment block, then looked down the Walworth Road, just about making out the traffic lights that led to his old flat. He toyed with walking to Reenie's, sitting at her kitchen table like he used to, flicking through *Inside Soap* and doing his teenage silent act while Reenie tutted as she ironed bed sheets. 'Why do I actually do this? Who's gonna see 'em?'

But he wanted to get drunk, and Reenie wouldn't have anything in apart from leftover congealed advocaat from Christmas. In his experience, only middle-class people had drinks in the cupboard that weren't meant to be drunk that very day. So instead he walked toward Kennington, quickly finding a small pub and installing himself in a quiet corner. With every drink – he alternated between pints of lager and double vodka-tonics – he turned over and over in his mind everything Trick had said in his videos, how the answer had been there all the time, waiting, if only Jake had ever watched. Looking at the table of empties before him, Jake decided he'd better quit while he could still speak. Outside, he looked up and down the road. South, toward Oval, Stockwell, Clapham and . . . home. *Their* home. It was suddenly imperative he be there. He ambled past the Costcutter, where a guy who smelled like biscuits, wearing what appeared to be three tracksuits at once, was propping up his bike. On the way into the shop, he shoved past Jake and told him, 'Move, wanker.' Jake shrank away and walked on, before turning and looking back at the bike. A proper boneshaker, like his teenage bike – rusted to hell, handles chipped and worn away – and its owner did not deserve an easy ride home. Stealing was bad, he knew, but walking to Balham was worse.

He zoomed down the road, cycling as carefully as drunkenness would allow, fearless even as buses rocketed by, forcing him to take refuge in the gutter and almost toppling him over the handlebars. He felt free again, as the months and years blew away and he was teenage Jake once more, singing 'Atomic' loud into the wind and whooping as another lorry honked its disapproval.

An abrupt wave of nausea made him swerve around Clapham Common, traffic lights blurring as water filled his eyes from the effort of not retching. But it was too late, he puked down himself, losing his grip on the bike. The glaring headlights of a bus coming toward him panicked him and he threw up again, jolting the bike hard to the left and hitting the kerb. The world seemed to spin – he was suddenly weightless, almost euphoric – and in those last milliseconds, he could've sworn he saw a familiar face, until he felt the crunch of the pavement and the last jerk of his stomach robbed him of his dignity yet again.

twenty-three.

Jake's head hurt, but not as much as the huge scrape on his back. He gingerly traced it with his fingers, squirming as his skin burned in protest. Where was he? Functional wardrobe, neutral pictures on the wall of vases of flowers or random areas of London, a distinct lack of clutter – a guest room, he assumed. But not his mum's. His mouth was parchment dry, throat raw with lingering scratches from alcohol's long, sharp nails. Someone was in there with him.

'Oh.' A voice he knew but couldn't place. Judging. 'It *lives*.'

The rustle of a beanbag as the stranger got up, and suddenly her face was in his. 'You look amazing, considering.' Kia. Jake had never been so happy to see her sarcastic leer. She'd been manoeuvring a very drunk Trick off the bus on Balham High Road, she said, when a complication came in the shape of Jake catapulting over the handlebars of the dilapidated old bike he was riding milliseconds earlier and skidding across the pavement before, quite brilliantly Kia thought, throwing up and then landing face down in it.

'It was dark as fuck so *thanks* for that memory,' sighed Kia.

'Thought you were dead. You D'Arcy boys love your booze, don't you?'

Somehow she'd guided Trick and Jake back to hers. Luckily her parents were away visiting friends in High Wycombe for a wild weekend of regional theatre and tapas.

When Kia had wondered whether they should strip down a puke-sodden Jake and throw him in the shower, Trick had slurred, 'I absolutely do *not* want to see my brother's knob, thanks!', before sloping off to the couch and falling fast asleep. Instead, Kia had led Jake upstairs, heaved off his shoes and trousers, carefully relieved him of his ruined shirt – nice body, she couldn't help but appreciate; what's a girl to do – and clothed him in one of her dad's dreadful holiday T-shirts, with 'IBIZA 4 EVER' emblazoned across it. Her father had never been to Ibiza.

'God, I'm an idiot.'

'One hundred points. Lucky to be alive. Riding a bike when drunk is *not* the one. Stupid.'

'I'm sick of waking up hungover. I've spent the last year drunk. I don't know what's happening to me.'

Kia went to fetch Jake a glass of water, coming back with a banana too. Jake tried to peel it but the sound was deafening and the effort exhausting.

Kia sat glaring. 'What's your problem, exactly, man? I know you split up with Amelia and stuff but . . . seriously. Why the meltdown?'

Jake's head was pounding. He begged for paracetamol, and as he washed it down, he considered Kia's question. 'Sometimes I think you kids have got it sorted. The world makes no sense to me. You're . . . fully equipped. You make it look easy.'

Kia couldn't believe her ears. *Kids*? Easy? Hoo, boy. Did she really have to give this lecture again? The constant attempts to debate or deny her existence in the media? The stares – real and imagined – wherever she went? The extra hour spent perfecting her make-up so she could 'pass'? Worrying what lighting would be like wherever she went? The fascination and insensitive gawping of people who knew her 'before' when they saw her again? It was inconceivable Jake had no idea about this – he read newspapers, had social media.

'There's more to this than people losing their shit because of which toilet I use, you know. I haven't got it sorted. I've grown a thick skin. Plenty haven't. And if by "you kids" – nice and patronising eff-why-eye – you're including Trick, you couldn't be more wrong.'

Jake leaned against the headboard, the cool metal soothing on his skin. 'So I'm beginning to discover. Where is he?'

'Why? You're not going for round two, are you? I don't think he can take it.'

'I . . . watched some of his videos. I saw . . . well, how hard he's had it.'

Kia sucked air between her teeth. 'Right, how does it feel to be famous?'

Jake wiped his eyes and gave a low, mournful moan. 'It's everything I imagined and more. Horrible. I never knew this, I swear. Why didn't he say?'

'He bares his heart and soul. He's inspiring, real, human . . . ' Kia paused ' . . . but he can't talk to you, can he? He's too busy "making it look easy", I guess, or maybe watching you be a best friend to literally every other gay person in the world apart from him.'

Jake thought of Trick's haunted face in that final video and felt himself choke up. 'That is about to change, I promise. Where is he?'

'In the kitchen feeling sorry for himself. Runs in the family. If you hurt him again, I'll cut you.'

Jake pulled back the covers, wincing at the grazes on his leg and also the fact that he was only in his underwear. When he finally reached the kitchen he saw Trick sitting at the breakfast bar, sulking and sipping a glass of orange juice.

'What you doing here?' he said, but Jake didn't reply. He walked over to him and grabbed him, wrapping his arms round him for the first time in for ever, holding him tightly, before kissing him on the top of his head.

Trick resisted for a second – 'Is somebody dead? Oh my God, why don't you have any jeans on? Yuk, Jake, God!' – before realising what was happening and giving into the hug, listening to his brother's deep breaths turn into light sobs.

'I love you, bro.'

'Um . . . okay.' Despite his outward embarrassment, Trick held him tighter. Then: 'Me too, Jake.'

'We're the same. It's gonna be okay, y'know? We're the same.'

'Well . . . ' Trick moved back and looked at Jake, a glint in his eye. 'Not *exactly* the same. My hair is nicer.'

Kia fluttered around them like cabin crew as the pair sat awkwardly at the breakfast bar trying to 'talk'. She refilled their glasses, placed yogurt and muesli in front of them, and considered going to the shop to buy croissants, before remembering she was not actually a waitress. The rest of the time, she leaned against the worktop, pretending to flick through her phone. She'd offered to leave them to it, but Trick had asked her to stay. He wasn't great with face-to-face. Tell him the camera was rolling and he morphed into a confident superstar at warp speed. In a threesome, lazing on sofas, he was hilarious and charming – but one-on-one . . . a baby.

'I watched your videos. You didn't unbox anything. I was disappointed.'

Trick was looking down at the floor, but Jake saw a smile. 'I don't *do* that any more.' He shrugged. 'And . . . what did you think?'

'I think I need to check the dictionary definition of a picnic.' Jake was relieved to see Trick's hint of a smile again. 'I wish you'd told me what was going on. I thought . . . you had it worked out. I've always admired your confidence.'

Trick looked like a baby as he sipped his juice. 'Nobody's ever shown admiration for me the same way *you* do.'

'Outsiders should stick together. I'm sorry I turned on you.'

Truck put his hands to his face. 'Oh my God, you watched *that* one.'

Jake smiled to see his brother embarrassed, not for the usual point-scoring, but because it made him realise how vulnerable he was. He felt close to him. 'I never realised you gave a fuck what I thought – what anyone thought.'

'I was very drunk. I would've said anything.'

Jake squirmed. Kia attempted to reach Trick via telepathy. Come on, baby, she beamed in his direction, you need to have this conversation.

Trick took a deep breath. 'You said some very shitty things to me.'

'I did. I'm sorry. I haven't stopped thinking about it.'

'Same.' Trick looked over to Kia, who winked in encouragement. 'I know I'm not nice to you. I can't explain it. You always . . . take it. Never go ape shit at me. Well, until the other day. Why not?'

Jake started to feel shaky. Why had he let it go, all those years? Didn't it matter his brother had such a low opinion of him? He seldom returned the sass, even though he thought of it. Frightened of hurting him? No, not that.

'Honestly? I didn't want to retaliate because I didn't want the argument we had on Saturday to happen. I was . . . frightened if I pressed you too hard about what your problem was . . . you'd tell me. I assumed you . . . uh . . . knew I was closeted.'

Trick gasped. 'You're kidding! I didn't have any clue. You wear so much *navy*. You can't mix cocktails. You're . . . *Not* like me.'

Jake laughed. 'No, I know I'm not, and that's the problem. I wanted to be like you, in a way.'

'You have the wrong shaped head for my outfits.'

Kia coughed.

Jake tried to make sense of what he was about to say. 'When Mum was pregnant, I hoped someone else like me in the family would come along, prove I wasn't a weirdo, maybe. Then there you were. A star is born. You were like me but . . . nothing like me.'

'So you could see I was gay and . . . what? Resented it?'

Jake looked into his brother's eyes, anime-huge, full of sorrow, his long lashes framing them like reeds round a lake. 'This isn't about you being gay or me being bi, not for me. No. I hated that you didn't seem to need me. Not at all. You seemed to be doing well on your own. I felt even more of an outsider.'

'I thought you hated me because I was camp and . . . ' He

looked down at his glittery fingernails. 'Like this. That you were embarrassed or scared people would think less of you. Then you came out, and I was, like, okay, but you were so horrible to me when I came out, and I didn't get it. I know how straight-acting gay men look at me, what they say.'

Jake sighed. 'I was a total tool. A whole toolkit, in fact. Adjustable spanners, pliers, the lot.'

Trick sat up straight, suddenly tapping into a new current of energy. 'Nah, don't apologise. I mean, yeah, be sorry you were a dick, but not for how you handled your coming-out. It's your business, like it was mine.' Kia's thought waves were getting through. 'Fucking *own* your sexuality, though; don't apologise like it's a disease.'

Kia beamed. *Attaboy.*

'When you came out, I thought . . . you were taking the piss, or doing it for attention.'

'Stealing your *thunder*!' Jake couldn't help but laugh.

'I know, I'm sor— Well, no apologies, but, yeah. You've got this masculine energy or whatever, and boys – I mean, *stupid* ones, but boys are boys – were queuing up for you. I'd been waiting all my life for it and you just . . . well . . . there you were.'

Jake placed his hands on Trick's bony shoulders. 'Look, however it seemed, I was doing my own head in the entire time, worrying I wasn't doing as great as you and . . . basically we're both idiots.'

Kia was a proud lioness watching them hug, as they made a pact to talk it out next time. When things got rough, they wouldn't be alone. But there was the implicit understanding there should never be a next time, because they knew each other now more than they had before.

'And I promise I'm going to watch your videos. All of them.'

'All of them? You've a lot of catching up to do. But there's a couple you should probably skip.'

'I'm afraid it might be too late.'

Trick's eyes narrowed. 'No, you definitely haven't seen the episode before last about heteronormativity and . . . family.'

'How do you know?'

Trick grimaced. 'We wouldn't be having this conversation; you'd be instructing lawyers. Ki . . . ?'

Kia came a step closer. 'Yes, honey?'

'Remind me to set that episode to "Private" as soon as we're done.'

Kia laughed. 'Sure. Let's keep things nice.'

'Just one thing, though, Jake.'

'Yes, bro?'

'Please . . . ' Trick's eyes widened ' . . . never, *ever*, call me "bro". It's too hetero; that's *not* who we are.'

As the brothers hugged again, Kia raised her glass of orange juice in a toast. One less battle to fight. Well, today anyway.

twenty-four.

Jake wasn't going to pretend that was all it took, but his parents coming home that Monday afternoon to find their two sons – one scratched and scarred from his drunken brush with a bicycle and the other pale and riding out post-booze tremors – in the back garden, chatting like . . . well, like brothers, had certainly helped clear most of the bad air. His dad came home first, immediately quizzing Jake over his bruises – 'Was this gaybashing? I can get the lads over to sort this; we can get some big dogs' – before joining them with a beer and listening in mild bewilderment as his boys tried to explain what the hell had been going on the last couple of decades. Shock registered on Vee's face as she poked her head round the back door, assuming that this rare conference of the male D'Arcys meant there'd been bad news.

'There she is. The originator.' Pat stood and pulled a chair out for his wife, who lowered herself into it gracefully, like she was opening parliament. Then they talked, like they never had before. Literally never. Nobody bolted away from the situation or slammed a door. It was hard for Jake and Trick to see the guilt on their parents' faces over mistakes made or things left unsaid. They'd never considered them like this, just humans, before. Apologies and explanations were only rare because usually nobody made a fuss, everybody got along, except Jake, and his way of dealing with it had been to clam up. Perhaps in recognition of this, Trick kept fairly quiet, handing the floor to Jake – another first, he realised as he smiled to himself. Right now, Jake wasn't making too bad a job of it.

'You're not responsible for how things, how *I*, turned out.' His mother's eyes searched his. What was she looking for? 'This is who I am and it makes me happy. *So* happy. Don't be unhappy on my behalf, or with each other.'

His mum spoke now. 'I don't like it when we row. You and me never do that.'

'But that's just it! The *freedom* to argue, to speak up, get it in the open – I never thought I would. I've been finding my way' – that old chestnut again, he needed new terminology – 'and I've got a way to go. Getting angry, fucking it up, they're luxuries. I'm much happier.'

Vee gripped her son's wrist. 'Are you sure? You . . . you're our first. I waited for you a long time. I'll never stop worrying. Same for Trick. He's my baby.' She reached over the table to grab her younger son's arm too and, for once, he didn't wrench it away in a flurry of eye rolling.

Trick clasped his free hand over his mother's. 'Can we just, like, agree, we can't change the past and do better from now on? I mean – ' he looked at Jake ' – Jesus, this is like being on daytime TV or something; like, I am so mortified right now, but can we start again?'

Pat nodded. 'We didn't always get it right. I know that. We didn't do enough. There's no answer. I don't . . . uh, do we. Uh?'

'What is it, Dad?'

'Well, I was reading in one of your mum's magazines about family therapy.'

Jake heard Trick say 'Jesus' under his breath. He appreciated his dad's effort, but knew what his mum and dad were like once someone asked them a question or gave them the chance to talk – two million Oscar acceptance speeches playing back to back. 'No, it'll be okay. Trick's right. Let's agree to try to understand each other a little better? Today is day zero. For everyone. Okay?'

Trick laughed, his pale, hungover face lighting up. 'It's not gonna be easy.'

'That's what we do, isn't it?' Jake felt a tingle as he said the word 'we'. 'It's never been easy, but at least it will be, uh, a different kind of not easy.'

At that moment, Margo walked in clutching Buddy's hand. On seeing the tableau before her, she groaned. 'Whatever this is, I'm glad I missed it.' And they laughed, in a kind of harmony, whose tune had always eluded Jake until right that moment. As his dad always said, 'Rome wasn't built in a day but for the right price you can get the scaffolding up before sunset.'

After so long spent being guarded and uptight, Jake gave being relaxed more of a go: chucking his socks into the laundry basket unballed and drinking apple juice straight from the carton were a start. Every so often, he'd leave a coffee on Rana's desk as he passed in the morning and half the time she smiled in acknowledgement and the other half there'd be a 'Thank you, Jake'. He asked or wanted no more than that. With Harry, though, he was still struggling. There was a thaw of sorts: they exchanged nods and vague small talk at team drinks but Jake made sure he never sat next to him, and if it looked like they would be left alone, Jake would give an exaggerated yawn and find an excuse to leave. Harry sometimes looked hurt by this obvious avoidance, but Jake felt it was safer than being in any situation where they talked about what had happened or, even worse, did it again. The main reason being, Jake was worried they *would* actually do it again. Despite everything, and there was a *lot* of everything to consider, there was that bond – their shared history stretching out between them like threads of caramel. Harry had been the first *proper*; the only one of note so far. Like his mother and her romantic reminiscences about childbirth, the bewildering aftermath of his encounter with Harry was starting to change shape, and Jake would find himself gazing at Harry surreptitiously across meeting rooms, in lifts, in the queue for the canteen, and feeling agitated in his presence. One Friday he was finishing an email to Marketing asking they not say 'y'all' and 'FML' when tweeting from the MTZ corporate account and debating whether his sign-off made it clear he thought they were imbeciles – he went for 'thanks in advance', ice-cold but demanded action – and felt a presence looming. He got a whiff of adolescent deodorant mixed with duty-free cologne, and knew it was Harry. He hated that the scent of him still gave him a buzz.

'What you doing this weekend, Jake?'

Jake did a quick scan of the office. Nobody else about. Hence Harry's question being so personal, perhaps. Any other Friday he would've said 'nothing much' and tried to shrug his way out of this confrontation with as few blushes as possible, but this weekend was different.

'Amelia is going travelling and having a leaving party, so I'm doing that tomorrow night.'

'Wow.' Any other person may have dispensed watered-down wisdom about how Jake must be feeling and how great it was he and Amelia were still friends, but Jake was relieved for the first time that Harry's condolences were frothy and shallow. 'Cool. Where's the party?'

Was he angling for an *invite*? Launching a catering business and hoping for an intro to take care of the buffet? This was weird. 'She's hired a room above the Crown in Soho.'

Harry broke into a beaming smile. He had tickets for a late-night comedy show round the corner, he said, and did Jake fancy joining him.

Jake looked into Harry's hopeful face, searching for any sign of what this was supposed to be about. This was a different Harry, a new expression. Not the lusty smirk of Cologne, or Brussels, or the matey grin of every other comedy show they'd gone to, it was . . . actually, it wasn't new. Jake had seen it before. That stare right through him, looking for something, like he was waiting to be asked a question. Christmas. Harry drunk, telling him he should stand up for LGBTQ people. What did he want him to say? All Jake could think was that he *did* want to join him. Bollocks. He held his nerve.

'Why are you asking me?' Harry went pale in realisation that this was not going to be easy. Jake motioned for him to sit.

'Look,' he said finally, rearranging himself in the chair with obvious discomfort, 'I've been meaning to talk to you.'

Jake rapped his fingers on the arms of his chair. '*Have* you?'

'I'm not good at talking about my feelings.'

'Or saying sorry.' This was rich coming from him, and he knew it, but still.

'No. But I'm sorry, I . . . yeah.'

Jake remembered Trick's video, how broken he was from being mistreated. These men had to *know.* 'Harry, you wanted to try it, and I let you. I'm mad at *myself*, to be honest. That first time in Cologne I was . . . confused, like I'd done something wrong. But I still let you, because I wanted to, and I'd fancied you for years.' It felt other-worldly to say that out loud. 'You knew it, didn't you? So you hear I'm bisexual and you think, Might as well. Is that what this is about?'

To Jake's surprise, Harry leaned over and placed his hand next to Jake's on the arm of his chair. Jake almost pulled his away, but Harry moved his hand a millimetre to the left and their hands touched. 'No, that's not it. I just wanna talk. I . . . I've never met anyone who . . . '

Jake stared at their hands so hard Harry instinctively withdrew his, like it was burned by a laser beam. Harry sighed. 'Can we start again?'

Jake breathed as evenly as he could. 'It depends where you want to start *from*, doesn't it?'

He stood up. As exhilarating as that night had been, he didn't want to be anyone's experiment; his days of being a project were done. 'Like I say, Harry, I have plans Saturday, but thanks for asking. See you Monday.'

As he strode away, he looked back to see Harry walking over to his own desk looking defeated and puzzled. Jake knew that face; he'd seen it in mirrors. He wanted to feel triumphant and empowered, but he didn't. He felt, as Margo was always warning him, like he'd not only taken a few steps back himself but also set Harry back one or two. Jake stopped, poked his head back round the door and shouted into the cavernous space: 'Have a good weekend, Harry.' He meant it.

*

It was a tough decision, not inviting her brother to her leaving party, but the last thing Amelia needed was any unnecessary drama. She'd last seen Freddie in the summer, making use of his sofa bed during the Edinburgh Festival. She thought she'd be sad to be back there without Jake, but if anything she felt re-energised. She'd sipped beer and spoken to strangers at pop-up bars, laughed in all the right places at comedy shows she went to alone, and applauded a little too loudly at subpar plays, to show she appreciated the effort. Freddie made it clear from the off he wasn't coming with her; he spent most of her visit out with friends paying over the odds for pub cocaine, and Amelia was happy to decline the invitation. On drugs, Freddie got very cloying and started calling her 'Me-Me' and asking if she loved him. But he was getting over an acrimonious break-up with Samir, who had turned out not to be as 'lovely' as she'd assumed, or perhaps he had finally seen through Freddie; Amelia knew that with her brother, there were at least six sides to every story. The one night she and Freddie had spent together, her brother had delivered the news that, the day they'd broken up, Samir had confessed he'd shared an elicit kiss with Jake at New Year. Amelia had taken a hearty glug of the wine in front of her, trying not to look like a tragic heroine; she certainly didn't feel like one.

'I don't give a fuck, Freddie.'

His look of disappointment had been a genuine thrill.

'Sorry to rob you of your moment, but who cares? I don't feel worse, or better; it's just a *fact*.'

She'd suspected Jake had slept with someone else

anyway – the man couldn't buy a tub of olives without trying three or four first, so he was hardly going to commit to a lifetime of bisexuality and walk away from their relationship without at least one attempt.

Amelia had stretched out on Freddie's floor, empowered by apathy, owning it. Why hadn't he told her earlier, when she'd needed it, when she could've channelled and processed her rage? Even though the kiss hadn't broken them up, it would've given her something to focus on and, fairly quickly, forget. Amelia had no time for Freddie's weedy excuse that he hadn't been able to find the words.

'Well, you found them now.' And she'd downed the wine, because the balance of power had shifted for the first time; she could no longer be in awe of someone so selfish. She didn't have to pretend Freddie always knew best any more. She was her own person.

So he wasn't here, to lurk in the shadows and pounce on Jake and cause a scene. Clean slate. No looking back. Voluntary redundancy and Rudi ditching her girlfriend were the most important factors in this decision to see the world – but Jake had his part to play, she had to admit. The alternative could've been so different. That's why she'd invited Jake's family to the party. She wanted to look them in the eye, these people whose lives she'd been a part of for four years, and show them she'd survived, was moving on. She would, along with Rudi, of course, be centre-stage for the first time in her life – and it felt great.

*

Jake looked at his watch. His date was running late. A buzz from his phone startled him. A text from his mother, finalising plans – more than likely making sure he was still coming.

Mum: We r getting a cab for
7.30 and Trick is following with
entourage an hour later.
R u bringing someone?
Mum xo

Jake: I am bringing a friend.
Entourage? xx

Mum: Yes Kia and Will and
another boy who I think is
a ***special*** friend 😉 but
too scared to ask in case he
does a YOU and clams up.
Is YOUR friend a
special one?!?
Mum xo

Ah, so she *hadn't* given up asking that question.

Jake: NO MOTHER.
Just a friend, please
take your wedding hat
back to the shop. xx

Right on cue, the doorbell. Jake opened the door, giving his date a salute – a habit he'd picked up watching Trick's videos. Bertie stood there looking nervous.

'I know I'm not a devastatingly handsome young buck with arms like tree trunks or a beguiling beauty with long legs and eyes bluer than the Seine, but will I do?'

Jake laughed. 'The perfect consort. Oh, and the Seine is kind of a grey-sludgy colour. Your eyes are just fine.'

In the cab on the way, Bertie listened as Jake recounted his set-to with Harry. 'That boy needs someone to talk to. Think of everyone you've got.'

But there was something getting in the way. Jake couldn't quite explain it.

'Oh, Jake, it's easy to see. You still fancy him. No biggie. Friendships can survive it. Look at your brother and his crush, the one you . . . '

That was a point: Jake remembered his mother saying Hot Will would be there. How was *that* going to play? He must've come back from university specially. 'Nothing happened! How many times . . . '

Bertie threw his head back in laughter. 'Fine. But be a friend to Harry if you can find it within you. Sounds like he needs one. You've more in common than you think. And what about our young gremlin Callum? You mended that bridge yet?'

Jake bristled at the mention of his name. Callum hadn't returned his messages. Not all sorrys could hit their targets – maybe sometimes it was for the best.

Jake tapped Margo on her right shoulder before ducking behind and appearing at her left.

'Why does that get you every time?'

Margo sighed. 'I pretend it does, to protect your fragile masculinity.'

'Ooh, someone's swallowed a dictionary.'

'You learn a lot about this kind of thing listening to girls in the changing rooms. Not that you'd know.'

Jake nodded over at Trick, Kia and their new crew, who were making a very big entrance, swathed in scarves, jewellery and, in one case, fairy lights. Embellishments, as Jake now knew them. 'Who are the new recruits?'

'Oh, that's Will and . . . Oh, I don't know the other one's name. Isaac, I think.'

Jake did a double-take at both the new boys. Neither of them looked anything like Hot Will. Was he in a dream? Was he in his own personal *Truman Show*, and the role of Hot Will had been recast with another actor and everyone else was pretending not to notice?

Margo saw his confusion. 'Oh, yeah, right. Hot Will is at university, isn't he? This is . . . the other one. He's back in the gang.' Jake could see why he hadn't been assigned 'hot' status – although he wasn't *that* bad. Margo carried on: 'There will always be another Will waiting in the wings. They're pretty interchangeable.'

Jake regarded the young people again, remembering Hot Will's cheery laugh and breezy self-confidence. 'I'm not sure that's entirely true. In fact, I'd say Hot Will was a one-off.'

He heard his mum and dad laughing uproariously and saw them standing with Bertie. A few weeks ago, this meeting of worlds would've terrified him, but now it was time to stop being a big baby. Was he ready to embrace being a D'Arcy at last? Maybe – just so long as he didn't have to wear a Christmas jumper.

As he approached, his mum was doing her 'rosé cackle', usually reserved for Boxing Day, around 8 p.m. 'Your friend Bertie was telling us about Grindr,' Vee screamed. 'It sounds *fabulous*. Toned bodies all lined up. I've never seen anything like it! Are *you* on it?'

Jake's eyes flicked to his dad's to read his expression, but he was chuckling. Jake was not ready for this level of scrutiny of his sex life, but his dad did like a bit of smut; maybe this was the common ground that had eluded them so long? Jake thought for a moment – he'd prefer to bond over football, to be honest. He shot dagger eyes at Bertie. 'Errrr, worth remembering that how we have sex and our . . . um . . . dating techniques aren't for joking about.'

Bertie nudged him. 'Oh, all right, *News at Ten*, calm down. I was offering some light education about the world their two magnificent sons now find themselves in.'

Mum's face suddenly caved a little. 'Will Trick be on there? Taking photos of . . . himself?' Jake saw the motherly concern – Trick was unlikely to ever be acknowledged as a sexual being in his own right. Jake decided to spare them this lecture tonight, but it was definitely in the post.

Bertie placed his hand on Vee's arm. 'You don't need to worry about either of them. They've got fantastic friends round them. And I *do* include myself in that! We'll look after them.'

'Good,' said Pat, his voice a croak, laden with emotional heft. And again: 'Good.'

'Jake, take a selfie of us!' Trick's repeated attempts to educate his mother on the correct definition of 'selfie' had been wasted. Jake took the photo.

'Done.'

Bertie sensed some family time was in order. 'I'll get some drinks, shall I? Back in a jiffy.'

While Bertie was at the bar, Jake brought his parents in closer. 'I don't want you to worry about all the, uh, sex stuff. But I can't *not* do it just because it might upset you. You don't need to think about it, no more than I . . . oh.'

Vee cackled. 'Did you just think about me and your dad . . . ? It has happened, you know. Still does. Just this morning, in fact.'

'Oh God. *God*. But, the same goes for Trick. Let him go on Grindr, meet men, make his own mistakes.'

Over his mum's shoulder, he saw Trick was already embarking on his next 'mistake' – aggressively kissing Isaac while Other Will and Kia looked on, fascinated.

Jake saw his mother's eyes go saucer-huge and decided to change tack. 'Have we ever talked this honestly before? *Ever*? No. And that's why it's gonna be all right.'

Pat pulled his son to him and gripped him for a second or two before springing back with a smile on his face. 'Gotcha. Lovely.'

Vee grabbed the large glass of Pinot Grigio blush from a returning Bertie. 'Thank fuck for that.' And when she laughed, it was like a shower of stars.

*

Kia came out of the loo, high-fiving Amelia who was passing on her way in, to see Trick standing with a pint in his hand.

'A pint?'

Trick grimaced. 'Dad bought me it. I felt too bad to ask him to change it for an Aperol Spritz.'

Kia whooped with laughter. 'Wow, the toxic masculinity jumped out.'

'Shut up. At least it's in a *glass*.'

Kia moved in closer to Trick. 'Have you not noticed?' she whispered. 'Jake seems to have ditched the uniform? He's wearing . . . colour.'

Trick peered over as if surveying the horizon, scanning his brother's outfit. Not a chino or Oxford shirt in sight.

'God, yeah, and it's all quite . . . well, it actually fits him, doesn't it? Hang on.' Trick's jaw dropped. 'Does he . . . ? Is Jake . . . buff?'

Kia laughed so hard she had to spit her vodka back into the glass. 'I *told* you there was a hench body under there.'

'That's disgusting.' He swigged his beer. 'Such a shame it's wasted on Jake, isn't it?'

Kia cackled. 'Hang on, I thought you two were doing okay these days?'

Trick turned to his friend in mock affront. 'We are! But . . . y'know, he's still *Jake*.'

'Truth.' Kia laughed again and checked her phone. 'Hot Will is in the group chat wanting to know how the night's going.'

Trick smiled faintly and gave a slight nod as if acknowledging the final crumbs of his crush on him.

'Yeah, I know. I saw.' He paused for effect, Kia noticed. 'I'll reply in a bit.'

'Leaving him on read?' Kia squeezed Trick's arm and put her phone back in her bag. 'You've grown, baby.'

Trick looked over at Isaac, who was throwing some very misguided shapes to the blaring hip-hop, but glanced over and gave a shy smile at being caught. Hot Will was always going to be a hard act to follow.

'I'm trying.'

*

'You know, you're doing all right.' Rudi held up her glass for Jake to clink. 'Taking to it like a duck to water. Or should that be *dick* to water? Where's your self-loathing? Your internalised homophobia?'

Jake winced, recalling the argument with Trick the

morning of Holly and Charlie's wedding, his dismissal of Callum, Harry's lost look as he'd walked away the day before. 'I have my moments. Too many. I've never *loathed* myself, just disappointed myself now and again. A lot. Still working on it.'

'Well, you came tonight and that's a big thing. Nice for Amelia.'

'I wasn't sure whether to stay away.'

Rudi glanced over at her friend, who was pretending not to look back over. 'No, you did the right thing. So what's next?'

'Next?'

'Now you're more comfortable in your skin, *working on things*, what now?'

Jake retreated to his mental holodeck, ticking things off his virtual to-do list. 'I'm going to get back in control of my life. Not be afraid.'

Rudi cooed. 'Oooh, my man got powerful.'

'And I'm gonna . . . be more patient. Give *people* a go. Imagine!'

Rudi laughed. 'Sounds peachy.'

'It may turn out to be the stupidest thing I've ever done.'

Rudi put her arm round Jake's back. 'Look at me and Amelia: sodding off to Thailand, no return ticket, vague plans for Australia but that's it. Renting my flat to a straight couple who listen only to Snow Patrol. *That's* the stupidest thing I've ever done – but I know it'll be the best one too. Now go on, scoot. Go talk to our girl.'

*

'I miss you, you know.'

'I miss you too.' Amelia smiled, meaning it. 'But I like being free more. I even enjoy watching *you* be free. Progress.'

'I just wanted to say—'

Amelia shook her head. 'I think we've done the apologies.'

'I wasn't actually going to say sorry. Not again.'

Amelia was a bit put out, but smiled like a minor royal. 'Okay, what then?'

'I wanted to say thank you. For everything. I had a nice time with you. I wish things had been different. You deserve . . . ' Jake's voice cracked the tiniest amount and Amelia was delighted to hear it. 'You deserve the world.'

Amelia thought carefully about her reply. Would she rather Jake be tormented for all eternity by what he'd done? Who'd benefit? Surely his punishment was right here, anyway, in this room, this world she was leaving. It would be so easy for her to stay. Brunches! Birthday gatherings! More weddings! Farewell parties like this, if any of them were ever brave enough to whip away the safety net! As dull as his life would now be, treated as a curiosity among his friends who did their damnedest not to make biphobic jokes in front of him, at least Jake could be himself. And she'd rather that than see him alone, miserable and lying to himself. The bastard. And yet: 'Thank you for saying that. And I *do* deserve the world. Fucking *totally*. That's why I'm off to find it.' She tried to read his face. Impossible. As ever. 'Friends?' Feeling wise and benevolent, she stuck out her hand. Jake grabbed it.

'For ever.'

'Now that I *will* hold you to.'

*

As Jake moved back through the room to rescue Bertie from having to look at his mother's pictures on her phone, he felt Margo tugging at his elbow.

'How are you getting on?'

'Oh, fine. I'll be okay.'

Margo rolled her eyes. 'So self-obsessed, as *per.* I meant with the drinks order you took from *me* about half an hour ago. I'm parched.' Her gaze tracked to the door, her mouth falling open slightly. 'Ooh. Who is *that*?'

At the door, looking hesitant, was Harry. What was he doing here?

'He's . . . a friend from work. Harry.'

'How good a friend?' Margo pouted in appreciation. 'He's *fit*.'

Jake began muttering explanations, but Margo hushed him.

'Look, whoever he is, bring him over, introduce him. Mum and Dad and . . . everybody . . . need to meet your friends. Properly. Like real families do. Get to know you.' Margo looked like a grown-up for the first time ever. Not his baby sister any more. 'Let us in. We're *nice*. Go get flash Harry. He looks lonely.'

He did look lonely. Jake knew that feeling. Giving Margo one last affectionate nudge, Jake made his way over to Harry, who saw him approach and smiled nervously, taking a step back. The conversation, and the road to reconciliation, began as they all must: 'Hello.'

acknowledgements.

I rambled too long in my acknowledgements for my first novel and if it's true what they say about books being like children, then you know how it is with the second child – you're more lax, let them do what they like. If they fall over and cut their knee, it's no big deal. (It *is* a big deal; I do not want my book to sustain any injury.)

The Magnificent Sons has been an incredible experience and, in a rare burst of efficiency, I would like to list those who helped make it possible and/or got me through it by offering help/advice/inspiration/commissions for freelance work to keep a roof over my head while I wrote it/hors d'oeuvres.

My partner Paul, my family and my wonderful, supportive friends: I'm so lucky to have you all – where would I be without you? | My amazing agent Becky Thomas | My marvellous editor Anna Boatman | Queen of publicity Clara Diaz | Eleanor Russell and everyone else at Little, Brown for their encouragement | Dominic Wakeford for the initial spot |

The Boyles and the Richardsons | Rob Copsey and Official Charts | Adam Kay | James Farrell | Jill Mansell | Alice Jones and everyone at The *i* | British *GQ* | The *Guardian* | Joe Stone | Nina Trickey | *Sunday Times Style* | Liz Vater and everyone at Stoke Newington Literary Festival | Amy Baker, Rosy Edwards and The Riff Raff | Alix Fox and Riyadh Khalaf | Maureen O'Hare and CNN Travel | Twitter UK | Kat Brown | Laura Jane Williams | Ally Gipps and Gaumont | Claire Woodward and Cassie Whittell at Croydon Lit Fest | Amy Stokes | Milton Keynes Literary Festival | Latitude | Henley Literary Festival | Aye Write! | Lewis Oakley | Michael Segalov | Rosie Wilby | Emma Gannon | Dame Joan Collins (She read the first one! I KNOW!) and Jeffrey Lane | Isabel Costello | Marina O'Loughlin | Hannah Verdier | Russell T Davies | Matthew Cain | Daisy Buchanan | John Marrs | Francesca Hornak | Nancy Pearl | Megan Nolan | Juno Dawson.

And last but not least . . . everyone who reads me. It can't happen without you.

The Magnificent Sons

extra content.

hello from the author.

As anyone who read my first novel, *The Last Romeo,* will know, I'm inspired by duality, by nobody quite being who they say they are – or even who they *think* they are themselves. No matter the image we project, we cannot control others' perceptions or prejudices. This is why the closet exists. People come out as lesbian, gay, transgender, bi, or non-binary all the time, yet no two events are ever the same – the sole comparison to a snowflake I'm willing to accept. Coming out tends to favour anticlimax over melodrama. Though it's a huge relief to get things off your chest, it can also be something dreary and functional you need to get through – think confirming your sexuality or gender to a medical professional or a hotel receptionist. Coming out can go well, it can go wrong, but it can never be unsaid, and it's always a work in progress.

The Magnificent Sons isn't autobiographical, but one of the best things about being an author is taking your own accumulated experiences, observations and morsels of gossip and saying, 'What if…?' I assume all authors do that, right? If not, maybe I'm doing authoring wrong?! I love to think through all the possibilities, turning a slight aside I heard 17 years ago into a character's entire life. What if one man was young, gay, confident and captivating, the world lying at his expensive sneakers. And what if his brother – older, unreadable and uncommunicative – was only just working out that he was bisexual? What might happen? Would they be treated the same? And so it goes. Usually, my constant overthinking is a hindrance, but writing fiction, it's literally my job! Excellent!

But if we're plugging into my own emotional hard drive, there are parts of me scattered throughout. I didn't play my cards quite so close to my chest as Jake; I desperately wanted a doll as a child, much to my family's bewilderment. The adorable, camp little boy in the bakery was real – I hope he's thriving now. Trick's 17th birthday party with teens vomiting into bin-bags was based on my own godson's party. Sadly, because Trick's birthday is in July, I had to leave out my favourite detail – drunk teenagers dry-humping the family Christmas tree. The Edinburgh street party scenes are based on my first gay kiss; Jake was already on his second, of course. Amelia and Jake's trip up the Eiffel Tower came from finding, among my ephemera, a visitor ticket for the Tower from 1999, from a disastrous romantic getaway with my final girlfriend. There's a photograph of me standing in front of it, my wide smile not reaching my eyes; I'm rail-thin and anxious, petrified not of the climb but a future I assume I can't change. Jake's thumping heart and rising panic in the elevator is my own.

I was an only child until I was 20. Fascinated by everyday sibling spats missing from my childhood, I was keen to explore the differing parenting styles and generational pressures and relationships between siblings. This idea that, depending which one you are, the eldest, or youngest, had it easier, is more spoiled, having more fun. (Margo, in the middle, is perhaps the wisest of all.) Putting both brothers on the LGBTQ+ spectrum pushed this generational chasm even further – ageism is as present in the LGBTQ+ community as it is everywhere else. I was a 'late' starter, coming out in my early twenties, decades of repression etched into my bones; I felt like I didn't come into my own for a long time. I'd see people much younger than me with buckets of confidence, who'd leapt out of the closet while at school and, mostly, found acceptance. I was thrilled for them, of course, but there were pangs of envy and regret at what I'd missed out on, even though, as the marvellous Kia points out to Jake, I was already 'six vitamin shots ahead'. But, of course, nobody's having quite as good a time as it seems.

Jake's bisexuality and existing relationship with Amelia further complicates matters, but these aren't just plot devices. I wanted to examine the prejudice many bisexual people face both from straight people and within the LGBTQ+ community – the cheap jokes, and accusations of greed and duplicity. Imagine discovering that coming out was not the answer you thought it would be, but the start of a new set of questions? Jake has *never* been himself – he's played a role, to avoid detection and prejudice. Once he comes out, he must now divine his true traits from the ones that are a product of years of pretending. Is Jake *really* sulky, moody and sensitive – or was this his armour, to keep an unforgiving world at bay? Readers tell me that main characters like Jake don't come along every day, and Amelia too aims to right a wrong I've felt in many coming-out stories about men – women tossed aside as collateral damage once the hero finds his destiny. Amelia's path to magnificence is just as important as the D'Arcy brothers' – it's no accident that in the final chapter, she's moving onto a new life, while Jake is still finding his place in his old one.

I enjoyed writing the arguments – I like letting characters lose control and say what they're thinking, things they never dared to think and, usually, what they don't mean. The final row between Jake and Trick, just as Jake is setting off for the wedding, is the first time the brothers are totally honest about how they see one another – and it's not pretty. Years of resentment spat out in anger, no going back, spent in minutes like fireworks. All built on misunderstanding and assumption. Further on, too, when Amelia lets Jake feel her rage, it's tough on him, but she deserves that moment – so often in life we hold back, often out of kindness, but sometimes, to appreciate the calm, and to rebuild, there needs to be an explosion.

Including incidents of homophobia and biphobia was necessary, I felt. In terms of equality and justice, we've come a fair way, but the view behind us is still the clearest and nearest. Most of these prejudices are challenged in the story, but sometimes they're not; I'm afraid that is the reality for many. The workplace incident where Jake's opinions are ignored; Callum's suspicious, judgmental friend Glanville; the clumsy and horrifying, yet well-meaning, remarks made by his parents and friends. I have, at one time or another, heard them all. Sometimes we're even fated to replicate the injustices we've experienced: Jake is oblivious to Harry's own journey unfolding, after all.

While there are serious themes at play, I wanted a feeling of lightness, so even in the darker moments, there's humour – just like life. The characters use jokes and withering putdowns to hide insecurities and show affection – even some of the most malicious exchanges come from a desire for understanding, or lashing out at being hurt. I'm fascinated by families, both biological ones bound by bloodlines and, as Armistead Maupin puts it, the 'logical' ones – the friendship groups we find ourselves in when our supposed loved ones can't accept who we are. I love to imagine the secrets they share, the hierarchies and allegiances, the resentment and joy.

The D'Arcy brothers may never understand each other fully, but every relationship has its own particular unknowns. All we can do is give someone the freedom and space to share them if they wish; that's what brings us closer together. It's about compassion, to pause and consider what someone might be going through – who are they trying to be? We're certainly under no obligation to make excuses for anyone's bad behaviour, but we can, at least, examine our own, and its impact on others.

The Magnificent Sons is, in a way, a love letter to families and friends and lovers – a celebration of the affinities and misunderstandings that fuel these bonds and tear them apart. How can we not be mesmerised by them, cut from the same DNA, or formed of common interest or shared history – so much like us, and yet so different? Brothers, sisters, daughters, sons – yet perfect strangers. And every last one of them magnificent in their own way.

Jake's playlist.

Jake's music is only ever heard on headphones – hi-spec ones he bought after months of meticulous research. Use speakers? Sing out loud? Too revealing, too open. He prefers to keep his tastes to himself so nobody can ruin them for him. But it's the playing-out-loud moments where Jake comes alive: mesmerised aged 17 as he watches Evan dance to the scratchy Fleetwood Mac LP; taking to the dance floor for the first time as Blondie's *Atomic* blares out; shouting out the words, drunk, as he speeds toward Balham on the stolen bike. (In case you didn't make the connection, the 'magnificent' of the title is inspired by the lyrics of *Atomic*, Jake's freedom cry.) Jake's never given himself permission to make noise, to take up space. But once he reveals his true self and starts on that journey, there's no stopping him – even if he hasn't perfected the moves yet.

Dreams
Fleetwood Mac

Somebody Else
The 1975

Thinkin Bout You
Frank Ocean

Kamikaze
Susanne Sundfør

Runaway
Kanye West, Pusha T

Atomic
Blondie

Sign of the Times
Post Precious

Black Belt
John Grant

Pink Lemonade
James Bay

Friends
Justin Bieber, BloodPop®

It's My Life
No Doubt

Find the extended playlist on
Spotify at bit.ly/mag_jake

Trick's playlist.

Depending on your age and experience, you'll either find Trick lovable, or a pain in the arse – most people thought the same about you when you were 17, by the way. His exuberance, barbed tongue and aesthetic obsessions might seem superficial, but inside he's desperately looking for his place in the world, trying to make the pieces fit together. As he says himself, 'I don't wanna make memories, I wanna make noise.' Trick's music is not just his manifesto, it's his heart worn firmly on sleeve, highs and lows and everything turned up to 11. Imagine his playlist booming out from behind a closed door, punctuated with the piercing laughter and screams of supposedly carefree teenagers trying to forget the world is on their shoulders.

King
Years & Years

17
MK

Blue Motorbike
Moto Boy

Bloom
Troye Sivan

Don't Kill My Vibe
Sigrid

Still Got Time
Zayn, PartyNextDoor

Hot Boyz
Missy Elliott

Touch It
Ariana Grande

Mr. Brightside
The Killers

Curious
Hayley Kiyoko

I Know A Place
MUNA

Find the extended playlist on
Spotify at bit.ly/mag_trick

Amelia's playlist.

There's no hiding it, at the start of her story, Amelia has settled. This is not who she thought she'd be. She's already waking up to this, though, reminiscing about her younger days and the women her best friends used to be, sharing secrets and passions and horror stories over late-night beers and cigarettes. Now, her friends are on accelerated paths to domesticity and Amelia is playing catch-up. Amelia's music library is her autobiography, soundtracking parties and heartbreaks. Every song's been talked over, its lyrics screamed out loud on the dance floor, blurting out of her battered bluetooth speakers. She's found comfort in nostalgia, but there's hope for the future too; the best years of her life await her, on the blank pages yet to be filled.

Write My Story
Olly Anna

Hit ‘Em up Style (Oops!)
Blu Cantrell

Dumb Love
Neil Frances

Casanova
Allie X

Only Girl (In The World)
Rihanna

The Runner
The Three Degrees

Tears Dry On Their Own
Amy Winehouse

New Rules
Dua Lipa

Ex's & Oh's
Elle King

no tears left to cry
Ariana Grande

Hang With Me
Robyn

Find the extended playlist on
Spotify at bit.ly/mag_amelia